Walking the Clouds

Volume 69

Sun Tracks
An American Indian Literary Series

Series Editor
Ofelia Zepeda

Editorial Committee
Larry Evers
Joy Harjo
Geary Hobson
N. Scott Momaday
Irvin Morris
Simon J. Ortiz
Kate Shanley
Leslie Marmon Silko
Luci Tapahonso

Walking the Clouds

An Anthology of Indigenous Science Fiction

Edited by Grace L. Dillon

THE UNIVERSITY OF
ARIZONA PRESS
TUCSON

THE UNIVERSITY OF ARIZONA PRESS

© 2012 Grace L. Dillon

www.uapress.arizona.edu

Library of Congress Cataloging-in-Publication Data

   Walking the clouds : an anthology of indigenous science fiction /
edited by Grace L. Dillon.
       p. cm. — (Sun tracks : an American Indian literary series ; v. 69)
   Includes bibliographical references.
   ISBN 978-0-8165-2982-7 (pbk. : alk. paper)
       1. Science fiction, American. 2. Indians of North America—Fiction. 3. American
fiction—20th century. 4. American fiction—21st century. I. Dillon, Grace L.

PS501.S85 vol.69
[PS648.S3]
813'.087620806—dc23

                                                      2011033427

Publication of this book is made possible in part by the proceeds of a permanent
endowment created with the assistance of a Challenge Grant from the National
Endowment for the Humanities, a federal agency.

Manufactured in the United States of America on acid-free, archival-quality paper
containing a minimum of 30% post-consumer waste and processed chlorine free.

With the moon
My young father comes to mind
Walking the clouds

—Gerald Vizenor, from *Empty Swings* (1967)

Contents

NATIVE APOCALYPSE

BISKAABIIYANG, "RETURNING TO OURSELVES"

Walking the Clouds

Imagining Indigenous Futurisms

$AT THE EDGE OF THE TWENTY-FIRST CENTURY, one of Canada's premier urban theater companies, Native Earth Performing Arts, staged *alterNatives,* a play about a liberal contemporary couple who throw a dinner party. Angel is a Native science fiction writer, and Colleen is a "non-practicing" Jewish intellectual who teaches Native literature. Their guests represent the apparent extremes of both societies—Angel's formerly close friends are radical Native activists, and Colleen associates with environmentally concerned vegetarians/veterinarians. Playwright Drew Hayden Taylor (Ojibway) satirizes many assumptions about contemporary Native experience, including a defense of science fiction (sf). Angel just wants to write sf because it's fun. He resists being backed into producing "the great Canadian aboriginal novel" that would transform him into "a window through which the rest of Canada can see [his] community." Angel views sf as a freeing arena and wonders why it should be reserved only for the likes of Arthur C. Clarke, William Gibson, and Ursula K. Le Guin, all of whom he greatly admires. "Unless there's a race requirement," he jests, "I like the concept of having no boundaries, of being able to create and develop any character, any environment or setting I want. . . . People want me to be ground-breaking, and I will be. But I'd rather do it my way, by becoming a financially comfortable writer of sci-fi who happens to be aboriginal."[1]

Angel's privileging of sf over "the Great Aboriginal Novel" asserts that sf provides an equally valid way to renew, recover, and extend

First Nations peoples' voices and traditions. This reader brings together Indigenous authors who explore this choice.[2] Their stories enclose "reservation realisms" in a fiction that sometimes fuses Indigenous sciences with the latest scientific theories available in public discourse, and sometimes undercuts the western limitations of science altogether. In this process of estrangement they raise the question, what exactly *is* science fiction? Does sf have the capacity to envision Native futures, Indigenous hopes, and dreams recovered by rethinking the past in a new framework?

As *alterNative*'s Angel might answer, "Why not?"

As Basil Johnston (Anishinaabe) might remind us, *w'daeb-a-wae*, "a telling of the truth," casts our voices and words only as far as vocabulary and perception allow.

Walking the Clouds opens up sf to reveal Native presence. It suggests that Indigenous sf is not so new—just overlooked, although largely accompanied by an emerging movement—and advocates that Indigenous authors should write more of it. We should do this as a way of positioning ourselves in a genre associated almost exclusively with "the increasing significance of the future to Western techno-cultural consciousness," as the editors of the popular *Wesleyan Anthology of Science Fiction* (2010) view the field. *Walking the Clouds* weds sf theory and Native intellectualism, Indigenous scientific literacy, and western techno-cultural science, scientific possibilities enmeshed with Skin thinking.[3] The stories offered here are thought experiments that confront issues of "Indianness" in a genre that emerged in the mid-nineteenth-century context of evolutionary theory and anthropology profoundly intertwined with colonial ideology, whose major interest was coming to grips with—or negating—the implications of these scientific mixes of "competition, adaptation, race, and destiny."[4] Historically, sf has tended to disregard the varieties of space-time thinking of traditional societies,[5] and it may still narrate the atrocities of colonialism as "adventure stories."[6] Its title also pays homage to Afrofuturisms, an established topic of study for sf scholars. As Mark Bould's introduction to a recent special edition of *Science Fiction Studies* frames the matter, what's intended is not relegating Afrofuturisms to a purely sf field, but rather recognizing that sf theory and Afrofuturisms may have much to gain by the exchange. The same is true of the approach here.[7]

Writers of Indigenous futurisms sometimes intentionally experiment with, sometimes intentionally dislodge, sometimes merely accompany, but invariably *change* the perimeters of sf.[8] Liberated from the constraints of genre expectations, or what "serious" Native authors are *supposed* to write, they have room to play with setting, character, and dialogue; to stretch boundaries; and, perhaps most significantly, to reenlist the science of indigeneity in a discourse that invites discerning readers to realize that Indigenous science is not just complementary to a perceived western enlightenment but is indeed integral to a refined twenty-first-century sensibility.

What better terrain than the field of sf to "engage colonial power in the spirit of a struggle for survival," the warrior ethic that Taiaiake Alfred (Kanien'kehaka) urges Natives to embrace as "thinkers, teachers, writers, and artists"? What better mindscape from which to "look at traditions in a critical way, not trying to take them down, but to test them and to make sure they're still strong"?[9]

The book is divided into sections corresponding to the major sf elements that *Walking the Clouds* reimagines: Native Slipstream; Contact; Indigenous Scientific Literacies and Environmental Sustainability; Native Apocalypse, Revolutions, and Futuristic Reconstructions of Sovereignties; and Biskaabiiyang, "Returning to Ourselves": Beyond the Shadow-Worlds of Postmodernity and the (Post)Colonial.

Native Slipstream

Native slipstream, a species of speculative fiction within the sf realm, infuses stories with time travel, alternate realities and multiverses, and alternative histories. As its name implies, Native slipstream views time as pasts, presents, and futures that flow together like currents in a navigable stream. It thus replicates nonlinear thinking about space-time.

In other contexts, the term *slipstream* often becomes a catchall for speculative writing that defies neat categorization. Victoria de Zwaan describes slipstream as "the overtly disruptive, experimental, and counter-realist surface of the text" and posits that slipstream is written by those who "play with and undermine the conventions of the [sf] genre" or by those who "could be discussed as sf because of their themes or techniques of estrangement."[10] Damien Broderick suggests that "slipstream slams comfortable expectations upside down and destabilize[s] our prejudices, and [does] so without preaching, for fun."[11] Native slipstream shares these features but is noteworthy for its reflection of a worldview. In other words, it is intended to describe writing that does not simply seem avant-garde but models a cultural experience of reality.

Native slipstream thinking, which has been around for millennia, anticipated recent cutting-edge physics, ironically suggesting that Natives have had things right all along. The closest approximation in quantum mechanics is the concept of the "multiverse," which posits that reality consists of a number of simultaneously existing alternate worlds and/or parallel worlds. Interested readers will enjoy John Gribbin's *In Search of the Multiverse: Parallel Worlds, Hidden Dimensions, and the Quest for the Frontiers of Reality* (2010) and David Deutsch's seminal *The Fabric of Reality: The Science of Parallel Universes and Its Implications* (1998). Deutsch's approach describes reality as "an infinite library full of copies of books that all start out the same way on page one, but in which the story in each book deviates more and more from the versions in the other books the farther into the book you read." The further twist of Deutsch's theory is that it "allows universes to merge back together . . . as if two of the books in the library have the same happy ending arrived at by different routes."[12]

Native slipstream exploits the possibilities of multiverses by reshaping time travel. Ultimately, the appeal may simply be "the fun" that Broderick lauds, but slipstream also appeals because it allows authors to recover the Native space of the past, to bring it to the attention of contemporary readers, and to build better futures. It captures moments of divergence and the consequences of that divergence. Vizenor's "Custer on the Slipstream" offers an alternate reality where Native peoples no longer suffer "the loathsome voice and evil manner of this devious loser," General George Armstrong Custer. Diane Glancy's "Aunt Parnetta's Electric Blisters" transforms spatial-temporal dislocations brought about by globalization, communications technologies, and electronic circuitry into a story of the heart's restoration. Stephen Graham Jones's *The Fast Red Road* navigates "Native time slots," "glitches," and "syndicated time loops" spanning from the thirteenth century to bioengineered Americas of tomorrow. Time slippages in Sherman Alexie's *Flight* teach that you can outrun the monster of revenge, move beyond the anger that turns righteous justice into senseless violence, and forgive. Typical of Native survivance stories, these slipstreams are tinged with sardonic humor and bittersweet hope.

The selections offered here only hint at the extent of Native slipstream. Recent Indigenous multimedia exemplify the trend: Archer Pechawis's (Cree) *Horse* is an award-winning "Custer on the slipstream" experimental film, where horses at the Battle of Little Big Horn discuss the outcome while mourning humans' loss of ability to "listen in"; Skawennati Fragnito's (Mohawk) "TimeTraveller™" is a machinima about a Mohawk time traveler who uncovers the Indigenous perspectives that mainstream history books don't care to recount; Cowboy Smithx's (Blackfoot) film *Chance* combines quantum physics with Napi's physics and science in time folds; Myron A. Lameman's (Beaver Lake Cree) short film *Mihko* offers an apocalyptic vision of the near future in the aftermath of Indigenous resistance to exploitation of the Alberta tar sands; Beth Aileen Lameman's (Irish, Anishinaabe, Métis) *The West Was Lost* offers an Aboriginal steampunk web comic that revisions the Windigo tradition in an alternative history; Jeff Barnaby's (Mi'gMaq) *File under Miscellaneous* presents a Skinrewired cyberpunk vision that explores the revitalization of Indigenous language while simultaneously restoring our knowledge that precontact written systems were consciously "erased" as part of the colonial agenda to eradicate Native self-sovereignty and identity; Helen Haig-Brown's (Tsilhqot'in) *Cave* presents an alternate world drawn directly from Tsilhqot'in storytelling and has been called the first sf film to be shot entirely in an Indigenous language.

Contact

Among the more familiar sf templates, stories of contact typically cast the Native/Indigenous/Aboriginal as alien/other and exploit the theme of conquest, otherwise known as "discovery." Either aliens invade humans or humans invade aliens, whether the terrain is geopolitical, psychological, sexual, or otherwise. Native writers who choose to experiment with sf thus confront the possibility of internal colonization, a semiotic of resistance and oppression that does little to address larger historical realities that have inalterably changed Native existence. When viewed as tales of survivance, however, Native-authored sf extends the *miinidiwag* tradition of ironic Native giveaway, of storytelling that challenges readers to recognize their positions with regard to the diasporic condition of contemporary Native peoples. Here the concept of survivance follows Gerald Vizenor's seminal discussion in *Fugitive Poses: Native American Indian Scenes of Absence and Presence*. Native survivance is "more than survival, more than endurance or mere response . . . survivance is an active repudiation of dominance, tragedy, and victimry."[13] Miinidiwag, the Native "giveaway," are curative stories told in an ironic way, ones that taunt the audience by implicating their part in the lesson conveyed. The trick is to avoid becoming "a mere archive, covering the earth with empty traces of a lost plenitude," a public memory that exists only through its exterior scaffolding and outward signs.[14]

Celu Amberstone's novella *Refugees* embraces the relevant contact themes almost in summary fashion. In this case, aliens have abducted earthlings and repopulated a new planet in an effort to sustain the human race. At face value, this would seem a beneficial act, and its effects embroil our narrator in the struggle to reconcile her biased trust of the colonizers with the skepticism of their latest crop of earth "seedlings." Gerry William's *The Black Ship* plays out hugely adventurous clashes between Home World Repletions and empire-seeking Anphorians typical of space opera. It thus follows a familiar contact template taken from trashy, pulp "sci-fi" origins "where larger-than-life protagonists encounter a variety of alien species, planetary cultures, futuristic technologies . . . and sublime physical phenomena" in a "plausible universe of plural, simultaneous, reversible spacetime continua."[15] William's spin on the contact motif inverts the pulp formula to show the drama from an Indigenous perspective, including the perception of the Home Worlds as already full of life to respect and relate to. This is a literary technique that Lisa Brooks (Abenaki), a Yale historian, has recently explored in *The Common Pot,* one that she discovered many eighteenth- and nineteenth-century Native writers were deploying to counteract the thinking of *terra nullius,* entering into an empty land. So, rather than a hollow earth (as even the subterranean adventures imitating the hollow earth theory might have it), the land itself is *wôlhanak* (in the Abenaki sense of "hollowed-out places"), "not empty spaces to be filled but deeply situated social and ecological environments." Further, the land is *aki,* "a self-sustaining vessel" requiring "participation from all its interwoven inhabitants," the "common pot" to be shared, "not an altruistic ideal but a practice that was necessary to human survival."[16] Simon Ortiz's experiment with contact narrative, "Men on the Moon," represents an important challenge to what Istvan Csicsery-Ronay characterizes as the American technological sublime, the awe-inducing expectation that humanity can create machines with the power to "annihilate time and space."[17] Quietly resolved, this story realigns the practiced way of living and knowledge that sees far more acutely the oil-slick refuse left behind by advancing, trampling space age science.

Indigenous Science and Sustainability

One aim of this book is to distinguish science fiction from other speculative writing typically associated with Native thinking, such as the time-traveling alternative worlds in Native slipstream and contact narratives. Here it is useful to return the "science" to sf, which should be recognized as the signature feature of the genre. The question arises, then, whether Indigenous peoples can lay claim to the term *science* (and, indeed, whether they should want or need to).

The third selection of readings juxtaposes western science with what can be thought of as "Indigenous scientific literacies" (known elsewhere by terms such as Aboriginal resource management, Indigenous resource management, and the politically controversial "traditional ecological knowledge," or TEK) to argue that Native/Indigenous/Aboriginal sustainable practices constitute a science despite their lack of resemblance to taxonomic western systems of thought. In contrast to the accelerating effect of techno-driven western scientific method, Indigenous scientific literacies represent practices used by Indigenous peoples over thousands of years to reenergize the natural environment while improving the interconnected relationships among all persons (animal, human, spirit, and even machine). Some of its features include sustainable forms of medicine, agriculture, architecture, and art. Since Indigenous scientific literacies historically are shaped by the diverse natural environments of the groups that use them, no single set of practices summarizes the possibilities. But many cultures shared the pattern of disseminating scientific knowledge in everyday teachings. In Anishinaabemowin, the word *gikendaasowin* begins to measure the prevalence and depth of scientific discourse. It is botanical knowledge, knowledge of the land, but it is also knowledge itself, teachings and ways of living. Storytelling was the medium of choice for transmitting and preserving traditional knowledge.

Interested readers will find ample discussion of the topic by researchers in multiple fields.[18] The title of a work by Wendy Makoons Geniusz (Cree raised Anishinaabe) stands out, however, as a common refrain in emerging movements today: *Our Knowledge Is Not Primitive*. That is the point. Methods that do not resemble western science are not de facto "primitive."[19]

Indigenous scientific literacies play key roles throughout Nalo Hopkinson's works. The excerpt from *Midnight Robber* introduces the practice in its simplest guise: a child comes under the tutelage of an Indigenous mentor who begins teaching her the science of survival, emphasizing the practical, day-to-day transmission of generational knowledge. Gerald Vizenor's *Darkness in St. Louis: Bearheart* implicitly criticizes the awe-struck neoshamanism that views Native people as impervious to the very real dangers of nature. The environment itself can be autonomous, resilient, and cruel; Native science employs practical everyday usage in mitigating its effects without resorting to romanticism (a claim often reserved for western science), which Vizenor views as a terminal creed. In Andrea Hairston's *Mindscape,* Indigenous scientific literacies reflect the emerging study of organic electronics, organic physics, and ethnopharmacology. Finally, Archie Weller's *Land of the Golden Clouds* extrapolates three thousand years into the future, where tribal song and storytelling persist as the way to teach and transmit Aboriginal science and medicine.

Native Apocalypse

It is almost commonplace to think that the Native Apocalypse, if contemplated seriously, has already taken place. Many forms of Indigenous futurisms posit the possibility of an optimistic future by imagining a reversal of circumstances, where Natives win or at least are centered in the narrative. Such alternate histories often have "well-known cataclysms" or "fairly resonant figures," according to Andy Duncan, largely so the reader will be able to distinguish between the fictional timeline and the real one.[20] Recurring elements in alternative Native stories include the Sand Creek Massacre of 1864, the Battle of Little Big Horn and Custer's demise (1876), the Ghost Dances after the Wounded Knee Massacre in 1890 (albeit many forms of Ghost Dances occurred historically prior to Wounded Knee), and the Oka uprisings of the 1990s at Kahnesatake. The Ghost Dance may be the most widespread image connected to Native Apocalypse, and it appears to varying degrees in many of the pieces in this collection.

Let's pause for a moment to clarify one possible Native conception of Apocalypse, in contrast to its association with the biblical canon. Lawrence Gross (Anishinaabe) contends that Anishinaabe culture is recovering from what he calls "post-apocalypse stress syndrome" and describes Apocalypse as the state of being *aakozi,* Anishinaabemowin for "he/she is sick" and, more to the point, "out of balance."[21] Native Apocalypse is really that state of imbalance, often perpetuated by "terminal creeds," the ideologies that Gerald Vizenor warns against in advocating survivance in the face of invisibility. Imbalance further implies a state of extremes, but within those extremes lies a middle ground and the seeds of *bimaadiziwin,* the state of balance, one of difference and provisionality, a condition of resistance and survival. Native apocalyptic storytelling, then, shows the ruptures, the scars, and the trauma in its effort ultimately to provide healing and a return to bimaadiziwin. This is the path to a sovereignty embedded in self-determination.

Readers interested in an overview of the Apocalypse as a trope in sf might consider Patrick B. Sharp's *Savage Perils: Racial Frontiers and Nuclear Apocalypse in American Culture*. His extensive genealogy of sf as nuclear frontier fiction provides a context for Indigenous futurisms, where contact and Apocalypse are reciprocal cause and effect. Here let a summary suffice to capture the dominant themes that mainstream sf has drawn from the real history of Eurowestern and Indigenous encounters:

Nuclear frontier fiction stories were defined by their landscape, which combined the wasteland imagery of literary Modernism with the frontier imagery of the nineteenth century in various combinations. With cities reduced to rubble-strewn wilderness, the survivors had to battle with manifestations of savagery in order to establish a new America out of the wreckage of the old. Drawing on Darwinist formulations of progress and the frontier, most nuclear frontier stories repeated the racism of Darwin's arguments that depicted superior Europeans winning the struggle to establish a new and better civilization.[22]

Sherman Alexie's "Distances" directly invokes the Ghost Dance and subsequently mixes a sense of nostalgia with Indian trapdoor humor, suggesting that a bitterly satiric approach is the valid response to the traumatic impact of apocalyptic eschatology on First Nations peoples. In the forlorn wasteland of William Sanders's "When This World Is All on Fire," Native bands diligently maintain their histories, dignities, and sovereignties while the invasive poor (often white) stream through their land; the story decenters the tendency in mainstream apocalyptic sf to pit a small and faithful band of the Eurowestern technologically elite against the descent into savagery that Sharp discusses. Zainab Amadahy's *The Moons of Palmares* encompasses a cycle from the onset of Apocalypse through revolution to a redesigned sovereignty. Misha's *Red Spider, White Web* closes the section by offering the traumatic experience of irrevocable losses suffered by both Native and Japanese as an *inversio* of nuclear frontier fiction.

Biskaabiiyang, "Returning to Ourselves"

It might go without saying that all forms of Indigenous futurisms are narratives of *biskaabiiyang,* an Anishinaabemowin word connoting the process of "returning to ourselves," which involves discovering how personally one is affected by colonization, discarding the emotional and psychological baggage carried from its impact, and recovering ancestral traditions in order to adapt in our post–Native Apocalypse world. This process is often called "decolonization," and as Linda Tuhiwai Smith (Maori) explains, it requires *changing* rather than *imitating* Eurowestern concepts.[23] *Walking the Clouds* confronts the structures of racism and colonialism *and* sf's own complicity in them. Authors who experiment with Indigenous futurisms can create "ethnoscapes" in the manner that Isiah Lavender has suggested: estranged worlds of the future in which the writer can "formulate an imaginary environment so as to foreground the intersection of race, technology and power,"[24] or sometimes, more to the point for the stories here, the intersection of Indigenous nations with other sovereignties, race, technology, and power.

Additionally, decolonization should be recognized as at least tangential to (post)colonial sf literature as a whole, and central to Indigenous futurisms as a path to biskaabiiyang. Amy Ransom provides a useful touchstone for discussions of oppositional postcolonial sf, foregrounding resistance to colonial authority.[25] Similarly, Michelle Reid's overview of postcolonialism asserts the view that sf writing is concerned with the "fantastic basis of colonial practice."[26] And John Rieder's *Colonialism and the Emergence of Science Fiction* offers a groundbreaking study of colonialism and imperialism in sf, arguing that fantasies of appropriation, subjugation of "lost races," and plundering of "discovered wealth" are not just historical features of the genre but persist in contemporary sf works.[27]

In the end, *Walking the Clouds* returns us to ourselves by encouraging Native writers to write about Native conditions in Native-centered worlds liberated by the imagination. These stories display features of self-reflexivity, defamiliarization, and the hyperreal present that Veronica Hollinger explains undergirds postmodern science fiction.[28] But those conditions are hardly new to Native experience. As Gerald Vizenor has stressed, postmodernism is already a condition for First Nations peoples, since they are seen as postindian if they do not resemble the iconic image of the late-nineteenth-century Plains Indian.[29]

Eden Robinson's "Terminal Avenue" collapses the black hole and event horizon on the modern "Indian problem." Leslie Marmon Silko's *Almanac of the Dead* reestablishes the Indigenous Americas as the culmination of Wovoka's Ghost Dance prophecy. Stephen Graham Jones's *The Bird Is Gone* revisits the pop culture icons of Tonto and the Lone Ranger. Robert Sullivan's "Star Waka" contemplates Indigenous space travelers' arrival on new planets.

Ultimately, all of the stories in this reader vacillate between the extremes of (post)colonial, postmodern Indigenous being, seeking balance.

May you find balance too.

Mino bimaatisiiwin!

The Native Slipstream

Custer on the Slipstream

GERALD VIZENOR

(1978)

> Slipstream raises fundamental epistemological and ontological
> questions about reality that most other forms of fiction are
> ill prepared to address.
> —*John Clute*

> I don't understand how time works anymore.
> —*Sherman Alexie,* Flight

IN THEIR 2006 ANTHOLOGY celebrating slipstream sf, James Patrick
Kelly and John Kessel recall Bruce Sterling's coinage of the term *slipstream* in his 1989 fanzine column *sf Eye*. Sterling is credited for an
attempt "to understand a kind of fiction . . . that was not true science
fiction, and yet bore some relation to science fiction."[1] Noticeably
absent from Sterling's original list of 135 so-called slipstream writers
is Native author, scholar, and activist Gerald Vizenor (Anishinaabe),
whose 1978 story "Custer in the Slipstream" unmistakably invokes
the genre. Nor is Vizenor included in Sterling and Person's updated
master list of 204 slipstreamers.[2] In fact, the updated list includes only
one Native author, Louise Erdrich (Ojibwe), despite the abundance of
slipstream elements in the works of Sherman Alexie (Coeur d'Alene),
Joseph Bruchac (Abenaki), Diane Glancy (Cherokee), Stephen Graham Jones (Piegan Blackfeet), Thomas King (Cherokee), N. Scott
Momaday (Kiowa), Eden Robinson (Haida/Haisla), Leslie Marmon

Silko (Laguna Pueblo), and Drew Hayden Taylor (Ojibwe), as well as Vizenor.

It's worth noting Vizenor as antecedent for the use of the term (which in fact was "coined" in the early 1900s as part of the jargon of the foundling aeronautics industry and received literary application at least as early as 1983 with the creation of Slipstream Press) not so much to correct the critical history of the idea as to draw attention to the inherent similarity between a now-familiar sf trope and a way of describing Native intellectual thinking, a subject of relevance to a broader interest in Native and Indigenous sf. Sterling and Vizenor make parallel efforts to articulate theories of a literary imagination. Sterling describes slipstream literature as "fantastic, surreal sometimes, speculative on occasion, but not rigorously so."[3] Vizenor illustrates the imaginative and creative nature of Native stories in typical trickster fashion by employing all of these slipstream elements, showing us a world where time and space are distorted, where shamanistic possession leads to surreal vision in which a reincarnated George Armstrong Custer comes "back to his time in consciousness . . . uncertain . . . if he could travel forever from the place he had been." Vizenor's slipstream narrative constitutes a survivance story that tribal people tell of a time when "the loathsome voice and evil manner of this devious loser [Custer] [that] prevails on hundreds of reservations" magically disappears into thin air, "slipping from grace in a slipstream."

If one can characterize Sterling's effort to coin a term that intended to describe something *other than* the prevailing genres of sf, fantasy, speculative fiction, magical realism, cyberpunk, et al.—in short, to put a label on writers whose craft defied neat categorization—readers must find intriguing the exclusion of Native authors, whose work remains even *more other than other* despite features that imply its status as an original slipstream literature.

Vizenor's "Custer on the Slipstream" provides two elements essential to an understanding of Native slipstream writing. First, Native slipstream provides a nonlinear way of thinking through complex cultural tensions like "Custerology," a term popularized in 1998 by Michael A. Elliott to capture America's ironic fascination with this historical figure who can be simultaneously viewed as a military hero by western standards and as a genocidal madman by Native Americans. Second, it conveys the very real psychological experience of slipping into various levels of awareness and consciousness, here conveyed as a state of falling down into deep dark pools of shamanic trances and possession.

So here, we kick off our slip down the rabbit hole of overlooked Indigenous sf with a seminal work that brings together two well-known yet never-before-aligned staples of Native American resistance and science fiction legerdemain: Custer as the poster child of the limitations of white oppression, and time travel through alternative realities.

General George Armstrong Custer, retouching the message that old generals never die, must hold the national record for resurrections. White people are stuck with his name, and his specter, in Custer, South Dakota and other places, but since the battle of the Little Bighorn the loathsome voice and evil manner of this devious loser prevail on hundreds of reservations. He is resurrected in humor and on white faces in the darkness.

The Chippewa, known as the Anishinabe in the language of the people, described the first white men as *kitchi mokaman*, which in translation means, the men with swords or "great knives." Since then the word has been shortened to *chamokaman* or *chamok* and the description has become depreciative and sardonic.

Farlie Border was a chamokaman and the resurrection of General George Custer. He lived for personal aggrandizement and worked for the United States Department of Labor. He was a proud and evil white man who exploited minorities and the poor for personal power and income. His manner, behind his needs for power, was devious. He laughed with unctuous humor. Federal agencies often found the most corrupt and incompetent administrators and paid them the highest salaries to work with the poor and disadvantaged. Custer and Border sought power and wealth in small places, and worked better under attack.

Farlie Border was resurrected as George Custer under the sign of Taurus, the second sign of the zodiac, but he was too stubborn to admit his celestial bearing. His personal gain games required the best tribal minds, sober and articulate, to survive and share the federal spoils. More ominous than the racial contests he staged in finding

and placing tribal people in new paraprofessional careers was his appearance in the modern world. His white hair and brackish blue eyes,
his gait and manner, the placement of his blunt white fingers when
he spoke, the smile and the evil curl on his thick lips, were all from
the tribal memories of General George Custer. The evil loser had
been resurrected in a federal program to serve tribal people and the
poor.

Tribal people who visited his office for the first time said later that
they could smell leather and blood and horses on the prairie. Someone in his department called him general, mister general, at a public
meeting for the poor. Border smiled and stacked his fingers one over
the others on the table like bodies.

"Crazy Horse is here," his tall blonde secretary told him one morning. "He said he has an appointment with you from the past, but
there is nothing on the calendar about him. . . . He looks too mean
to think about before lunch."

"What ever turns him on. . . . First place a call to Clement Beaulieu
and then send in the mean one when I am through talking to Beaulieu," said Border.

General Border passed most of his federal administrative time in a
padded high-back office chair. He pitched backward in his chair and
bounced the tips of his fingers together when he listened. The drapes
were drawn closed. The floor was covered with an expensive thick
bone-white carpet. A picture of a black panther, the animal, was
mounted on one wall. Two posters were taped on the other wall
opposite the window. One encouraged tribal people, through eccle-
siastical shame, not to drop out of high school. The second poster
pictured one sad tribal child, suffering from hunger and various dis-
eases, walking without shoes on the hard earth. The printed message,
"walk a mile in his moccasins," had been crossed out and changed to
read, "don't walk in my moccasins now, I think I stepped in something." His sinister smile seemed to spread over the entire room.

"Beaulieu. . . . You mixedblood bastard."

"Nothing is certain," responded Beaulieu.

"Lunch?" asked Border.

"No."

"Selfish bastard. . . . Then at least tell me what Alinsky said last
night. What are the new rules for radicals?" asked Border, pitching

back in his high-back chair and closing his eyes to listen. He preferred telephone conversations with people because visual contacts made him nervous.

It was spring and the winter dreams of radicals and racial ideologies were budding into abstract forms. Saul Minsky, the radical organizer and street-tough theoretician, was on his "zookeeper mentality" tour and had spoken at the Lutheran Redeemer Church in Minneapolis to a collection of fair-minded liberals. He said it was the issue and the action, not the skin color that made the difference in organizing for social changes.

"Alinsky blessed himself with cigarette smoke," said Beaulieu. "He smokes too much. He toured through the usual zookeeper shit . . . his social worker shockers . . . and then defined power as amoral, power as having the ability to act. The liberals loved him. You should have been there. . . . Why do you fight being the great white liberal you are?"

"Be serious, Beaulieu," said Border.

"Yes, this is a revolution, right?" said the mixedblood tribal organizer. "I remember two great lines from his speech: the tongue has a way of trapping the mind, and we are tranquilized by our own vocabulary. . . . He *is* one of the word warriors."

"More?"

"Never expect people to move without self-interest. . . . The white liberals there had no trouble knowing what that meant. Neither do you there, Farlie Custer."

Silence.

"He also said color made the difference . . ."

"The difference in what?"

"The difference in issues and actions."

"Bullshit! No white man said that," said Border.

"Listen to this," explained Beaulieu. "I was putting you on, color makes no difference for the moment, but the best part of the evening was a spontaneous speech made by an old bow and arrow, as George Mitchell says, one of the arrowstocracy. He called himself Sitting Bull one time and Crazy Horse the second time, one of the prairie arrowstocracy, and he moved forward through the old church with a loud voice, interrupting Alinsky. Saul took another cigarette and listened. No one had the courage to tell him to stop. He spoke your name."

Beaulieu remembered how silent the church was when the old arrowstocrat spoke:

"My people call me Sitting Bull. Listen here, who told you white skins to sit there feeling smug and stingy as ticks on a mongrel when you should be out there, in the streets with the rats and cockroaches, all over this land, burning down the Bureau of Indian Affairs?

"The Bureau is yours, your government made it up, and it is killing us while you sit in here talking and talking like ducks on a crowded pond. The white man has been killing us since he first drifted off course and got lost on the shores of our great mother earth. . . .

"Now our pockets are empty and mother earth is polluted and stripped for coal and iron. Why are you all sitting here listening to talking about talking from a white man? My name is Crazy Horse, remember that, you'll hear it again. My people are the proud Sioux. Listen, there are things to tell now. The white man puts himself in our way everywhere. Look at that Border and the Bureau, Custer is sitting everywhere holding up the Indians. Now all the original people on our mother earth go through white men and stand in lines for everything. The white man tries to make us like you to sit and listen to white people talking about talking about money and things and good places to live away from the poor.

"What would the white man do if he didn't have our problems to talk about? Think about all the people who are paid to talk about us and our so-called problems. Who would social workers be without us? Tell me this. Who would they be? They'd be out of work, that's where they'd be now. . . .

"But they are wrong, all wrong. The land will be ours again. Watch and see the land come back to us again. The earth will revolt and everything will be covered over with new earth and all the whites will disappear, but we will be with the animals again, we will be waiting in the trees and up on the sacred mountains. We will never assimilate in places like this. This church . . .

"There just ain't enough jobs in the Bureau of Indian Affairs to keep us all quiet. Everywhere else the government restores the nations they defeat in wars. Do you know why the Indian nations, the proudest people in the whole world, were never restored? Do you know why? You, all you white faces, do you know? The answer is simple, see how dumb white people are. This is the answer, listen now, because we were never defeated, never defeated, that is the answer. . . .

"Everywhere else in the world the white government sends food and medicine to people who are hungry and sick but not to the Indians. We get nothing, nothing, because the white man never defeated us, but he makes his living on us being poor. The white man needs us to be poor for his sick soul. We got nothing because we have never been defeated, remember that. . . .

"The white government puts people everywhere in our way, trying to defeat us with words now and meetings so we can be helped. But we still dance, see. The road to evil and hell will never be laid with feathers from our sacred eagles. We are the people of the wind and water and mountains and we will not be talked into defeat, because we know the secrets of mother earth, we talk in the tongues of the sacred earth and animals. We are still dancing. When we stop dancing then you can restore us. . . .

"Remember me. Remember me talking here. My face is here before you. My name is Crazy Horse and when I talk the earth talks through me in a vision. I am Crazy Horse. . . ."

When he stopped talking he lowered his head, fitted his straw hat on his head over his braids, drew his scarred finger under his nose, and then walked in a slow shuffle down the center of the church and through the center doors to the outside.

Alinsky lighted another cigarette.

"Catch you later, Custer," said Beaulieu.

"Fuck you, Beaulieu," said Farlie Border, dropping the telephone and stroking his white beard. He sat back and remembered the first time he encountered a tribal person. The experience still haunts him at night. It was in northern Wisconsin where his parents had a summer cabin. Border had seen people with dark skin from a distance, his parents called them savages, but it was not until he was fifteen that he had his first real personal encounter.

He was watching the sun setting behind the red pines across the lake when he heard several dogs barking. Young Border opened the door of the cabin and no sooner had he focused on four reservation mongrels chasing a domestic black cat than the animals turned around twice and ran past him into the cabin. The four mongrels knocked him down in the door. He stood up again, the cat reversed the course and he was knocked down a second time when the dogs came out of the cabin. Then, in a rage, he took his rifle, which was mounted near the back door, and shot at the cat and two mongrels before an old tribal man grabbed his arm and knocked him to the ground. Border rolled over and sprang back on his feet ready to fight, but reconsidered when he came face to face with four tribal people. The faces smiled at him and pointed at his white hair. At first the tribal people teased him, speaking part of the time in a tribal language. They called him an old woman with white hair, but then, recognizing a historical resurrection, he was named General George Custer.

"Custer, you killed our animals."

"Wild animals," said Border to the four faces.

"Everything is wild, little Custer."

"But the mongrels attacked me," pleaded Border.

"Now you must pay for our animals."

"You must pay us for the wild," said another face.

"How much?" asked Border.

"Ten thousand dollars," said a third dark face.

"How much?"

"Ten million dollars," said a fourth dark face.

"What did you say?" Border asked again.

"Then return the land to wild," said the old man.

"What wild?"

"Your cabin and the land is ours."

Border resisted their demanding voices and became arrogant and hostile. He demanded that his rifle be returned and made a detracting remark about tribal people. The tribal faces smiled and mocked his words and manners, and then touched him again and pulled at his white hair. Border was furious and lunged at the old man, but the old tribal shaman stepped aside like a trickster. Border tripped and fell to the ground.

"This is wild land," said the old man. "This has been tribal land since the beginning of the world. . . . What you know is nothing. Custer has taken your heart."

Border spit on the old man.

"Custer has returned," said the old man.

"Rotten savages," said Border.

The sun had set behind the red pines.

Silence.

The old man motioned with his hands and then hummed ho ho ha ha ha haaaa. . . . Border was weakened under the gaze of the old man. Then he was overcome with dizziness. Moments later, he has never been sure how much time passed, he regained consciousness. His rifle was gone. His eyes were crossed and his vision was weakened. He could not see straight for several hours. Border still dreams about falling with the setting sun into deep black pools, like the deep dark eyes of the old tribal man who possessed him with his shamanic powers.

Border bounced his fingers together.

The office was too warm.

"My name is Crazy Horse," he said, standing inside the office door on the bone-white carpet. "Sitting Bull and Crazy Horse and I have come down here to see you alone. . . . I came on the rails not on relocation. Need some cash now, not much, but enough to make it for a time. . . . And some work, hard to find work, like your work, whatever you can find me to do well."

Border turned in his high-back chair. Looking toward the floor, avoiding eye contact, he saw that Crazy Horse was wearing scuffed cowboy boots and tight blue jeans. His crotch was stained and his shirt was threadbare at the elbows. He rolled his own cigarettes and carried a leather pouch of loose tobacco lashed to his belt.

"Crazy Horse is the name. . . ."

Border said nothing. While he watched his hands he thought about the old tribal man at the cabin. Crazy Horse cracked his knuckles and then hooked his thumbs under his belt. Tattoos, wearing thin on his fingers, spelled "love" on the left and "hate" on the right hand.

Crazy Horse waited on the white carpet. The longer he waited for recognition the more he smiled. He bumped the brim of his western straw hat with his thumb, tipping it back from his forehead. His right ear moved with ease when he smiled. Animals knew more about smiling than people, animals knew that when he smiled and moved his ear in a certain way, it meant that he was in spiritual control of the situation. He survived much better when white people did not speak, because words, too many words, loosened his concentration and visual power.

Silence.

Border was breathing faster. The veins in his neck throbbed harder and his stomach rose in sudden shifts beneath his light-blue summer suit. Border turned and looked into the face of the stranger. His eyes were deep black pools. Border could not shift his focus from Crazy Horse. He was being drawn into the dark pools, the unknown, he was falling in his vision. His arms tingled and his head buzzed, but before he slipped from consciousness into the deep dark pools of tribal shamanism, he sprang from his chair with the last of his energy, like a cat, leaped across the white carpet and struck at the tribal face with his white fists again and again until he lost his vision and consciousness. He was peaceful then. Face down on the deep white carpet he could smell the prairie earth that dropped from the boots of the shaman.

"Border, wake up . . . wake up, wake up."

Silence.

Border came back to his time in consciousness, but he was uncertain, he wondered if he could travel forever from the place he had been on the floor. His vision was weak, colors were less distinct, sunlight was blurred as it fell through the windows in the outer offices, blurred as it was when the old tribal man hexed him at the cabin. He did recognize the shapes of familiar faces around him, his fellow federal employees. The women rubbed his arms and face, and then the men lifted him into his high-back chair.

Silence.

"Where is that man?" asked Border.

"What man?"

"That man called Crazy Horse."

"Crazy Horse?"

"Crazy Horse, peculiar name of course," his secretary explained. "Well, he waited for a few minutes, not too long, and then left while you were on the telephone . . . but he did say he would be back sometime."

Farlie Border shivered in his sleep for months. His dreams were about people falling into deep pools, dark pools, people he could not reach. In some dreams he saw his own face in the pools, slipping under before he could reach himself. To balance his fear and boredom with his work he turned to visual and mechanical thrills. He ingested hallucinogenic drugs, subsidized bizarre sexual acts, bought a police radio so he could be at the scene of accidents, and drove a powerful motorcycle.

Border disappeared late in the summer. White people said he was teaching at a college for women, but tribal rumors held that his vision crossed coming around a curve at high speed on his motorcycle and he died in the wind space behind a grain truck . . . slipping from grace in a slipstream.

Aunt Parnetta's Electric Blisters

DIANE GLANCY

(1990)

> For the old-time people, time was not a series of ticks of a clock,
> one following the other. For the old-time people time was
> round—like a tortilla; time had specified moments and specific
> locations so that the beloved ancestors who had passed on were
> not annihilated by death, but only relocated. . . . All times go on
> existing side by side for all eternity. No moment is lost or
> destroyed. There are no future times or past times; there are
> *always all* the times, which differ slightly, as the locations
> on the tortilla differ slightly.
> —*Leslie Marmon Silko*

DIANE GLANCY (CHEROKEE) bases her sense of time on ideas she gleaned when auditing a physics course: time as a rubber band, stretchable, or as little loops. Millions of years can be

kinked up and crawled over. There are wormholes you can fall down and get lost in and then come back up and move on and travel. So time is certainly not really circular, and it's certainly not linear. There are lapses and times within times, and coils, and other geometrical patterns that time can follow. It can undulate, and be wavelike, going back and forth . . . History is a multiplicity . . . [akin to] the unrolling of many scrolls . . . going back and retrieving what was there but has not had a voice.[1]

This view of time infuses the central sf element in "Aunt Parnetta's Electric Blisters": the kinked-up, coiled, rutting hog of a fridge, which sometimes slipstreams Custer and Little Big Horn, sometimes Talequah, the capital of the Cherokee nation, sometimes the old road there (and the Trail of Tears), and sometimes the repositioning of the heart of Aunt Parnetta herself.

A ceremonial tale of everyday rituals to be told anytime, since the fridge is where it is "always winter," Glancy's Native slipstream encompasses the importance of nature, animal transformations, the Great Spirit, family, the intrusion of the dream world, ancestors speaking and not being held down by physical borders—all contributing to a kind of "spirit DNA that brings us into line."[2] The interactions of human–animal–machine in this story call to mind Jim Jarmusch's *Dead Man,* where the frozen stasis of the American frontier industrial Machine Town at the film's opening contrasts sharply with the vibrancy and advanced technologies of the remote Makah village at its close. Which civilization serves a more utilitarian purpose? Which will break down more easily?

Glancy's comments on the story address the affinity between technology and Native culture:

> I was happy "Aunt Parnetta's Electric Blisters" was in the Norton sf reader. I hadn't thought of the story in terms of sf, but after it appeared there, I understood. The story is about technology and primitivism in folk culture. A glossy white box in which it is winter year around. A magical place in which things are preserved. It seems the visions of the spirit world that often appear in Native culture are close to the imagery of video art I see in my grandchildren's screen. Electricity is a trickster. There is magic to it. I remember a [Northern Arapaho] sculptor named Ernie Whiteman who made spirits with neon tubes of lighting. I liked his neon art. There again, that combination of tradition and technology.

ℋ

Some stories can be told only in winter
This is not one of them
because the fridge is for Parnetta
where it's always winter.

Hey chekta! All this and now the refrigerator broke. Uncle Filo scratched the long gray hairs that hung in a tattered braid on his back. All that foot stomping and fancy dancing. Old warriors still at it.

"But when did it help?" Aunt Parnetta asked. The fridge ran all through the cold winter when she could have set the milk and eggs in the snow. The fish and meat from the last hunt. The fridge had walked through the spring when she had her quilt and beading money. Now her penny jar was empty, and it was hot, and the glossy white box broke. The coffin! If Grandpa died, they could put him in it with his war ax and tomahawk. His old dog even. But how would she get a new fridge?

The repairman said he couldn't repair it. Whu chutah! Filo loaded his rifle and sent a bullet right through it. Well, he said, a man had to take revenge. Had to stand against civilization. He watched the summer sky for change as though the stars were white leaves across the hill. Would the stars fall? Would Filo have to rake them when cool weather came again? Filo coughed and scratched his shirt pocket as though something crawled deep within his breastbone. His heart maybe, if he ever found it. Aunt Parnetta stood at the sink, soaking the sheets before she washed them.

"Dern't nothin' we dude ever work?" Parnetta asked, poking the sheets with her stick.

"We bought that ferge back twenty yars," Filo told her. "And it nerked since then."

"Weld, dernd," she answered. "Could have goned longer til the frost cobered us. Culb ha' set the milk ertside. But nowd. It weren't werk that far."

"Nope," Filo commented. "It weren't."

Parnetta looked at her beadwork. Her hands flopped at her sides. She couldn't have it done for a long time. She looked at the white patent-leathery box. Big enough for the both of them. For the cow if it died.

"Set it out in the backyard with the last one we had."

They drove to Tahlequah that afternoon, Filo's truck squirting dust and pinging rocks.

They parked in front of the hardware store on Muskogee Street. The regiments of stoves, fridges, washers, dryers, stood like white soldiers. The Yellow Hair Custer was there to command them. Little Big Horn. Whu chutah! The prices! Three hundred crackers.

"Some mord than thad," Filo surmised, his flannel shirt-collar tucked under itself, his braid sideways like a rattler on his back.

"Filo, I dern't think we shulb decide terday."

"No," the immediate answer stummed from his mouth like a roach from under the baseboard in the kitchen.

"We're just lookin'?"

"Of course," said Custer.

They walked to the door leaving the stoves, washers, dryers, the televisions all blaring together, and the fridges lined up for battle.

Filo lifted his hand from the rattled truck.

"Surrender," Parnetta said. "Izend thad the way id always iz?"

The truck spurted and spattered and shook Filo and Aunt Parnetta before Filo got it backed into the street. The forward gear didn't buck as much as the backward.

When they got home, Filo took the back off the fridge and looked at the motor. It could move a load of hay up the road if it had wheels. Could freeze half the fish in the pond. The minute coils, the twisting intestines of the fridge like the hog he butchered last winter, also with a bullet hole in its head.

"Nothin we dude nerks." Parnetta watched him from the kitchen window. "Everythin' against uz," she grumbled to herself.

Filo got his war feather from the shed, put it in his crooked braid. He stomped his feet, hooted. Filo, the medicine man, transcended to the spirit world for the refrigerator. He shook each kink and bolt. The spirit of cold itself. He whooped and warred in the yard for nearly half an hour.

"Not with a bullet hole in it." Parnetta shook her head and wiped the sweat from her face.

He got his wrench and hacksaw, the ax and hammer. It was dead now for sure. Parnetta knew it at the sink. It was the thing that would be buried in the backyard. "Like most of us libed," Aunt Parnetta talked to herself. "Filled with our own workings, not doint what we shulb."

Parnetta hung the sheets in the yard, white and square as the fridge itself.

The new refrigerator came in a delivery truck. It stood in the kitchen. Bought on time at a bargain. Cheapest in the store. Filo made sure of it. The interest over five years would be as much as the fridge. Aunt Parnetta tried to explain it to him. The men set the fridge where Parnetta instructed them. They adjusted and leveled the little hog feet. They gave Parnetta the packet of information, the guarantee. Then drove off in victory. The new smell of the gleaming white inside as though cleansed by cedar from the Keetowah fire.

Aunt Parnetta had Filo take her to the grocery store on the old road to Tahlequah. She loaded the cart with milk and butter. Frozen waffles. Orange juice. Anything that had to be kept cool. The fridge made noise, she thought, she would get used to it. But in the night, she heard the fridge. It seemed to fill her dreams. She had trouble going to sleep, even on the clean white sheets, and she had trouble staying asleep. The fridge was like a giant hog in the kitchen. Rutting and snorting all night. She got up once and unplugged it. Waking early the next morn to plug it in again before the milk and eggs got warm.

"That ferge bother yeu, Filo?" she asked.

"Nord."

Aunt Parnetta peeled her potatoes outside. She mended Filo's shirts under the shade tree. She didn't soak anything in the kitchen sink anymore, not even the sheets or Filo's socks. There were things she just had to endure, she grumped. That's the way it was.

When the grandchildren visited, she had them run in the kitchen for whatever she needed. They picnicked on the old watermelon table in the backyard. She put up the old teepee for them to sleep in.

"Late in the summer fer that?" Filo quizzed her.

"Nert. It waz nert to get homesick for the summer that's leabing us like the childurn." She gratified him with her keen sense. Parnetta could think up anything for what she wanted to do.

Several nights Filo returned to their bed, with its geese-in-flight-over-the-swamp pattern quilt, but Aunt Parnetta stayed in the teepee under the stars.

"We bined muried thurdy yars. Git in the house," Filo said one night under the white leaves of the stars.

"I can't sleep 'cause of that wild hog in the kitchen," Aunt Parnetta said. "I tald yeu that."

"Hey chekta!" Filo answered her. "Why didn't yeu teld me so I knowd whad yeu said." Filo covered the white box of the fridge with the geese quilt and an old Indian blanket he got from the shed. "Werd yeu stayed out thar all winder?"

"Til the beast we got in thar dies."

"Hawly gizard," Filo spurted. "Thard be anuther twendy yars!"

Aunt Parnetta was comforted by the bedroom that night. Old Filo's snore after he made his snorting love to her. The gray-and-blue-striped wallpaper with its watermarks. The stovepipe curling up to the wall like a hog tail. The bureau dresser with a little doily and her hairbrush. Pictures by their grandchildren. A turquoise coyote and a ghostly figure the boy told her was Running Wind.

She fell into a light sleep where the white stars blew down from the sky, flapping like the white sheets on the line. She nudged Filo to get his rake. He turned sharply against her. Parnetta woke and sat on the edge of the bed.

"Yeu wand me to cuber the ferge wid something else?" Filo asked from his sleep.

"No," Aunt Parnetta answered him. "Nod unless id be the polar ice cap."

Now it was an old trip to Minnesota when she was a girl. Parnetta saw herself in a plaid shirt and braids. Had her hair been that dark? Now it was streaked with gray. Everything was like a child's drawing. Exaggerated. The way dreams were sometimes. A sun in the left corner of the picture. The trail of chimney smoke from the narrow house. It was cold. So cold that everything creaked. She heard cars running late into the night. Early mornings, steam growled out of the exhaust. The pane of window glass in the front door had been somewhere else. Old lettering showed up in the frost. Bones remembered their aches in the cold. Teeth, their hurt. The way Parnetta remembered every bad thing that happened. She dwelled on it.

The cold place was shriveled to the small upright rectangle in her chest, holding the fish her grandson caught in the river. That's where the cold place was. Right inside her heart. No longer pumping like the blinker lights she saw in town. She was the Minnesota winter she remembered as a child. The electricity it took to keep her cold! The energy. The moon over her like a ceiling light. Stars were holes where the rain came in. The dripping buckets. All of them like Parnetta. The *hurrrrrrrrr* of the fridge. Off. On. All night. That white box. Wild boar! Think of it. She didn't always know why she was disgruntled. She just was. She saw herself as the fridge. A frozen fish stiff as a brick. The Great Spirit had her pegged. Could she find her heart, maybe, if she looked somewhere in her chest?

Hurrrrrrrr. Rat-tat-at-rat. Hurrr. The fridge came on again, and startled, she woke and teetered slightly on the edge of the bed while it growled.

But she was a stranger in this world. An Indian in a white man's land. "Even the ferge's whate," Parnetta told the Great Spirit.

"Wasn't everybody a stranger and pilgrim?" The Great Spirit seemed to speak to her, or it was her own thoughts wandering in her head from her dreams.

"No," Parnetta insisted. Some people were at home on this earth, moving with ease. She would ask the Great Spirit more about it later. When he finally yanked the life out of her like the pin in a grenade.

Suddenly Parnetta realized that she was always moaning like the fridge. Maybe she irritated the Great Spirit like the white box irritated her. Did she sound that way to anyone else? Was that the Spirit's revenge? She was stuck with the cheapest box in the store. In fact, in her fears, wasn't it a white boar which would tear into the room and eat her soon as she got good and asleep?

Hadn't she seen the worst in things? Didn't she weigh herself in the winter with her coat on? Sometimes wrapped in the blanket also?

"Filo?" She turned to him. But he was out cold. Farther away than Minnesota.

"No. Just think about it, Parnetta," her thoughts seemed to say. The Spirit had blessed her life. But inside the white refrigerator of herself—inside the coils, an ice river surged. A glacier mowed its way across a continent. Everything frozen for eons. In need of a Keetowah fire. Heat. The warmth of the Great Spirit. Filo was only a spark. He could not warm her. Even though he tried.

Maybe the Great Spirit had done her a favor. Hope like white sparks of stars glistened in her head. The electric blisters. *Temporary!* She could shut up. She belonged to the Spirit. He had just unplugged her a minute. Took his rifle right through her head.

The leaves growled and spewed white sparks in the sky. It was a volcano from the moon. Erupting in the heavens. Sending down its white sparks like the pinwheels Filo used to nail on trees. It was the bright sparks of the Keetowah fire, the holy bonfire from which smaller fires burned, spreading the purification of the Great Spirit into each house. Into each hard, old pinecone heart.

from *The Fast Red Road*

A Plainsong

STEPHEN GRAHAM JONES

(2000)

> Your past is a skeleton walking one step behind you, and your
> future is a skeleton walking one step in front of you. . . . And they
> can trap you in the in-between, between touching and becoming . . .
> keep walking, keep moving. . . . See, it is always now. That's what
> Indian time is. The past, the future, all of it is wrapped up in the
> now. That's how it is. *We are trapped in the now.*
> —*Sherman Alexie*

STEPHEN GRAHAM JONES (PIEGAN BLACKFEET) says that "science
fiction's always been the bulls-eye I'm lobbing darts at. I was going to
say it saved me, but that's kind of a lie. It'd really be Louis L'Amour
who saved me, him and Robert Jordan, finding me when I was eleven,
twelve, showing me this whole other world out there, in my head. I
came over to science fiction soon enough, though. I mean, change
the outfits, and L'Amour's Sacketts are space explorers, yeah? But,
after that version of Old West, space and the future—sometimes even
the Hyperborean Age—tended to be more inclusive, and not just on
the deck of the *Enterprise*. And, once I lucked into Samuel Delaney,
into Philip K. Dick, into Asimov and Clarke and Bradbury, my world
kind of opened up."

As a tour de force in Native slipstream, his debut novel *The Fast Red Road: A Plainsong* offers a tongue-in-cheek take on the so-called pan-Indian Red Road to wisdom and enlightenment. Interspersing alternative histories of the ends of various possible "americas" with prognostications on the resurgence of a possible future "america," the novel begins as a fast and furious Indian road trip in the vein of popular Native films like *Powwow Highway* and *Smoke Signals*. But it also deftly invokes the black apocalyptic humor of Thomas Pynchon's nuclear age in *Gravity's Rainbow,* while also calling to mind the rapidly escalating time slippages of Philip K. Dick's *Ubik*. Jones's Red Road stretches out a series of "Custer on slipstream" events, "Native time slots," "glitches," and "syndicated time loops," whiplashing us between the thirteenth century to imaginable tomorrows, with visits among culture-jamming medieval Goliard clerics and massacre victims at Wounded Knee, Nagasaki, and Hiroshima spaced in between.

The scene offered here takes place in Clovis, New Mexico, where a Native archeological dig of a Precambrian site is abruptly co-opted by nearby university academics. Amerindian Larry is the owner of the construction company overseeing the dig. Charlie Ward is grandfather, turtle-man trickster, who frequently shape-shifts into various animals; he owns a red Ford Cutlass that can transform into a spaceship or tunnel into the earth like a submarine. Pidgin is a mixedblood Blackfeet Indian who is trying to inter his dad's body nine years after a government lab finally releases it from clinical experimentation, "no cavity unviolated, and a seam-ridden heart . . . back in the wrong side of his chest where it had always been."

Jones says this about the story:

> *Fast Red Road*'s got man-eating cannabis plants, coyotes too small to be seen, and headlights that stay in the clouds for decades—zygotes in the sky. To me it's a reality that's all melted together, a place where every cubic inch has three square feet of meaning packed in, so that the physical laws we think we know, they've got no choice but to bend back on themselves, let us see the real underbelly of the world. A running cartoon where none of the old rules apply, where the television channel can change all around you, but the story, this cycle Pidgin's hopefully at the tail end of if he can just hold on, it's supposed to be the thing that

thrusts through all the levels of reality, kind of splats onto the coffee table in front of whoever's watching this cartoon, right onto that burrito. Or there's another part in here where Pidgin's in his head, falling down through awning after awning, wondering if he's ever even going to hit the ground. That's the reader, maybe, the guy in the convenience store who picked this burrito up in the first place, zapped it for about ten seconds too long so that it woke up, looked through the window at him.

That sense of "the physical laws we think we know" having "no choice but to bend back on themselves" hints at Jones's juxtaposition of Native thinking and scientific theory—specifically, Fermat's Last Theorem and the so-called new religion of superstring theory via quantum mechanics. Jones's short story "The Man Who Could Time Travel" presents a more Borgesian puzzle of the complexity of that stock sf scenario. But many of his survivance stories and novels, including *The Fast Red Road* and *The Long Trial of Nolan Dugatti* (2008), resonate with the work of quantum physicists F. David Peat and David Bohm, who have worked with the Blackfoot, Mi'kmaq, Cree, and Anishinaabe in identifying common ground between Eurowestern science and Native worldviews. So, for example, "Blackfoot physics" includes other spaces and times interpenetrated and coexisting with our own, comparable to the multiverses and parallel universes touted by science writers like John Gribbin. Interested readers may want to access Peat's *Blackfoot Physics* (2005) or its earlier iteration, *Blackfoot Physics: A Journey into the Native American Universe* (1995). Suffice it here to point out that Jones's dexterity with scientific elegance is completely in line with the best in sf tradition.

In the rearview mirror Larry's star jacket reared lifeless and hulking. Pidgin slung it into the pit too, held close to his thigh the banktube he'd plundered against his will. In the Cutlass he inspected it as morbid duty dictated: it was Cline Stob's resistance piece in duplicate—the original on brittle engineering paper with unidle pictograms, the copy on vellum in Larry's grand hand, both undeciphered. And there was another thing too, under them, a photograph from the first generation of cameras, when shutter speed could be sundialed in. A barefoot

Indian with a wide scarf tied around his head. The exotic. He was mounted on a white horse and the saddle was English, polished to brown glass, mane and tail combed with care. The Indian's camera-side bare foot was hooked lightly in the stirrups, his knee bent at the proper angle, his back held military straight. He had been posed. The photo was worn at the edges where Larry had held it, looking into it for something. There were no words on the back. It existed out of time. Pidgin left it in the tube with the letter because maybe it was nonlinear medicine against the algorithm, an antidote of some kind.

Pidgin didn't want the tube, the cylindrical parcel. He knew what it was worth.

He sat in the Cutlass again, burdened, surrounded by Clovis. When Charlie Ward appeared by the driverside door, gas can in one hand, cases of looted spirit gum in the other, Pidgin said he wasn't going to let this bullshit consume him. He slung his hand around the headliner to show. Charlie Ward grunted that he understood. He said he was going west for a windshield, grandson. Pidgin said he could do that, he could do that. It was settled. Charlie Ward gassed the car back up and they were in motion again, gutting the asphalt with the rock snail, the car sitting lowrider-deep in the road, dragging sparks. It wasn't a fast getaway. They screeched slow and halting around corners, the Cutlass stalling over and over, vacuum-locked, the chain too hot to touch anymore. Finally at the edge of town some weak link snapped and the snail cartwheeled into a field, moving faster in death than it ever had in life, and Pidgin and Charlie Ward slingshot ahead, freed, blowing spirit bubbles that stuck in their hair, coated their chins, tangled their fingers in stringy grey matter. The new religion. Pidgin watched the upturned bowl of the sky for missing pieces spanned like crane wings. He asked where Charlie Ward had been, and Charlie Ward shrugged, said back and forth. His security guard outfit was fresh pressed, had crisp ridges down the arms and legs. The tin badge shone.

"You going to arrest me, yeah?" Pidgin asked.

Charlie Ward replied with his foot, buried it deeper yet in the Cutlass. It didn't respond. Their speed was legal, and there were keys in the ignition. They were two longhairs going from place to place now, crossing no state lines even. Looking for a windshield. Charlie Ward told all the same stories in all the same order: cars cars cars, the occasional Mexican Wasp. The bandit-black Trans-Am and Hopiland was third from the end in the coup succession, and Pidgin was a nameless passenger in it, a white-knuckled accomplice, both feet on the dash. It was an attitude of reluctance. He watched his depersonalized self in Charlie Ward's tale, asked him to tell it again, felt himself already becoming the uneasy rider in the windshield story they were currently making. Each movement became heavy, labored with eventual description. The effort needed to sustain even the vagaries of a breathing pattern put him to sleep, where he dreamed he was in the Cutlass heading west, looking for the windshield that would solve it all. Charlie Ward was talking and driving and driving and talking.

When Pidgin woke it was an incomplete action, and he had to claw up through layers and layers of false wakenings. On the bench seat again, the nap real between his real fingers, he tried to claw up even further, out of New Mexico, but he was plateaued. The Cutlass was motionless. Charlie Ward called it Chaves County, but that didn't matter; there was a sign out Pidgin's window. It read A-1 AUTO SALVAGE, had a UFO stenciled in in the background, the two A-1 mechanics dismantling it for parts, tinkering those parts into Edsels and Studebakers and Saabs, in that order. The UFO was a familiar disc of light in the sky to Pidgin. He clamped onto the dash, not breathing, not doing anything until Charlie Ward reached across the seat, touched Pidgin's line of underlip hair. Charlie Ward was wearing a polished bone thimble on the reaching thumb when he did it, touched Pidgin. It was unaccountable; it was an old man trick: the thimble on hairstub made a jawdeep scratching sound that pried Pidgin's fingers from the dash vinyl and pushed him out of the car by the marrow. It wasn't light yet, but close. Charlie Ward said she was always open, that was a thing about her.

"She?"

"Her."

They got no further without proper names. They walked through the gate, were met by no junkyard dogs.

There was a kerosene lamp hung on the open trunk of a makeless car. It guttered yellow with their entrance gust and Pidgin understood what Larry had meant about the senses expanding. He could no longer reel them back in. Two manshapes stepped as one from behind two wrecked panel vans. "I think they're calling to you," Charlie Ward said, and then eased down a carwide aisle of parts, unqueried. The two men were the mechanics from the sign. Both flat-eyed and dark-skinned. The one who approached from the north wore a Thoth-Amon shirt and stage boots; the one from the south had a motocross breastplate and was poking a screen into the top of a Dr Pepper can. They sat in the lee of a third panel van and smoked, passed the can around twice before there were any words, any introductions. The Thoth-Amon mechanic began it. He asked Pidgin if he knew of the two of them. Pidgin shook his head no. Thoth-Amon shrugged it off, said in days past they had been the Skag Brothers, the Phillips Head Brothers, and the dual subject of an image-driven documentary called *Glory Dog*. Now they were Killbourne and Cornbleu, of Aughtman Wrecking Services. Pidgin said he was Pidgin. Cornbleu rustled against his bumper-stickered breastplate and said they weren't without the occasional briefing: they knew of Pidgin.

"From Clovis, yeah?" he said.

Pidgin nodded.

Cornbleu held up the can for inspection, said the pot too, it was from Clovis. "We even bought it from a fucking *pirate,*" he said, "here in the big NM, understand?" He laughed, lost his smoke, covered one eye then the other, left conversational room for appreciation or awe or acknowledgment. Pidgin had none of the three to give anymore. Killbourne filled the empty space with tightlipped staring. Cornbleu turned his head away, leading with the tripartite brow of his right eye. It was a ducking motion. Killbourne continued his glare and explained that there were still a few procedural wrinkles to iron out: they'd only won the A-1 contract six months ago, only met her a few weeks back. Their duties here were vague.

Pidgin backpedaled. "Her?" he asked for the second time.

Cornbleu said it, still looking away: "Jackie. Jackie Feather, man. Jacqueline. The sweetheart of yesterday's rodeo. The Salvage Queen, y'know, shit. Used to do seances and shit over in Texas? That's how she financed this place, the yard. Bought it for less than two grand twenty years ago, then made it into this. *That* her."

Pidgin nodded that he had seen her once, yes—indelible, shuffling. "I didn't come here for a seance, though," he said, "that would be about the last thing I need."

Cornbleu used his whole forearm to wipe his nose. "She'll *tell* you what you need, compadre. Count on that."

Killbourne rubbed his nose, stepped between them, said it was a good contract they had with her, as far as contracts went. But too, it was kind of long-term temporary, would only last until they got together enough stake money to produce their TV pilot, in which they would be reincarnated yet again and sold wholesale to the public thirty minutes at a time. He made Pidgin guess the title and Pidgin guessed The Tonto Talk Show, with Cato on gongs. It got the necessary laughs. Killbourne passed the Dr Pepper can back to Pidgin, said to cash it if it needed cashing.

Pidgin negotiated the can to his face, rolled the lighter wheel four times slow, making sixteen sparks. Cornbleu laughed, said the sacred herb was getting to their honored guest already. Killbourne corrected: the THC was just doing the rete mirabile shuffle with Pidgin's psyche. It was a necessary dance. Without it none of this would make sense. Tonic clonic was a single word the way he said it, ran together in the middle. Cornbleu acted it out with his hand, from a sitting position.

Pidgin watched from an internal distance, trying to deal with the time lag involved, and said it was too late; he was already convulsed on the insides, spasmed out. He offered the spirit gum around. Killbourne and Cornbleu lined their hatbands with it with Hendrixian precision, said they were loyal. Dawn was miles away, an inchoate glow. Charlie Ward a metal noise rooting in the distance, an old man picking over trucks with his windshield measurements scrawled over the leathery back of his hand.

Cornbleu pulled Pidgin back into their three-pointed circle, pulled him back with a name.

"Glory Dog the Series," he said, underlining *series,* spitting it like a bad taste, getting the jump on Killbourne. Killbourne swelled. He said it was better than Red Noise or Indian Time, no? Or, what, Young Pagans in Love? They were at it in silence, dagger-eyed and ham-fisted, maybe real brothers even. Pidgin looked past their rivalry and saw the insistent hem of a densely beaded dress, the flash of a slim ankle, but then it was gone behind a car husk. Killbourne said to ignore it for now. They had a little more ground to cover first: Cornbleu produced the pilot episode of their long teleplay from inside his plastic breastplate. There were mimeographs, enough for all. Glory Dog the Series. It left them blue-fingered like jail. The working title of the first episode was multiple choice either *The* Glitch, *Our* Glitch, or, in a different hand, Glitchman Rex.

"Only three?" Pidgin asked as Killbourne backed away, framing with thumbs and index fingers, but got no response. The shot was him and Cornbleu. Cornbleu narrated the introductions in rapidfire sentences, detailed the fast-cut glam shots that would orient the viewer to their Indian locale, the Native time slot. First there was a lone vole keeping nervous time, acting like he was on medicine. Next was a Ouida bird caught in a tailspin, which panned down to a shot which foregrounded the beauty and the economy of the dog travois. Last, of course, was the animated Pocahontas dancing and singing off-center, double D at least, piped like a prima donna, seen first on a hand-held television set in a Roman Catholic stadium and then suddenly on all the sets the crowd was locked to. There were one-way dotted lines drawn from the tiny screen to the eye, and as the screen became the monitor of a video game, the eye became Iron Eyes Cody himself, roadside, thinking in Italian. The first season in a visual capsule. Cornbleu called it a spring-loaded suppository.

Pidgin didn't laugh; he was to play himself for most of it. He had scripted lines to follow, written in longhand, in a cursive peyote allowed. But still. He dropped the teleplay. Behind him Killbourne was warming up a decrepit theramin, and right beside him Cornbleu was wrestling from his breastplate a jawharp strung with catgut. He got it out, and after a few false starts they fell into a zydeco-influenced getaway beat that would accompany Pidgin, scrambling across time. Cornbleu told Pidgin he was the good guy here, remember, but Pidgin kicked the teleplay away, blew at it, refused to touch it with bare skin, and his antics cued a laugh track. When his back was turned to the canned laughter and to the idea of a camera Killbourne stood for, Cornbleu stage-whispered that Pidgin was doing fine, perfect, he was a natural Nature's Child.

Pidgin shook his head no, no, was rewarded with another laugh track, with one man laughing long and Spanish in the mezzanine. Pidgin cast about for the Mexican Paiute, for the Y on his father's chest that didn't need a question mark. Killbourne said to look at the camera, look at the camera. Pidgin found the teleplay in his hands again, leading him by the lips. He pantomimed the back and forth with Cornbleu, read his lines about how *The* Glitch had occurred circa 1610 or so, and those three core figures involved never died but transmigrated over the centuries, athanasiaed, cursed by instant karma to walk the earth, atone, make germ-line repairs, kill the damned butterfly, get back on that good red road and burn some serious rubber. He explained it to Cornbleu the Fawning Initiate first by way of failing sestinas and villanelles, and when that didn't work he retreated to the *Wargames* computer: the historical characters were jumping from actor to actor, running through all the options over and over, faster and faster, trying to escape the cycle, unbalance it somehow, spin it off track. But each time. The cast multiplied around them yet the triangle held, wouldn't go away, informed them all. It was different but the same: Pocahontas and her captain and the old chief, the first domino.

Cornbleu nodded, agreeing, pretend-seeing what had been within reach the whole time, imitating Pidgin it seemed, improvising with him, and when Pidgin studied the teleplay to find his place, the next line Sally had written for him, he saw that the cursive he had been reading was just the lowercase letter *A* over and over with a light touch, a weak pen, a hurried hand. There were no words there, only the shape of a mouth, of his mouth in the moment before he had said it all from nothing, nowhere. He exited stage left before the mechanical applause could start, removed himself from the shot, hid in one of the panel vans that still smelled of prohibition-era beerbread. When Killbourne approached to console or to prompt, Pidgin stopped him, said enough already, enough.

Killbourne held his hands up, palm out.

From his recess Pidgin said he supposed Golias was slotted for a guest appearance in episode two, after hours in the make-up trailer? Killbourne shook his head no with a smile, said Golias was old hat, European, African of late. Episode two was to be more about the Dog Days of summer, when the snakes were blind with their own milky skin, striking at anything, at heat. It was to be a nature digression for the sake of ratings—that's what the audience would expect from the Native timeslot—and would segue directly into the previews for the third episode, which would shufflestep from nature to the historical players by revealing their Platonic plight—how they were denied total recall, anamnesis, how they started each time wiped clean, yet still had at least the *potential* for rememory locked in their collective unconsciouses. It influenced their unthinking actions, so that they knocked the domino over again and again.

"And the fourth?" Pidgin asked, weary of his own voice.

"The fourth," Killbourne said, "the fourth episode is really like the next step from the second episode, like there it branched into two threes, get it?" Pidgin nodded; Sally had hardwired him to understand things being the same in number yet distinct. Killbourne rolled on, explained that the so-called fourth episode would be about a conscious renouncement of harquebuses and Spanish horses; it would be a format for the return to the old meaning of Dog Days, when Indians didn't need anything European, when horses were dogs. People would listen.

"Slow-ass going on foot, though," Pidgin said, the desperate hole-puncher.

Killbourne shook his head no, it wasn't. "They got around," he said, "the old old Indians," holding both hands over imaginary ski poles that weren't ski poles, but the top part of stilts. "You know what I'm talking about here."

Pidgin turned in the direction of the Cutlass, in the direction of the volatile banktube forced under the bench seat like a pipe bomb. It was dramatic head movement and for once he hadn't meant it to be.

"How much are they paying you," Pidgin asked, Rhine's hungry hands on him again, "the truckers?"

"Cash on delivery," Cornbleu said from the background.

"I don't want to be on your TV program," Pidgin told Killbourne, "on any damn program."

Killbourne said he already was. He shook the script like a rattle, made a meek face, tendered an apology with cheek muscles. Pidgin didn't accept. That would be the first step. He said he wasn't looking at the Cutlass for any particular reason; he was just looking for Charlie Ward, and Charlie Ward was looking for a windshield, and that was all.

Killbourne nodded at the beaded dress hem undeniable four cars away, lifting and falling in the breeze occasioned by the predawn temperature dip. "Now," he said, "she's waiting. I guess you can either go to her, or . . ." He indicated the Cutlass, the banktube that needed guarding.

Pidgin crawled from the panel van, kept his back to it, looked back once to Killbourne who had him framed with his hands, the frame tilted diagonal, his feet meanwhile easing Cutlass-ward. If Pidgin ever needed to be two people. He flipped coins in his head and drew mental straws and finally just leaned uphill, away from Killbourne, away from both of them, then covered the last two car widths in a bound, a two-legged pounce. The dress he had picked over the bank-tube was in motion too, though, ahead of him already. It was a young girl, the Kiowa-Comanche girl from Four Corners, the postdoc's tiny dancer, the automaton's grand-daughter. She hadn't aged. Pidgin wove in behind her and understood he had both feet fully in the amusement park now, was feeling his way down funhouse walls hammered out of junked cars. His distorted reflection in the chrome bumpers assaulted him, gave him a new kinesthetic, made him move like he looked. He rolled after the girl like a ragdoll, and it was because she let him, because she re-presented herself each time he lost her. He chased her and chased her, and she ran through the fluid dance steps she'd lured the postdoc in with, and then she ran on, to California, where she concealed herself in a pay-sweat and waited with the long, eightfold sight of a spider.

Pidgin could draw no closer than ten car lengths. It was enough. The postdoc wandered in, kneeling to catalogue the occasional hubcap-as-cultural artifact, counting his money against the pay-sweat sign, pulling the flap closed behind him. The white back of his index finger was the last thing of his in the world, and then it too slipped away and he left no brilliant, unfading afterimage. Moments later the sleeping-bag-covered frame shook itself awake. The postdoc screamed from within, a muffled plaint, and Pidgin felt his eyebrows grin at the situation, grin with the tiny dancer, for her, but it was false complicity. She emerged, undizzy with her deed, and began aging fast. Pidgin wheeled on swivelhips and fell into motion, his natural state. She was chasing him now, only her legs were getting longer and longer. Pidgin clambered over cartops and under shelves of bumpers and alternator innards. He rolled tires behind him and stood hoods in the teen dancer's way. She vaulted over most of the tires though, used the hoods as springboards to dive through the rest, and finally cornered Pidgin at the complicated door of a schoolbus sitting on its frame. PISD, Portales Independent School District, an extra *S* and *E* done with spraypaint long ago, forced into the narrow space between the last two letters.

The sky wasn't yet light except in the distance. Pidgin felt his way in, huddled against the emergency exit in the rear that wouldn't kick open. The girl-become-a-woman entered the bus through the folding door, closed it behind her, then began tearing the covers off the seats and wrapping herself in them, deep. She was still aging. Inside of ten steps she was the Salvage Queen, bent with years, her silver-black hair queued into a hard topknot, her weight focused over a single aluminum cane, bowing that cane. She didn't advance. She matched Pidgin stillness for stillness, directed her lined face out the unbroken window. Pidgin followed. There was Charlie Ward, singing the sun up, a crackless windshield tucked under his arm, duct-taped at likely stress points. Horse-thief in the a.m.

"The night's almost over," the Salvage Queen said, then looked back to Pidgin, leaning hard and nonchalant on the exit lever, legs crossed at the ankle. "You wear his cowboy clothes well," she added.

"That's because he's dead," Pidgin said. "Cultural hand-me-downs and all. That anthropologist guy you killed would have loved it."

"Squiggly Leni," the Salvage Queen said, fondly. "The Slay."

Pidgin tried to contain a smile he didn't think he had in him anymore.

"What?" the Salvage Queen asked, looking around.

"I thought you were talking about my uncle, at first," Pidgin said, "the *Slob*."

The Salvage Queen leaned on her cane with both hands, let it guide her down to the edge of one of the seats. Pidgin sat too. She affected bemusement with him. "He came to me once, too, you know," she said, "your uncle. Looking for her."

Pidgin quit smiling.

"Your mother, I mean," the Salvage Queen finished, turning to the front of the bus again, where there was a woman wrapped in a kimono, sitting alone. Staring stubbornly forward, shoulders stiff.

Pidgin closed his eyes, shook his head no, the Salvage Queen had it all wrong: he was looking for his father. Big lanky white guy. Nearly ten years dead.

"You do miss her, though," the Salvage Queen said, "like she misses you," and Pidgin's non-answer counted against him. She had used the present tense, *was* using the present tense. They sat like that for Pidgin didn't know how long, Pidgin afraid to speak, not trusting his voice, the Salvage Queen not interrupting him, Marina Trigo staring straight ahead.

"You don't understand," Pidgin finally said. "I just want out of all this." He rattled the emergency exit lever to show.

The Salvage Queen said she would give Pidgin a song to take with him, then, if that's what he wanted so bad. Instead of everything else. She removed from her shawls a pen and paper, scrawled and talked, said Pidgin's *Glory Dog* monologue reminded her of the old days, before she passed the mantle on to the next set, when she was still in temporary love with the Captain Smith of her time. Pidgin said the herb and peyote had made that monologue up, it was only bullshit. He apologized for saying bullshit. The Salvage Queen wrote slow. She licked her pentip as if it were a pencil she was writing with. She shook her head no, said she'd seen *The Screling,* after all, they all had. That was what it was all about, all right, where it started: circa 1610. John Smith and his Indian princess. Pidgin covered his face with both hands. His fingers were twitching. The protective sac around his awareness was being pierced at many points, and *The Screling*'s BIA office was rushing in, the end of the story Pocahontas started. "No," he said, letting it rise in his voice, against the Salvage Queen, "*no*. It wasn't like it was. The video lied. I got away, see. I got adamnway."

The Salvage Queen regarded him, said *yes*.

Her eyes glistened with it.

Pidgin held his hand out for the song because he knew it was the ticket home, out, because maybe he'd paid for it by saying *no* for her, but at the last moment her hand closed on the paper scrap, and the interknuckle regions of her fingers sprouted golden hair like wheat. Pidgin told her he didn't deserve this. He'd done nothing; he'd chanced on a grave robbery, seen a ghoul when he wasn't looking for one. He followed her shawled arm up from the back of her fingers and her features were rearranging themselves yet again. She could get no older though. There was only one place left to go. Pidgin backed to the exit door as her hard topknot submerged, was replaced by nascent-yellow sidehair. It was an unsubtle gender swap. Pidgin shook his head no and watched through a spyhole burrowed in the aevum, and she came at him in pieces, and the pieces ordered themselves into Redfield's Custer, a hard hand on his curved military sabre.

He sniffed the early morning air, considered it, then looked at this crumpled song in his fingers, held it at bifocal range. "Toe the line or don't," he read with the last of the Salvage Queen's voice, dropping the ticket underfoot with a grin, "and that was all she wrote."

"I got away from you," Pidgin said.

"You sure about that?" Custer said.

Pidgin pulled on the exit lever until it broke off. Custer's harsh laughter rolled down the aisle, and Custer was approaching behind it, a direct military maneuver, all nineteenth-century brinkmanship swept out the complicated door. He drew his seventh-cavalry sabre. It gleamed. Pidgin closed his eyes and opened them, did it again, again, but still Custer persisted, approached. "No," Pidgin said, keeping his back to the wall, "no." Custer shook his head yes, though, yes. His legs were long, striding, a sound. He was in his prime, in his element. Pidgin said it one last time—that he got away—and then stepped forward, with the exit lever held low heavy and half-reluctant at thigh level, half impatient. The line was toed. Like the Salvage Queen had said in her song. Pidgin tested the lever for weight, balance. It was there like it had to be. When Custer was two armlengths out, already a smell, Pidgin said aloud that he could run no more, he was out of time to traipse over, and was goddamn tired of traipsing anyways. It was a warning. His voice was as even as he could make it. Custer slowed, chewed the insides of his cheeks, appraised Pidgin, shook his head no but was unsure, his neck begrudging movement.

Pidgin drew closer, within reach, should he need it. Custer smiled one side of his face and extended the sabre between them, keeping things civilized, leaving time and space for his joke about this Indian kid with the deadwhite father, had Pidgin heard it?

Pidgin stepped back without meaning to.

Custer nodded, said this kid then, one day his dad's talking long-distance on the phone, to the late Marty Robbins, so the kid has to go outside.

"To wax the shelters."

"To wax the shelters, yeah. Stop me if you know this one."

"It doesn't sound like a joke," Pidgin said.

Custer told him to just wait, it's a riot. So this kid's out there, waxing whichever shelter, when a lady walks up out of nowhere. A census-taker of all people. She knocks on the door, and, because the phone reaches that far, this kid's father puts Marty Robbins on hold, chocks

the screen open with his foot, and immediately gets into a yelling
match with this federal employee about who she's really working for
and why. Typical stuff with him. But then the census-taker backs up
from the fight before it can get out of hand, says she just want to collect the facts here, please, then points across the shelters at the kid, so
dark in the sun, so Indian.

And standing there in the unlit door of the trailer the father's so
white he glows.

"Him," the lady says, "he's not yours, anyway, is he?" her pencil
cocked to record his answer, and the father looks along her finger to
the kid, standing there waiting to be claimed. Expecting to be claimed.
But then the father stares for longer than it should take, as if seeing
the kid for the first time all over. Finally he just shrugs and shakes his
head no. Probably no.

"He was just trying to mess up her data," Pidgin said to Custer,
when it was over.

"Tell yourself what you like," Custer said back. "But just because you
never had a mother, don't go thinking the world owes you a father
or anything."

Pidgin was breathing hard now. "How do you know?" he said to
Custer, a schoolyard comeback, and Custer said this was the funny
part, the punchline, get ready. Keeping the sabre between them the
whole time, he loosened the chin-strap from his gaudy hat, pushed it
off the back of his head, leaned his paunch out, then calmly removed
his sideburns.

Until he was Cline.

He winked at Pidgin, and Pidgin shook his head no.

"Daddy's home," Custer said in a low voice, applying pressure to
Pidgin's sternum with the sharp point of his sabre, and Pidgin reflex-
ively batted the sabre away with his lever. The lever's weight carried
it through to bare seatback. It buried itself there. Pidgin placed a foot
on the seatback to extract it from the springs and the stiff foam, never
looking away from Custer, standing there like Cline.

"You're not him," Pidgin said, insisted, terrified by what it would
mean if he was, ready to give up if he was, accept all the benign inevi-
tability of colonization BS he'd been spoonfed, forget the ending
originally written for *The Screling,* where the aliens come to colonize
america with their advanced weaponry, and america tries to conscript

Indians to fight, and the Indians just laugh while the credits roll. Under his father's insistent stare, Pidgin already was already forgetting it, even how it sounded, all of it, but then for an instant he saw through the disguise—the disguises—how Custer was just Birdfinger here, pretending to be Cline. Like always. Even down to the sidehair, the gut.

Pidgin laughed to himself, and when Birdfinger-as-Redfield-as-Custer-as-Cline cast a meaningful eye to the front of the bus, where the cardboard cut-out of Marina Trigo had been and still was, Pidgin shook his head no one final time.

"You don't know her," he said.

Birdfinger-as-Redfield-as-Custer-as-Cline grinned the part of his face Pidgin could see, disagreed with a suggestive waggle of his eyebrows.

"I do know who you are, though," Pidgin said. *"Uncle."* The blond figure turned to him then, nostrils dilating evenly, the blood draining from his lips, the dash from his posture. Everything else Pidgin took away with the rising backswing of the lever. It caught Birdfinger-as-Redfield-as-Custer-as-Cline in the fatty part of the throat, glancing across the larynx, felling him over a seatback. First he was on his knees though, his head nodding once to Pidgin in something like acknowledgment, thanks almost.

And *then* he fell. Like orchestra. Pidgin breathed in catches when it was done. His fingers were still twitching. The blond figure held his throat hard, trying for breath, for air, voice, words. There were none, though. His right leg pedaled a missing bicycle. Pidgin checked outside, for Charlie Ward in the new light, and when he redirected to the figure, saw the Salvage Queen there now, her side rising and falling in strained rasps, shawls spread around her like opera blood.

The world drew to a standstill, balanced on a sharp point.

What had he done, what had she done? Pidgin rearranged the names in his mind, to Custer-as-Redfield-as-Birdfinger-as-Cline, using him to get to her. But why? And there were so many other options too. All of which left her dying facedown at his feet. By his hand. Her aluminum cane bent, not a sabre, never a sabre. Pidgin let the lever slip away, and it rebounded off the rubber flooring, settled against the wall.

What had he done here.

What had he done just because his father lied to a census-taker once, because his uncle drew a picture of Marina Trigo once. Because the dead wouldn't rest for him.

He watched the Salvage Queen struggle for a few moments, then swallowed, unnarrowed his vision, and felt from seat to seat in the dim interior, making his way to the front of the bus—proud, unproud. Numb. The cardboard cut-out of his mother corrugated on the frontside, blank. Waiting to be filled in with memories Pidgin didn't have. He stepped down from it all without looking back, exited by the proper door and into the morning. He sang under his breath as he went, and his song was like this:

> toe the line or don't
> and that was all she wrote.

His new stage name would be Lido, not Golias. Lido who had struck an old woman down when she approached with a ticket in her hand. Low light didn't justify it, vague historical melodrama didn't justify it. But then again. God. New Mexico was too much with him; he was daisy-chained across twelve days. His breath was corrosive.

Meaning his cartilage-white trachea was intact, functioning to some degree. Pidgin touched it gingerly, and as he did, laughter carried across the husks of many cars. It was hollow, procreative. Pidgin rocked back and forth, sang his song of power until Charlie Ward approached.

"Did she find you?" Charlie Ward asked, the banktube there in his rear pocket, safe all along.

Pidgin held it all behind his eyes, nodded, looked away.

He had done it.

It was real.

The ride back to Clovis was the last time. Pidgin sat in the passenger seat and Charlie Ward didn't speak. Pidgin became larger and smaller with each breath. They balanced the windshield across their laps. Mars rusting in the early morning light. Charlie Ward slid his thin leather belt from his jeans and held it out the window, whipped the Cutlass faster, faster, his dyed-black hair unbraiding in the fifty-five mile per hour wind, and they never had to stop for gas. Pidgin's breath caught once, reliving it, but he didn't confess to Charlie Ward, and Boz Scaggs didn't come over the radio, and nothing rose from the asphalt to halt their progress, their regress.

Pidgin said his mother's name aloud and Charlie Ward didn't ask him about it, apologized instead for Pidgin having missed the interment. Pidgin said no apologies: it started when he left Utah, or maybe it started at WWI, or 1610, or the thirteenth century.

"At least you filled in that hole," Charlie Ward offered, and Pidgin nodded, unnodded; Cline Stob was still out there, after almost ten years of clinical death. Pidgin had failed even at that, and was still failing. He held the idea of a shovel steady over the dash because a shovel could repair the glitch in his recent past. He was thinking in glitch-terms now. He told Charlie Ward to ask him what he did for fun. "So what do you do for fun?" Charlie Ward asked, but then Pidgin couldn't bring himself to answer because one answer was that he clubbed junkyard proprietresses into the afterlife. It had almost been a confession. His hand remained over the dash, holding nothing, and he watched his actions become antics and half-feared a laugh track. Someone's grandmother was dying in the faded yellow bus of his mind. His throat constricted; the color and the texture of the road surface changed.

In Clovis, Charlie Ward coasted to the bus stop, shifted the windshield to the seat, groaned out of the Cutlass. Pidgin followed by way of the driverside door, child-style, framing himself for a moment with both hands on either side of the doorframe so he could pull himself the rest of the way out. Reentry. It was like he was arriving all over, hadn't been here for seven-odd years. He stepped down, let the heat loosen his joints, tighten the skin around his eyes. Here he was. The Unemerald City, the Land of Disenchantment, The Greatest Medicine Show on Earth. Unmade in Clovis New Mexico. Charlie Ward opened the trunk, and in the trunk was the paisley suitcase, and the paisley suitcase was the only thing that could have been there. He set it by Pidgin's leg.

He nodded goodbye grandson to Pidgin.

Pidgin nodded back yes.

Here he was.

from *Flight*

SHERMAN ALEXIE

(2007)

> We have to acknowledge and face historical facts; there is no use
> or sense in denying that colonialism has affected us in very serious
> and critical ways; in fact, it is self-defeating to do so. Colonialism
> has driven us to the verge of vanishing; at times, in fact, we have
> succumbed and accepted banishment and invisibility! However,
> we are still "Indians" . . .
> —*Simon J. Ortiz*

TIME SLIPPAGE AND ALTERNATIVE FUTURES are stock elements of
mainstream sf, but these elements also are typical of thought experiments by Native authors. In *Flight*, National Book Award winner Sherman Alexie (Coeur d'Alene) creates an Indian Holden Caulfield who
introduces the narrative by directing the reader, "Call me Zits," a dis-
paraging moniker that mixes teenage angst and bravado. "Everybody
calls me Zits," he continues. "That's not my real name, of course. My
real name isn't important." An orphaned fifteen-year-old escapee from
bad foster homes, whose mother was Irish and whose father was an
Indian "[from] this or that tribe [from] this or that reservation," Zits
jumps from one time slippage identity shift to another in a dizzying
trip through representative moments in Native American history.
In the aggregate, these slippages represent rites of passage that allow
him to move beyond the self-loathing of internal colonization that

Alexie might argue typifies reservation youth today (precisely his target audience) and toward a more holistic sense of self and place. Ultimately, his experience of past and future lives helps him reject the chance to participate in a Columbine-like random killing spree at a Seattle bank. He is taken in by a sympathetic police sergeant and, as a narrative frame reflecting his internal struggle with self-identification, is able by the final line of the novel to ask his new mentor, "Please, call me Michael. My real name is Michael."

Much like the figure of the alien ethnographer in Andrea Hairston's "Griots of the Galaxy," who "drops in" to possess sentient bodies on Earth to study our culture firsthand, but who arrives with no idea of "who" she has become and who must therefore fake familiarity with the mysterious narrative of her stolen identity until another identity comes along, Alexie's Michael "drops in" to several characters during the course of his adventures. His array of shifting identities also parallels the popular early 1990s television series *Quantum Leap*. Michael manifests five characters: (1) Hank Storm, murderous FBI agent who kills an upstart reservation Indian, recalling events surrounding the violent 1970s on the Pine Ridge Reservation in South Dakota; (2) a twelve- or thirteen-year-old "old time Indian kid" (63) camped with the families of warriors who defeated Custer's Seventh Cavalry at the Battle of Little Big Horn; (3) Gus, a grizzled old Indian hunter on the nineteenth-century American plains, whose experiences in turn recall the massacre at Wounded Knee; (4) Jimmy, a flight instructor from the near future, who unwittingly trains his Muslim friend Abbad for a terrorist mission reminiscent of the 9/11 hijackings; (5) and, finally, a contemporary Seattle street drunk who turns out to be Michael's own father. Each vignette serves to challenge stereotypes of Eurowestern–Native encounters. Hank Storm turns out to be a loving husband and father, while the Indian he kills was in fact betrayed and given up for sacrifice by other Indians; the "old-time Indian kid" is forced to murder a captured cavalry soldier as a rite of passage that Michael recognizes as barbaric and, ultimately, unjust; Gus witnesses a young white soldier commit mutiny and risk death to save an Indian boy from a genocidal raid; as his father, Michael communes with a white businessman who uncharacteristically meets his expectation for genuine personal contact instead of simply offering a condescending "handout." In this final slippage, Michael glimpses the forces that account for his father's behavior and gets a chance to see his own likely future if he continues on the same self-destructive path.

The following excerpt telescopes the novel's sf elements in depicting Michael's slip out of present time and into alternate reality. Look closely for it. He's there; he's not.

𝒜

When I open my eyes, I'm standing in a bank in downtown Seattle. Yes, that bank.

I have two pistols in my coat, a paint gun and a .38 special.

Yes, those guns.

I'm supposed to pull them out and shoot everybody I see.

Yes, I'm supposed to kill for Justice.

I did it before: a long time ago, a little while ago, a second ago. I don't understand how time works anymore.

There's that man again, the one who told me I wasn't real.

I think he's wrong; I think I am real.

I have returned to my body. And my ugly face. And my anger. And my loneliness.

And then I think, Maybe I never left my body at all. Maybe I never left this bank. Maybe I've been standing here for hours, minutes, seconds, trying to decide what I should do.

Do I pull out my guns and shoot all these people?

Do I shoot that little boy over there with his mother? He is maybe five years old. He has blue eyes and blond hair. He's wearing good shoes. A jean jacket. Khaki pants. Blue shirt. He's beautiful. A beautiful little man. His mother, also blond and blue-eyed, smiles down at him. She loves him. She sees me watching them and she smiles at me. For me. She wants me to know how much she loves her son. She's proud of the little guy.

Did my mother love me like that? I hope so.

I wave at the little boy. He waves back.

I hate him for being loved so well.

I want to be him.

I close my eyes and try to step inside his body. But it doesn't work. I cannot be him.

I open my eyes. I think all the people in this bank are better than I am. They have better lives than I do. Or maybe they don't. Maybe we're all lonely. Maybe some of them also hurtle through time and see war, war, war. Maybe we're all in this together.

I turn around and walk out of the bank. I step out onto First Avenue.

It's not really raining, but this is Seattle. There are only fifty-eight sunny days a year in our city. So it always feels like it's just about to rain, even when the sun is out.

I used to hate the rain. But now I want it to pour. I want it to storm. I want to be clean.

I am surrounded by people who trust me to be a respectful stranger. Am I trustworthy? Are any of us trustworthy? I hope so.

I remember my first day of school. Kindergarten. My mother walked me there. It was only six blocks away from our apartment, but six blocks is forever to a child.

As we walked, my mother talked to me.

"It's going to be okay," she said. "School is a good thing. You're going to have lots of friends. And you'll learn so much. And the teachers will take care of you, okay? I love you, okay? You'll be okay. I'm going to wait right here for you. All day, I'll wait right here."

She was wrong, of course. School was not good for me.

I never made friends.

I didn't learn much.

I was not okay.

And my mother didn't wait for me. She died.

After she died, I went to live with her sister, my aunt. Yes, that's the dirtiest secret I own.

This is what I don't tell anybody. I don't talk about it. I don't dream about it. I don't want anybody to know. My aunt was supposed to take care of me. She had promised her sister she would take care of me. She was the only family I had. My father was gone. My mother was gone. My grandparents were gone. Everybody was gone. My aunt was all I had.

Aunt Zooey. Auntie Z.

She lived in an apartment with her boyfriend. A man who smelled of onions and beer. A man who leaned over my bed in the middle of the night. A man who hurt me. I told Auntie Z.

She slapped me.

I told Auntie Z again.

She slapped me again.

I was six years old. I cried for my mother. Like a lost dog, I howled all night. I could not stop crying. I missed my mother.

My mommy. My mommy. My mommy.

I cried for one week. Then two weeks. Then three weeks.

Every night, Auntie Z rushed into my room, shook me, slapped me, and screamed at me.

Stop crying, stop crying, stop crying.

I miss her, too. I miss her, too. I miss her, too.

She's not coming back. She's not coming back. She's not coming back.

Some nights, her boyfriend came to see me. He hurt me and whispered to me in the dark.

Don't tell anybody, don't tell anybody, don't tell anybody.

Everybody knows you're a liar. Everybody knows you're a liar. Everybody knows you're a liar.

Nobody loves you anymore. Nobody loves you anymore. Nobody loves you anymore.

I learned how to stop crying.

I learned how to hide inside of myself.

I learned how to be somebody else.

I learned how to be cold and numb.

When I was eight years old, I ran away for the first time.

When I was nine, I poured lighter fluid on my aunt's boyfriend and tried to set him on fire. He woke up and punched me into the hospital. They sent him to jail.

After he got out of jail, he left my aunt. She blamed me.

When I was ten, Auntie Z gave me twenty dollars and sent me to buy some hamburgers and fries. When I got back to the apartment, she was gone. She never came back.

When I was eleven, I ran away from my first foster home and got drunk in the street with three homeless Indians from Alaska.

When I was twelve, I ran away from my seventh foster home.

When I was thirteen, I smoked crack for the first time. When I was fourteen, I stole a car and wrecked it into a building beneath the Alaska Way Viaduct.

When I was fifteen, I met a kid named Justice who taught me how to shoot guns.

But I am tired of hurting people. I am tired of being hurt.

I need help.

I walk from street to street, looking for help. I walk past Pike Place Market and Nordstrom's. I walk past Gameworks and the Space Needle. I walk past Lake Washington and Lake Union. I walk for miles. I walk for days. I walk for years.

I don't understand how time works anymore.

I walk until I see a police car parked in front of a restaurant.

I walk inside.

It's a cheap diner. Eight tables. Two waitresses. A cook, in the back.

At one of the tables sit two cops, Officer Dave and his partner. They've arrested me more often than any other duo.

I walk up to them.

"Officer Dave," I say.

"Hey, Zits," he says. "What's going on?"

I want to tell him the entire story. I want to tell him that I fell through time and have only now returned. I want to tell him I learned a valuable lesson. But I don't know what that lesson is. It's too complicated, too strange. Or maybe it really is simple. Maybe it's so simple it makes me feel stupid to say it.

Maybe you're not supposed to kill. No matter who tells you to do it. No matter how good or bad the reason. Maybe you're supposed to believe that all life is sacred.

"Officer Dave," I say, and raise my hands high in the air, "I want you to know that I respect you. And I'm here for a good reason. I'm raising my hands up because I have two guns inside my coat. One of them is just a paint gun, but the other one is real."

Officer Dave and his partner quickly get to their feet. Their hands touch their guns, ready to pull them out of their holsters.

"This isn't funny, Zits," Officer Dave says. "You say stuff like that, you're going to get shot."

I start laughing.

"What's so funny?" Officer Dave asks.

"I'm not trying to be funny," I say. "And I don't want to get shot. I really do have two guns. I want you to take them from me. Please, take them away."

Officer Dave takes my guns.

And then he takes me to the police station. He stands nearby as a detective interviews me. He's a big black man with big eyeglasses. He calls it an interview. It's really an interrogation. I don't mind. I guess I deserve to be interrogated.

"Where did you get the guns?" Detective Eyeglasses asks.

"I got them from a kid named Justice," I say. "Was Justice his first or last name?"

"He just called himself Justice. That's all. He said he gave himself the name."

"You don't know his real name?"

"No."

"Where did you meet him?"

"In jail."

"When was this?"

"A few months ago, I guess. Don't really remember. I've been in jail a lot."

"Okay, so you met him in jail. But you don't remember exactly when. And you say his name is Justice. But that's not his real name."

"Yeah."

"None of that information helps us much, does it? It's not very specific, is it?"

"No, I guess not."

I can tell that Detective Eyeglasses doesn't believe me. He thinks I invented Justice.

"You say this guy named Justice is the one who told you to go to the bank and kill people?" Eyeglasses asks me.

"Yeah," I say.

The detective stares at me hard, like his eyes were twin suns. I feel burned.

He pulls a TV cart into the room and plays a video for me. It's a copy of the bank security tape.

Eyeglasses, Officer Dave, and I watch a kid named Zits walk into the bank and stand near a huge potted plant.

I laugh.

"What's so funny?" Eyeglasses asks.

"I just look stupid next to that big plant. Look at me, I'm trying to hide behind it."

It's true. I'm using it for cover. Eyeglasses and Officer Dave have to laugh, too. It is funny. But it's only funny because I didn't do what

I was supposed to do. It's only funny because I'm alive to watch it. It's only funny because everybody in that bank is still alive.

So maybe it's not really funny at all.

Maybe we're all laughing because it's so fucking unfunny.

In the video, I pat my coat once, twice, three times. "What are you doing?" Eyeglasses asks.

"I'm checking to see if my guns are still there," I say.

"Are you thinking about using them?"

"Yeah."

"But you didn't. Why not?"

On the video, my image disappears for a second. I'm gone. And then I reappear.

"Whoa," Officer Dave says. "Did you see that?" The detective rewinds the tape. Presses PLAY. I'm there in the bank. Then I'm gone—*poof*. And then I reappear.

"That's weird," Officer Dave says.

"Aw, it's just a flaw in the tape," Eyeglasses says. "They reuse these tapes over and over. The quality goes down. They got weird bumps and cuts in them."

Eyeglasses is probably right.

On the video, I am staring at the little blond boy and his mother. I smile and wave.

"Who is that?" Eyeglasses asks me.

"It's just a boy and his mother," I say.

"Do you know them?"

"No."

"Then why are you being so friendly to them?"

"They were beautiful," I say.

Detective Eyeglasses snorts at me. He thinks I'm goofy. But Officer Dave smiles. He must be a father.

"Do you know where we might find this Justice?" Eyeglasses asks me.

"Maybe," I say. "We lived together in this warehouse down in SoDo."

"Jesus," he says. "Why didn't you tell us this before?"

"You didn't ask."

I lead them to the warehouse. I wait outside with two rookie cops while Dave and Eyeglasses and a SWAT team check out the whole building.

Nobody is there.

Pretty soon, Eyeglasses comes out and takes me upstairs to the room where Justice and I lived for a few weeks.

There are empty cans, bottles, and plastic containers. There are two beds made out of newspaper and cardboard. There are newspaper photos and magazine articles taped on the walls. All the people in those photos and articles have crosshairs painted over their faces. They were all targets.

"This is where you and Justice lived?" Eyeglasses asks me.

"Yeah."

"Well, if he was here, he's gone now."

"Yeah."

I know that I won't see Justice again.

Eyeglasses stares at me hard. He's good at staring hard. "Zits," he says. "I'm happy you changed your mind about using those guns."

I'm happy, too, but I can't say that.

Contact

from *Refugees*

CELU AMBERSTONE

(2004)

> To bring an alien culture to its knees, you steal the Native stories
> and fill them with lies. You desecrate sacred symbols and replace
> ancestral wisdom with your story of the world. You obsess
> the benighted Natives with being like you, until they finally
> forget themselves and become you. Why waste bullets when a
> cultural bomb will do? Stealing the future is an old story,
> a universal cliché.
> —*Andrea Hairston*

CELU AMBERSTONE (CHEROKEE) acts as a cultural ethnographer of sovereign Indigenous nations near Vancouver, British Columbia. Like Richard Van Camp (Dogrib) and Daniel Heath Justice (Cherokee), she promotes genre fiction in sf, fantasy, and horror written by Native and Aboriginal writers, especially those aligned with Native-owned presses such as Kegedonce, often conducting her advocacy among the members of Canada's Association of Speculative Fiction Professionals (www.sfcanada.ca).

"For me Aboriginal sf isn't about robots and sterile Euro-American physics and astronomy," she says. "Having the advantage of being bilingual or at least bicultural, Aboriginal writers have the ability to think 'outside the box.' Our fiction is alive with new possibilities inspired by our cultural heritage, fiction that can offer new insights to our troubled world. As Indigenous peoples, we understand that the specters of corporate greed and colonialism still haunt Earth's future. It is our responsibility to offer humanity a new vision of the universe."

Her novella *Refugees,* from which the following excerpt is taken, interpolates what may be the most recognizable element of sf: the story of contact between aliens and Indigenous people. Here she takes up the relocation narrative that accompanies many contact stories, as her narrator, Qwalshina, provides first-person accounts of what happens when Benefactors intercede to protect Earth from the disastrous husbandry of its human population. Her style participates in a tradition of Native literature, what Thomas King (Cherokee) might describe as "associational literature," one that devalues the spectacle of hero and villain, favoring instead a concentration on the common members of the community.

Whether the aliens are to be trusted or not often creates the suspense in sf contact tales; in some instances, simply unveiling the nonhumanoid alien form hidden under the guise of human appearance is enough to cast strong doubts, as in the early 1980s miniseries *V,* which was remade in 2009 for the ABC network. There's just something about an alien we think looks like us peeling back his skin to reveal his true reptilian identity that taps into horrific primordial memory. But what happens, as in *Refugees,* when a lizard race of Benefactors, who have populated a new world with at least seven generations of transplanted Indigenous Earthlings, ostensibly to protect Earth's seed, encounters violent resistance from newly exiled urban Indians from Vancouver?

The tension between the Indigenous rooted and the Indigenous routed frustrates Qwalshina, who has bought into the notion that a benign tyrant is better than self-determination that might end in extinction. She has been convinced that her people's traditions have been preserved despite the Benefactors' intercessions. The new transplants may feel that the Benefactors merely tolerate these traditions as a means of controlling the population. The events of the story cause Qwalshina to question how beneficent the Benefactors really are, as the fosterlings recently brought from Earth resist colonization.

Rain-Comes-Back Moon, sun-turning 4
Jimtalbot and Bethbrant were troubled by a crazy rumor they'd heard, and came this evening to ask me if it might be true.

"One of the guys from Earth living at Black Rock Village said that Earth isn't really destroyed," Jimtalbot told me.

I looked into their troubled faces and felt a shiver run down my spine. "What? Why would he say such a thing? Of course the Earth Mother is gone. Why else would our Benefactors have brought you here?"

"Why indeed, Qwalshina?" Jimtalbot said. "Could the—uh—Benefactors be planning some weird experiment? Something that they need live humans, or human body parts, for?"

I was shocked, speechless. "Experiment? No, of course not. That's preposterous. Who said such a thing? I must tell Dra'hada; who is it?"

Their expressions became closed at that point. Jimtalbot mumbled that he didn't know the man's name, but I was sure he was lying to me. He looked at Bethbrant and they started to walk away, but I stopped them. "Please wait. If you don't wish me to tell Dra'hada, Jimtalbot, I won't, but listen to me. There is no truth to this rumor. I felt Earth Mother's death agony myself—through the Communion—we all did. The pain was almost unbearable. Truly She is gone. And there is no planned experiment. Our Benefactors only wish us well."

"If your people were also a part of their design, you might not be aware of the experiment either," Bethbrant said.

"No, we would know if they were using us in that way. We have been here for generations. My father was a man of the Tsa'La'Gui people. His ancestors were brought here when pale-skinned invaders from across a big ocean came and took their land. My mother's people came here long before my father's. They were Crunich and lived on the island of Erin before the black-robed ones with their dead god came and stole the island's soul. There are others from Earth Mother here too, rescued from disaster as you were. Our Benefactors wish only good for us. And, no matter our origin on Earth, we are all one people now, the children of Tallav'Wahir. There has never been any experiment. Please believe me."

When I finished talking to them, they seemed convinced that it was all a crazy, made-up lie. But later the children told me that a group of our charges walked down the beach together to talk something over in private. Did I do right to promise not to tell Dra'hada? This is very troubling. I must go to the Mother Stone and tell Her my concerns.

Falling Leaves Moon, sun-turning 5
Sleek's tattooed friend and six other youths have developed a terrible
case of the itch. No common healing remedy has worked. Poor lads—
I know they're miserable—and I shouldn't laugh at their misfor-
tunes, but it *is* funny to watch them trying to scratch all those hard-
to-reach places. Rain's twins were in on the scheme. One of them
finally broke down and confessed. About half of the stolen uiskajac
was brought back. Granny is keeping the offenders in suspense for one
more night, but she told me privately that she would forgive them,
and give them a healing salve tomorrow.

Falling Leaves Moon, sun-turning 25
Sleek and I took the children for a walk on the knoll today. We piled
up great mountains of leaves and had fun jumping into them. I tired
before they did, but felt so good just watching them. I think my new
daughter loves playing like a child when none of her Earth friends are
around to ridicule her. She is recreating the happy childhood she
didn't have on Earth, and it is a joy to see her so.

In the dappled light under the trees, her face suddenly seemed to
metamorphose into that of an ancient. Expressing wisdom far beyond
years, she said to me, "I had fun with you today, but I'm not Tukta,
Qwalshina. Please try to remember that." There was no anger in her
voice for once; the smells of tree resin, spicy siba, and a lazy afternoon had drained her of hostility.

Later we gathered siba fruit and roasted it on sticks over an open
fire, and everyone sang songs. I found myself wishing Tukta could have
been there to share the day with us. When we were heading home the
children raced ahead as usual, but Sleek waited for me on the trail
and fell into step beside me as I passed. I smiled and she returned the
gesture.

Startled, I paused on the trail and faced her. "I know. . . . I had fun
today and I'm glad you are who you are. I wouldn't want it any other
way."

"Mmm. . . . Then stop calling me Tukta."

"I don't," I protested.

She gave me a reproachful look, her eyes luminous and sad. "You're
not even aware that you're doing it, are you?"

Was I? Oh, Mother, was I confusing her with my daughter in the

physical world as well as in my mind? "I'm sorry, Sleek, I didn't realize I'd been doing that. Do I do it often?"

She made a noncommittal sound which I took to be acceptance of
my apology. "Not often, but sometimes—like today—you forget!"
She shrugged, looked away, and brushed her hand across a feathery
tree branch. We'd chopped off the dyed blue parts of her hair some
time back, and now soft brown waves hung down past her shoulders.
Up ahead, one of the children called to her at that point, and she
raced down the trail to catch up with the others.

I kept walking at a slower pace, thinking. I hadn't realized I'd been
doing that. Her gentle rebuke caused me to question my own insecurities. It wasn't fair to Sleek if I was indeed trying to mold her into
another's image for my own comfort. Why did I continue to cling to
the past? Why couldn't I go on with my life—what was I afraid of? I
will have to guard my tongue and my thoughts more carefully in
future. I must go see Granny Night Wind; maybe she can guide me
through this difficult time.

Frost Moon, sun-turning 15
It's getting very cold at night now. We arrived back in the village by
the lake yesterday afternoon, our pack beasts heavy-laden from the
annual hunt. Soon we will hold the last harvest feast. Everyone is
excited. After the festivities we will pack up everything important
and leave this exposed, stormy beach. When the blue snows pile up
outside, we will be safe in our warm underground lodges up the shel-
tered valley in the hills.

Frost Moon, sun-turning 28
I walked to the Mother Stone today to say farewell till our return in
Awakening Moon. The seasons have turned and the dark time is upon
us once again. In the shadows along the path specters of other races
that once lived here too materialized, and watched me with solemn
red eyes. Their voices whispered to me on the cool wind, but I couldn't
understand their alien speech. What happened to those born to this
world? Our Benefactors don't know. . . .

Along with my blood, I poured out to the Mother my hopes and
fears for the future. I hope She heard and will bless us. We are all that
is left of humanity now. Can we survive? Or will this land one day

absorb us back into itself as she has others who have walked these hills? Such thoughts deepened the chill in my bones, and I hurried back to the warmth of my family's compound. I want us all to live, and be happy.

The last harvest feast is tonight after the communal prayers. I'm resolved to set aside my dark mood and be happy. My pregnant daughter and others from across the lake are coming for the festivities. Oh, it will be good to see her. I mustn't waste any more time, Sun Fire needs help with baking.

Cold Moon, sun-turning 1

I'm a little achy this morning—too much good food, dancing—and definitely too much uiskajac. What a wonderful party. I danced till I thought my feet would fall off. It was too cold for lovemaking under the stars, but the sweet pleasure under our warm blankets was just as good. I want to laze around in bed today, but the village will begin the packing for our move. And I have to say farewell to our departing guests. My daughter looks radiant—she is due in the Awakening Moon. What a good omen. I will miss her though. I wish I could be with her during this time. I hope she waits to have the child till I can come to her.

Sleek has disappeared again—just when I need her the most. . . .

Cold Moon, sun-turning 12

During the good weather, we were able to distract our charges with work and games played down on the beach in the evenings. Now that the blue snows are here, some of them have started whining about computer games and videos again. I talked to Tomcowan today about a theater project. Maybe that will help keep them amused.

Cold Moon, sun-turning 14

As a compromise, Dra'hada is willing to send for some of the high-tech equipment now in storage. If our new charges agree to study in our school, they will be allowed limited time on the equipment for entertainment pursuits. Twace and the others are dubious about the schooling part, but Dra'hada was firm with them. The Long Sleep Moons are a strain on everyone; I hope the play practices and Dra'hada's machines will help it pass in tranquility.

Ice Moon, sun-turning 2

We are teaching those who wish to learn the discipline of "The Communion." In the long nights when the snows are heavy on the land above, we journey underground, to the warm cave of the Mother. There we lie together on the floor of a large chamber, our limbs touching, and we slide into the sweet reverie that is the Deep Communion with Tallav'Wahir. We leave our bodies in the warm darkness and allow our spirits to swim upon the Great Starry River. We journey to other worlds and visit with friends light years away. None of our charges can travel so far, but for those who are willing to try, we have hope that someday they will master the technique well enough to join us.

Ice Moon, sun-turning 7

Tomcowan's play was a success. It was written and performed by our charges. And I am so proud; my new daughter is such a good actress. She seemed to shine like a jewel when we offered her our praise. Our fosterlings told us the story of their lives in the lost city of Vancouver. Parts were funny, and some things were sad. Much of it I didn't understand, but in spite of that, the performance was very moving. The elders will tell stories of our own history tonight. I hope our fosterlings will like them. There is so much for us to share and weave together if we are to become one people.

Ice Moon, sun-turning 15

In the aftermath of Tomcowan's play, an air of desolation has settled over our charges. It is very disheartening. The long, gloomy days indoors have given the memories of their lost home an unexpected poignancy. More fights today.

Just now I found Jimtalbot staring moodily into the flames of our fire. I sat beside him and asked why he and the others were still grieving for such a horrible place.

He looked at me with his sorrowful blue eyes and said, "It wasn't all bad there, Qwalshina. My wife and I lived comfortably in a nice house by the ocean. Along with the bad, there was a lot of good too. Art, music, fine literature, advances in science and medicine—we had a lot to be proud of. As hard as it was for people like Sleek and Twace back home, I think they miss it as much as I do."

"Yes, I'm sure they do, and I can't understand that either."

He shrugged. "Home is home, no matter how bad it is, and you can't stop caring when it's gone—if it's gone!"

If it's gone? I didn't want to get bogged down in that conversation again, so I began a new topic. "Caring? Why didn't the people of your city care enough to protect suffering children who starved on your city streets? Why didn't they care enough to honor the Earth Mother and not destroy her gifts to you? Can you honestly say that life here has been so terrible that you would wish to go back?"

He was silent for a long time, just staring into the flames. Finally he tossed another stick onto the fire and shook his head. "I don't know, Qwalshina."

"Don't know?" I was confused and upset myself by then, so I left him. Vancouver sounded like such a terrible place. How could they possibly miss it and want to return?

Ice Moon, sun-turning 19

The rumors about Earth have surfaced again, and this time I'm sure Dra'hada has heard them. Perhaps the play wasn't such a good idea after all. Everyone is getting tired of the cold and the confinement. The books have been read and reread, lessons and amusements are boring, and food and drink grow stale. Tempers are short. I try to sleep as much as I can. For us, this time is a natural phenomenon to be endured. For our charges, it is a torment beyond belief. Our warm dark homes anger or depress them. The snow is too deep, not the right color, too cold—the litany is endless. I'm going back to my bed.

Sun-Comes-Back Moon, sun-turning 7

When I lie upon my communion mat and close my eyes, I can feel the deep stirring in the land, and my body responds to it gladly. The sap is rising, and the snow melting, and my daughter tells me her belly is nearly bursting. The sun is warm on my back when I collect the overflowing buckets of sap from the trees in the sugar bush. And, wonder of wonders, our Sun Fire is pregnant again. Tree is taking a lot of teasing for starting a new family at his age, but we are so pleased. This time the baby—all the babies—will be healthy, I just know it.

Sun-Comes-Back Moon, sun-turning 28

One of the great ships from the Homeworld is coming. Dra'hada is ecstatic. Poor creature—this past year-turning has been so hard on him. What with all the villagers' and fosterlings' complaints to sort out and the unease of the Mother's Spirit Guardians to placate, it is no wonder that our Benefactor has aged visibly. It will do all of us good to have Benefactors from the Homeworld here for the renewal ceremonies. Perhaps they will be able to put those rumors about Earth's survival to rest once and for all.

The ship will be here by the time the snow is gone, so Dra'hada tells me. I wonder if they will bring a new mate for our dear teacher. It will be a great celebration; other villages are coming to join us. Everyone is excited, even our young fosterlings.

Awakening Moon, sun-turning 4

We are back in our village by the lake again. Our compound survived the storm season without needing many repairs. That is good because the ship will be here soon, and there is so much to do before our guests arrive.

During all the confusion, Sleek went missing again. When she crept back into the compound just before the evening meal, I was so angry I shouted at her. She of course shouted right back. Why, oh why, does she continue to be so irresponsible! I'm trying not to compare her to Tukta, but it is so hard.

Awakening Moon, sun-turning 10

My heart is on the ground. The village is overflowing with guests. I'm trying very hard not to let my personal tragedy spoil the festive mood for others. My daughter's baby was born deformed and was— oh, I can't even write down the words. . . . The tragedy happened the night before last; her husband's aunt told me when she arrived today. Tears blur my vision as I try to write this. Oh, Mother, how could this happen—again.

Tukta, my dear sweet Tukta! I want desperately to go to her, take her in my arms, and kiss away the pain. But I can't, not until after the ceremonies are over. What am I thinking of? She isn't a child any-more. I can't make this terrible hurt go away by my presence. And I have obligations to the people that take precedence over personal concerns. I must stay; I must be here to greet our Benefactors when the ship comes tomorrow. The Renewal Ceremony at the Mother Stone this year will be very important.

Awakening Moon, sun-turning 11
When I looked into the faces of our guests from the Homeworld today, I felt such a rage building up inside me that I could hardly breathe at times. Granny Night Wind sensed my disharmony, and made me drink a potion to settle my spirit. This new emotion I feel frightens me. What if we are living a lie—what if the people from Earth are right? I hate them! Why did they have to come here? Maybe they should have been left to die on their god-cursed world!

Awakening Moon, sun-turning 12
The compound is quiet tonight; we took in no guests for the feasting. I can hear the sounds of merriment going on around us as I write this. The little ones don't understand. Sun Fire has taken them to the fire down on the beach. I am glad. My old man Tree is resting in the bedroom behind me. His nearness right now is a comfort.

To my surprise, Sleek hasn't joined the revelers. She was standing in the doorway when I looked up from my pad. I wanted to say something encouraging to her, but I feel too dead inside to make the effort.

She watched me for a long moment in silence, then said, "I-I'm sorry about your daughter, Qwalshina. Sun Fire said something went wrong and the baby's dead. Is that true—or did the damned lizards kill it?"

Her unspoken thought seemed to ring in my mind: filthy lizards, I told you they couldn't be trusted. Suddenly I felt my anger leap up like oil poured onto flames. I hated her at that moment with all my heart, and maybe she felt it, because she staggered backward and grabbed the doorpost for support. Why was she here—and healthy? Why had she, an unfit mother, had a healthy baby, when my dear sweet Tukta could not? Tukta loves her new husband, I thought, and now our Benefactors will probably want her to choose a new mate— it is unfair.

When I gave no answer and only glared at her, Sleek's expression crumpled, and she disappeared back into the night.

After she was gone, Tree came out of the bedroom. He didn't reproach me for my cruelty; he only took me in his arms and led me to our bed. I lay down beside him, buried my face in the warmth of his chest, and cried.

When I could control myself enough to speak, I said, "I'm so ashamed. The one time she tried to comfort someone else, I was unkind to her. Like a mean-spirited hag I pushed her away. Why was I so cruel to her, Tree? I don't understand her or myself anymore."

"Hush now, my flower," Tree soothed. "You are tired, and grieving. People say and do things that they don't truly mean at such a time. I know you care about her, and she does too. I will speak to her tomorrow. Go to sleep, my heart, all will be well."

I drifted into sleep, as he suggested, but deep in my heart I knew all would not be well—not for a long time—and maybe not ever again.

Awakening Moon, sun-turning 13
The most terrible thing has happened. Oh, it is so terrible I can hardly think of it without bursting into tears all over again. Sleek is dead, and so are ten others, one of them a native man from Cold Spring village. Tallav'Wahir, forgive me. I saw her sneaking out of our compound, and I did nothing to stop her. Did I drive her into joining those foolish people with my hard looks and resentment? Was I just another mother who failed her?

It was late in the afternoon when it happened. Most of our visiting Benefactors and other guests had taken air cars down the lake to visit Black Rock Village. I was just helping Sun Fire settle the children for their naps when a loud rumbling whine brought me and most of the adults still in the village racing to the shore. The great ship resting on the sand was making terrible noises, and trembling violently by the time we arrived. From within its opened hatchway we heard screaming—human screaming.

We looked at one another, our eyes round as soup bowls. Then all the noise and trembling stopped as abruptly as it started. We waited, but nothing further happened. Finally, Granny Night Wind and I walked to the stairway and called out to the crew left on duty inside. At first no one answered, but when the old woman started up the stairs, a weak voice from within warned her to come no closer. We exchanged glances, and then I said to the people in the ship, "Honored Benefactors, is something wrong? Can we help you?"

"No, you can't help. Come no closer—it may kill you too if you try to enter."

Kill us? I was taller than Granny; I peered into the dimness of the open hatch. My nose caught the metallic scent of blood before I saw it. There on the floor, blood—red blood. The Benefactors' blood is brown. I shivered, a claw of fear tearing at my heart. What had happened in there? Oh, Mother, where was Sleek? I turned back to Granny. Had she seen the blood on the floor too? I stepped down off the stair, my mind in shock. People called to me, but I couldn't answer. I heard the sound of the air cars returning, and then people running past me. I swayed and would have fallen, but suddenly Tree's arms were around me, hugging me to his chest. "Qwalshina, what's happened?"

He was warm and solid, smelling of budding leaves and smoky leather. Against his chest, I shook my head. No words could get past the aching gulp in my throat.

The visiting Benefactors rushed into their ship, and soon after Dra'hada appeared and told us to return to our homes. He wouldn't answer the shouted questions put to him. "Everything is in order now. No need to fear. Go back to your homes. Tonight at the Big Sing I will tell you all that has happened."

Granny Night Wind added her own urging to the gathered people, and soon most drifted away. I stayed; I refused to let Tree and Sun Fire lead me away. When Dra'hada came over to us, I clutched his scaly hand and urged, "Please, honored teacher, tell me what has happened."

Dra'hada's headcrest drooped, and he patted my hand. "Go home, Qwalshina. You can't do anything to help here. Go home with your family."

"Damn you, I'm not a child. Tell me what's happened. Is Sleek in there?" I heard Tree and Sun Fire's gasps of surprise at my disrespect, but I was too frightened to care. I had to know.

For just a moment Dra'hada's headcrest flattened, and I saw the gleam of long teeth under his parted black lips. I shuddered, but stood my ground. I had to know. Then he let go his own anger and looked at me solemnly. "I never assumed you were a child, Qwalshina; I am sorry if you think that. All right, I will tell you. Yes, Sleek is in there—dead."

I continued to stare at him, willing him to finish it. He sighed and finally continued, "It seems that the rumor about Earth still existing took root stronger in other villages than it did here. All during the harsh weather this cancer has been growing among the new refugees. A man named Carljameson wanted to take our ship and go back to Earth. There were others who helped him try. What they didn't know, or couldn't understand, is that the great ships from the Homeworld are sentient beings. They aren't shells of dead metal like the machines of Earth. When our crew was threatened, the ship itself responded by killing the intruders in a most painful way."

Dra'hada refused to tell me the details. He could sense how upset I was, and told Tree to take me home. Later I learned Carljameson and his war band forced their way on board the ship with the help of the man from Cold Spring. They stole weapons from somewhere and injured one of our Benefactors during the struggle. With so many new people here, and everybody celebrating, no one took note of the conspirators' odd behavior.

Ah, why didn't I go after Sleek when I saw her leave? I was selfish and careless. I was grieving for my daughter, and I was so tired of fighting with Sleek. I blame myself in part for her tragic death. Could I have done more to make her a part of our family?

Awakening Moon, sun-turning 14
There is a great council being held among our Benefactors aboard the ship. Communications with the Homeworld have been established. Because of the man from Cold Spring's involvement, not only the newcomers' fate, but also our own, will depend on the council's decision.

Some of our Benefactors claim that we are a genetically flawed species. We should all be eliminated, and this world reseeded with another more stable species. Others like our dear Dra'hada counsel that that is too harsh a decision. We have lived here the required seven generations and more. We are not to blame for the assault. They counsel that those of us who have bred true to the Ancient Way should be allowed to continue on, either as we are or interbred with another compatible species to improve our bloodlines.

They are meeting on the ship now.

Around me, the land continues to sing its ancient song of renewal. The Mother will not intercede for us with our Benefactors. She is wise, but in the passionless way of ancient stone. In the darkness last night the people met in the village square to sing the Awakening songs, as we have always done. Tears in my eyes, I lifted up my voice with the rest. I was afraid—we all were. Just before dawn I climbed to the Mother Stone.

What will the day bring to my people, life or termination? I lean my head against the stone's solid bulk and breathe in the smells of new growth and the thawing mud in the lake. Blood. The old people say it is the carrier of ancestral memory and our future's promise. The stone is cold. I'm shivering as I open a wound on my forearm and make my offering. My blood is red, an alien color on this world.

from *The Black Ship*

GERRY WILLIAM

(1994)

> The destruction of the Indians of the Americas was, far and away,
> the most massive act of genocide in the history of the world.
> —*David E. Stannard*

> [T]he destruction and assimilation by western industrialism of
> every culture it comes in contact with, has been represented in
> science fiction for a long time.
> —*Ursula K. Le Guin*

GERRY WILLIAM (Spallumcheen Indian Band, Enderby, British Columbia) has worked with various Native organizations throughout his life and has taught at En'owkin International School of Writing in Penticton, British Columbia. His publications include the historical novel *The Woman in the Trees* (2004) and the science fiction novel *The Black Ship* (1994), which is excerpted here.

William is an avid reader of sf, a genre that he contends is still too rarely explored by First Nations writers. SF offers a variety of techniques and structures "needed if the future is to be explored in a meaningful way." He specializes in "space fiction," a subgenre in which plot predominates over characterization, and he compares space fiction to the work of Charles Dickens, whose "revelations of all slices of the society he knew is what his stories are about, and why they continue to be enjoyed to this day":

The grand gestures of people in critical leadership positions can be juxtaposed with the ordinary soldiers, farmers, bureaucrats, etc. that make up the world being described. In my own small way I try to honor this type of writing. One is indebted to the society one grows up in, and one also owes it to that society to follow the traditions established. Constantly challenging those traditions brings on an instability that if carried too far can destroy the good parts of a culture just as much as the parts being questioned. There is a responsibility here that is true to the tribal traditions I grew up in—respect for one's family, tribe, and elders is just as important as trying to find one's own way. It's been noted that in western novels one finds oneself by leaving home, while in Native American storytelling one finds oneself by returning home.

Space fiction encourages writers to challenge boundaries, which can help them to avoid becoming formulaic. By challenging, I mean writing that forces a writer to question his or her own fundamental beliefs time and again, and to write stories from viewpoints that might be diametrically different from anything the writer might do in his or her own life.

William thoroughly enjoys maintaining the "traditions" of space opera and points out how its techniques complement First Nations traditions. He approaches space fiction from an Okanagan perspective, in particular with the Okanagan sense of time in space-time traditions of aurality. He explains that his writing follows "the Okanagan beliefs that linear time is something from western paradigms. Time in our stories is not circular, but perhaps more in keeping with the Irish tribal traditions of the cone, where time spirals along a path which never repeats, but is also always there in the past, present and future." The space-time shifts of "the black ship" featured in his debut novel illustrate this conception, as Enid Bluestreak follows a spiraling trajectory through memories conveyed in the narrative.

William also employs the Okanagan traditions of aurality in his space fiction:

The storyteller interacts with his or her audience and becomes as much a part of the story as the events being dramatized. Storytelling does not enter into the direct thoughts and feelings of characters, unless those thoughts and feelings are externally expressed by words, postures, and actions. One can guess at those thoughts and feelings, but as with a play on a stage, the audience sees only the actions and hears only the voices of the actors, from which they must interpret everything else. Western fiction is so different. Time and again the reader is taken directly into the minds and feelings of characters, and many times those thoughts and feelings are not externally demonstrated or expressed. Telling, not showing, dominates this type of writing, a voyeuristic trip that goes beyond observation into knowing everything about a character, including motivations, feelings, philosophy, and beliefs, something which is not possible either in "real" life or in storytelling. James Joyce's *Ulysses* is dominated by telling, not showing, and he sets a precedent that I instinctively shy away from.

STANDARD YEAR 2478

Enid settled into her commander's chair and stared at the row of buttons that lined one arm of the chair. David, who came onto the bridge, showed her the functions of each button. Enid was a quick learner and waved David away once she had learned the chair's operations. The communication center of her flagship, *Stars End*, keyed in her identification. She then took time to study the four other people who were her bridge crew for the next few weeks.

Besides David, she had Janet Carstairs, her combat major, as security chief, a decision that was automatic once she chose David. Two others were assigned to manage the exchange between the computers and the bridge. Given the complex engines that drove this ship, the computer did most of the navigation but still relied on humans for the more delicate operations. Enid had been on this bridge once during a training session a year ago. That three-week session came in handy now.

"Admiral, we're ready to proceed to Brian's Planet."

Enid gave the signal to depart. In moments, the stars spun in their orbits and then became single streaks of light centered on the middle of the forward screen. They would remain there for the two days it would take to reach Brian's Planet.

Through habit Enid crossed her legs under her chair, her right foot beating a steady rhythm against the cushioned floor. As she went through a series of routine checklists, her thoughts lingered on the worlds of Repletia. She had studied what was known of them and talked to many people about them. Some of these people were soldiers who told tales of heroism and bravery against the Repletians. One soldier showed his battle scars, a testament to his being the sole survivor of a battle just off the outer rim of the Byron Nebula. When they found him aboard a scarred and broken cruiser, he was hardly alive. Afterwards, when asked for details, the man talked of demons and a rage that seemed inhuman.

"There's no doubt in my mind that we need to wipe them all out. They don't deserve to live."

Enid stared at the man in disbelief. "Are you saying that we should kill them all—men, women, and children?"

The soldier stirred uneasily in his seat but stared back at Enid. "No offense intended, Sir, but those Repletians don't know when to quit. They make human sacrifices to their gods, that's a fact."

"I see. Tell me, have you ever witnessed any sacrifices?"

"No, I can't say that I have, Sir. But why else would they skin their victims?"

"Skin their victims!" Enid was shocked. "I hadn't heard of that one."

"Sir, we found some of our people aboard a burnt-out freighter. They put up a good fight, but it was hopeless. They had no skins left. Our medics said they were still alive when it happened."

"My God."

"Yes, Sir. That's exactly what we felt. You can't blame our boys for attacking the first group of Pletes we found a day later."

"Yes, your report said that. How did you lose?" The soldier took a deep breath before he continued, "We had come out of our third jump after finding the freighter. We landed right in the middle of about fifty of their ships. Naturally we had to shoot or be destroyed."

"Naturally. How many did you get before they beat you?"

"That's the funny thing. They seemed to be waiting for us. There's no way they could've known and yet they had our fleet surrounded.

I've never seen so many Plete ships at one place. It's almost as if they knew we would land just where we did."

"If they did, they're one up on us. We don't have the technology to pinpoint our missions that closely."

"I know that. Our boys knew that. I guess the Pletes weren't told. Anyway, we opened fire, but they beat us to the punch. A third of our fleet went down in the first volley. After that, it was a run-and-shoot battle. We never had a chance. They kept coming and coming and coming. No mercy was shown; they weren't even interested in capturing our ships."

The soldier wiped a bead of sweat from his upper lip. Janet Carstairs kept still in the corner of the room where she stood, but she watched the soldier's every move. Enid waited while he took a big gulp of water.

"We scattered after we saw the flagship break up. They came after us, three or four of their ships ganging up on one of ours. We couldn't jump because they were too close and never gave us distance. We fired with everything we had, but they were so quick we only got a few of them."

"And you're certain they were Repletians?"

The young man looked shocked. "Who else could it have been? Of course they were Pletes. No one else fights that way."

The next person she talked to was a Repletian servant who had been in the service of a patrician family for fifty years. He stood before her, his stance showing his nervousness. His stocky figure swayed slightly from side to side. Enid knew he wasn't happy to be here, but neither could he disobey an order from the head of his family, an ex-naval officer who was glad to perform this small service for the military.

"Your name is Blue Strike?"

"Yes, Ma'am, or should I say, Yes, Sir?"

"Call me neither. 'Admiral' will do."

"Yes, Admiral."

"It's said that you grew up free."

Blue Strike looked down at his feet and said nothing. "Is this true?"

"Yes, Ma'am. I mean, Admiral."

"Where did you grow up?"

"Can't rightly say, Admiral. My memory isn't as it should be."

"Can you make a guess?"

"A guess, Admiral?"

Enid shifted her weight and threw a glance at David, whose face stayed neutral. "A guess, Blue Strike."

Blue Strike frowned as he thought hard for a few moments. Then he smiled and looked up at her. "I guess, Admiral, that I grew up somewhere in Sector Four."

"I see. That's where the Home Worlds of Repletia are."

"Yes, Admiral, that's what they say."

"And what are your memories of those times?"

"Memories, Admiral? I can't rightly say that I have any. None, that is, that would mean much to someone like yourself, Admiral."

"What makes you say that?"

"Well, you see, unless you know your family, there isn't much I could say that would mean much."

"My family? What has my family got to do with what I want to know?"

Blue Strike again looked at his feet, and this time he stared absently at them. After another awkward silence, Enid leaned forward in her seat, and the tone of her voice snapped Blue Strike's head up. "Mister, look up when I ask you questions. I said, what has my family got to do with this?"

Blue Strike took a half step back and glanced nervously behind himself. He hesitated and licked his lips. "Admiral, it's like this. We all have a family, and what you know is through what your family knows."

"Are we talking about mysticism here?"

"I don't rightly know what you mean by that word, Admiral. I do know that you won't get what you need from me. I'm not your family."

"Of course you're not my family. Besides, my parents died years ago in a crash."

Blue Strike shrugged his shoulders. "Not that family, Admiral. I'm talking about your real family."

The bridge was empty of everyone but Blue Strike and Enid's four bridge officers, but Enid still felt the heat of emotions on her face. What he said stirred something in her that she didn't understand. She told herself that the man before her was talking nonsense. "My real family, Blue Strike? What do you know of my real family? They died when I was young. I loved them. If you're talking about my biological parents, there's nothing to say. They don't belong in this conversation."

Blue Strike said nothing to this. He stole a quick glance towards David and then towards the straight, still figure of the combat major. Then he waited, staring again at his feet.

In the background, the low hum of activity gave Enid a pleasure she hadn't always felt. She noticed Blue Strike's austere yet well-kept clothes. His angular face seemed peaceful in its remoteness, and Enid knew she wouldn't get anything from this man that he didn't want to give her.

"Don't go far, Blue Strike. I may need you at a later time."

"I go nowhere I'm not permitted, Admiral. I'm in no haste. My fast lasts another three days."

"Fast?"

"It's right that we fast once a season to find joy in what we have."

Enid had heard of this ritual but decided to let the matter rest. She had other things to consider and waved him away. He made a bow and in a low voice he said, "When I give to you, I give myself."

Now her thoughts returned to Blue Strike and his reticence. This fasting thing, for example. How many Repletians followed ways that were set thousands of years ago on the First Home World of Humanity? Enid asked David to watch the bridge before she entered the main body of the flagship, one guard ten paces before her and the combat major trailing five paces behind. Most of the long halls were empty, their steel-grey walls muting the sounds of passage. Their angularity added to the air of military purpose that usually gave Enid a dim sense of comfort, but she walked down the halls today without any sense of ease. She missed the people who'd swarmed through here mere hours before when the ship was loaded with supplies and as staff reported for duty.

Enid was Repletian by blood, she knew that, but until she met Blue Strike she never thought of her bloodline as an issue. That others reacted badly towards her for her ancestry, she thought was their problem, and by extension, their weakness. She felt nothing but contempt for people who allowed their emotions to rule their actions; and yet, now, her military training and beliefs were of no help to her. She felt like retreating to her quarters and drawing something, anything, to escape from her thoughts for a while. Only the presence of Janet Carstairs kept her from doing this. She had to play out her role as the admiral. So she continued down the long silent corridors while wondering what worried her so much about Blue Strike's seemingly innocuous comments.

When she returned to the bridge David relinquished the command chair. Enid read the fleet's status reports; most of the fleet was gathering at Brian's Planet as planned. The border worlds had heard of what happened in Sector Five and the disappearance of the Fifth Fleet. Everyone braced for an all-out war with the Repletians. Enid hoped that an escalation of the fighting, which so far had been limited to border fights, wouldn't happen. She knew that her promotion was part of such a hope. The Anphorian Council hoped that the Repletians would wait before firing on a fleet led by one of its own.

Yet, there were so many questions about the destruction of the Fifth Fleet. For one, Repletians tended to use hit-and-run methods that suited their smaller ships. They had never tried to attack a fleet head-on, nor did the council think they had the strength to do so.

As her officers gathered on the bridge, Enid's thoughts were only half on her duties. A part of her mused on the red lights of her panel. She idly tapped her pencil on the arm of her chair to a tune she dimly recalled from her childhood, one of the few things she could remember of her past.

Men on the Moon

SIMON ORTIZ

(1999)

> The reach of imperialism into "our heads" challenges those who
> belong to colonized communities to understand how this
> occurred, partly because we perceive a need to decolonize our
> minds, to recover ourselves, to claim a space in which to develop
> a sense of authentic humanity.
> —*Linda Tuhiwai Smith (Maori)*

OUR FINAL INSTALLMENT in the "Contact" section, Simon J. Ortiz's
"Men on the Moon," shares skepticism for a common sf trope, the
discovery of "new worlds" that offer plunder and adventure to technologically advanced colonizers. The story quietly questions assump-
tions about Native peoples' "technoprimitivism" by juxtaposing the
television imagery of the first lunar landing with an elder's dream of
a machine monster on the moon. "It's a dream," he warns, "but the
truth." Ortiz's imagery masters technosurrealism by likening the greatest advancement in western science at the time to a traditional *Skquuyuh mahkina,* great and powerful but of evil origins, a living entity
to beware. The sublime wonder typical in pulp sf contact narratives
is inverted from an Indigenous perspective, which sees nothing of
new worlds discovered, only rupture as the old world is catastrophi-
cally changed.

Simon J. Ortiz (Acoma Pueblo), Professor of English at Arizona
State University, prolific writer of more than two dozen volumes of

Indigenous poetry, prose fiction, children's literature, and nonfiction, has played pivotal roles in bringing cultural studies and Native American literatures to mainstream attention, and in offering generous mentorship for many involved in the current Native intellectual movement's attention to Native-centered theory. He also has succeeded in getting the scholarly community to reframe its thinking about Indigenous peoples transnationally, unifying tribal, national, hemispheric, and global perspectives.

Darko Suvin's concept of "cognitive estrangement," a typical sf strategy, guides the reader through the story, as we meet an old man—Faustin, a grandfather—who is unfamiliar with both television and the English language, and thus depends on a grandson's translations, explanations, and possible teasing about the momentous *Apollo 11* mission. The televisual images and montage scenes of white smoke and *mahkinas,* huge machines, compound Nana's uneasiness with Mericanos who laboriously quest for knowledge in an arena where they believe there is no life.[1] This irony perhaps informs Nana's perspective on the wonders of the technological sublime conceived "to better mankind" and the astronauts' overwrought efforts to discover "where everything began a long time ago and how everything was made in the beginning." Surprised at the lengths they'll go to in search of answers to simple questions, he wonders, "Hasn't anyone ever told them?"

Ortiz flips the elitism of those immersed in the technological sublime, the testing grounds of the atom bomb, the testing out of space travel, and the search for the "tiniest bit of life" on other planets. This allegorical and abstract story in fact is linked to a sequence that explores the specifics of Kerr-McGee Corporation, an actual petroleum products company that began operations in Depression-era Oklahoma and went on to operate large uranium mines in the US Southwest in the 1960s and 1970s. One site was the Ambrosia Lake mine in New Mexico on Acoma Pueblo land. Presciently, Ortiz's "Men on the Moon," which he originally began in the sixties before revising for publication in the 1999 collection that shares its title, anticipates Kerr-McGee's development into a subsidiary of Anadarko Petroleum and Western Gas Reserves, and Ambrosia's subsequent dubious status as one of the largest uranium tailings in the Western world.[2]

The full cycle of the history of Eurowestern contact thus lies beneath the surface of Ortiz's marvelous little allegory. After making the people's land lifeless, the colonizers take their final trip to a life-less land.

⁂

I

Joselita brought her father, Faustin, the TV on Father's Day. She brought it over after Sunday mass, and she had her son hook up the antenna. She plugged the TV cord into the wall socket.

Faustin sat on a worn couch. He was covered with an old coat. He had worn that coat for twenty years.

It's ready. Turn it on and I'll adjust the antenna, Amarosho told his mother. The TV warmed up and then the screen flickered into dull light. It was snowing. Amarosho tuned it a bit. It snowed less and then a picture formed.

Look, Naishtiya, Joselita said. She touched her father's hand and pointed at the TV.

I'll turn the antenna a bit and you tell me when the picture is clear, Amarosho said. He climbed on the roof again.

After a while the picture turned clearer. It's better! his mother shouted. There was only the tiniest bit of snow falling.

That's about the best it can get, I guess, Amarosho said. Maybe it'll clear up on the other channels. He turned the selector. It was clearer on another channel.

There were two men struggling mightily with each other. Wrestling, Amarosho said.

Do you want to watch wrestling? Two men are fighting, Nana. One of them is Apache Red. Chisheh tsah, he told his grandfather.

The old man stirred. He had been staring intently into the TV. He wondered why there was so much snow at first. Now there were two men fighting. One of them was a Chisheh—an Apache—and the other was a Mericano. There were people shouting excitedly and clapping hands within the TV.

The two men backed away from each other for a moment and then they clenched again. They wheeled mightily and suddenly one threw the other. The old man smiled. He wondered why they were fighting.

Something else showed on the TV screen. A bottle of wine was being poured. The old man liked the pouring sound and he moved his mouth and lips. Someone was selling wine.

The two fighting men came back on the TV. They struggled with each other, and after a while one of them didn't get up. And then another man came and held up the hand of the Apache, who was dancing around in a feathered headdress.

It's over, Amarosho announced. Apache Red won the fight, Nana.

The Chisheh won. Faustin stared at the other fighter, a light-haired man who looked totally exhausted and angry with himself. The old man didn't like the Apache too much. He wanted them to fight again.

After a few minutes, something else appeared on the TV.

What is that? Faustin asked. In the TV picture was an object with smoke coming from it. It was standing upright.

Men are going to the moon, Nana, Amarosho said. That's *Apollo*. It's going to fly three men to the moon.

That thing is going to fly to the moon?

Yes, Nana, his grandson said.

What is it called again? Faustin asked.

Apollo, a spaceship rocket, Joselita told her father.

The *Apollo* spaceship stood on the ground, emitting clouds of something, something that looked like smoke.

A man was talking, telling about the plans for the flight, what would happen, that it was almost time. Faustin could not understand the man very well because he didn't know many words in the language of the Mericano.

He must be talking about that thing flying in the air? he said.

Yes. It's about ready to fly away to the moon.

Faustin remembered that the evening before he had looked at the sky and seen that the moon was almost in the middle phase. He wondered if it was important that the men get to the moon.

Are those men looking for something on the moon, Nana? he asked his grandson.

They're trying to find out what's on the moon, Nana. What kind of dirt and rocks there are and to see if there's any water. Scientist men don't believe there is any life on the moon. The men are looking for knowledge, Amarosho said to Faustin.

Faustin wondered if the men had run out of places to look for knowledge on the earth. Do they know if they'll find knowledge? he asked.

They have some already. They've gone before and come back. They're going again.

Did they bring any back?

They brought back some rocks, Amarosho said.

Rocks. Faustin laughed quietly. The American scientist men went to search for knowledge on the moon and they brought back rocks. He kind of thought that perhaps Amarosho was joking with him. His grandson had gone to Indian School for a number of years, and sometimes he would tell his grandfather some strange and funny things.

The old man was suspicious. Sometimes they joked around. Rocks. You sure that's all they brought back? he said. Rocks!

That's right, Nana, only rocks and some dirt and pictures they made of what it looks like on the moon.

The TV picture was filled with the rocket spaceship close-up now. Men were sitting and standing and moving around some machinery, and the TV voice had become more urgent. The old man watched the activity in the picture intently but with a slight smile on his face.

Suddenly it became very quiet, and the TV voice was firm and commanding and curiously pleading. Ten, nine, eight, seven, six, five, four, three, two, one, liftoff. The white smoke became furious, and a muted rumble shook through the TV. The rocket was trembling and the voice was trembling.

It was really happening, the old man marveled. Somewhere inside of that cylinder with a point at its top and long slender wings were three men who were flying to the moon.

The rocket rose from the ground. There were enormous clouds of smoke and the picture shook. Even the old man became tense, and he grasped the edge of the couch. The rocket spaceship rose and rose.

There's fire coming out of the rocket, Amarosho explained. That's what makes it fly.

Fire. Faustin had wondered what made it fly. He had seen pictures of other flying machines. They had long wings, and someone had explained to him that there was machinery inside which spun metal blades that made the machines fly. He had wondered what made this thing fly. He hoped his grandson wasn't joking him.

After a while there was nothing but the sky. The rocket *Apollo* had disappeared. It hadn't taken very long, and the voice on the TV wasn't excited anymore. In fact, the voice was very calm and almost bored.

I have to go now, Naishtiya, Joselita told her father. I have things
to do.

Me too, Amarosho said.

Wait, the old man said, wait. What shall I do with this thing?
What is it you call it?

TV, his daughter said. You watch it. You turn it on and you watch it.

I mean how do you stop it? Does it stop like the radio, like the mahkina? It stops?

This way, Nana, Amarosho said and showed his grandfather. He
turned a round knob on the TV and the picture went away.

He turned the knob again, and the picture flickered on again. Were
you afraid this one-eye would be looking at you all the time? Amarosho laughed and gently patted the old man's shoulder.

Faustin was relieved. Joselita and her son left. Faustin watched the
TV picture for a while. A lot of activity was going on, a lot of men
were moving among machinery, and a couple of men were talking.
And then the spaceship rocket was shown again.

The old man watched it rise and fly away again. It disappeared
again. There was nothing but the sky. He turned the knob and the
picture died away. He turned it on and the picture came on again. He
turned it off. He went outside and to a fence a short distance from
his home. When he finished peeing, he zipped up his pants and studied the sky for a while.

II

That night, he dreamed.

Flintwing Boy was watching a Skquuyuh mahkina come down a
hill. The mahkina made a humming noise. It was walking. It shone
in the sunlight. Flintwing Boy moved to a better position to see. The
mahkina kept on moving toward him.

The Skquuyuh mahkina drew closer. Its metal legs stepped upon
trees and crushed growing flowers and grass. A deer bounded away
frightened. Tsushki came running to Flintwing Boy.

Anahweh, Tsushki cried, trying to catch his breath.

What is it, Anahweh?

You've been running, Flintwing Boy said.

The coyote was staring at the thing, which was coming toward them. There was wild fear in his eyes.

What is that, Anahweh? What is that thing? Tsushki gasped.

It looks like a mahkina, but I've never seen one quite like it before. It must be some kind of Skquuyuh mahkina, Anahweh, Flintwing Boy said. When he saw that Tsushki was trembling with fear, he said, Sit down, Anahweh. Rest yourself. We'll find out soon enough.

The Skquuyuh mahkina was undeterred. It walked over and through everything. It splashed through a stream of clear water. The water boiled and streaks of oil flowed downstream. It split a juniper tree in half with a terrible crash. It crushed a boulder into dust with a sound of heavy metal. Nothing stopped the Skquuyuh mahkina. It hummed.

Anahweh, Tsushki cried, what can we do?

Flintwing Boy reached into the bag hanging at his side. He took out an object. It was a flint arrowhead. He took out some cornfood.

Come over here, Anahweh. Come over here. Be calm, he motioned to the frightened coyote. He touched the coyote in several places on his body with the arrowhead and put cornfood in the palm of his hand.

This way, Flintwing Boy said. He closed Tsushki's fingers over the cornfood. They stood facing east. Flintwing Boy said, We humble ourselves again. We look in your direction for guidance. We ask for your protection. We humble our poor bodies and spirits because only you are the power and the source and the knowledge. Help us, then. That is all we ask.

Flintwing Boy and Tsushki breathed on the cornfood, then took in the breath of all the directions and gave the cornfood unto the ground.

Now the ground trembled with the awesome power of the Skquuyuh mahkina. Its humming vibrated against everything.

Flintwing Boy reached over his shoulder and took several arrows from his quiver. He inspected them carefully and without any rush he fit one to his bowstring.

And now, Anahweh, Flintwing Boy said, you must go and tell everyone. Describe what you have seen. The people must talk among themselves and learn what this is about, and decide what they will do. You must hurry, but you must not alarm the people. Tell them I am here to meet the Skquuyuh mahkina. Later I will give them my report.

Tsushki turned and began to run. He stopped several yards away. Hahtrudzaimeh! he called to Flintwing Boy. Like a man of courage, Anahweh, like our people.

The old man stirred in his sleep. A dog was barking. He awoke fully and got out of his bed and went outside. The moon was past the midpoint, and it would be daylight in a few hours.

III

Later, the spaceship reached the moon.

Amarosho was with his grandfather Faustin. They watched a TV replay of two men walking on the moon.

So that's the men on the moon, Faustin said.

Yes, Nana, there they are, Amarosho said.

There were two men inside of heavy clothing, and they carried heavy-looking equipment on their backs.

The TV picture showed a closeup of one of them and indeed there was a man's face inside of glass. The face moved its mouth and smiled and spoke, but the voice seemed to be separate from the face.

It must be cold, Faustin said. They have on heavy clothing.

It's supposed to be very cold and very hot on the moon. They wear special clothes and other things for protection from the cold and heat, Amarosho said.

The men on the moon were moving slowly. One of them skipped like a boy, and he floated alongside the other.

The old man wondered if they were underwater. They seem to be able to float, he said.

The information I have heard is that a man weighs less on the moon than he does on earth, Amarosho said to his grandfather. Much less, and he floats. And there is no air on the moon for them to breathe, so those boxes on their backs carry air for them to breathe.

A man weighs less on the moon, the old man thought. And there is no air on the moon except for the boxes on their backs. He looked at Amarosho, but his grandson did not seem to be joking with him.

The land on the moon looked very dry. It looked like it had not rained for a long, long time. There were no trees, no plants, no grass. Nothing but dirt and rocks, a desert.

Amarosho had told him that men on earth—scientists—believed there was no life on the moon. Yet those men were trying to find knowledge on the moon. Faustin wondered if perhaps they had special tools with which they could find knowledge even if they believed there was no life on the moon.

The mahkina sat on the desert. It didn't make a sound. Its metal feet were planted flat on the ground. It looked somewhat awkward. Faustin searched around the mahkina, but there didn't seem to be anything except the dry land on the TV. He couldn't figure out the mahkina. He wasn't sure whether it moved and could cause harm. He didn't want to ask his grandson that question.

After a while, one of the bulky men was digging in the ground. He carried a long, thin tool with which he scooped up dirt and put it into a container. He did this for a while.

Is he going to bring the dirt back to earth too? Faustin asked. I think he is, Nana, Amarosho said. Maybe he'll get some rocks too. Watch.

Indeed, several minutes later, the man lumbered over to a pile of rocks and gathered several handsized ones. He held them out proudly. They looked just like rocks from around anyplace. The voice on the TV seemed to be excited about the rocks.

They will study the rocks, too, for knowledge?

Yes, Nana.

What will they use the knowledge for, Nana?

They say they will use it to better mankind, Nana. I've heard that. And to learn more about the universe in which we live. Also, some of the scientists say the knowledge will be useful in finding out where everything began a long time ago and how everything was made in the beginning.

Faustin looked with a smile at his grandson. He said, You are telling me the true facts, aren't you?

Why, yes, Nana. That's what they say. I'm not just making it up, Amarosho said.

Well then, do they say why they need to know where and how everything began? Hasn't anyone ever told them?

I think other people have tried to tell them but they want to find out for themselves, and also they claim they don't know enough and need to know more and for certain, Amarosho said.

The man in the bulky suit had a small pickax in his hand. He was striking at a boulder. The breathing of the man could be heard clearly. He seemed to be working very hard and was very tired.

Faustin had once watched a work crew of Mericano drilling for water. They had brought a tall mahkina with a loud motor. The mahkina would raise a limb at its center to its very top and then drop it with a heavy and loud metal clang. The mahkina and its men sat at one spot for several days, and finally they found water.

The water had bubbled out weakly, gray-looking, and did not look drinkable at all. And then the Mericano workmen lowered the mahkina, put their equipment away, and drove away. The water stopped flowing. After a couple of days, Faustin went and checked out the place.

There was nothing there except a pile of gray dirt and an indentation in the ground. The ground was already dry, and there were dark spots of oil-soaked dirt.

Faustin decided to tell Amarosho about the dream he had had.

After the old man finished, Amarosho said, Old man, you're telling me the truth now, aren't you? You know that you've become somewhat of a liar. He was teasing his grandfather.

Yes, Nana. I have told you the truth as it occurred to me that night. Everything happened like that except I might not have recalled everything about it.

That's some story, Nana, but it's a dream.

It's a dream, but it's the truth, Faustin said.

I believe you, Nana, his grandson said.

IV

Some time after that the spacemen returned to earth. Amarosho told his grandfather they had splashed down in the ocean.

Are they alright? Faustin asked.

Yes, Amarosho said. They have devices to keep them safe. Are they in their homes now?

No, I think they have to be someplace where they can't contaminate anything. If they brought back something from the moon that they weren't supposed to, they won't pass it on to someone else, Amarosho said to his grandfather.

What would that something be?

Something harmful, Nana.

In that dry desert land of the moon there might be something harmful, the old man said. I didn't see any strange insects or trees or even cactus. What would that harmful thing be, Nana?

Disease which might harm people on earth, Amarosho said.

You said there was the belief by the men that there is no life on the moon. Is there life after all? Faustin asked.

There might be the tiniest bit of life.

Yes, I see now, Nana. If the men find even the tiniest bit of life on the moon, then they will believe, the old man said.

Yes. Something like that.

Faustin figured it out now. The Mericano men had taken that trip in a spaceship rocket to the moon to find even the tiniest bit of life. And when they found even the tiniest bit of life, even if it was harmful, they would believe that they had found knowledge. Yes, that must be the way it was.

He remembered his dream clearly now. The old man was relieved.

When are those two men fighting again, Nana? he asked Amarosho.

What two men?

Those two men who were fighting with each other the day those Mericano spaceship men were flying to the moon.

Oh, those men. I don't know, Nana. Maybe next Sunday. You like them?

Yes. I think the next time I will be cheering for the Chisheh. He'll win again. He'll beat the Mericano again, Faustin said.

Indigenous Science and Sustainability

from *Midnight Robber*

NALO HOPKINSON

(2000)

Native healers as keepers of knowledge were keen observers of the
natural world, with knowledge equivalent to today's naturalists,
botanists, and ecologists.
—*Gregory Cajete (Tewa, Santa Clara, Pueblo Nation)*

ACCLAIMED AUTHOR OF SF and speculative fiction, and coeditor
with Uppinder Mehan of the breakout anthology showcasing sf writers of color *So Long Been Dreaming: Postcolonial Science Fiction and
Fantasy* (2004), Nalo Hopkinson (Taino/Arawak and Afro-Caribbean
descent) continues to inspire, encourage, and elevate emerging voices
in the field. *Midnight Robber,* the novel excerpted here, re-forms Taino
tales, as its narrator explicitly states. At the same time, Hopkinson
creates landscape and bush on an sf future world and/or parallel world
(in keeping with Taino thinking about our four worlds aligned side-
by-side). Called New Half-Way Tree, the setting replicates features
not only of the Caribbean (Hopkinson's home in her youth) but also
of northern Aboriginal Canada (near her current residence in Toronto)
and the Australian Aborigine bush. Mirroring this multitude of geo-
graphical sources, Hopkinson also innovates linguistically by combining Jamaican, Trinidadian, and Guianan languages. These techniques
have the effect of placing the reader in worlds that split apart the
colonizer-versus-colonized binary that occurs in much sf. Diverging

from stereotypical scenes of Indigenous contact with colonial power, New Half-Way Tree boasts a diverse and intermingling array of creatures, all of whom vie for the rights and responsibilities of "personhood": the Indigenous animal persons (known as the *douen* and *hinte*), the people persons exiled from their home planet and relocated to this new world (whom the douen call Tallpeople), machine persons (Granny Nanny Anansi and her *eshu*), and spirit-persons (such as Bush Poopa, Father Bush, master of the forest). The interactions among Indigenous or diasporic Aboriginal peoples and animal-persons engage colonizers in conflicted (sometimes ambivalent and violent) negotiations that potentially evolve into positive exchanges of commodities and customs. Ultimately, the story reflects Hopkinson's timeless imagination, which offers a vision of future technology in the Indigenous tradition of teaching through storytelling and ceremony.

The novel could find itself parsed into any of the sections in this reader. It is fundamentally a contact narrative and as such is about the apocalyptic and diasporic experience of Aboriginal peoples. The passage excerpted illustrates the concept of Indigenous scientific literacies, a defining element throughout Hopkinson's works, including *Brown Girl in the Ring* (1998), *The Salt Roads* (2004), *The New Moon's Arms* (2007), and the post-cyberpunk *Midnight Robber* (2000). The excerpt here highlights intersections between colonizer and colonized, specifically the reciprocal gift-giving exchange between animals and humans, or, more accurately, between nonhuman persons and humans. A mainstay of the novel is the emphasis on symbiosis among all elements of nature, a relationship that human-persons sadly have lost. For example, the douen expression, "Take one, give back two," which is voiced throughout the novel, is an essential tenet of sustainability that teaches us to replenish resources or risk losing them. As in Taino and Arawak thinking, one must learn to steal, to wrestle secrets through trial and error, and "learn how to make use of cultivation, weaving, hunting and fishing for the benefit of mankind."[1] The excerpt foreshadows multiple Indigenous scientific literacies in, for example, the concern over the Tallpeople's introduction of non-Indigenous invasive species to the Aboriginal environment. Rather than seeking to eradicate the new flora, the douen embrace the opportunity to experiment in adaptation and grafting. In addition, reciprocal altruism—or learning and modeling sustainable behavior from observing animal species—occurs here and in many of Hopkinson's novels.

We enter the story where Tan-Tan and her father, Antonio, newly arrived human-person exiles to New Half-Way Tree, find themselves lost on an unfamiliar trail in this brave new world and must rely on an Indigenous douen named Chichibud for survival. Antonio sees the strange creature as an annoyance if not a threat, while young Tan-Tan, Hopkinson's iteration of the Caribbean folklore hero known as the Robber King, offers a more nuanced response to an Indigenous mentor who provides safe passage through the bush.

ℛ

The light was too red and the air smelled wrong. The shift pod had disappeared and left Tan-Tan and the daddy she couldn't recognize no more in this strange place. They were in a bush with no food and no shelter. Everything was changed.

"Allyou climb the Tree to visit we?" The high, clear voice was coming from behind Tan-Tan. She whipped round. Someone strange was standing there. Tan-Tan screamed and jumped behind Antonio.

Antonio grabbed Tan-Tan's arm and took a step back. "What you want?" he asked.

It made a hissing noise *shu-shu* and said, "That all depend on what you have to trade."

"Not we. We come with we two long arms just so."

Tan-Tan peeked out. The creature was only about as tall as she. It smelled like leaves. Its head was shaped funny; long and narrow like a bird's. It was ugly for so! Its eyes were on either side of its head, not in front of its face like people eyes. It had two arms like them, with hands. Each hand had four fingers with swollen fingertips. Slung across its leathery chest was a gourd on a strap. It carried a slingshot in one hand and had a pouch round its waist. It wore no clothing, but Tan-Tan couldn't see genitalia, just something looking like a pocket of flesh at its crotch. A long knife in a holder was strapped onto one muscular thigh. But it was the creature's legs that amazed Tan-Tan the most. They looked like goat feet; thin and bent backwards in the middle. Its feet had four long toes with thick, hard nails. "Eshu," she muttered, "a-what that?"

Static, then a headache burst upon her brain. Eshu didn't answer.

The jokey-looking beast bobbed its head at them, like any lizard. "I think you two must be want plenty, yes? Water, and food, and your own people? What you go give me if I take you where it have people like you?"

At the word "water," Tan-Tan realized that she'd had nothing to drink since the cocoa-tea Nursie had given her that afternoon, and she'd only sipped that; a whole lifetime away, it seemed now.

"Daddy, I thirsty."

"Hush your mouth, Tan-Tan. We don't know nothing about this beast."

The creature said, "Beast that could talk and know it own mind. Oonuh tallpeople quick to name what is people and what is beast. Last time I asking you: safe passage through this bush?"

"Why I making deal with some leggobeast that look like bat masque it own self? How I know you go do what you say?"

"Because is so we do business here. Give me something that I want, I go keep my pact with you. Douen people does keep their word."

Douen! Nursie had told Tan-Tan douen stories. Douens were children who'd died before they had their naming ceremonies. They came back from the dead as jumbies with their heads on backwards. They lived in the bush. Tan-Tan looked at the douen's head, then its feet. They seemed to attach the right way, even though its knees were backwards.

The creature made the *shu-shu* noise again. "Too besides, allyou taste nasty too bad, bitter aloe taste. Better to take you to live with your people."

Antonio made a worried frown. Then: "All right," he said. "Let me see what I have to trade with you." He searched his jacket pockets and pulled out a pen. "What about this?"

One of the douen's eyes rolled to inspect the pen. A bright green frill sprang up round its neck. It stepped up too close to Antonio. Antonio moved back. The douen followed, said, "Country booky come to town you think I is? Used to sweet we long time ago, when oonuh tallpeople give we pen and bead necklace. Something more useful, mister. Allyou does come with plenty thing when you get exile here."

"Nobody know we was leaving Toussaint. I ain't think to bring nothing with we."

"Me ain't business with that."

Worriedly, Antonio started searching his pockets again. Tan-Tan saw him ease a flask of rum part way out of his back pants pocket then put it back in. He patted his chest pocket, looked down at himself. "Here. What about my shoes-them?" He bent over and ran his finger down the seam that would release his shoe from his foot.

"Foolish. Is a two-day hike." Its frill deflated against its neck, leaving what looked like a necklace of green beads. "Leave on your shoes and come."

"What?"

"You will owe me. Come. Allyou want water?"

That was what Tan-Tan had been waiting to hear. "Yes, please, mister," she piped up. *Mister?* she wondered.

The douen laughed *shu-shu*. "This one barely rip open he egg yet, and he talking bold-face! Your son this, tallpeople?"

"My daughter. Leave she alone."

"He, she; oonuh all the same."

Antonio shot the douen a puzzled look.

"She want water," the creature said.

"Let me taste it first."

Antonio took a few swallows from the gourd the douen handed him. He nodded, then held it for Tan-Tan to drink. The water was warm and a little slimy. She didn't care, she drank until her throat wasn't dry any more.

The douen said, "Never see a tallpeople pickney climb the halfway tree before. What crime you do, pickney, to get cast away?"

"Never you mind," growled Antonio.

The creature didn't reply. It took the gourd back. It sniffed at Daddy, then at Tan-Tan. She moved away from its pointy snout, hands jumping protectively to cross in front of her body. But it just grunted at them and started off through the bush, hacking a path with its knife. Tan-Tan remembered Nursie's stories about how douens led people into the bush to get lost and die. She started to feel scared all over again. She called silently for eshu. Her headache flared, then quieted. She reached for Antonio's hand. "Daddy," she whispered. "Where eshu?"

"Back on Toussaint, child. We leave all that behind now."

She didn't understand. Eshu was always there. She bit her bottom lip, peered into the bush where the douen had disappeared. "We have to go with that funny man?"

"Yes, doux-doux. It say it taking we to we own people."

"For true? It not going to lost we?"

"I don't know, doux-doux. Just come."

They followed the path the creature had left. Red heat beat down. Branches jooked. The space the creature was clearing through the bush was short so till Antonio had to rip off the foliage above his own head to make room to pass through. By the time they caught up to the douen, Antonio was panting with the exertion and scratched from jutting twigs. "Is what you did call this place?" he asked.

"New Half-Way Tree oonuh call it."

"But," said Tan-Tan, "we not halfway. We come all the way and reach now." The douen blinked at her. Its eyes were very large. She didn't like it looking at her. She shouldn't have said anything. Nervously she giggled at her own joke.

Antonio stopped her with a look. He said, "How you know where to find we? The shift pod does land at the same place every time?"

"No. Douen does know when and where a next one going to land. Taste it in the air. Whichever douen reach there first, him get first right of trade with the new tallpeople. Bring we good business, oonuh. A tallpeople gave me a shirt one time. Front does close up when you run your finger along it. I give it to the weavers in my village. Them will study how to make more."

"How come you could speak the same way like we?"

"Yes. Anglopatwa, Francopatwa, Hispanopatwa, and Papiamento. Right? We learn all oonuh speech, for oonuh don't learn we own."

"And why you call yourself 'douen'?"

"Allyou call we so. Is we legs."

The ringing in Tan-Tan's ears, which had never quite stopped since the shift pod had deposited them here, was getting louder. She shook her head to try to clear it. She had begun to feel chilly. She wrapped her arms round herself.

The douen noticed, sniffed in her direction. It raised one twisted leg and scratched behind its shoulder blade. "Mister, watch at your pickney-girl. Is so allyou does do for cold."

Antonio stared down at her with a look like he didn't know what to do.

"Allyou people blood too hot for this place," said the douen. Now it was holding the foot up in front of its face, inspecting between its long toes to see if its scratching had unearthed anything. Its toes flicked, shaking dust off themselves as agilely as fingers. It put its foot back on the ground, looked at Antonio. "Give she something warm to wear."

"Me done tell you, me don't have nothing!"

The creature reached into the pouch at its waist and pulled out a cloth like the one it was wearing. It was saffron yellow, Tan-Tan's favourite color.

"Here, small tallperson."

Tan-Tan pressed up against Daddy's legs. She looked doubtfully at the cloth. Antonio took it, peered at it, smelt it. He shook it out and put it round her shoulders. "Thanks," he said grudgingly.

"My wife make those cloths," the douen said to Tan-Tan.

A dead douen baby could have wife?

"With every thread she weave," the douen continued, "she weave a magic to give warmth to who wear the cloth. Is true; I does see she do it."

Tan-Tan took a hard look at the little person. She wished she could talk to eshu. The douen's eyes-at-the-sides couldn't look at her straight on; it cocked its head like a bird's to return the stare, like a parrot. She smiled a little. No, it didn't look like a dead child. Too besides, it didn't have no Panama hat like a real douen. She began to feel warmer, wrapped in its wife's magic cloth. "What you name?" she asked the douen.

"Eh-eh! The pickney offering trail debt." He bent, sniffed her hair. "You have manners. Me name Chichibud. And what you name?"

"Tan-Tan," she said, feeling shy.

"Sweet name. The noise Cousin Lizard does make when he wooing he mate."

"It have lizards here?"

Chichibud looked round the gloomy bush, picked up a twig and flung it at a crenellated tree trunk. A liver-red something slithered out of the way. It was many-legged like a centipede, long as Daddy's forearm, thick around as his wrist.

"Fuck," Antonio muttered.

"No, I make mistake," said Chichibud. "Foot snake that, not a lizard. *Shu-shu.*"

He peered round again, then pointed to a tree in front of them. "Look." The tree had brownish purple bark and long twist-up leaves fluttering in the air like ropes of blood floating in water.

"I ain't see nothing."

"Look at the tree trunk. Just above that knothole there." Tan-Tan squinted and stared at the tree, but still couldn't make anything out.

Chichibud picked up a rockstone from the ground and flung it at the tree. "Show yourself, cousin!"

A little lizard reared up on its hind legs to scuttle out of the way, then just as quickly settled still again on the tree.

Tan-Tan laughed. "I see he! He like the ones from back home, just a different color." The lizard was purple like the bark, but with streaks of pink the same strange color as the sunlight. When he was quiet he looked just like a piece of tree bark with the sun dappling it.

"Tallpeople say your world not so different from the real world," the douen told her.

Yes it was. Plenty different. "Why you call the lizard `cousin'?"

"Old people tell we douen and lizards related. So we treat them good. We never kill a lizard."

Antonio said impatiently, "The place you taking we; is what it name?"

"We go keep hiking," Chichibud told them. They moved off through the bush again. He answered Antonio's question: "It name Junjuh."

The parasitic fungus that grew wherever it was moist.

"Nasty name," Antonio mumbled.

"One of oonuh tell me about junjuh mold. It does grow where nothing else can't catch: When no soil not there, it put roots down in the rock, and all rainwater and river water pound down on it, it does thrive. No matter what you do, it does grow back."

As they walked, Chichibud showed them how to see the bush around them. He took them over to a low plant with pointy leaves. In the dusky sunlight they could just make out dark blue flowers with red tongues. "Devil bush this."

"I know it!" Tan-Tan said. "We have it back home, but the flowers does be red."

"The one back home like this?" Carefully, Chichibud picked a leaf off the plant. He held it up to the light so they could see the tiny, near-transparent needles that bristled on its underside. "Poison thorn.

If you skin touch it, bad blister. Skin drop off. Our bush doctors smoke it. Give them visions. It does talk to them and tell them which plants does heal. Some of oonuh smoke it too, but never hear the voice of the herb, just the voices of your own dreams."

From then on, Tan-Tan kept casting her eyes to the ground to make sure she wouldn't brush up a devil bush.

Chichibud said to Antonio, "You bring any lighter with you? Any glass bottle?"

"Nothing, me tell you!"

"Too bad for you. Woulda trade you plenty for those; bowls to eat out of, hammock to sleep in."

A few minutes later Chichibud pulled down a vine from a tree as they were walking under it. The vine had juicy red leaves and bright green flowers. "Water vine. You could squeeze the leaves and drink from them. If you dry the vine, you could twist it together to make rope." Chichibud picked two-three of the leaves and squeezed them in his hand. "You want to try, pickney?" But before he could drip the water into her mouth, Antonio dashed the leaves out of his hand.

"Don't give she nothing to eat without I tell you to!" Antonio shouted angrily.

Chichibud fell into a crouch. He said nothing, but bobbed his head like a parrot. His eyes went opaque and then clear again, like someone opening and closing a jalousie window shutter. The frill at his neck rose. Somehow he seemed to have grown bigger, fiercer. Tan-Tan edged behind her daddy again. Them was going to fight! Maybe Daddy still had some of the poison he'd used on Uncle Quashee. That would serve the nasty leggobeast right.

"Man," Chichibud replied, his voice growly, "you under trail debt, your pickney declare it. Is liard you calling me liard?"

"I don't want her to eat nothing that might make she sick."

"Oh-hoh." Chichibud straightened up. He was back to his normal size. How he do that? "You watching out for your pickney. Is a good thing to do. But we under trail debt, I tell you. You go get safe to Junjuh. I won't make your child come to harm."

Antonio just grunted. Tan-Tan knew that particular set of his jaw. He was still vex. Chichibud tugged down a length of vine, showed it to Antonio first, then said to Tan-Tan, "Water vine only grow on this tree here, the lionheart tree with the wood too tough to cut. But if you see a vine looking just like this, only the flowers tiny-tiny, don't touch it! Allyou call it jumbie dumb cane. Juice from it make your tongue swell up in your head. Can't talk. Sometimes suffocate and dead."

They hiked on through the bush. It was sweaty work, but Tan-Tan still felt chilly. Her ears tingled. She was only watching the ground below her feet for the devil bush and the bush above her head for jumbie dumb cane. Chichibud stopped them yet again. "What you see?" he said, pointing to the ground ahead. Like all the ground they'd tromped so far, what wasn't covered with a thick carpet of ruddy dead leaves was blanketed with a fine, reddish green growth like moss. Gnarled trees with narrow trunks twisted their way out of it, reaching towards the too-red sun. It looked just like the rest of the bush.

Antonio sucked his teeth. "Look, I ain't business with your bush nonsense, yes. Take we to this Junjuh."

But as Tan-Tan had looked where Chichibud was pointing, she had slowly discerned something different through the mess of leaf and mold and stem. She tapped Chichibud on the shoulder. "Mister, I see some little lines, like the tracks badjack ants does leave in the sand."

Gently, Chichibud touched her forehead with the back of his hand, once, twice. "Good, little tallpeople. Sense behind you eyes. That is sugar-maggot trails. If you follow them, you could find their nest. Boil them to sweeten your tea." Chichibud looked at Antonio. "You must learn how to live in this place, tallpeople, or not survive."

They hiked and they hiked. They had to stop one time for Tan-Tan to make water. They kept walking. Tan-Tan pulled Chichibud's wife's cloth tighter round her, wishing she could feel warm. She peered through the dimness of the bush ahead. "Look, Daddy! Bamboo like back home."

Antonio turned wary eyes on the tall, jointed reeds growing thick as arms up towards the light. There was a whole stand of them. The shifting shadows caused by the narrow leaves blowing in the breeze hurt Tan-Tan's eyes. The hollow stems clacked against each other and made her head pound. Antonio frowned. "How bamboo reach here? Is from Toussaint." He looked to Chichibud for explanation.

"Tallpeople bring it. Plenty other bush too."

They hiked on and on until Tan-Tan couldn't make her legs move any more; Antonio had to carry her. As Daddy gathered her into his arms, Tan-Tan could feel how he was shivering too. He turned to the douen: "So where this village you only telling me about all the time? Like you is douen in truth, trying to lead we deeper into the bush and get we lost?"

"Your people tell me story. Where you come from, you could hire people to carry you *where* you going. You could go fast in magic carriage with nobody to pull it. Here, tallpeople have only your own two feet to carry you. By myself I get to Junjuh in one day. With new exiles, longer. Allyou making I move slow. Not reaching tonight. Tomorrow morning. After we sleep."

"And so is what? Where we going to stay?"

"Right here. I go show you how to make the bush your home for the night."

"And suppose it rain?" Antonio challenged him.

"It ain't go rain. I woulda smell it coming. We looking for a clearing with a tree spreading wide over it."

A few more minutes' walk. The douen passed one tree by; it had too many beasts living in its trunk. Then another; it would drop strange, wriggling fruit on their heads while they tried to sleep. Finally they came upon two trees growing close together. Chichibud pointed to lumpy brown growths in the branches of one tree. "Halwa fruit. Dinner." The other tree was broad-trunked with fire-red leaves. It had thick spreading branches, the shade of which made a clear space in the bush beneath them. "This one good. Let we make camp," Chichibud told them. He led them under its branches.

The sun was setting. The dying light reflected off the tree's leaves and made Tan-Tan's eyes ache, so she looked down. Blood-red shadows were darkening and lengthening along the ground. She could hear things rustling in the gloom where they couldn't see. She was frightened. She shook her head to clear its ringing.

Antonio let Tan-Tan down. The douen told her, "Pickney, pick up as much dry stick as you could find for the fire. Don't go far. Stay around these two trees."

Chichibud went to the halwa tree and shinnied up its trunk. Tan-Tan could hear him moving through the branches.

"Down below! Catch!"

Daddy went and stood below the tree, hands stretched out. Chichibud threw down two heavy round fruits, big as Daddy's head. Daddy caught them, making a small explosion of air from his lips as he did.

No sound came from the douen for a few minutes. Then from another part of the foliage came a *wap!* like something hitting against the tree trunk. He let something else drop into Daddy's hands, something big so like the halwa fruit, but floppy and flabby. Daddy looked good at the hairy body he was holding, cried out, "Oh, God!" and dropped it on the ground. In the incarnadine evening light the blood covering his hands looked black. Tan-Tan shuddered. Antonio was only whimpering, "Oh, God! Oh, God, what a place!" and wiping the blood off on his pants.

Chichibud sprang down from the tree, licking his hands. He peered at Tan-Tan and then at Antonio. "New tallpeople always 'fraid the dead." He laughed *shu-shu-shu*. "Is meat for dinner."

Antonio flew at the little douen man, yanked him into the air by the throat, and gave him one good shake. "Jokey story done right now," Antonio said. "What you do that for?" Chichibud snapped at Antonio's face and reached for his knife. Antonio let him go.

The douen's throat was smeared with blood from Antonio's hands. He wiped it off and sucked it from his palm. His tongue was skinny like a whip. "In the bush, you catch food when you see it. Manicou, allyou call that beast. Allyou bring it here."

The large rodent lying on the ground had a naked tail. Tan-Tan remembered the tail she'd hallucinated growing and losing again in the shift pod. The thing on the ground looked fat and healthy. Its head was all mashed up. "What happen to it?"

"I kill he," Chichibud replied. "Grab he quick by the tail and swing he head against the tree trunk. You hear when it hit?"

"Yes." She imagined the head splitting apart like a dropped watermelon. She felt ill.

"Every noise you hear in the bush mean something. Bush Poopa don't like ignorance."

"Bush Poopa?"

"Father Bush, master of the forest."

Antonio had had enough of the lesson. "We setting up this camp, or what?" He helped Tan-Tan find twigs for the fire. They made a big pile on the ground in the clearing, beside the halwa fruit and the ratthing. Antonio crouched down right there, just watching Chichibud. Tan-Tan knotted Chichibud's wife's cloth around her shoulders. She picked up one of the heavy halwa fruit and pressed her nose against it. The smell made her mouth water.

Chichibud had come back into the clearing with three sturdy staves, fresh cut. He put them beside the trunk of the red-leaved tree and spread a cloth from his pouch on the ground. He jammed the staves into the ground round the groundsheet. They met and crossed in the air like steepled fingers. Chichibud pulled out one more cloth and shook it out. It was much larger than the others. How had it fit inside that little pouch? Like it was magic too, yes? Tan-Tan wondered what else he could have in there. He threw the cloth over the staves. It stretched down to the ground. He shook some pegs out of the endless pouch, looked round himself, saw Antonio watching at him. "Find a rock to pound these pegs in with."

Sullenly Antonio stood up and cast round until he'd found a good rockstone. "Here."

Chichibud pounded the pegs through the stretched cloth, solidly into the ground. They had a tent. Chichibud straightened up and stretched his back, just like any man.

"If you ever sleep out in the bush like this by yourself, check the tree first. Any hole in the trunk, look for a next tree. Might have poison snake or ground puppy living in there."

Chichibud showed them how to start a fire with three sticks for kindling and a piece of vine for friction. By the time the fire had caught it was full dark. The dancing flames were pinkish and the burning wood had a slight smell of old socks, but Tan-Tan felt cheered by the circle of flickering light the fire threw. She moved nearer, rinsed her chilled hands in the heat flowing from the fire. The itching in her ears eased if she turned them to the warmth, one side of her head, then the other. One ear was more itchy.

Chichibud built a wooden spit over the fire. He skinned and gutted the rat-thing. Tan-Tan's stomach writhed at the sight of the raw, split-open rat, but she couldn't look away. This was a thing she'd not seen before, how the meat that fed her was a living being one minute and then violently dead. The smell of it was personal, inescapable, like the scent that rose in the steam from her own self when she stepped into a hot bath. They had broken open the animal's secret body just to eat it.

Chichibud chopped off their supper's head. He smeared the empty body cavity with herbs from his pouch, then with a quick motion jooked the spit through it. Tan-Tan started at the wet ripping sound. Chichibud put the meat above the fire to cook.

"Here, Tan-Tan. Turn the handle slow, cook it even all around."

He wrapped up the guts and the head in the creature's skin. "I soon come back," he told them. "Taking this far away so other beasts don't smell it and come after we."

He disappeared into the bush, rustling branches as he went.

"Nasty little leggobeast goat man," Antonio muttered. "You all right, doux-doux?"

"I don't like the dark. My ears itching me. Let we go back home nuh, Daddy?"

"No way back home, sweetness. The shift pod gone. Here go have to be home now."

Tan-Tan sniffled and jerked the meat round and round on its spit.

"I here," Antonio said. "I go look after you. And I won't make the goat man hurt you, neither."

Tan-Tan was more 'fraid ground puppy than Chichibud, but she didn't say so. Antonio sighed and pulled out his flask of rum. He took a swig.

Chichibud returned just as the browning, smoking meat had begun to smell like food. He praised Tan-Tan for turning the spit so diligently, then took the halwa fruit-them and broke them open. Tan-Tan's belly grumbled at the smell. It favored coconut, vanilla and nutmeg. Same way so the kitchen back home smelled when Cookie was making gizada pastry with shaved coconut and brown sugar.

"It best raw, this meat," Chichibud told her, "but oonuh prefer it burned by fire."

He hauled out three flat stones from his pouch and put them on top of some of the live coals close to the outside of the fire. "Far away from the meat, yes? So the meat juice wouldn't splatter?" He balanced the fruit on the stones. In the firelight, Tan-Tan could make out the brown fleshy inside of the fruit halves. Little-little, the sweet gizada fragrance got stronger. It floated in and round the rich scent of the cooking meat till Tan-Tan could feel the hunger-water springing in her mouth. She feel to just rip off a piece of manicou flesh and stuff it down, half-cooked just so. She reached towards the spit, but Chichibud gently took her fingers. Antonio stood up and came over to them.

"It hot," said Chichibud. "You a-go burn your fingers and make me break trail debt." From his pouch he took a parcel wrapped in parchment paper and unwrapped it. It had a square of something dry and brown inside. With his knife, Chichibud cut off strips for the three of them. He distributed them then bit into his own. When Antonio saw Chichibud eating, he started to chew on his own piece one time. Chichibud said, "Is dry tree frog meat." Antonio cursed and spat the jerky out of his mouth. He tossed the rest into the bush. Chichibud just watched him.

Tan-Tan bit into the dried meat. It was salty and chewy. She tore off a piece with her teeth. It tasted good.

A little time more, and Chichibud told them that the meat was cooked. He set out three broad halwa leaves around the fire as plates. He pulled out a little brown cloth from his endless pouch and used it to juggle the hot fruit halves onto the leaves. Then with his knife he sliced off three slabs of rat-thing and put them beside the fruit.

"Pickney, everything hot. Go slow until it cool. Use your fingers to scrape out the fruit. Don't swallow the seeds, you might choke." He put two long fingers into his halwa fruit and pulled out a shiny purple seed, round like a pebble.

"I go be careful, Chichibud." Tan-Tan scooped out a piece of fruit, pulled out the seed and put it on her leaf plate. She put the fruit in her mouth. It come in sweet and sticky and hot. The lovely gizada taste slid warmly down her throat. The meat was good too, moist and tender, and the spice Chichibud had rubbed on it tasted like big-leaf thyme. Tan-Tan began to feel better.

Antonio picked up his halwa fruit half with both hands and dropped it again, blowing on his burnt hands. "Motherass!"

Chichibud laughed his *shu-shu* laughter. Antonio glared at him and started to dig out pieces of fruit, blowing on his fingers and spitting the seeds out everywhere.

"Don't spit them into the fire," Chichibud warned. But Antonio just cut his eye in contempt and shot one seed from his mouth *prraps!* into the middle of the flames-them.

"Back! Behind the tree!" Chichibud grabbed Tan-Tan's arm and they both scrambled quick to get behind the trunk of the tree, Chichibud hopping on his backwards legs like a kangaroo. But Antonio took his cool time, doing a swaggerboy walk towards them. "What stupidness this is now?" he grumbled.

With a gunshot noise, a little ball of fire exploded from the flames. Only because the sound made Antonio duck that the seed didn't lash him in the head. It landed on top of the tent. By its glow Tan-Tan could see the tent fabric smouldering. With shrill, birdlike sounds, Chichibud rushed over and quickly flicked the burning ember onto the ground. His ruff was puffed out full. Tan-Tan stared at it, fascinated. Chichibud growled at Antonio, who shrank back, muttering sullenly, "All right, all right! Don't give me no blasted fatigue. How I was to know the damned thing would explode?"

"I tell you not to spit it in the fire. I know this bush, not you. You ignorant, you is bush-baby self. If you not going to listen when I talk, I leave you right here."

Antonio made a loud, impatient *steuups* behind his teeth. He went back to the fire and continued eating his share of the meal. Chichibud inspected the tent. "Just a little hole," he said to Tan-Tan. "I can mend it." His ruff had deflated again. Tan-Tan ran her fingers over the cloth and was surprised at how thin and light it felt.

They went back to their dinner. Antonio looked up as they approached. "All right," he said to Chichibud. "It have anything else we have to know to pass the night in this motherass bush behind God back?"

"Don't let the fire go out," Chichibud replied. "Light will frighten away the mako jumbie and the ground puppy, and grit fly like the flame. Fly into it instead of into we eyes. You and me going to sleep in shift."

"All right," Antonio said. He looked unhappy.

"You catch the first sleep," Chichibud told him. "Little bit, I wake you up."

Tan-Tan and Antonio curled up under their shelter, sharing the cloth Chichibud had lent to Tan-Tan. The firelight danced against the sides of the tent.

"Daddy? How Mummy go find we here? How she go know which Toussaint we come to?"

But Antonio was already snoring. Truth to tell, Tan-Tan was missing Nursie and eshu just as much as Ione. All now so, if she was going to bed back home, she and eshu would have just finished singing a song; "Jane and Louisa" maybe, or "Little Sally Water." Nursie would have had Tan-Tan pick a nightie from her dresser drawer to put on. Tan-Tan could almost smell the bunch of sweet dried khus-khus grass that Nursie kept inside the drawer to freshen her clothing.

She would pick the yellow nightie. Then Nursie would have hot eggnog sent from the kitchen for both of them, with nutmeg in it to cool their blood. The smell would spice the air, not like in this strange red land where the air smelled like sulphur matches all the time.

Tan-Tan swallowed, pretending she could taste the hot drink. Swallowing cleared her ears a little. *Now Nursie was combing out Tan-Tan's thick black hair. She was plaiting it into two so it wouldn't knot up at night. Nursie and eshu was singing "Las Solas Market" for her. When the song finished, Nursie kissed her goodnight. Tan-Tan was snuggling down inside the blankets. Eshu wished her good dreams and outed the light.*

The wetness on Tan-Tan's face felt hot, then cool against her skin. She snuffled, trying not to wake Antonio. She clutched her side of the yellow blanket round herself and finally managed to fall asleep.

from *Darkness in St. Louis: Bearheart*

GERALD VIZENOR

(1978)

> I am suggesting to you that there has to be a Fourth World in order
> for mankind to survive. . . . a political mechanism, an economic
> mechanism and perhaps a cultural mechanism to establish for our-
> selves as people, world people, a framework of survival and equality,
> dignity and pride for . . . all indigenous minorities of the world.
> —*George Manuel (Shuswap), World Council of Indigenous Peoples,*
> *Copenhagen, 1975*

> The regeneration in *Darkness* [*in Saint Louis: Bearheart*] will not
> come from violence, from a defeat of evil by good, of "savagery"
> by "civilization," but from the efforts of the pilgrims to survive
> the violence and reach the fourth world.
> —*James H. Cox*

GERALD VIZENOR'S (ANISHINAABE) 1978 sf novel, *Darkness in Saint Louis: Bearheart* (later published as *Bearheart: The Heirship Chronicles*), explored the economics of what then seemed an alternative but plausible world of depleted resources where the environment harshly responds to human exploitation. Only some three decades later, such a world no longer seems an imaginative prophecy, but a reality that science warns we must address.

Vizenor describes the novel as "a grand satirical reversal [of] a western expansion encountering the savage":

Now we have, some five hundred years later, the end of that civilization which depended exclusively on petroleum, and now we have Native Americans moving south, encountering the white savages, the people who had it, and now don't know what to do, now that they have nothing . . . the country has abandoned all other institutional affiliations and sources of solace, is completely dependent upon an immediate and situational and gratifying economic system and resources, and something as simple as a shortage of gasoline throws the country completely at its violent mercies. It has no other institutions to return to, but a kind of fundamental savagism, which was always a part of Western civilization.

So, here we have this complete breakdown. And it reaches to the sanctuaries on reservations. Once again, the federal government in cooperation, within this novel, with the tribal government needs timber, because it has no other resources. . . . In the middle of this are a group of people who are trying to figure out a way to survive. One thing they have to do is move. Well, they are thrown out of this center . . . they are driven out, and it's their episodes and experiences on their way to a southwestern transformation.[1]

Vizenor's presentation of a group of pilgrims "trying to figure out a way to survive" has often been aligned with Chaucer's *Canterbury Tales,* but the pilgrims who wander through the terrain in *Bearheart* do not go leisurely; they must make a series of life-threatening dives past blasts of lightning "to walk through the thunderbirds" over a red earth that was "steaming and smelled of ozone," a landscape where round houses are made from "cottonwoods and oak trees split and exploded with lightning." "Our lives are electrical," says one pilgrim, so survival means walking "between strokes [of lightning] to be alive."

At its root the novel warns of the economic threats that an Indigenous Fourth World faces when its sovereignty stands in the way of a government gone mad without its gasoline. Anishinaabe Proude Cedarfaire's sacred cedar grove has gained the attention of agents who work for the stopgap policy of switching from oil to lumber. The following excerpt presents the motivation that causes Cedarfaire and his wife to begin their pilgrimage.

$\mathcal{R}$

If Green Machines

The clown crows were raucous. Two officials from the federal government were riding through the sovereign cedar nation on dark green fenderless machines. The government had issued pedal machines for official transportation when gasoline was no longer available for automobiles. One of the pedalers was a young woman dressed in a coarse turtleneck sweater. The second pedaler was an older man with short blunt fingers. It was a warm afternoon in late summer. The sun was drawn in deep angles through the cedar trees.

Fourth Proude walked into the woods with the mongrels when he heard the government pedalers. He watched from a wilding distance. The woman pumped her government machine over the soft cedar earth to the log cabin. She stopped near the woodpile, leaning her machine against a tree. Her legs were muscular. The older man had dismounted and was walking his machine through the woods. His stamina had been altered in automobiles. The woman waited for him, smiling, with one hand on her hip and the other resting on the top of her firm buttocks.

The clown crows were swooping and flapping after the federal man. When he reached the woodpile and the woman the crows retreated and waited in the trees. Black blotches in the cedar.

"Government service ratings should be based on stamina," the woman carped at the breathless man. "No wonder our government fell apart with weaklings like you sitting behind desks and using up the gas driving three blocks to lunch." He ignored her, but smiled in agreement as he had learned to do in interpersonal service training, and then, when the subject of his weakness had passed, he made historical reference to his honorable and dedicated service to past federal programs and administrations. Their laughter was strident and mechanical. The dogs nudged each other. Proude, waiting in the distance, looked over to the crows. The clown crows yawned and poked at their black claws.

"No one seems to be home," said the federal man, after knocking three times on the open door of the cabin. "Jordan Coward at the tribal headquarters said the old cedar man never left the place." The federals called into the cabin. The woman squinted through her blue tinted glasses.

"The door is open . . . there can be no harm in waiting inside," the federal woman said, stepping into the cabin and pulling out a chair near the wood stove. Rather than sitting, she moved around the small cabin, looking and touching personal objects with her fingertips. "These people own so little . . . there is nothing here but little shrines."

Proude circled around the cabin through the cedar trees. The dogs and clown crows moved with him in silence. Rosina was stretched out on her back near the shore of the lake watching the thin clouds pass through the cedar boughs.

"The government people are here," he said as he sat next to her.

"They wobbled through the cedar on their slow machines to tell us the government wants the circus."

Rosina rolled on her side to watch his face and eyes as he spoke. Sometimes his words were so distant. "What did you tell them?" she asked.

"They said we would not mind if they waited for us in the cabin . . . They are there now comparing their lives with ours for the afternoon."

Proude told his wife he did not wish to speak with strangers now, he did not want to know what official words would be told until he knew more about their insecurities. He would be a clown, he said, a compassionate trickster for the afternoon, a bear from the cedar. When his voice and personal energies changed with the thoughts about trickeries the clown crows cocked their black heads at each other.

Rosina walked around the cabin to the western boundaries of the circus where the federals had entered the cedar woods. She rested against a tree and waited.

Proude circled around the cabin on the eastern side, stopping at the *migis* sandridge where he dipped his face under the water and opened his eyes. The pebbles and sandgems cracked in the angular iridescent sunbeams. He wiped his face with his blue shirt and strode into the woods toward the cabin. The mongrels moved with him. He stopped near the cabin on the north side, the winter side, the sunless side of moss and fern, the side of moths, the hoarfrost side, and roared ha ha ha haaaa four times as a bear.

The dogs ran off in five directions, circling each other near the cabin, yelping and howling. The clown crows crowed in shrill voices and swooped on the cabin. When the federals ran out of the cabin to see what was the matter, the crows swooped again and cawed at them. The dogs ran into the woods howling.

Proude moved to the west side of the cabin next, the black side, the sunset side, the direction of the thunderbirds and summer storms, and the side the federals had entered. The mongrels and clown crows waited out of sight. Proude roared ha ha ha haaaa again and snarled four times. The dogs howled in the distance and then, when the federals ran out of the cabin the second time, the crows called in their loudest voices while hopping and flapping from tree to tree in front of the cabin.

The federal man was so unnerved by the sounds of bears and harsh crows that he picked up his machine and started running, not pedaling, in the wrong direction out of the woods. The federal woman stopped him and encouraged him to return to the cabin. She reminded him of their responsibilities as elite employees of the federal government.

Proude circled to the south side of the cabin, the summer side, the flower side, yellow and green, and snarled and roared four times again. The dogs howled and the crows flapped again. When the federals came out of the cabin for the third time, Proude snarled several more times with his deepest bear voice. The federal man could not be stopped the third time. He ran out of the woods in the right direction with the federal woman following on her machine. Pumping with her stout legs the federal woman was the first to reach the brown cedar ghost border of the circus. Exhausted and near heart failure, the federal man slumped out of the cedar woods, vowing never to return to the wilderness with bad news.

The federals pedaled their machines down the dirt roads on the reservation to the tribal center where they told Jordan Coward, elected president of the reservation government, about their harrowing experiences with the bears in the cedar. Coward first laughed and then his mood changed and he cursed them, calling them louts, addlebrained, beefwitted, and sapheaded federals, while he paced back and forth on the squeaking oak floors of his office in the old federal school building. Spume from his hostile words gathered on his bulbous purple lips.

from *Mindscape*

ANDREA HAIRSTON

(2006)

> The imminent and expected destruction of the life cycle of world
> ecology can be prevented by a radical shift in outlook from our
> present naive conception of this world as a testing ground of
> abstract morality to a more mature view of the universe as
> a comprehensive matrix of life forms.
> —*Vine Deloria Jr.,* God is Red

ANDREA HAIRSTON, Professor of Theatre and Afro-American Studies at Smith College, has written numerous Afrofuturist plays and will be familiar to sf readers more recently through her exploration of African American, African diasporic, and Native negotiations and exchanges in the short story "Griots of the Galaxy" (2004), in the sf novel *Mindscape* excerpted here, and in her novel *Redwood and Wildfire* (2011). These narratives feature Black Seminole characters (Jay Silverfeather, Aaron Dunklebrot, and Aidan, respectively) whose experiences illustrate the intersections between Native and African ancestries. Of all three works, *Mindscape* provides the strongest invective on the sometimes unconscious imperialisms hidden in forms of western science. On the one hand, it addresses the nineteenth-century pseudoscience of polygenesis, whose critics—including W. E. B. Du Bois and Charles Eastman (Santee Sioux)—decried its placement of Native and African peoples on the barbaric end of a genetic measuring stick of civilization. On the other hand, the novel tackles a contemporary tendency: "the eulogizing of Africa, proclaiming her demise, mourning the impossibility of any sort of African survival." Hairston explains the motivation for her concern:

> Decolonizing the African (Native) spirit was a hopeless futile fantasy. I wanted to imagine something else. In the minds of those folks writing these eulogies, the colonized enter science as refugees from their magical worlds—prisoners of superstition, hostages of the colonizer, slaves of the master narrative. Modernity and post-modernity, although products of colonialism, displace the colonized to the past, to history, to people who once were whole and have now been shattered by their backwardness, their poor competitive adaptation, their lack of science and democracy, their inept economics. The colonizers have consumed the colonized and define the future. So caught up in the past, still trying to survive history, how can the colonized imagine a future? How can a future be imagined that contains the remnants of their broken spirits? This is the kind of challenge I like as a writer.

In *Mindscape,* Hairston imagines a Barrier that mysteriously appears on Earth one hundred years into our twenty-first-century future. This Barrier is a trans-organism, an emergent life-form that operates on a vast, intergalactic, interdimensional scale quite dissimilar to the Earth's interconnected and, by comparison, place-bound ecosystem. The Barrier creates separations among peoples and regions and is too dangerous to breach, providing only spontaneous seasonal openings that permit trade. Civilizations now consist largely of refugee camps residing in the Zones of New Ouagadougou (twenty-first-century capital of Burkina Faso in West Africa), Lost Santos (western portions of the United States), and Paradigma (portions of Europe, particularly Germany). Despite the difficulty of contact among the Zones, they share one common tie: the life-threatening "fire virus" that accompanied the appearance of the Barrier and now threatens worldwide pandemic.

The single antidote to this postapocalyptic fever appears to be a potion of fire ants and malanga fruit brewed up by a new cast of healers, the Vermittlers in New Ouagadougou. Since the abrupt seasonal openings of the Barrier are very risky, globally all have come to rely upon the Vermittlers, phase-shifters of the Barrier dimensions whose griot-sculpt-singing has the power to form temporary passages connecting the Zones.

One among them, the Wovoka, has gone renegade and attracted lizard-embedded Ghost Dancers living in the *mako sica,* Lakota for "badland," surrounding the environs of Los Santos. These Ghost Dancers, who are born-again Sioux, Indians "under deep cover," are puzzlingly immune to the fire virus. Both groups, the Vermittlers and the Ghost Dancers, are singers and dancers who experience trances, speak in tongues, and wield a symbiotic relationship with the Barrier itself. The Ghost Dancers look forward to the day when the souls of the dead and loved ones will return from the Barrier. The Vermittlers resulted from scientific experiment and therefore are considered posthuman and mutant by many. Both groups operate as go-betweens and negotiators and are much needed despite being treated as suspect and *murahachibu,* outcast.

This imaginative conflation of marvelous sf elements along with race theory helps *Mindscape* cross over many of our themes, including contact and apocalyptic (post)colonial allegory. Its commingling of newer fields of physics, such as organic electronics and ethnopharmacology, makes it particularly well suited for discussions of Indigenous scientific literacy. Take, for example, its treatment of the mutualist and parasitic behaviors of plants. As a central metaphor for the new existence that must emerge from (post)colonial intersections, Hairston chooses the Alora, whose flower and leaf provide a stimulant with healing power when eaten together, but poison if eaten separately. This example suggests the symbiogenesis that all figures in the novel must embrace in order to survive and informs the creation of the central character Saint Celestina, a genetic hybrid of two scientists, one Native and one West African. Symbiogenesis creates Celestina, and Celestina creates the interzonal peace treaty that begins the transforming of sovereignties in the novel.

The excerpt here replicates a letter from Lawanda Kitt to her friend and lover Honoré. A Paradigma ambassador, Kitt has been sent to Los Santos to maintain goodwill for the peacekeeping interzonal alliance. Her ethnic speech and dark looks are met with derisiveness, as she becomes increasingly devastated by what she sees as the "spirit assault" on Indians and African slaves that has taken place for over five hundred years in this Zone. Encouraged by the Ghost Dancers' enigmatic messages, she reports on her visit to Paradise Healthway, the central medical locus for those stricken by Barrier fever.

Cross-Barrier Transmission/Personal (October 5, Barrier Year 115)
From: Lawanda
To: Sweet, Sweet Major

You are some cold dark matter! Your personal transmission be about as close to absolute zero as a human can get. Why am I all surprised? We been together a coupla years, been all insida each other, and I don't even know your name. Is that top secret too? Or one of the rules you don't be breakin'? Captain won't tell neither. So, what, all y'all just a rank in the secret service of the Prime Minister and nothin' else? Well damn, why ain't you a colonel or a general by now?

I do appreciate the diplomat info & instruc you sent and your up-front concern for my mental health. Haven't gone insane yet, but gettin' close. I had a coupla Celestina "visions" too, but it ain't nothin' some human contact wouldn't cure. I'd settle for live Electro exchange—my private channel be wide open 24-7, you just ain't tunin' in. What's the deal?

Los Santos folk got some funky personal Electros (the few who can afford it). Steada minipads & headphones, alotta of 'em wear monster half-masks. Look like bugs or aliens, and you never know what channel they be on. It's rude and they ain't got enough attention span to be spreadin' it 'cross ten Electro channels plus real life. I know you do split-channel too, Major, but there's alotta you to go around. I mean, I always know you're there, somewhere.

Never thought I'd be achin' for your face on a damn Electroscreen.

Armando got me four weeks "on location"—jitterbuggin' thru Sol, Angel City, Paramount Way, Nuevo Nada, plus a day trip to the Vegas-suck-down-site. Studios gonna wine and dine me, show me the sights, a few Entertainment adventures 'fore I hit Studio City and real negotiations. Armando and Hitchcock, the general secretary of this region who wear his lunch steada eat it, cook up this bullshit runaround to keep me outa they business. But Captain say I got these goons by the balls. Maybe the Captain's more objective . . . cuz I feel like I dashed offa cliff and I'm runnin' on air.

Sorry. I'm procrastinatin'.

Ghost Dancers send me a second invite—over the Electro this time—to check out healthcare for Extras. Word is Ghost Dancers ain't just religious fanatics committin' ritual suicide to bring back a dead past. They hooked up with rebel Extras and fought Los Santos' ganglords even though they didn't sign the Treaty. Some gangstas is still gunnin' for the Wovoka and other born-again Sioux leaders, so Indians be under real deep cover. You can't just search 'em out on the Interweb. But they sure know how to get to me.

Anyhow, yesterday on this born-again tip, Captain and me is unofficially walkin' 'round Paradise Healthway, a Extra "hospital" in the wasteland halfway between Angel City and Sol. Our visit be so unofficial, we have to leave the resta the squad and the bio-corder at the transport fifty meters from the entrance (which I know is risky and stupid, but . . .)

Paradise Healthway useta be a holdin' station for the organ market, where folk waited 'round to get chopped up. Ain't nothin' but nasty shacks and a big red circus tent surrounded by a steel mesh quarantine wall with half-ass power net shieldin' to keep folk in and out. Under the raggedy big top, patients be stacked on triple-decker shelves like aboard a slave ship, lyin' in they own (and everybody else's) puke, pus, and shit. We gotta shuffle down the slimy aisles sideways, single file, and we be bumpin' into patients' heads and feet all the way. Spaceage drug-proof viruses and bacteria be havin' a field day. Folk rottin' away in front of my eyes. That make it hard to tell what landed 'em here in the first place. (I'ma send touch-up drawin's with the official report tomorrow. Hard to mind-doodle in my enviro-suit.) Why'n't they just do these suckers quick and get it over with?

Old folks say God don't like ugly. Which God is that I wonder?

Los Santos be so corrupt, anti-Treaty folk don't even bother to front. We talkin' bodacious scammin'. Gangbangers hijack shipments of herbs and supplies. Doctors, nurses, orderlies be collectin' hefty paychecks, don't never show for they shifts. I scoped the login records—just a few guards at the gate for lockdown. Healthway's Ouagadougian medical envoy, Zumbi, is a sorry-ass novice who couldn't make it thru *Healer First Aid,* forget the *Final Lessons,* and he gotta cover ten of these wasteland quarantine camps. That's ten thousand square kilometers and over twenty thousand sick people. Why'd the Healer Council send him? New O's settin' people up big-time. I mean, Zumbi's heart be in the right place. He claim me and the Captain is tourist thrill-seekers and walk us past the guards. He even guide us thru the Electro-maze of records, highlightin' invisible corruption. Ready to do whatever he can, but there ain't no tiger in his tank. Yellow skin gone gray, stringy hair in knots, hands shakin', one eye hangin' down slack—he look real sick hisself. Not much better than the patient he standin' over.

"Gene art backfiring," Zumbi say. "A lot of that recently. Not a pretty sight." A orderly, one of the healthier lookin' patients, dump the body in a waste bin 'fore I get a good look. "All I do is bury the dead," Zumbi complain. That's a metaphor, he mean throw the dead at the Barrier. I think sometimes he be tossin' live ones too. We walk by a little boy, look like he eat a bomb and explode. I'm starin' at him and can't move. "Fire virus," Zumbi say, steady mumblin' to hisself in old German or Swahili. You know how Healers be with metaphors and dead languages. He don't stop to check the kid out, just signal for somebody to dump him.

"This can't be happenin'. Elleni found a cure for fire virus: ants and that nasty tropical fruit, malangi?" I say, but Zumbi don't hear me. My Electro be on a private channel to the Captain.

"Malanga." The Captain push me to move on. "It doesn't seem that they have the fire virus cure here, does it?"

I'm 'bout to jump bad 'bout Healer shipments and greenhouses in the wasteland when the little boy open his big brown eyes and blink long dark lashes twice. He reach his hand out to me. I jerk back cuz I don't want him touchin' even my enviro-suit. His sallow cheeks flush a moment with color. "They said you were coming." Kid talk so quiet I gotta amplify the sound to the max. "I didn't believe them." He try to hand me a scrap of outprint. "I made you a picture." I have to force myself to snatch the slimy thang and shove it in my enviro-suit pocket. "Nothing ever happens like they say." Kid's voice ain't nothin' but air. "You're not a dream, are you?"

"I'm real, I'm here," I say, but only the Captain hear me.

Boy look down at hisself, insides splattered all over yellow underwear and naked knees. His face twist up, like he tryin' to cry or scream.

Then the spirit leave his eyes, and his face go hard. The patient-orderly stumble up, draggin' a long, thin cart behind her. She roll the kid and his beddin' up in the lime green plastic they use for Barrier bio-waste.

"Said he wanted to be buried in the Promised Land," Zumbi say. I look at him funny, so he explain—"Dancer name for the Barrier. I try to grant last wishes. Everybody wants the Promised Land now."

Kid don't weigh nothin'. Orderly toss him on top the cart and stumble off.

I got on my high-tech suit & helmet with the vacuum seal; ventilator runnin' at max s'posed to keep me cool, collected, and germ-free, and still I'm gettin' sick all over myself. Everybody moanin', groanin', and gaggin'. Me too. How can people do each other like this? I gotta get outa this funky hellhole posthaste.

Captain grab my arm and say, "Nothing we could have done for him."

I switch my Electro to public speaker and make up a big lie for slack-eyed Zumbi, like I'ma meet up with hotshots and talk Treaty talk, try to do somethin' 'bout this health crisis mess. I break bad for a second, almost chokin' up with tears. "No way am I goin' just grin, shuffle alotta Electro outprint, and let folk croak in they own shit, when we got cures! No fuckin' way!" Now why I say alla that?

These terminally sick people hear me BSin' and think I'm a acupuncture ace workin' Chi "vital essence" like Elleni, come to replace the dip-dip, slack-eyed novice who be one step from the grave hisself. These terminals *believe* I'ma channel Chi and make 'em well with my bare hands. If they can just get me to touch they naked skin, spit down they throats, or stick acupuncture needles in they skulls, they won't have to suffer and die. Maybe they even live forever. Gangstas believe any ole no-sense crap. Proof ain't a issue at all. Plus they can't tell a ethnic throwback from a shaman/*Vermittler*. False hope wash over 'em like a flash flood. Alluva sudden I got this horde of half-dead, crippled-up folk chasin' me down narrow aisles in a circus tent. Woulduv been funny 'cept we slip-pin' and slidin' thru bodily fluids and stumblin' 'round patients that ain't exactly mobile. Zumbi try to restrain 'em, but the mob beat him back and keep on comin'. You'd think sick folk'd be kinda slow too, but that ain't necessarily so. Runnin' as fast as we can, we knock over the pitiful medical equipment Zumbi done scrounged up and step on folk who don't even scream.

Finally we bust out the tent into the open and head for the gate. A coupla gangsta guards watch the show from a catwalk along the quarantine wall and crack up. Like we antique slapstick Entertainment, Whetstone Cops or somethin'. Please. Captain turn and shoot a volley over the sick folk's heads. Mob don't stop but a second or two, then they get a surge of adrenaline and pick up speed. Crutches, splints, and filthy, ole-timey bandages flappin' in the wind—I ain't seen no recon-skin. It's a ghastly sight: me and the Captain chargin' thru the wasteland in frontuva Day of the Dead parade. Gangsta at the quarantine gate think this the funniest joke he done ever seen. We ten meters away, and he crackin' up, closin' the gate on us, and chargin' up the power nets. I keep on runnin' cuz I don't believe any of this shit really be happenin'. Captain runnin' right beside me, but with a plan. Gangstas be underestimatin' your dream team, Major. Captain deploy one of your fancy scramblers and fuck up gate man's electromagnetism. He don't know what hit him. Power net shieldin' fizzle, gate swing open, automatic weapons drop offline. We run by the creep and don't explain shit.

"Can't be a power-out!" He mumblin' and fumblin' all over hisself, talkin' 'bout goddamned witchdoctors, like we zapped his retarded ass with magic! He don't notice the horde of livin' dead comin' right at him. Captain get our transport up and runnin' with the remote and be whisperin' commands to the home squad when we hear weapons explode behind us. Captain shove me toward the transport and swing 'round, weapons armed, ready to fight and die for me. That trip me right out.

But ain't nobody comin' at us! The crazy sick folk who breached the quarantine perimeter be trashin' the gatehouse. Three gangsta guards is up on the catwalk usin' personal weapons to shoot 'em down. A fourth guard be wavin' his weapon and screechin' at 'em to go back. I'm hangin' at our transport power nets, paralyzed. I scope the fourth guard jump down into the mob. He have to shoot a few but then they snap to and start listenin' to him. Folk stagger and fall back toward the gate. Gangstas on the catwalk steady, shootin' 'em down like it's Electro-spiel even after the Extras be inside the quarantine wall! Fourth guard curse out his trigger-happy cohorts while he herdin' Extras into the big tent and shacks, bullets zingin' by his helmet, folk droppin' all 'round him. Compu-grid come back online and gate swing shut. Three gangstas on the wall still shootin'. Now they got lasers too, and Extras bust out in flames. I wonder if the fourth guard on the ground goin' make it. Mob startin' to trample itself.

More ugly, and God don't do nothin'.

Captain hustle me inside the transport, say it's not good to watch atrocity, 'specially when you can't do nothin'. I'm beyond worthless at this point, fallin' all over myself. My mind's on the run. I don't wanna think or feel anythin'. Somehow the Captain get us both sterilized and outa that wasteland in less than three minutes.

"I'm getting too old for this crap." She shiver. "Way too old."

I stare at her, grateful for somethin' to do sides relive the freak show. In all this time, don't know that I ever *really* look at her before. Just kinda takin' her for granted, like a invisible force at my back. Who look at the wind? You just watch what it do. So I stare at her good now. Captain got a short cap of silky white hair, dark velvet skin, not one wrinkle, and muscles that look industrial strength like yours, Major. Her ancestors been 'round the world to make that face or at least all over the Pacific. She the kinda lady you draw walkin' on water and boxin' with God. I gotta smile cuz for a second I feel like me and her can turn this mess around. "Too old? For what?" I ask.

"Ghost Dancers, anybody could have set us up back there."

"Naw, Ghost Dancers be hookin' us up with the truth, tryin' to open our eyes."

"That's politics. I'm security. I don't trust anybody. I know better than to just walk into a situation like that."

I try to get her to say more, but she don't talk the whole trip back to Angel City. She already say enuf for me to know the Day of the Dead parade really mess her up—comin' face to face with the Evil Empire, you know what I'm sayin'?

Nobody back home would believe this, like a refugee camp in hell. Before the Treaty, Los Santos thugs be workin' terminal Extras to death on action-adventure and snuff Entertainment, or be marchin' em into the Barrier. Now they marchin' em into Paradise Healthway, which definitely ain't my idea of the promised land, more like middle passage to the grave. The Treaty is a bust! What the hell good is all that cyber-static declarin' no more Death Percent or gang rapes? All the Treaty really mean is unrestricted junk trade and alotta thrill seekers on the loose. Celestina must be squirmin' in her grave.

I ain't tell Jenassi diddly squat 'bout Paradise. He'd wanna get a payoff, not do a shakedown. Him and most thug leaders in Los Santos be livin' very high drama. It's like I'm stuck in a bad Entertainment. Nothin' seem real. Cartoon characters, Electro-spiel victims, surreal shit. I keep wonderin' where are the real people at? Guess I'm worryin' 'bout the kinda character I'm playin' too. I'm so over my head it ain't funny.

What am I s'posed to do with alla this, Major?

Some big shot's throwin' a gala for us tonight, to make out like he ain't anti-Treaty. Fireworks got me jumpin' out my skin already. Jenassi be the guest of honor. He want me to dress up and slink in there on his arm. Afterward everybody goin' party back at Jenassi's place. He don't never wanna be seen in public with me, so what's up with that? Captain got me mad-dog suspicious. And I'm still pissed at you, but mostly just missin' your chocolate kisses and whirlwind hugs. I wanna curl up insida you, like in the eye of a storm and let the resta the world rush on by. Ain't that pathetic? I just wish I knew how this story was goin' go down. Course, maybe it's better not to know. The ole folks say—a coward, he die a million times, a brave man only once.

Love you, Lawanda

from *Land of the Golden Clouds*

ARCHIE WELLER

(1998)

> My view is that the landscape, the place is dangerous—*that* to me
> is more of a traditional sense of environment than taking up the
> kind of Western romance of the environment as pristine and
> beautiful and a reservoir of hope and resurrection.
> —*Gerald Vizenor*

AUSTRALIAN AUTHOR ARCHIE WELLER'S (Koori) debut novel, *The Day of the Dog* (1981), received both the Australian/Vogel Literary Award and the Western Australian Premier's Book Award in fiction before being adapted into the film *Blackfellas* (1991), which subsequently added two Australian Film Institute awards to the array of critical acclaim. He followed his initial literary success with a short-story collection, *Going Home* (1986), before turning to sf for his second novel, *Land of the Golden Clouds* (1998). Later works include the multiple-award-winning film script *Confessions of a Headhunter,* co-authored with Sally Riley (Wiradjuri). It brought Weller another Western Australian Premier's Book Award and also the Cinema Nova Award, an Australian Film Institute Award for Best Short Fiction Film, as well as the Best Short Film of 2001 Award from the Film Critics Circle of Australia. His latest effort is another short-story collection called *The Window Seat* (2010). Throughout this body of work, Weller's consistent theme is the Indigenous experience in Australia.

Land of the Golden Clouds extrapolates Weller's thinking about contemporary Aboriginality to an Australia set three thousand years in the future. Weller jam-packs this world with numerous races, most notably Ilkari, or "People of the Sun," peaceful healers largely, who have developed a complex system of storytelling and song to detail their histories and their knowledge of the area; the Keepers of the Trees, who are revered for their knowledge of medicine and healing; the Islanders; Rastafarians; and Maroons of the Caribbean. Of mixed Aboriginal and European descent, the Ilkari, who have been strongly influenced by the Keepers' stories, rituals, and ceremonies, represent the "whitest" of these groups, and their darker counterparts clearly have the upper hand in developing technologies and the capacity for survival.

While differences exist among these Indigenous populations, all but the Island visitants can trace their lineage to various nations of Australian Aboriginals, raising the question posed by many of Weller's works: What constitutes authentic Aboriginal identity? As Brian Attebery points out in "Aboriginality in Science Fiction," Weller offers two different visions of Aboriginal futures: "On the one hand, the Keepers of the Trees remain apart, preserving the myths and disciplines of nomadic life that have kept their ancestors alive for millennia. On the other hand, descendants of Aboriginal people and the stories those descendants tell provide the basis for a new hybrid humanity. Neither cultural pattern is marked within the narrative as the right or only way to be Aboriginal."[1] A mainstay of Aboriginal identity seems to exist in what China Miéville characterizes as "magicking science" in *The Scar*.[2] While it is based on close connection to the land and simple technology in comparison to the stock space travel variety familiar from mainstream sf, it remains the most sustainable and effective, exemplifying Indigenous scientific literacy.

The backstory to this excerpt: Rastafarian pirates and Maroons armed with metallic weapons have arrived in silver spaceships ready to negotiate for resources and to conduct trade. The Indigenous peoples have greeted them as gods. The passage here brings their multiple cultures and beliefs into conflict on a bush trail and makes clear that Indigenous scientific literacy prevails in times of crisis.

ℛ

They traveled the river for perhaps a week, going ever onwards towards the setting sun as Red Mond informed them the stars had told him to do. Sometimes the tall grass came right down to the river's edge, but mostly it kept well back as though afraid of the murmuring river. There were signs everywhere of animal life, if none of human, and in the distance small herds could be seen. There were antelope of several kinds and zebra, vast herds of wild horses and, of course, kangaroo in their hundreds. There was also a sign of the occasional bear and, once, Akar Black Head smelled the strong odor of a lion on the air—but no sign of it was seen.

One day, when the sky was gradually gathering up scurrying fluffy clouds in its huge blue hands, when the nights were getting colder while the days were becoming shorter, Kareen and Surrey Anne sauntered out to search for medicinal plants. By rights, an Earth Mother should have been wary of a child of the sun but these two women were both the healers of their two different groups and they had formed a warm affiance.

Bees buzzed busily amongst the flowers that still grew on the wild herbs and their fragrant scents blessed the air. For a while there were only the sounds of their snipping off the leaves or flowers and their heavy breathing as they exerted themselves.

"The river looks inviting. We should go for a swim later," Kareen said. "It is a good feeling to have water all around you instead of sunlight," she added, before remembering that being a Sun child probably the opposite would apply to her charcoal companion.

"I-an'-I a go make cake fe Port Rial birthdate. Is why me gatherin' 'erbs now," Surrey Anne explained, unconsciously fingering her brilliant purple necklace—his gift to her on *her* birthdate.

"A birthday? For the skinny one?" Kareen said surprised. "Then we must make him something special," she said decisively. She pointed in the direction of a clump of tall straggly reeds that bent weary heads towards the slowly swirling currents of the river. "There could be some duck eggs in there. That would be a pleasant taste for him."

They ambled over to the reeds. When they arrived they surprised a small deer who sprang past them on agile feet. It so startled Surrey

Anne that she fell over and the look on her face sent the taller, older woman into fits of giggling mirth.

They waded through the shallows and—sure enough—nestled in amongst the reeds in a wide curved nest were some twelve, large, white eggs. Kareen smiled as she chose six small gifts from Sister Earth to one of her nieces, this Sun child who still worshipped her partner's birthday.

She turned her smiling face to make some mild joke about this— about High Ones living forever so what was the point of a birthday—when a rustling in the reeds behind her stayed her thoughts. As she rose from where she bent over the nest a throaty cough caused her instantly to freeze while her grey eyes dilated in fear.

The cough turned into an angry scream as a large male leopard— beautiful in its dappled coat, terrifying with its sharp claws and glistening teeth—deprived of the small deer he had been stalking, leapt upon the women. The creature's scream was echoed by Surrey Anne. Kareen had no time to do anything, for the leopard had chosen her as his victim. Now its warm, soft, stinking body pressed down on her as teeth and claws sought to still her squirming.

Surrey Anne dragged her gun from off her shoulder and with shaking hands aimed it at the roaring cat not three feet away as she relived the horror of The Syrian's death. But when she pulled the trigger nothing happened! She pulled it again but there was only a harmless click.

Another leopard, smaller than the first, came streaking across the grass towards its fat, sweet-smelling meal. The stench of fear in the air only served to make this female more excited at the thrill of the kill. Kareen, fighting for her life with only her fists and feet, kicking and punching the rank, heaving sides of the bigger leopard, had a split-second image of Surrey Anne's raw terror before she was bowled over by the creature. Kareen had another second to reflect that these were just ordinary people, after all, who had no magic powers over all the creations of Sister Earth. Her whole world fell apart and such was this revelation to the Earth Mother's soul that she almost gave up there and then. But a searing rake of the vicious claws across her breast and shoulder jerked her into the moment.

Using her great strength she rolled out from under the leopard, gushing blood. She clung for dear life to the neck so the teeth and claws could not reach her. At the same time she tried to exert pressure on the neck to break it. The graceful animal was an accomplished killing machine and his muscles were too sinewy for her to grasp. Besides she was weak from loss of blood.

He tossed and twisted and then, at last, managed to hurl her off and sink teeth into her other shoulder. She gasped with the pain of it all while his powerful jaws worried her body, shaking her like a puppy with a cloth doll—like the doll she had had as a child not so long ago. She felt herself slipping into unconsciousness and into the cruel embrace of sudden death that would be so sweet for her, if it would mean the pain would go away. . . . The most horrifying sound now was the contented rumble of the leopard's purring as it tore away at her still-living flesh.

A spear, sharp and bright, flashed briefly in the sun before burying itself deep into the leopard's head, entering through its ear. It fell across Kareen, instantly dead.

The female had been temporarily stopped from her murderous course by Surrey Anne's swinging gun. But then it had fastened its teeth into the coat Kareen had given her—the lion's coat which her lover Yellow Eyes had made for her from his story. It started to drag her away into the tall grass and she felt herself fainting from fear. Knowing that at any moment the saliva-flecked teeth would rip into her flesh and the cruel green eyes, alight with primitive rage, would gloat over her pathetic death throes, turning her into a quivering mess, she lost all control of her body—and almost her mind.

Then there was a fierce cry and someone was beside her. Through her tears of fright and pain she glimpsed burnished red hair afire in the sun's rays. A heavy club smashed into those green eyes and when the leopard let go of her and crouched to face this new enemy, another figure approached from the other side and brown hands jabbed a sword into her mottled splotchy side and she sank with a strangled growl down to the grass to die.

Culvato and Red Mond Star Light stood, chests heaving together as one. Then they turned distressed eyes upon one another just as an anguished cry escaped from Akar Black Head as he arrived too late.

"Kareen! My Kareen!" he cried.

Over by the fallen male leopard the big form of the Ilkari warrior knelt down tentatively.

"Is she dead?" Red Mond asked in a shocked whisper.

"She breathes," Culvato whispered back.

"We must get her back to camp at once and stop her bleeding. The High One? Can she be hurt?" Red Mond said and moved to the side of the shocked, dazed Surrey Anne.

Now Nanny and Mungart came running. The five carefully picked up the wounded Kareen and did their best to staunch the freely flowing blood. Nanny wrapped a comforting arm around her country-woman's shoulders and led her stumbling away, murmuring to her in their singsong language.

As the four men carried Kareen into the camp, Mungart's *coo-ee* was answered by his brother, who came running from the long grass. He had been out hunting but even he had heard the terrified screams and had set off at a lope, leaving the fat kangaroos to live another day.

Red Mond was beside himself with grief. "Come back, cousin-mine!

"Don't leave me alone in this strange cruel land where beauty is only a disguise for unspeakable evil," he lamented.

Weerluk skidded to a halt beside them, his dark eyes concerned. In bursts of musical language his brother explained what had happened. Then Weerluk turned and ran towards the river.

Culvato gently prised Red Mond away from the quietly moaning form. Her tawny hair was clotted with blood and her left breast was ripped to ruination. The white bones of both her shoulders lay bare where the beast had gnawed away at her. Her usually calm grey eyes had dilated from shock and pain and she recognized no one.

Akar Black Head knelt beside her once more and carefully took off her tattered skin coat. His eyes looked up at Culvato's, so devoid of their cynicism and anger that it was another shock to the Gypsy. "She will die. We have no knowledge of medicine and, besides, the wound is too deep and severe," he said softly.

"Nooooo!" came Red Mond's scream. "This was not what I read in the stars!"

"Read in the stars!" snorted Akar Black Head, and his violence, never far from the surface, returned. "There is *nothing* to read in the stars. Do you see what happens when you follow these 'High Ones'? Kareen would never have let herself become so relaxed if she did not think she had the love of a Goddess to get her out of trouble. Where is the sword she wears? Hanging on a tree by her camp, because she has the love of a High One to protect her. See what that love has brought her!" he shouted.

But before his anger could spill over, Weerluk arrived panting from the river. In his hands he carried fine white clay and this he pressed rapidly into the cruel wounds, thus staunching the blood flow. He ignored the others gathered there as he spoke to Mungart, who nodded and silently left. Then he turned dark eyes to Red Mond's distressed brown ones.

"Brother, we have medicine here. A cure as old as the land. We will comfort your cousin and she will not die."

His voice was calm and soft as he stared into the distraught face. Of the two brothers he had been the most wary and the most unfriendly, keeping much to himself.

He had seen that, although they were all different and often argued among themselves, they were all united in their respect and love for this red-headed one. He had wondered which Keeper of the Trees had been ancestor and what his Totem would be. He knew this white one, who was not really white, had the magic and the beliefs Weerluk's people possessed.

He had also noticed and watched the gentleness of the big, tawny-haired woman who had a name not dissimilar to one of their own women's names—Kareen. She loved the land as much as did the women of his family. He had slipped out after her at times and studied her ceremonies.

This was why he forgot about all those crowded around him and bent over the woman, quiet now the clay, cool and soothing, had eased her suffering.

That very morning Mungart had killed a fat emu and even now he had been cooking it on their fire in preparation for tonight.

Now he came back with several furs taken recently from the many possums that lived in the trees along the river and a small container of emu oil that bubbled softly and sent its pungent odor to the air. Also he had some of the sacred red clay, which his people called wilgi, hot from the fire.

Carefully, on the great wound of her shoulder, Weerluk placed some possum furs and then he bound it up with other furs. The wound on her breast and other shoulder was just as succinctly washed clean while Mungart mixed the warm red clay with the emu oil. This putty

Mungart applied to the wounds and then another possum skin was wrapped around them.

"We must keep this warm at all times. But we cannot stay here," Weerluk said to Red Mond.

His brother looked up from where he mixed more emu oil with wilgi and said something Red Mond could not follow. They seemed to have an argument for a moment before an unhappy Mungart capitulated, shaking his head.

"We must take you to the Silver City. There you will find medicine more powerful than ours perhaps. There, at least, you will be with your people."

"What is this place?" Red Mond wished to know.

"It is a huge camp beside the banks of a huge river—bigger than this one."

"What do you mean 'my people'?"

"They are white, like you."

"So were the people in the hills."

"We told you of their dangers, brother. You would not listen." Weerluk's dark somber eyes never left his own and Red Mond had to agree the Keeper was right.

She watches Culvato come towards them where they gather around the stricken Surrey Anne. The coat Kareen had given her has saved her life, Port Rial cries out joyfully. But he is the only one happy. Cudjo Accompong is grey with rage as he berates the young girl for failing to check her weapon. An empty gun is useless! How can they expect to survive this trip if they don't take care of their weapons! They are the most powerful people on this Island, don't they see! Only because they have the weaponry to destroy a whole culture if need be. But what use is that power if you walk around with no bullets in your gun!

To be killed by a leopard—a wild animal. What stupidity! Has she forgotten already the fate that befell Clarendon Jon in the Northlands and Porky and The Syrian here?

"But him country beautiful yah, Ras! No danger dey about," Surrey Anne wept.

"You see him danger!" Cudjo cried.

"Enough! Leave she alone. Her already face him one leopard t'day, maan!" Port Rial butted in suddenly. "She friend dyin' deh."

It is unusual for the little pirate to face up to a confrontation. His whole mode of life is based on one of stealthy attack and quick withdrawal. Still, the greatest treasure he possesses now is the laughter and smiles of Surrey Anne. He will fight to the death to protect them.

"Jackal growl at him lion," *Cudjo says wonderingly, as he moves into battle stance.*

"Jackal him steal de lion meal many a time before, me seh," *Port Rial says bravely, not stepping out of the giant's shadow.*

It is her way to let arguments come out before she assumes control. It is good to argue and get everything out in the open, especially when she had such diverse and fiery people on the crew. But now she must intervene. She has never had to stand in for Port Rial, who has only ever been interested in his treasure, his sacred smoke, his singing and dancing and, of course, Surrey Anne after Clarendon Jon Cannu was killed.

"She bungo-girl fe havin' him gun empty. But she alive," *she says.* "We in Babylon an' the temptations of he be everywhere. We mus' keep each other's company an' stand backaback."

She is worried over Cudjo Accompong's remark—made in anger it is true—about how they are the most powerful people on this Island. It is true, but has the charade of playing a God finally turned into reality for the giant Ras Tafarian? He is not noted for his love of white men—or indeed of any-one not truly of his faith. Is he becoming carried away with the fearsome hold he has on these ignorant people of different Races? That is how the Muslims rose in power on their own Island and is one of the reasons they left, to escape the strict laws being enforced on parts of their home.

"Every hill has only one tiger," *she murmurs in warning to the giant.*

"One love, sisthren." *He smiles back. But it is a haughty smile.*

She is glad to see Culvato come across towards them. Cudjo shrugs and grins.

"Wha' magic me woman Saint Catherine leave she Captain? So you a go bewitch de bwoy. Will you take him from him home a fi you beloved Island? Or will she Captain leave him gaspin' like him fish dey pon shore?"

Port Rial laughs out loud and even Surrey Anne manages a watery smile. So she has defused the argument at the price of her dignity.

And what will you do, strong and independent Nanny, warrior of the Maroon? When the war is over and it is time to pick up your dead (if dead there be) and go home to the quiet green trees and glades of your Maroon community? Will you pluck him like a flower only to watch him dry up and die, or will you carry on home alone and just die a little yourself as you did when The Baptist was murdered?

It was a somber group that left in the cold light of early morning. There were those among them who could not understand the fickleness of these High Ones who could destroy a whole village of men, women and children at a whim because of the death of one youth, yet could stand back and not use their magic when the most peaceful and kindest among them was mauled by one of her own creatures.

Before they left, Culvato and Akar Black Head skinned the two cats—and it was not lost to them that these were the same Devils who took away Joda's father. It was their intention to make them into a wonderful blanket as a gift for when she recovered: Kareen, beloved member of their clan, friend and Earth Mother to them all.

Native Apocalypse

Distances

SHERMAN ALEXIE

(1993)

Survivance is an active sense of presence, the continuance of
Native stories, not a mere reaction or a survivable name. Native
survivance stories are renunciations of dominance, tragedy, and
victimry. Survivance means the right of succession or reversion
of an estate, and in that sense, the estate of Native survivancy.
— *Gerald Vizenor*

HEAVILY SATIRIC, SHERMAN ALEXIE'S "Distances" intertextualizes
the popular paradigm of Asimov's "robots run amok" in a renewed
Wovokan sf narrative of "Indian Traditionalism run amok." The Indian
trapdoor humor of this piece invites a closer look at the great Apocalypse supposedly presaged by the historical Ghost Dance prophe-
sied by Northern Paiute holy man Jack Wilson, known as Wovoka,
as well as the tradition of transmission within Native literature itself.

Wovoka had a vision of resurrected Natives and the expunging of
all whites from North America. To achieve the end times of white
supremacy, Wovoka instructed the people to conduct round dances,
known as Ghost Dances. Predictably, the Ghost Dance was outlawed
by the US government. Significant as a symbol of unification among
all Native peoples despite tribal affiliation, the Ghost Dance has
become iconic of Native hope and resistance and is treated amply
throughout the literature—we see its influence here in "Distances," in

the earlier excerpt from Andrea Hairston's *Mindscape,* and in the later excerpt from Leslie Marmon Silko's *Almanac of the Dead.*

"Distances" imagines a postapocalyptic landscape in post–Ghost Dance terms—that is, the state of things after the Wovoka prophecy has come to pass. The Others, huge emanations or ancestral persons from ten thousand years ago, "taller than the clouds . . . faster than memory," come back to haunt the remaining Urbans, the city Indians who survived and made their way out to the reservations after the effects of the Ghost Dance became manifest, and the Skins, those living on the res when it happened. In this world, electrical circuitry is cautiously destroyed if not already obliterated, and a tribal council determines what is evil under the prevailing policy that all white-man artifacts are sinful, while Skins counsel together on who should burn. The sense of Native Apocalypse extends beyond the more commonplace sf Armageddon or end-of-the-world scenarios drawn from a Eurowestern biblical tradition, which informs mainstream sf in notable instances such as Cormac McCarthy's *The Road* (2006), Albert and Allen Hughes's 2010 film *The Book of Eli,* and television series such as *Survivors,* a BBC venture of the mid-1970s that was reenvisioned in 2008 by Adrian Hodges for subsequent global distribution. Often triggered by specific events such as nuclear warfare, biological disaster, cosmological phenomena, or abrupt ecological "takeovers," sf postapocalyptic narratives feed into the desire for a new frontier and a new start. The Native Apocalypse typified by the Wovoka tradition is often marked by the nostalgia of what was irrecoverably lost in contrast to any hope for a brighter future. It is this more nuanced sense of irony over loss that underpins Alexie's satiric adaptation of Wovoka tradition.

All Indians must dance, everywhere, keep on dancing. Pretty soon in next spring Great Spirit come. He bring back all game of every kind. The game be thick everywhere. All dead Indians come back and live again. Old blind Indian see again and get young and have fine time. When Great Spirit comes this way, then all the Indians go to mountains, high up away from whites. Whites can't hurt Indians then. Then while Indians way up high big flood comes like water and all white people die, get drowned. After that, water go away and then nobody but Indians everywhere and

game all kinds thick. Then medicine man tell Indians to send
word to all Indians to keep up dancing and the good time will
come. Indians who don't dance, who don't believe in this word,
will grow little, just about a foot high, and stay that way. Some of
them will be turned into wood and burned in fire.
    —*Wovoka, the Paiute Ghost Dance Messiah*

After this happened, after it began, I decided Custer could have,
must have, pressed the button, cut down all the trees, opened up
holes in the ozone, flooded the earth. Since most of the white men
died and most of the Indians lived, I decided only Custer could have
done something that backward. Or maybe it was because the Ghost
Dance finally worked.

Last night we burned another house. The Tribal Council has ruled
that anything to do with the whites has to be destroyed. Sometimes
while we are carrying furniture out of a house to be burned, all of us
naked, I have to laugh out loud. I wonder if this is how it looked all
those years ago when we savage Indians were slaughtering those helpless settlers. We must have been freezing, buried by cold then, too.

I found a little transistor radio in a closet. It's one of those yellow
waterproof radios that children always used to have. I know that most
of the electrical circuitry was destroyed, all the batteries dead, all the
wires shorted, all the dams burst, but I wonder if this radio still works.
It was hidden away in a closet under a pile of old quilts, so maybe it
was protected. I was too scared to turn it on, though. What would I
hear? Farm reports, sports scores, silence?

There's this woman I love, Tremble Dancer, but she's one of the
Urbans. Urbans are the city Indians who survived and made their way
out to the reservation after it all fell apart. There must have been over
a hundred when they first arrived, but most of them have died since.
Now there are only a dozen Urbans left, and they're all sick. The
really sick ones look like they are five hundred years old. They look
like they have lived forever; they look like they'll die soon.

Tremble Dancer isn't sick yet, but she does have burns and scars all
over her legs. When she dances around the fire at night, she shakes
from the pain. Once when she fell, I caught her and we looked hard
at each other. I thought I could see half of her life, something I could
remember, something I could never forget.

The Skins, Indians who lived on the reservation when it happened, can never marry Urbans. The Tribal Council made that rule because of the sickness in the Urbans. One of the original Urbans was pregnant when she arrived on the reservation and gave birth to a monster. The Tribal Council doesn't want that to happen again.

Sometimes I ride my clumsy horse out to Noah Chirapkin's tipi. He's the only Skin I know that has traveled off the reservation since it happened.

"There was no sound," he told me once. "I rode for days and days but there were no cars moving, no planes, no bulldozers, no trees. I walked through a city that was empty, walked from one side to the other, and it took me a second. I just blinked my eyes and the city was gone, behind me. I found a single plant, a black flower, in the shadow of Little Falls Dam. It was forty years before I found another one, growing between the walls of an old house on the coast."

Last night I dreamed about television. I woke up crying.

The weather is changed, changing, becoming new. At night it is cold, so cold that fingers can freeze into a face that is touched. During the day, our sun holds us tight against the ground. All the old people die, choosing to drown in their own water rather than die of thirst. All their bodies are evil, the Tribal Council decided. We burn the bodies on the football field, on the fifty-yard line one week, in an end zone the next. I hear rumors that relatives of the dead might be killed and burned, too. The Tribal Council decided it's a white man's disease in their blood. It's a wristwatch that has fallen between their ribs, slowing, stopping. I'm happy my grandparents and parents died before all of this happened. I'm happy I'm an orphan.

Sometimes Tremble Dancer waits for me at the tree, all we have left. We take off our clothes, loincloth, box dress. We climb the branches of the tree and hold each other, watching for the Tribal Council. Sometimes her skin will flake, fall off, float to the ground. Sometimes I taste parts of her breaking off into my mouth. It is the taste of blood, dust, sap, sun.

"My legs are leaving me," Tremble Dancer told me once. "Then it will be my arms, my eyes, my fingers, the small of my back.

"I am jealous of what you have," she told me, pointing at the parts of my body and telling me what they do.

Last night we burned another house. I saw a painting of Jesus Christ lying on the floor.

He's white. Jesus is white.

While the house was burning, I could see flames, colors, every color but white. I don't know what it means, don't understand fire, the burns on Tremble Dancer's legs, the ash left to cool after the house has been reduced.

I want to know why Jesus isn't a flame.

Last night I dreamed about television. I woke up crying.

While I lie in my tipi pretending to be asleep under the half-blankets of dog and cat skin, I hear the horses exploding. I hear the screams of children who are taken.

The Others have come from a thousand years ago, their braids gray and broken with age. They have come with arrow, bow, stone ax, large hands.

"Do you remember me?" they sing above the noise, our noise.

"Do you still fear me?" they shout above the singing, our singing.

I run from my tipi across the ground toward the tree, climb the branches to watch the Others. There is one, taller than the clouds, who doesn't ride a pony, who runs across the dust, faster than my memory.

Sometimes they come back. The Others, carrying salmon, water. Once, they took Noah Chirapkin, tied him down to the ground, poured water down his throat until he drowned. The tallest Other, the giant, took Tremble Dancer away, brought her back with a big belly. She smelled of salt, old blood. She gave birth, salmon flopped from her, salmon growing larger.

When she died, her hands bled seawater from the palms.

At the Tribal Council meeting last night, Judas WildShoe gave a watch he found to the tribal chairman.

"A white man artifact, a sin," the chairman said, put the watch in his pouch.

I remember watches. They measured time in seconds, minutes, hours. They measured time exactly, coldly. I measure time with my breath, the sound of my hands across my own skin.

I make mistakes.

Last night I held my transistor radio in my hands, gently, as if it were alive. I examined it closely, searching for some flaw, some obvious damage. But there was nothing, no imperfection I could see. If there was something wrong, it was not evident by the smooth, hard plastic of the outside. All the mistakes would be on the inside, where you couldn't see, couldn't reach.

I held that radio and turned it on, turned the volume to maximum, until all I could hear was the in and out, in again, of my breath.

When This World Is All on Fire

WILLIAM SANDERS

(2000, published 2001)

> [W]hen you've gone through five hundred years of genocidal
> experiences, when you know that the other world that surrounds
> you wants your death and that's all it wants, you get bitter. And
> you don't get over it. It starts getting passed on almost genetically.
> It makes for wit, for incredible wit. But under the wit there
> is a bite.
> —*Paula Gunn Allen*

> We are those people, survivors in this postapocalyptic frontier.
> —*Daniel Heath Justice (Cherokee)*

APOCALYPTIC TALES USUALLY PORTRAY a future scenario related
to the abuse of advanced technologies, such as the aftermath of
nuclear bombs detonated with terrorist intent on US soil. Native sf
often points out that historically the apocalypse has already occurred.
Sanders's story has that underlining, echoing Indian Territory humor
through the ironic language of embattled tribal sovereignty in the
tradition of Cherokee genealogist Emmet Starr (1870–1930), whose
classic *History of the Cherokee Indians* (1921) sought to avoid erasure
of his people or, in Starr's words, served "the purpose of perpetuating
some of the facts relative to the Cherokee tribe, that might otherwise

be lost."[1] Recently, Native intellectuals have praised this seminal work in the spirit of imagining Indigenous futurisms, lauding Starr for writing "*of* the past, but *to* the future, to the never-quenched fire of the Cherokee."[2] Nevertheless, the mainstream opinion emphasizes apocalyptic disenfranchisement: "The simple truth was that [Starr] was a man whose country was gone, destroyed as completely as if it had been bombed from the face of the earth. To Starr, and other Cherokees of his age, the end of the Nation was a catastrophic blow."[3]

Often labeled as an sf writer because of his many stories of alternative worlds, Sanders wrote "When This World Is All on Fire" in the tradition of apocalyptic vision, warning of the dangers of climate change in our near future. SF readers will recognize concern for the environmental consequences of unbridled technology, shared by many writers, and the emphasis on global climate change most notably with Octavia Butler's *Parable of the Sower* (1993) and *Parable of the Talents* (1998). These forms of extrapolation are often called "cautionary tales" in sf, but Sanders points out the error in associating sf only with "what if" scenarios set in far-off (and therefore not so frightening) futures:

> The story "When This World Is All on Fire" just barely qualifies as sf, since its basic premise is not some future development that might or might not happen (and may not even be possible according to our present scientific knowledge), but something that's already in the process of happening; all I did was speculate a bit on how some of the details might develop.
>
> And that was always the appeal of sf for me: a means of using imaginary future events and situations to talk about the present-day real world. For example, "When This World Is All on Fire" was one of several stories I wrote with the idea of helping call attention to the ongoing abuse of the environment, in the present case global warming. Not that I really believed it would do any good, but you do what you can.

Sanders tends to tinge humility with sardonic tones, but his work, in this story in particular, calls to mind Louis Owens's (Choctaw/Cherokee) contrast of the "egosystemic" culture of modern industrialized nations with the "ecosystemic" culture of Native peoples who feel neither removed from nor superior to nature, recognizing themselves as an essential "part of that complex of relationships we call the environment."[4]

It's worth considering the story's apocalyptic elements in light of our author's Cherokee background. In *Our Fire Survives the Storm: A Literary History of the Cherokee* (2006), Daniel Heath Justice points out that in their search for a home during the relocation, the Cherokee trekked to "the Darkening Lands of the West, where the spirits of the dead reside" (55). The West is the place of the dead, and the recognition of Apocalypse lies long in the bones and memories of the Cherokee people. The West for Cherokees is named *Uswinhiyi*, the Darkening Land (or Nightland), and is home to Tsusginai, the Ghost Country, home of the dead, a place of fear and darkness. In this sense, all that's left postrelocation is the West, the place left over when all the world reemerges after apocalyptic fire.

"Squatters," Jimmy Lonekiller said as he swung the jeep off the narrow old blacktop onto the narrower and older gravel side road. "I can't believe we got squatters again."

Sitting beside him, bracing himself against the bumping and bouncing, Sergeant Davis Blackbear said, "Better get used to it. We kick this bunch out, there'll be more."

Jimmy Lonekiller nodded. "Guess that's right," he said. "They're not gonna give up, are they?"

He was a husky, dark-skinned young man, and tall for a Cherokee; among the women of the reservation he was generally considered something of a hunk. His khaki uniform was neat and crisply pressed, despite the oppressive heat. Davis Blackbear, feeling his own shirt wilting and sticking to his skin, wondered how he did it. Maybe full-bloods didn't sweat as much. Or maybe it was something to do with being young.

Davis said, "Would you? Give up, I mean, if you were in their shoes?"

Jimmy didn't reply for a moment, being busy fighting the wheel as the jeep slammed over a series of potholes. They were on a really bad stretch now, the road narrowed to a single-lane dirt snaketrack; the overhanging trees on either side, heavy with dust-greyed festoons of kudzu vine, shut out the sun without doing anything much about the heat. This was an out-of-the-way part of the reservation; Davis had had to check the map at the tribal police headquarters to make sure he knew how to get here.

The road began to climb, now, up the side of a steep hill. The jeep slowed to not much better than walking speed; the locally distilled alcohol might burn cooler and cleaner than gasoline but it had no power at all. Jimmy Lonekiller spoke then: "Don't guess I would, you put it that way. Got to go somewhere, poor bastards."

They were speaking English; Davis was Oklahoma Cherokee, having moved to the North Carolina reservation only a dozen years ago, when he married a Qualla Band woman. He could understand the Eastern dialect fairly well by now, enough for cop purposes anyway, but he still wasn't up to a real conversation.

"Still," Jimmy went on, "you got to admit it's a hell of a thing. Twenty-first century, better than five hundred years after Columbus, and here we are again with white people trying to settle on our land. What little bit we've got left," he said, glancing around at the dusty woods. "There's gotta be somewhere else they can go."

"Except," Davis said, "somebody's already there too."

"Probably so," Jimmy admitted. "Seems like they're running out of places for people to be."

He steered the jeep around a rutted hairpin bend, while Davis turned the last phrase over in his mind, enjoying the simple precision of it: running out of places for people to be, that was the exact and very well-put truth. Half of Louisiana and more than half of Florida under water now, the rest of the coastline inundated, Miami and Mobile and Savannah and most of Houston, and, despite great and expensive efforts, New Orleans too.

And lots more land, farther inland, that might as well be submerged for all the good it did anybody: all that once-rich farm country in southern Georgia and Alabama and Mississippi, too hot and dry now to grow anything, harrowed by tornadoes and dust storms, while raging fires destroyed the last remnants of the pine forests and the cypress groves of the dried-up swamplands. Not to mention the quake, last year, shattering Memphis and eastern Arkansas, demolishing the levees and turning the Mississippi loose on what was left of the Delta country. Seemed everybody either had way too much water or not enough.

He'd heard a black preacher, on the radio, declare that it was all God's judgment on the South because of slavery and racism. But that was bullshit; plenty of other parts of the country were getting it just as bad. Like Manhattan, or San Francisco—and he didn't even want to think about what it must be like in places like Arizona. And Africa, oh, Jesus. Nobody in the world wanted to think about Africa now.

The road leveled out at the top of the hill and he pointed. "Pull over there. I want to do a quick scout before we drive up."

Jimmy stopped the jeep and Davis climbed out and stood in the middle of the dirt road. "Well," Jimmy said, getting out too, "I wish somebody else would get the job of running them off now and then." He gave Davis a mocking look. "It's what I get, letting myself get partnered with an old 'breed. Everybody knows why Ridge always puts you in charge of the evictions."

Davis didn't rise to the bait; he knew what Jimmy was getting at. It was something of a standing joke among the reservation police that Davis always got any jobs that involved dealing with white people. Captain Ridge claimed it was because of his years of experience on the Tulsa PD, but Jimmy and others claimed it was really because he was quarter-blood and didn't look all that Indian and therefore might make whites less nervous.

In his own estimation he didn't look particularly Indian or white or anything else, just an average-size man with a big bony face and too many wrinkles and dark brown hair that was now getting heavily streaked with gray. He doubted that his appearance inspired much confidence in people of any race.

The dust cloud was beginning to settle over the road behind them. A black-and-white van appeared, moving slowly, and pulled to a stop behind the jeep. Corporal Roy Smoke stuck his head out the window and said, "Here?"

"For now," Davis told him. "I'm going to go have a look, scope out the scene before we move in. You guys wait here." He turned. "Jimmy, you come with me."

The heat was brutal as they walked down the road, even in the shady patches. At the bottom of the hill, though, Davis led the way off the road and up a dry creek bed, and back in the woods it was a little cooler. Away from the road, there wasn't enough sunlight for the kudzu vines to take over, and beneath the trees the light was pleasantly soft and green. Still too damn dry, Davis thought, feeling leaves and twigs crunching under his boot soles. Another good reason to get this eviction done quickly; squatters tended to be careless with fire. The last bad woods fire on the reservation, a couple of months ago, had been started by a squatter family trying to cook a stolen hog.

They left the creek bed and walked through the woods, heading roughly eastward. "Hell," Jimmy murmured, "I know where this is now. They're on the old Birdshooter place, huh? Shit, nobody's lived there for years. Too rocky to grow anything, no water since the creek went dry."

Davis motioned for silence. Moving more slowly now, trying to step quietly though it wasn't easy in the dry underbrush, they worked their way to the crest of a low ridge. Through the trees, Davis could see a cleared area beyond. Motioning to Jimmy to wait, he moved up to the edge of the woods and paused in the shadow of a half-grown oak, and that was when he heard the singing.

At first he didn't even recognize it as singing; the sound was so high and clear and true that he took it for some sort of instrument. But after a second he realized it was a human voice, though a voice like none he'd ever heard. He couldn't make out the words, but the sound alone was enough to make the hair stand up on his arms and neck, and the air suddenly felt cooler under the trees.

It took Davis a moment to get unstuck; he blinked rapidly and took a deep breath. Then, very cautiously, he peered around the trunk of the oak.

The clearing wasn't very big; wasn't very clear, either, any more, having been taken over by brush and weeds. In the middle stood the ruins of a small frame house, its windows smashed and its roof fallen in.

Near the wrecked house sat a green pickup truck, its bed covered with a boxy, homemade-looking camper shell—plywood, it looked like from where Davis stood, and painted a dull uneven gray. The truck's own finish was badly faded and scabbed with rust; the near front fender was crumpled. Davis couldn't see any license plates.

A kind of lean-to had been erected at the rear of the truck, a sagging blue plastic tarp with guy-ropes tied to trees and bushes. As Davis watched, a lean, long-faced man in bib overalls and a red baseball cap came out from under the tarp and stood looking about.

Then the red-haired girl came around the front of the truck, still singing, the words clear now:

Oh, when this world is all on fire
Where you gonna go?
Where you gonna go?

She was, Davis guessed, maybe twelve or thirteen, though he couldn't really tell at this distance. Not much of her, anyway; he didn't figure she'd go over eighty pounds or so. Her light blue dress was short and sleeveless, revealing thin pale arms and legs. All in all it didn't seem possible for all that sound to be coming from such a wispy little girl; and yet there was no doubt about it, he could see her mouth moving:

Oh, when this world is all on fire
(she sang again) *Where you gonna go?*

The tune was a simple one, an old-fashioned modal-sounding melody line, slow and without a pronounced rhythm. It didn't matter; nothing mattered but that voice. It soared through the still mountain air like a whippoorwill calling beside a running stream. Davis felt his throat go very tight.

Run to the mountains to hide your face
Never find no hiding place
Oh, when this world is all on fire
Where you gonna go?

The man in the baseball cap put his hands on his hips. "Eva May!" he shouted.

The girl stopped singing and turned. Her red hair hung down her back almost to her waist. "Yes, Daddy?" she called.

"Quit the damn fooling around," the man yelled. His voice was rough, with the practiced anger of the permanently angry man. "Go help your brother with the fire."

Fire? Davis spotted it then, a thin trace of bluish-white smoke rising from somewhere on the far side of the parked truck. "Shit!" he said soundlessly, and turned and began picking his way back down the brushy slope.

"What's happening?" Jimmy Lonekiller said as Davis reappeared. "What was that music? Sounded like—"

"Quiet," Davis said. "Come on. We need to hurry.

"Go," Davis said to Jimmy as they turned off the road and up the brush-choked track through the trees. "No use trying to sneak up. They've heard us coming by now."

Sure enough, the squatters were already standing in the middle of the clearing, watching, as the jeep bumped to a stop in front of them. The man in the red baseball cap stood in the middle, his face dark with anger. Beside him stood a washed-out-looking blond woman in a faded flower-print dress, and, next to her, a tall teenage boy wearing ragged jeans and no shirt. The boy's hair had been cropped down almost flush with his scalp.

The woman was holding a small baby to her chest. Great, Davis thought with a flash of anger, just what a bunch of homeless drifters needed. Running out of places for people to be, but not out of people, hell, no. . . .

The red-haired girl was standing off to one side, arms folded. Close up, Davis revised his estimate of her age; she had to be in her middle to late teens at least. There didn't appear to be much of a body under that thin blue dress, but it was definitely not that of a child. Her face, as she watched the two men get out of the jeep, was calm and without expression.

The van came rocking and swaying up the trail and stopped behind the jeep. Davis waited while Roy Smoke and the other four men got out—quite a force to evict one raggedy-ass family, but Captain Ridge believed in being careful—and then he walked over to the waiting squatters and said, "Morning. Where you folks from?"

The man in the red baseball cap spat on the ground, not taking his eyes off Davis. "Go to hell, Indian."

Oh oh. Going to be like that, was it? Davis said formally, "Sir, you're on Cherokee reservation land. Camping isn't allowed except by permit and in designated areas. I'll have to ask you to move out."

The woman said, "Oh, why can't you leave us alone? We're not hurting anybody. You people have all this land, why won't you share it?"

We tried that, lady, Davis thought, and look where it got us. Aloud

he said, "Ma'am, the laws are made by the government of the Cherokee nation. I just enforce them."

"Nation!" The man snorted. "Bunch of woods niggers, hogging
good land while white people starve. You got no right."

"I'm not here to argue about it," Davis said. "I'm just here to tell
you you've got to move on."

The boy spoke up suddenly. "You planning to make us?"

Davis looked at him. Seventeen or eighteen, he guessed, punk-mean
around the eyes and that Johnny Pissoff stance that they seemed to
develop at that age; ropy muscles showing under bare white skin, fore-
arms rippling visibly as he clenched both fists.

"Yes," Davis told him. "If necessary, we'll move you."

To the father—he assumed—he added, "I'm hoping you won't make
it necessary. If you like, we'll give you a hand—"

He didn't get to finish. That was when the boy came at him, fists
up, head hunched down between his shoulders, screaming as he
charged: "*Redskin motherfu—*"

Davis shifted his weight, caught the wild swing in a cross-arm block,
grasped the kid's wrist and elbow and pivoted, all in one smooth
motion. The boy yelped in pain as he hit the ground, and then grunted
as Jimmy Lonekiller landed on top of him, handcuffs ready.

The man in the red cap had taken a step forward, but he stopped
as Roy Smoke moved in front of him and tapped him gently on the
chest with his nightstick. "No," Roy said, "you don't want to do that.
Stand still, now."

Davis said, "Wait up, Jimmy," and then to the man in the red cap,
"All right, there's two ways we can do this. We can take this boy to
Cherokee town and charge him with assaulting an officer, and he can
spend the next couple of months helping us fix the roads. Probably
do him a world of good."

"No," the woman cried. The baby in her arms was wailing now, a
thin weak piping against her chest, but she made no move to quiet
it. "Please, no."

"Or," Davis went on, "you can move out of here, right now, without any more trouble, and I'll let you take him with you."

The girl, he noticed, hadn't moved the whole time, just stood there
watching with no particular expression on her face, except that there

might be a tiny trace of a smile on her lips as she looked at the boy on the ground.

"No," the woman said again. "Vernon, no, you can't let them take Ricky—"

"All right," the man said. "We'll go, Indian. Let him up. He won't give you no more trouble. Ricky, behave yourself or I'll whup your ass."

Davis nodded to Jimmy Lonekiller, who released the kid. "Understand this," Davis said, "we don't give second warnings. If you're found on Cherokee land again, you'll be arrested, your vehicle will be impounded, and you might do a little time."

The boy was getting to his feet, rubbing his arm. The woman started to move toward him but the man said, "He's all right, damn it. Get busy packing up." He turned his head and scowled at the girl. "You too, Eva May."

Davis watched as the squatters began taking down the tarp. The girl's long red hair fairly glowed in the midday sun; he felt a crazy impulse to go over and touch it. He wished she'd sing some more, but he didn't imagine she felt like singing now.

He said, "Roy, have somebody kill that fire. Make sure it's dead and buried. This place is a woods fire waiting to happen."

Davis lived in a not very big trailer on the outskirts of Cherokee town. Once he had had a regular house, but after his wife had taken off, a few years ago, with that white lawyer from Gatlinburg, he'd moved out and let a young married couple have the place.

The trailer's air conditioning was just about shot, worn out from the constant unequal battle with the heat, but after the sun went down it wasn't too bad except on the hottest summer nights. Davis took off his uniform and hung it up and stretched out on the bed while darkness fell outside and the owls began calling in the trees. Sweating, waiting for the temperature to drop, he closed his eyes and heard again in his mind, over the rattle of the laboring air conditioner:

>   *Oh, when this world is all on fire*
>   *Where you gonna go?*
>   *Where you gonna go?*

It was the following week when he saw the girl again.

He was driving through Waynesville, taking one of the force's antique computers for repairs, when he saw her crossing the street up ahead. Even at half a block's distance, he was sure it was the same girl; there couldn't be another head of hair like that in these mountains. She was even wearing what looked like the same blue dress.

But he was caught in slow traffic, and she disappeared around the corner before he could get any closer. Sighing, making a face at himself for acting like a fool, he drove on. By the time he got to the computer shop he had convinced himself it had all been his imagination.

He dropped off the computer and headed back through town, taking it easy and keeping a wary eye on the traffic, wondering as always how so many people still managed to drive, despite fuel shortages and sky-high prices; and all the new restrictions, not that anybody paid them any mind, the government having all it could do just keeping the country more or less together.

An ancient minivan, a mattress roped to its roof, made a sudden left turn from the opposite lane. Davis hit the brakes, cursing—a fenderbender in a tribal patrol car, that would really make the day— and that was when he saw the red-haired girl coming up the sidewalk on the other side of the street.

Some asshole behind him was honking; Davis put the car in motion again, going slow, looking for a parking place. There was a spot up near the next corner and he turned into it and got out and locked up the cruiser, all without stopping to think what he thought he was doing or why he was doing it.

He crossed the street and looked along the sidewalk, but he couldn't see the girl anywhere. He began walking back the way she'd been going, looking this way and that. The street was mostly lined with an assortment of small stores—leftovers, probably, from the days when Waynesville had been a busy tourist resort, before tourism became a meaningless concept—and he peered in through a few shop windows, without any luck.

He walked a couple of blocks that way and then decided she couldn't have gotten any farther in that little time. He turned and went back, and stopped at the corner and looked up and down the cross street, wondering if she could have gone that way. Fine Indian you are, he thought, one skinny little white girl with hair like a brush fire and you keep losing her.

Standing there, he became aware of a growing small commotion across the street, noises coming from the open door of the shop on the corner: voices raised, a sound of scuffling. A woman shouted, "No you don't—"

He ran across the street, dodging an oncoming BMW, and into the shop. It was an automatic cop reaction, unconnected to his search; but then immediately he saw the girl, struggling in the grip of a large steely-haired woman in a long black dress. "Stop fighting me," the woman was saying in a high strident voice. "Give me that, young lady. I'm calling the police—"

Davis said, "What's going on here?"

The woman looked around. "Oh," she said, looking pleased, not letting go the girl's arm. "I'm glad to see you, officer. I've got a little shoplifter for you."

The girl was looking at Davis too. If she recognized him she gave no sign. Her face was flushed, no doubt from the struggle, but still as expressionless as ever.

"What did she take?" Davis asked.

"This." The woman reached up and pried the girl's right hand open, revealing something shiny. "See, she's still holding it!"

Davis stepped forward and took the object from the girl's hand: a cheap-looking little pendant, silver or more likely silver-plated, in the shape of a running dog, with a flimsy neck chain attached.

"I want her arrested," the woman said. "I'll be glad to press charges. I'm tired of these people, coming around here ruining this town, stealing everyone blind."

Davis said, "I'm sorry, ma'am, I don't have any jurisdiction here. You'll need to call the local police."

She blinked, doing a kind of ladylike double-take, looking at Davis's uniform. "Oh. Excuse me, I thought—" She managed to stop before actually saying, "I thought you were a real policeman." It was there on her face, though.

Davis looked again at the pendant, turning it over in his hand, finding the little white price tag stuck on the back of the running dog: $34.95. A ripoff even in the present wildly inflated money; but after a moment he reached for his wallet and said, "Ma'am, how about if I just pay you for it?"

The woman started to speak and then stopped, her eyes locking on the wallet in his hand. Not doing much business these days, he guessed; who had money to waste on junk like this?

While she hesitated, Davis pulled out two twenties and laid them on the nearby countertop. "With a little extra to pay for your trouble," he added.

That did it. She let go the girl's arm and scooped up the money with the speed of a professional gambler. "All right," she said, "but get her out of here!"

The girl stood still, staring at Davis. The woman said, "I mean it! Right now!"

Davis tilted his head in the direction of the door. The girl nodded and started to move, not particularly fast. Davis followed her, hearing the woman's voice behind him: "And if you ever come back—"

Out on the sidewalk, Davis said, "I'm parked down this way."

She looked at him. "You arresting me?"

Her speaking voice—he realized suddenly that this was the first time he'd heard it—was surprisingly ordinary; soft and high, rather pleasant, but nothing to suggest what it could do in song. There was no fear in it, or in her face; she might have been asking what time it was.

Davis shook his head. "Like I told that woman, I don't have any authority here."

"So you can't make me go with you."

"No." he said. "But I'd say you need to get clear of this area pretty fast. She's liable to change her mind and call the law after all."

"Guess that's right. Okay." She fell in beside him, sticking her hands in the pockets of the blue dress. He noticed her feet were barely covered by a pair of old tennis shoes, so ragged they were practically sandals. "Never rode in a police car 'fore."

As they came up to the parked cruiser he stopped and held out his hand. "Here. You might as well have this."

She took the pendant and held it up in front of her face, looking at it, swinging it from side to side. After a moment she lipped the chain over her head and tucked the pendant down the front of her dress. "Better hide it," she said. "Ricky sees it, he'll steal it for sure."

He said, "Not much of a thing to get arrested for."

She shrugged. "I like dogs. We had a dog, back home in Georgia, before we had to move. Daddy wouldn't let me take him along."

"Still," he said, "you could have gone to jail."

She shrugged, a slight movement of her small shoulders. "So? Wouldn't be no worse than how I got to live now."

"Yes it would," he told her. "You've got no idea what it's like in those forced-labor camps. How old are you?"

"Seventeen," she said. "Well, next month."

"Then you're an adult, as far's the law's concerned. Better watch it from now on." He opened the right door. "Get in."

She climbed into the car and he closed the door and went around. As he slid in under the wheel she said, "Okay, I know what comes next. Where do you want to go?"

"What?" Davis looked at her, momentarily baffled. "Well, I was just going to take you home. Wherever your family—"

"Oh, come on." Her voice held an edge of scorn now. "You didn't get me out of there for nothing. You want something, just like everybody always does, and I know what it is because there ain't nothing else I got. Well, all right," she said. "I don't guess I mind. So where do you want to go to do it?"

For a moment Davis was literally speechless. The idea simply hadn't occurred to him; he hadn't thought of her in that way at all. It surprised him, now he considered it. After all, she was a pretty young girl—you could have said beautiful, in a way—and he had been living alone for a long time. Yet so it was; he felt no stirrings of that kind toward this girl, not even now with her close up and practically offering herself.

When he could speak he said, "No, no. Not that. Believe me."

"Really?" She looked very skeptical. "Then what *do* you want?"

"Right now," he said, "I want to buy you a pair of shoes."

An hour or so later, coming out of the discount shoe store out by the highway, she said, "I know what this is all about. You feel bad because you run us off, back last week."

"No." Davis's voice held maybe a little bit more certainty than he felt, but he added, "Just doing my job. Anyway, you couldn't have stayed there. No water, nothing to eat, how would you live?"

"You still didn't have no right to run us off."

"Sure I did. It's our land," he said. "All we've got left."

She opened her mouth and he said, "Look, we're not going to talk about it, all right?"

They walked in silence the rest of the way across the parking lot. She kept looking down at her feet, admiring the new shoes. They weren't much, really, just basic white no-name sport shoes, but he supposed they looked pretty fine to her. At that they hadn't been all that cheap. In fact between the shoes and the pendant he'd managed to go through a couple days' pay. Not that he was likely to get paid any time soon; the tribe had been broke for a long time.

As he started the car, she said, "You sure you don't want to, you know, do it?"

He looked at her and she turned sidewise in the seat, moving her thin pale legs slightly apart, shifting her narrow hips. "Hey," she said, "somebody's gotta be the first. Might as well be you."

Her mouth quirked. "If it ain't you it'll prob'ly be Ricky. He sure keeps trying."

With some difficulty Davis said, "Turn around, please, and do up your safety belt."

"All right." She giggled softly. "Just don't know what it is you want from me, that's all."

He didn't respond until they were out of the parking lot and rolling down the road, back into Waynesville. Then he said, "Would you sing for me?"

"What?" Her voice registered real surprise. "Sing? You mean right now, right here in the car?"

"Yes," Davis said. "Please."

"Well, I be damn." She brushed back her hair and studied him for a minute. "You mean it, don't you? All right . . . what you want me to sing? If I know it."

"That song you were singing that morning up on the reservation," he said. "Just before we arrived."

She thought about it. "Oh," she said. "You mean—"

She tilted her head back and out it came, like a flood of clear spring water:

Oh, when this world is all on fire
Where you gonna go?

"Yes," Davis said very softly. "That's it. Sing it. Please."

Her family was staying in a refugee camp on the other side of town; a great hideous sprawl of cars and trucks and buses and campers and trailers of all makes and ages and states of repair, bright nylon tents and crude plastic-tarp shelters and pathetic, soggy arrangements of cardboard boxes, spread out over a once-beautiful valley.

"You better just drop me off here," the girl said as he turned off the road.

"That's okay," Davis said. "Which way do I go?"

At her reluctant direction, he steered slowly down a narrow muddy lane between parked vehicles and outlandish shelters, stopping now and then as children darted across in front of the car. People came out and stared as the big police cruiser rolled past. Somebody threw something unidentifiable, that bounced off the windshield leaving a yellowish smear. By now Davis was pretty sure this hadn't been a good idea.

But the girl said, "Up there," and there it was, the old truck with the homemade camper bed and the blue plastic awning rigged out behind, just like before. He stopped the car and got out and went around to open the passenger door.

The air was thick with wood smoke and the exhausts of worn-out engines, and the pervasive reek of human waste. The ground underfoot was soggy with mud and spilled motor oil and God knew what else. Davis looked around at the squalid scene, remembering what this area used to look like, only a few years ago. Now, it looked like the sort of thing they used to show on the news, in countries you'd never heard of. The refugee camps in Kosovo, during his long-ago army days, hadn't been this bad.

Beyond, up on the mountainsides, sunlight glinted on the windows of expensive houses. A lot of locals had thought it was wonderful, back when the rich people first started buying up land and building homes up in the mountain country, getting away from the heat and the flooding. They hadn't been as happy about the second invasion, a year or so later, by people bringing nothing but their desperation. . . .

Davis shook his head and opened the door. Even the depressing scene couldn't really get him down, right now. It had been an amazing experience, almost religious, driving along with that voice filling the dusty interior of the old cruiser; he felt light and loose, as if coming off a marijuana high. He found himself smiling—

A voice behind him said, "What the hell?" and then, "Eva May!"

He turned and saw the man standing there beside the truck, still wearing the red cap and the angry face. "Hello," he said, trying to look friendly or at least inoffensive. "Just giving your daughter a lift from town. Don't worry, she's not in any trouble—"

"Hell she's not," the man said, looking past Davis. "Eva May, git your ass out of that thing! What you doing riding around with this God-damn woods nigger?"

The girl swung her feet out of the car. Davis started to give her a hand but decided that might be a bad move right now. She got out and stepped past Davis. "It's all right, Daddy," she said. "He didn't do nothing bad. Look, he bought me some new shoes!"

"No shit." The man looked down at her feet, at the new shoes standing out white and clean against the muddy ground. "New shoes, huh? Git 'em off."

She stopped. "But Daddy—"

His hand came up fast; it made an audible crack against the side of her face. As she stumbled backward against the side of the truck he said, "God damn it, I *said* take them shoes off."

He spun about to face Davis. "You don't like that, Indian? Maybe you wanta do something about it?"

Davis did, in fact, want very much to beat this worthless *yoneg* within half an inch of his life. But he forced himself to stand still and keep his hands down at his sides. Start a punch-out in here, and almost certainly he'd wind up taking on half the men in the camp. Or using the gun on his belt, which would bring down a whole new kind of disaster.

Even then he might have gone for it, but he knew that anything he did to the man would later be taken out on Eva May. It was a pattern all too familiar to any cop.

She had one shoe off now and was jerking at the other, standing on one foot, leaning against the trailer, sobbing. She got it off and the man jerked it out of her hand. "Here." He half-turned and threw the shoe, hard, off somewhere beyond the old school bus that was parked across the lane. He bent down and picked up the other shoe and hurled it in the opposite direction.

"Ain't no damn Indian buying *nothing* for my kid," he said. "Or going anywhere *near* her. You understand that, Chief?"

From inside the camper came the sound of a baby crying. A woman's voice said, "Vernon? What's going on, Vernon?"

"Now," the man said, "you git out of here, woods nigger."

The blood was singing in Davis's ears and there was a taste in his mouth like old pennies. Still he managed to check himself, and to keep his voice steady as he said, "Sir, whatever you think of me, your daughter has a great gift. She should have the opportunity—"

"Listen close, Indian." The man's voice was low, now, and very intense. "You shut your mouth and you git back in that car and you drive outta here, right damn *now,* or else I'm gon' find out if you got the guts to use that gun. Plenty white men around here, be glad to help stomp your dirty red ass."

Davis glanced at Eva May, who was still leaning against the truck, weeping and holding the side of her face. Her bare white feet were already spotted with mud.

And then, because there was nothing else to do, he got back in the car and drove away. He didn't look back. There was nothing there he wanted to see; nothing he wouldn't already be seeing for a long time to come.

"Blackbear," Captain Ridge said, next morning. "I don't believe this."

He was seated at his desk in his office, looking up at Davis. His big dark face was not that of a happy man.

"I got a call just now," he said, "from the sheriff's office over in Waynesville. Seems a reservation officer, man about your size and wearing sergeant's stripes, picked up a teenage girl on the street. Made her get into a patrol car, tried to get her to have sex, even bought her presents to entice her. When she refused he took her back to the refugee camp and made threats against her family."

Davis said, "Captain—"

"No," Captain Ridge said, and slapped a hand down on his desk top. "No, Blackbear, I don't want to hear it. See, you're about to tell me it's a lot of bullshit, and I *know* it's a lot of bullshit, and it doesn't make a damn bit of difference. You listen to me, Blackbear. Whoever those people are, you stay away from them. You stay out of Waynesville, till I tell you different. On duty or off, I don't care."

He leaned back in his chair. "Because if you show up there again, you're going to be arrested—the sheriff just warned me—and there won't be a thing I can do about it. And you know what kind of chance you'll have in court over there. They like us even less than they do the squatters."

Davis said, "All right. I wasn't planning on it anyway."

But of course he went back. Later, he thought that the only surprising thing was that he waited as long as he did.

He went on Sunday morning. It was an off-duty day and he drove his own car; that, plus the nondescript civilian clothes he wore, ought to cut down the chances of his being recognized. He stopped at an all-hours one-stop in Maggie Valley and bought a pair of cheap sunglasses and a butt-ugly blue mesh-back cap with an emblem of a jumping fish on the front. Pulling the cap down low, checking himself out in the old Dodge's mirror, he decided he looked like a damn fool, but as camouflage it ought to help.

But when he got to the refugee camp he found it had all been for nothing. The truck was gone and so was Eva May's family; an elderly couple in a Buick were already setting up camp in the spot. No, they said, they didn't know anything; the place had been empty when they got here, just a little while ago.

Davis made a few cautious inquiries, without finding out much more. The woman in the school bus across the lane said she'd heard them leaving a little before daylight. She had no idea where they'd gone and doubted if anyone else did.

"People come and go," she said. "There's no keeping track. And they weren't what you'd call friendly neighbors."

Well, Davis thought as he drove back to the reservation, so much for that. He felt sad and empty inside, and disgusted with himself for feeling that way. Good thing the bars and liquor stores weren't open on Sunday; he could easily go on a serious drunk right now.

He was coming over the mountains east of Cherokee when he saw the smoke.

It was the worst fire of the decade. And could have been much worse; if the wind had shifted just right, it might have taken out the whole reservation. As it was, it was three days before the fire front crossed the reservation border and became somebody else's problem.

For Davis Blackbear it was a very long three days. Afterward, he estimated that he might have gotten three or four hours of sleep the whole time. None of the tribal police got any real time off, the whole time; it was one job after another, evacuating people from the fire's path, setting up roadblocks, keeping traffic unsnarled and, in the rare times there was nothing else to do, joining the brutally overworked firefighting crews. By now almost every able-bodied man in the tribe was helping fight the blaze; or else already out of action, being treated for burns or smoke inhalation or heat stroke.

At last the fire ate its way over the reservation boundary and into the national parkland beyond; and a few hours later, as Wednesday's sun slid down over the mountains, Davis Blackbear returned to his trailer and fell across the bed, without bothering to remove his sweaty uniform or even to kick off his ruined shoes. And lay like a dead man through the rest of the day and all through the night, until the next morning's light came in the trailer's windows; and then he got up and undressed and went back to bed and slept some more.

A little before noon he woke again, and knew before he opened his eyes what he was going to do.

Captain Ridge had told him to take the day off and rest up; but Ridge wasn't around when Davis came by the station, and nobody paid any attention when Davis left his car and drove off in one of the jeeps. Or stopped him when he drove past the roadblocks that were still in place around the fire zone; everybody was too exhausted to ask unnecessary questions.

It was a little disorienting, driving across the still-smoking land; the destruction had been so complete that nothing was recognizable. He almost missed a couple of turns before he found the place he was looking for.

A big green pickup truck was parked beside the road, bearing the insignia of the US Forest Service. A big stocky white man in a green uniform stood beside it, watching as Davis drove up and parked the jeep and got out. "Afternoon," he said.

He stuck out a hand as Davis walked across the road. "Bob Lindblad," he said as Davis shook his hand. "Fire inspector. They sent me down to have a look, seeing as it's on federal land now."

He looked around and shook his head. "Hell of a thing," he said, and wiped his forehead with the back of his hand.

It certainly was a strange-looking scene. On the northeast side of the road there was nothing but ruin, an ash-covered desolation studded with charred tree stumps, stretching up the hillside and over the ridge and out of sight. The other side of the road, however, appeared untouched; except for a thin coating of powdery ash on the bushes and the kudzu vines, it looked exactly as it had when Davis had come this way a couple of weeks ago.

The Forest Service man said, "Anybody live around here?"

"Not close, no. Used to be a family named Birdshooter, lived up that way, but they moved out a long time ago."

Lindblad nodded. "I saw some house foundations."

Davis said, "This was where it started?"

"Where it *was* started," Lindblad said. "Yes."

"Somebody set it?"

"No question about it." Lindblad waved a big hand. "Signs all over the place. They set it at half a dozen points along this road. The wind was at their backs, out of the southwest—that's why the other side of the road didn't take—so they weren't in any danger. Bastards," he added.

Davis said, "Find anything to show who did it?"

Lindblad shook his head. "Been too much traffic up and down this road, last few days, to make any sense of the tracks. I'm still looking, though."

"All right if I look around too?" Davis asked.

"Sure. Just holler," Lindblad said, "if you find anything. I'll be somewhere close by."

He walked off up the hill, his shoes kicking up little white puffs of ash. Davis watched him a minute and then started to walk along the road, looking at the chewed-up surface. The Forest Service guy was right, he thought, no way in hell could anybody sort out all these tracks and ruts. Over on the unburned downhill side, somebody had almost gone into the ditch—

Davis almost missed it. A single step left or right, or the sun at a different angle, and he'd never have seen the tiny shininess at the bottom of the brush-choked ditch. He bent down and groped, pushing aside a clod of roadway dirt, and felt something tangle around his fingers. He tugged gently and it came free. He straightened up and held up his hand in front of his face.

The sun glinted off the little silver dog as it swung from side to side at the end of the broken chain.

Up on the hillside, Lindblad called, "Find anything?"

Davis turned and looked. Lindblad was poking around near the ruins of the old house, nearly hidden by a couple of black tree stubs. His back was to the road.

"No," Davis yelled back, walking across the road. "Not a thing."

He drew back his arm and hurled the pendant high out over the black-and-gray waste. It flashed for an instant against the sky before vanishing, falling somewhere on the burned earth.

from *The Moons of Palmares*

ZAINAB AMADAHY

(1997)

> Are First Nations peoples supposed to be portrayed only in
> westerns, as the losers to the greater good of manifest destiny? . . .
> [S]cience fiction is the only genre that suggests that First Nations
> peoples and their cultures have a future that has not been
> assimilated into the dominant society. This feature of science
> fiction is significant to First Nations individuals.
> —*Sierra S. Adare (Cherokee/Choctaw)*

ZAINAB AMADAHY (Cherokee and African American ancestry) came
to Canada from the United States in 1975 and has worked or volun-
teered in the fields of anti-apartheid activism, nonprofit housing management, women's programming, immigrant services, fundraising,
medical technology, and community business development. This experience of strong activism translates well into her experiments with speculative fiction, or, as she terms it, "spec fiction." This is, for her, the
best genre for "exploring social issues like colonialism, racism and the
dominant social concept of empowerment."

Expressing what Jace Weaver (Cherokee) might call the Native
"communitist" outlook, one oriented to community and activism,
Amadahy describes her aesthetic:

> I further like empowering Indigenous and other racialized char-
> acters who too rarely get to be protagonists as well as mentors,

love interests, and antagonists to each other. In fact, we are often disappeared/genocided from the majority of spec fiction out there. When we do appear, our cultures, histories, and bodies are too often "othered" and "alienized," and we and our stories exist only for the purposes of enabling the protagonist's transformation or providing contrast to the values and behaviors of other characters. While we can celebrate that things are changing, there is still a ways to go. Through my stories I get to posit alternative ways of organizing communities, economies, and political systems, which we two-leggeds desperately need right now. I can subversively teach history and current affairs from a rarely validated perspective. Though my effectiveness at doing so can be critiqued, I aspire to write in a way that views possible alternatives through the lens of a relationship framework, where I can demonstrate our connectivity to and interdependence with each other and the rest of our Relations.

Adopting the literary device of writing slave narrative to preserve the memory of insurrection, Amadahy follows notable speculative fiction authors including Ishmael Reed (*Flight to Canada,* 1976), Samuel Delany (*Tales of Neveryon,* 1979), and Octavia Butler (*Patternmaster,* 1976). In the novel excerpted here, Amadahy creates a distant future adventure set on a faraway world, the world of the Palmarans, or people of Palmares, a name taken from a settlement of escaped slaves in nineteenth-century Brazil. Amadahy also makes use of the timeless tale of a technologically superior culture colonizing an Indigenous population to exploit natural resources. In this case, the colonizers are called the Terran Consortium, and their mantra is "keep the quilidon flowing." Quilidon is a precious natural resource, and Terran anthropologists theorize that "traditional cultures from around Earth had made Palmares an amalgam as rare as the mineral its citizens mined."

Politics on Palmares are familiar enough. The Palmarans ask for home rule, which the Terran Consortium will allow as long as treaties guarantee its right to maintain a protected base of operations on the planet. And, of course, the Consortium sends in a contingent of Peacekeepers to assure that its terms are met. The Palmaran political party Menchista demands that the Consortium leave the planet altogether for reasons of both environmental justice and genuine sovereignty. One of the party's leaders, geology professor Sixto Masika, argues that the overly extensive mining of the three moons of Palmares has resulted in lands lost through volcanic and quake activity. Expressing a fundamental Indigenous point of view based on the commonality of shared experiences, elsewhere in Amadahy's novel the character Masika points out that "colonizers throughout history have recognized the cost-effectiveness of indirect control. Give people the right to elect their own leaders, fund their own security forces, health care and education, but maintain control of their resources and you can still call the tune. It's an old strategy—once called neo-colonialism by dissidents on Earth. Political independence alone means little."

As the excerpt begins, Major Leith Eaglefeather (Cherokee), a Peacekeeper of the Terran Consortium who conducts more trustworthy negotiations with the Palmarans than his fellow comrades do, comes into closer contact with Masika's quilombo (from Angolan Kimbudu *kilombo,* designating an Indigenous community: specifically, recalling historically a community of escaped African slaves who joined with various Indigenous peoples in resisting colonization in pre-nineteenth-century Maroon settlements). Confronted by members of the Beloved Path (Masika's inclination) and the Kituhwas, an activist group descended from the Earth-time Chickasauga and Maroon backgrounds, he is kidnapped. Eaglefeather is at the point of escaping when an unexpected quake hits the community.

Young Joachim lay still and quiet now, in the arms of his mother, her head wrapped in a crude blood-stained dressing. She was not among the worst of the injured, so she sat quietly as two overwhelmed paramedics ministered to others.

A handful of able-bodied, and not so able-bodied, neighbors sifted through heaps of rubble looking for survivors. A few residents were still unaccounted for.

The newborn baby boy cradled in Jamal Breiche's arms was also still and quiet. Holding the sleeping baby made him feel less useless than he had at its birth. He could only watch helplessly as the young paramedic cursed in frustration. Though still a girl as far as Jamal was concerned, she had fought to keep the mother alive, but within minutes she'd had to focus her efforts on saving the unborn baby, for it was clear the mother would not survive.

He looked around him. Bodies ringed the field. His house, although damaged, was one of the handful that were still standing. Keoki, who had survived with a mild concussion, pronounced three of the five structurally safe, including Jamal's. Eventually the survivors would move into them, Jamal knew, and his tiles and furniture would be under assault again. He cursed himself for being a cranky old man.

A medi-skip was lifting off from the makeshift skip-strip in the center of the field. It would ferry the more seriously injured and return with supplies. On the far side of the courtyard, Jamal saw the slow-moving figure of Tuyet Chowdhury. She spoke briefly to a woman who was awkwardly trying to bandage her hand. Letting the bandage dangle, the woman pointed to Jamal. Tuyet hurried towards him, slowing only to skirt a wide crack in the earth. When she reached him, he silently handed her the baby.

Tuyet carefully took the sleeping baby, studying its face intently. Jamal remembered examining his own newborns just that way many years ago. Lately, he had been looking forward to becoming a grandparent. Only months ago, he had been jealous of Tuyet's joy at the news that her son's partner was pregnant.

"Thank you, Jamal," Tuyet whispered. "It's amazing he can sleep through this. Is he all right?"

"He wasn't sleeping a moment ago. The paramedic is sure there's no damage to his lungs."

Under other circumstances, Tuyet would have given a proud grandmotherly smile. She nodded. "Is there any hope my son will be found alive?"

They turned toward the wreckage that had once been the home of Tuyet Chowdhury's son and his partner. Sixto Masika was among those digging in the rubble, looking for survivors. They would be digging for some time. The scene spoke for itself. Tuyet nodded again. Drawing the baby close, she walked toward the rubble to watch the digging.

Jamal lurched over to the landing strip. The medi-skip was due back soon. Surely there was something he could do to help.

He was helping to unload medical equipment and supplies when he overheard the pilot tell the young paramedic that the quilombo's hospital could handle no more casualties. The skip would be flying out empty. The young paramedic began to argue with the pilot. The rains were scheduled to begin in an hour, and, dammit, they couldn't just leave people out in the open. Jamal could see she was exhausted. "Let him go," he said. "We can move those who can be moved to my house and to the others that are still standing."

The moving of the injured had just gotten under way when Jamal spotted Magaly, with Huseni and Rahim in tow. She looked dazed as she stopped to take in the ruins. Then she reddened in anger and rushed at Sixto. She and Jamal reached his side at the same time.

"Where's the major?" Magaly said. Sixto exchanged a quick look with Jamal. "He'd better be dead," she warned, as Sixto hesitated.

"He escaped," Jamal calmly told her, "but he's on foot. He won't get far."

"He'd better not or we're all up the Cygnus gravity well without a thruster. We'll be heading back to the base. Rahim, you take a ground-skip through the Huseni, fly a skip up around Goree. I'll take the underside of the cliff."

"If you have access to a skip, I think there are better uses for it," Sixto said. "Communications are down. Supplies and medical personnel need transport. The Tubman hospital is full. The injured are going to have to be taken for care outside of the quilombo."

"I understand that. But our lives are at stake if Major Eaglefeather makes it back to Simcoe." Her expression remained unchanged. Sixto and Jamal watched her soberly. "I'll be back as soon as I can."

Sixto set his jaw and blinked. "Don't kill him. Otherwise you're no better than they are."

"Not to mention you would have murder charges hanging over your head," Jamal added pointedly. "Imhotep extradites people for that, you know."

An incoming stratoskip drowned out her response. The skip did not bear the medi-serv emblem. They waited for it to land. Jamal was relieved to see his two children climb out. The major followed. Tariq called for a stretcher for Jung-Min. When it became apparent that they were the full complement of the stratoskip's passenger manifest, Jamal knew that Priya Said was dead.

Sixto bolted for Jamal's daughter. The two clung to each other as paramedics took over the care of Jung-Min. Jamal hugged his son, feeling Tariq's tension drain. The major waited by the skip.

Magaly walked up to the major. The others fell silent. "Why did you come back? You could have been halfway to the base by now."

"He could have been all the way there, if he'd taken our skip," Zaria said.

"He had the chance and didn't."

Tariq agreed. "He helped us with Jung-Min and others we found injured on the way back."

"Your arm's bleeding again," Jamal said. "You should have one of the paramedics take a look."

"They're busy. I'll be all right," the major said softly.

A low rumbling began, followed by familiar vibrations. A child screamed, setting off a chain of cries and shouts.

"It's only a tremor!" Jamal called out. "Keep calm, everyone." He staggered off into the courtyard, imploring people not to panic.

The aftershock subsided and with it the clamor in the courtyard. Jamal went on directing the moving of the injured into the houses. Sixto, with Huseni and Rahim, returned to the ruins. As Zaria looked for something useful to do, Magaly cursed angrily.

"Damn! Our communications are still jammed, so we can't contact Imhotep to find out if we should expect more aftershocks."

"That can be fixed." The major had said little since he decided to help them and nothing on the way to Tubman, just gazed silently out the windscreen as they flew over the devastation. Zaria had been too preoccupied with the crisis to wonder what he might be thinking.

"The jamming is designed to break up the signal into particles so that no one can make sense of it."

"So we've noticed," said Magaly.

"But it's not randomized. The base would have figured you wouldn't be able to reprogram your comnet to compensate, so it didn't bother. Your receivers can be set to reassemble the jumbled signal into something intelligible. I can do it for you."

"Will you?" Zaria asked. The major was offering to commit treason. He nodded without enthusiasm. "Take me to a receiver."

"Right this way," said Tariq. The two men climbed back into the stratoskip. With Tariq piloting, they lifted off.

"What's gotten into him?" Magaly asked Zaria.

"He's becoming disillusioned, I think. He was shocked to find out that the Peacekeepers had deliberately jammed our comnet, so we wouldn't have time to prepare for the quake."

"Sure," Magaly snorted. "Didn't he give the order to jam us in the first place? Days ago?"

"I don't think he did," Zaria said tightly and walked away to help her father.

The comnet was finally online, the image blurred. Evidently, the major had been successful in re-programming the quilombo's receivers. In the only room of Jamal's house not crammed with the injured, Zaria tapped at the console, fine-tuning the reception. Her father had just joined her. It was the first break they'd taken since the quake hit fourteen hours earlier.

The comcasts said there were twenty-six known dead in Tubman, with seventy people still missing. Fires were now under control. The imager panned across the ruins. Relief efforts were receiving official support from Imhotep. The nearest quilombos had sent medi-skips to treat and fly out the injured. Militia contingents would be arriving to set up temporary shelters for those left homeless. The base and compound, it was reported, had experienced little damage and only minor casualties.

The Palmaran Governing Council had called an emergency debate on its response to what was believed to have been the Peacekeepers' jamming of the comnet. The Peacekeepers denied responsibility for what their spokesperson called "communication interference" and cited natural causes as the likely cause. They offered to help in the relief efforts. Nevertheless, demonstrations had broken out in quilombos across the planet, with protesters calling for everything from reparations to independence to war.

Then came a hurried interview with Sixto Masika, Professor of Geology, Tubman University. Zaria leaned forward in her chair.

The comcaster summarized Sixto's comments. Professor Masika was disappointed that people were talking in terms of vengeance, she said. Then the comcast switched to a clip of his interview.

"The quake," he explained, "was caused by the wide-scale mining of our moons. The moons are losing mass and their orbits are shifting, and with them the gravitational forces. The volcanic eruptions, the tsunamis, the quakes we've had for the last two decades are the result. And it will get worse. The Consortium and the Peacekeepers have to go. Pressuring them into better relations with us is irrelevant. The mining has got to stop."

The clip stopped. His views, said the comcaster, were controversial and not widely accepted by experts. "Although," she conceded, "more and more Palmarans are calling for Terran withdrawal. This is Imelda Hranov reporting from Tubman Quilombo."

Zaria muted the audio and looked at Jamal exasperatedly. "Well, it took her about two seconds to discredit everything he said."

"If you think the comcast's bad, forget checking out Peacecom," he told her.

A tired-looking young man in a paramedic jumpsuit appeared at the doorway. "Elder Jamal, there you are. I've just spoken to the hospital. No beds are available and they don't expect to have any available any time soon. We'll have to spend the night here."

"Don't worry," Jamal assured him. He welcomed the change from the suspicion and distrust he usually met as a Terran and former Peacekeeper. The paramedic nodded his thanks. "Oh, by the way, that Peacekeeper is downstairs asking for you." His contempt for the major was clear in his tone. Too tired to take issue with him, Jamal and Zaria went down to greet the major.

After re-programming the quilombo's main receivers, the major had left the Tariq to join a search party looking for survivors at the badly damaged bibliotek, the region's major reference center. No one had talked to him about his change of heart. He had wanted to help with relief efforts and that had been taken at face value. Earlier, Jamal had offered him a place to sleep for the night, and he had returned. He stood just outside the cottage, exhausted and alone, black uniform caked in red mud, chestnut stubble shading his jaw.

Jamal led him through the room that had earlier served as his cell. Three quake victims lay on cots, their accusing stares tracking the major's self-conscious movements. A dozen others, propped on cushions on the floor, glowered at the major. Jamal said firmly, "Major! Looks like you've been on a dig. The comnet's working fine. We just turned off the comcast."

The major shook his head slowly. "Guess you've given up on your furniture."

Jamal paused in confusion. "You were worried my blood would stain it," the major said with a tight smile. Jamal, now beset by questions coming from the room of injured about the comcast, had no time to answer the major. How many were dead? they wanted to know. How many injured? How many homeless? What was the damage? What was being done about relief? What was the government going to do? What about the Consortium? Was there news of this one's partner, that one's son?

Zaria took the major by the arm and led him to the patio, away from the voices. She pressed the button on the wall and the door slid shut behind them. "Imhotep has declared us a disaster area," she said. "They're sending in relief supplies and workers. And they want an official apology from the Peacekeepers, who still deny they jammed us."

"They're lying."

"We know that," she said. "Everyone does. But there isn't much we can do about it."

She wondered if he would be willing to tell the public what he knew of the jamming, but before she could ask, she saw someone walking into the courtyard.

A young blond man wearing a paramedic jumpsuit stepped up to them.

Hanif Bjorndahl. "Well, well," she mumbled, ignoring the major's perplexed look, "just in time."

Bjorndahl's face wore a look of determination. "Hello, Zaria," he said briskly, intending to forge past them.

"Hanif?" Zaria blocked his path. "Glad to see no harm has come to you. Can the hospital spare you?"

"The hospital sent me."

"Good. I guess things are calming down a bit."

"Somewhat," he said, trying unsuccessfully to get past.

"This is Major Leith Eaglefeather of the Peacekeepers," Zaria said, waving her hand in the major's direction.

Bjorndahl did not look at the major. "Excuse me," he said to Zaria.

"Hanif," she pleaded, her green eyes fixed on his. "Please."

"He won't believe me."

The major watched, frowning.

"What have you got to lose?" she asked.

"Bjorndahl? Corporal Hanif Bjorndahl?" the major interrupted, his face alight with recognition. "I read about you. You're listed as missing in action."

"Is that so?" Bjorndahl asked, bristling.

"Yes." The major felt too tired to make an issue of Bjorndahl's desertion.

"Tell him, Hanif. He's got to know."

Bjorndahl sighed. "I worked with Major Reynolds, your predecessor. I did not agree with many of her, uh, methods."

"Such as?"

"Her interrogation techniques." Bjorndahl glanced at Zaria, who nodded for him to go on.

"Yes? Go on," the major urged.

"She used torture to get information and confessions."

"I assume by that you mean she mistreated prisoners. Did you report her?"

Bjorndahl sighed again. "No, sir. I mean, no, sir, that's not what I meant. When I said torture, I meant torture."

"All the more reason to report her to Major Stojic or the colonel, if what you say is true."

"The colonel knew, sir." In the face of the major's presumption of authority, Bjorndahl had suddenly become submissive. Peacekeeper training ran deep.

The major hesitated before his next question. "Just what are we talking about here?"

With a nod, Zaria prompted Bjorndahl. "Tell him, Hanif."

"She set up a special interrogation room, in the docking section, Compartment Two. She put in a neuro-link, operated from a control console in an adjacent room. The link stimulates the brain's pain centers. The victim feels intense pain, but there's no tissue damage, nothing shows."

The major kept his voice level. "I've heard that some Palmarans claim that the base has such a device, but I didn't believe them and I don't believe you."

"I assure you, Major, it exists. It has been used. Many times."

"On whom?"

"People Major Reynolds considered terrorists. Those who lived through it were shipped to prison camps on the asteroid belt near Jupiter."

"So you have no proof?"

Zaria spoke up. "A year ago, we liberated two Kituhwa comrades en route to a prisoner transport headed off-planet. In their debriefing, they told us they had been tortured with the device. Even we doubted their story, thinking they were suffering from some kind of post-traumatic disorder. You see, the technique leaves no physical scars behind. The symptoms of stress are not significantly different from those of any former prisoner. We were prepared to dismiss the matter, when Corporal Bjorndahl walked into the quilombo."

Bjorndahl continued, "I couldn't stand it any more. I saw a woman being tortured to death. I had warned them. She was old, had a weak heart. They wanted to know about her daughter. The death certificate read natural causes. I left that day."

"You didn't report this to anyone?"

"Like I said, the colonel knew."

"You could have gone over his head."

Bjorndahl shook his head and turned to Zaria. "I told you he wouldn't believe me."

"Major," Zaria insisted, "this goes well beyond Colonel Welch and the Peacekeepers at Simcoe. Only the Peacekeepers' high command on Earth could have developed such a device. And that would have required secret funding. My guess is that the Terran government contracted with the Consortium to build and test it here on Palmares."

"That's a big jump," the major said. "I can believe that the Consortium is corrupt and that the Peacekeepers stationed here are their willing accomplices. But you're suggesting a Terran conspiracy. When I get back to the base, I'll certainly look into his charges about Major Reynolds. But as for the Terran government . . ." He turned to Bjorndahl. "Come back with me, Corporal. I can help you cut a deal, get the charges against you dropped if you agree to testify against Colonel Welch."

Bjorndahl stepped back and shook his head vehemently. "I'm not going back, Major. Never. My life is here now." Then he quickly stepped inside Jamal's house.

Zaria's look made the major uncomfortable. "I might not be able to do much about this if he won't agree to come back with me."

Her hands slapped her sides in exasperation. "What does it take, Major? What does it take?"

His face flushed with anger, he squinted in the sunlight. "What do you want me to do?"

She frowned. "Your ancestors were indigenous North Americans. You must have read your history."

"My history?" he said, puzzled by the sudden change of topic.

"Do you remember anything about the struggles against the Europeans?"

"What's that got to do with this?"

"As people after people encountered the Europeans, they debated what to do. Whether to respond peacefully or violently. Whether to cooperate or resist. Whether to be assimilated, or not. Some peoples cooperated. Some resisted peacefully, others not so peacefully. Some withdrew to other territory, even as the land shrank before them till there was nowhere to go. Different people had different responses. And not one worked. They were decimated. In some cases, entire civilizations disappeared."

"Your point being?"

She regarded him soberly. "There are only fifteen million people on this planet, Major. Whether we fight openly or not, we don't stand a chance against Terran Peacekeepers."

"You think it will come to that?"

"It has."

"If you're right, then whatever I do will make no difference to the outcome of your struggle."

"That could be true. But some of us don't feel as if we have a choice. We take a stand, because we have to."

"Did you save my life in the hope I would join you?"

"That was Sixto's hope."

"But you gave the order that kept me alive. Why?"

She wasn't sure herself what the answer was. "I don't know. I just— I couldn't let them kill you." She turned away.

"Ho, there!" called Sixto, from the distance. He sprinted toward them, a cloth sack bouncing over one shoulder. Bounding onto the patio, he kissed Zaria's lips with a smack.

Zaria turned back to look at the major, her arms folded across her chest. Glancing from one to the other, Sixto stepped back from Zaria.

"Seems I intercepted something."

The major said nothing.

"We just talked to Hanif," Zaria explained. "Our major here is, shall we say, skeptical."

"I see," Sixto said.

She wondered if he really did. "I have work to do. See you later," she said to Sixto and went inside.

from *Red Spider, White Web*

MISHA

(1990)

> My people will sleep for one hundred years, but when they awake,
> it will be the artists who give them their spirit back.
> —*Louis Riel (Métis)*

MISHA NOGHA (MÉTIS) has published numerous short stories with Oregon's Native press, Wordcraft, which featured the novel *Red Spider, White Web* in its Wordcraft Speculative Writers Series. She is well regarded in the sf field, and her short story "Chippoke Na Gomi" (1989) was featured in the 2010 *Wesleyan Anthology of Science Fiction,* putting Misha in the company of "over a 150 years' worth of the best science fiction ever collected in a single volume."

"As a Métis who cut my ideological teeth on the Rebellion of Louis Riel, I am naturally attracted to Science Fiction," says Misha. "As sf writer Philip K. Dick put it, 'Writing sf is a way to rebel.' SF is a rebellious art form, and it needs writers and readers and bad attitudes—an attitude of 'Why?' or 'How come?' or 'Who says?' Carrying the tribal heritage of Métis, 'People Who Own Themselves' or people who belong to no one, or feral, I am a rebel and a renegade shapeshifter, changing my skin every hour and walking between the red earth and blue sky; a violet integration of two worlds, yet belonging to neither."

In *Red Spider, White Web,* Indigenous tribalism interpenetrates the cyberpunk and postcyberpunk face of neotribalism, to borrow from Michel Maffesoli's discussion of our postmodern landscape in *The Time of the Tribes* (1996). As cultural institutions begin to fail serving their traditional purposes, according to Maffesoli, nostalgia will lead people to fill the vacuum with old ways, including social formations that recall tribal society. Certainly in this novel, new tribes proliferate: the Pinkies, the wiggers, the zombies, the Mikans, and even the artists. Here Misha's take on neotribalism reminds one of other sf luminaries, such as Neal Stephenson's phyles in *Diamond Age* (1995) and his steampunk story "Excerpt from the Third and Last Volume of *Tribes of the Pacific Coast*" (1995), and, of course, the numerous tribes and bands that form and fade within weeks in the Sprawl, a dystopic environment pervasive in William Gibson's trilogy, *Neuromancer* (1984), *Count Zero* (1986), and *Mona Lisa Overdrive* (1988). Misha's neotribes also resemble *bosozoku,* speed tribes or underground versions of Japanese subculture often linked to the Yakuza, as Karl Taro explains in *Speed Tribes: Days and Nights with Japan's Next Generation* (1995).

In this future, reservations do exist, but they are closed, the ghost-haunted realm of genetic tribes who lived on Nature Conservancy lands. In fact, all things rural are disappearing, as one Native artist, Tommy, declares: "There's nothing out there but those closed-down genetic reservations, frozen deserts and howling winds."

Kumo, a Native female artist and the Red Spider of the narrative, discovers that Tommy and she are not simply genetic experiments, but rather "twins of the same litter." These two artists illustrate Donna Haraway's concept of the cyborg as an amalgam of animal-human-machine: Tommy is thought to consist of stolen metal and skin, invoking Takayuki Tatsumi, who connects postmodern sensibilities with a so-called metallocentric imagination in the provocative examination of the "Japanoid" fusion of Japanese American culture in *Full Metal Apache* (2006). With her wolverine masks (recalling the layered masks of kabuki theater and the Native masks seen in Gerald Vizenor's *Darkness in St. Louis: Bearheart*), her feral musk-scent that both repels and attracts, her sinuous movements more animal than human, her body casing with Neoyakuza Yugi's tattooed spider of eight legs on her back, Kumo is both insect and predatory mammal to colleagues and artists.

In this excerpt, the postwar aesthetics of kitsch and appropriation
of Native art forms are powerfully undermined as Kumo heads to market for another day. Misha has this to say about the selection:

> In RSWW I investigated a couple of my favorite themes. First,
> I wanted to write a modern trickster tale (in truth all my fic-
> tional characters are modern tricksters). I also wanted to make
> a social commentary about the great corporate windigo, postu-
> late the fate of humanimals, cyber people, and enhanced human
> beings, and question what makes a human, human. So in RSWW
> I created Kumo, a modern trickster who is a product of gene
> splicing of human and wolverine DNA. An experiment started
> and then dropped by corporate scientists, she and others like
> her were left to fend on their own, without help, without hope,
> and without an identity. Kumo is a totally disenfranchised crea-
> ture, disrespected and disowned by the very world that created
> her. In order to survive, to tell her story, to share her vision, she
> becomes a free-range, feral, and *non-government-approved* artist.
> While Kumo honors her animal side *and* her human side through
> her art, she strives to transcend her genetics and create good
> things for all "peoples." In this scene at the market she is wearing
> layer upon layer of shape-shifter masks, each of which is stripped
> away to reveal her true essence, a new creature, of flesh and
> spirit, a sort of—humanimal. Kumo also shows her trickster self
> in this scene, and like most tricksters, the joke is just as much on
> herself as it is on her audience. Like me, Kumo is a sport, a rebel
> and a renegade by genetics and by nature.

At LaurelHurst Station 508, the gates were already open. Even the
stoic Motler showed signs of nervousness at the piked, iron slats. The
train tracks led in at one gateside and concrete pedestrian tracks led
in at another. The skin visible beneath Motler's eyepieces was shiny
with sweat. His animalistic mask looked spooked. He whispered to
Kumo, "I don't like them wiredogs."

Kumo nodded and glanced up at the airborne police dogs, clever
surveillance devices to keep riots under control. Every pair of cops on
a beat had one.

She looked up at the crest atop the gates, a dancing rocky mountain goat in flaking white paint on a green and orange insignia. Just beyond the gates lay pick-up sticks of rusted rails, wheels, scrapped engines, twisted, graffiti-covered boxcars, leaf springs, and stacks of rotting ties. Floating over the station were two green and orange fabric tubes, gigantic wind socks that wriggled with the current.

"Calling heaven, calling heaven. Over." Motler joked.

Suddenly, an artist carrying a mask came running out of the gates, slammed into Kumo, and darted off to the left. Kumo rolled away to get out of the path of booted, strobing Friendly Navvy police. A sudden burst of fire and a scream made Kumo wince.

She stood up slowly. "Kerist," she said, picking up the red mask that had fallen in the impact. She held it out to Motler. It was Carmelo's.

Motler knocked it out of her hand as if it were poisonous. "That poor sucker was off it. Jerk causing trouble for the lot of us." Motler was coolly irritated.

Kumo bit the inside of her cheek and held back a hard lump in her throat. She glanced at Motler, cataloging all this new bright data. She didn't have anything to say.

The tracks before them were cluttered with the sorry hulks of the abandoned trains, so she got onto the sidewalk and went in through the gates.

"Pauvre. Carmelo-o-o," she hissed under her breath. She jerked the strings of her emotions upright. She could mawk about it later, not at market. "You can call heaven all ya want, Mot, but something tells me this ain't it."

Motler nodded, and cleared his throat. "Better make yer offering pretty quick."

Kumo snorted. A group of Dogton garbage distributors walked by and jeered at them.

"Low-life scum. Poison!" they shouted, without much conviction. Dogtons usually only made market on Thursdays and Saturdays.

Once past the initial gates, they both had to stop and stare. "Well, well, well, Kumo, looks like your holo was accepted after all."

As they watched, a giant white-skinned holo of a woman opened her thighs so they could walk right into the black cunt which led into the art show.

Kumo gave a tiny nod of satisfaction as she went through the contracting, holographic door.

Once inside she stopped and took a deep breath. Her palms sweated and her heart ran up against her chest and she trembled violently. She was suddenly seized with the urge to turn and run. Instead, she went straight to the bay of the huge station. The place was already swarming with craftsmen, and punctuated here and there by real artists.

A rack of magnetic pool balls clattered by, rolled up the sides of the lockers, rushed back down again, split up and careened off in various directions.

"Dammit—late again," Kumo muttered under her breath. "Wot's it matter?" Motler was coming on to automatic. Once past the initial nervousness of Navvys and wiredogs, as well as the sharp jolt of Ramirez's demise, he was content. He lived for the market.

An eight-wheeled bicycle of blue argon lights hurtled by, and Kumo jumped back to miss being run down by it.

She stepped over one of Dori's pieces, a huge matrix of transparent tubing, shaped into a human circulation system full of hot pink "blood" that covered a good twenty feet of the station floor.

Duke's "living marine life" swam through the crowd. Holographic jellyfish bobbed while snub-nosed sharks whipped their tails and circled. Kumo liked this display best of all, never tired of the weaving fish.

Through all this, Kumo followed on Motler's boot heels. Nobody stayed in his way.

"I have to fight for a fucking booth spot every market day."

"Set it up next to mine then," Motler spoke tersely.

Kumo followed Motler to his locker and watched as he pulled all of it out in a heap. The echoes of voices, laughter, cursing, dropped metal and shouts all slammed into Kumo's ears and she shuddered in revulsion. The old smell of unwashed bodies, of clone leathers, of cigarettes and synthetic sushi clammed onto her senses like a wet blanket. She detested the actual market with the very fabric of her soul. Yet here was the only legal place left for her to make art.

Kumo pulled back into real-time, stared at the stinking apparatus of Motler and laughed, "Fuck that. I can't stand the stench of your genius."

"Sissy," Motler snarled at her, knowing Kumo usually rose to a tease.

A kinetic sculpture, a sort of rubber wave, undulated past them. It was one of Carmelo's.

"No, forget it—whatever poor cadavers you're grinding up in that display of yours—I don't want to see or smell em." Her lips curled back against her red gums. She thought of Carmelo once again and shuddered. He bought his one-way ticket. Did she admire him for that?

She lifted her head and sniffed.

"I ain't doing that right now. I ain't chopping up the rats' livers," Motler protested with great feeling. He had this toy, this new thing he was doing that he wasn't telling Kumo about. He'd gotten bits of machinery, a *Brain Box,* from Tommy who'd scarfed it from a junk pile at the Bell Factory.

Kumo sensed the whole market was sooty with fear.

Motler grabbed his booth set-up. It was uniquely Motler's—nobody else would dare touch it because of his art with the rats. The rats' livers were chopped up and boiled. The steam emitting from them was run through a spectrograph. The rats killed by poison showed some violent colorations. "Nah, lately been beating out masterpieces with canvas and acid. I kinda airgun it on." He smiled thinking of the brain machine.

Kumo snorted, "Metzger did the same in London—1961."

Motler growled, "Wal his canvas weren't made of clone skin now was it?"

Kumo shrugged. "So yours smells worse. Who's center attraction for today, eh?"

"David's set, eh? Yeah—that bloody hermie is damn good too." Motler got a soft look in his eyes.

Kumo nodded. "I'm setting my booth over by the brick steps. On the other side of the stadium from you, Motler."

"All right then—I'll give ya a hand—since I kept you late with gabbing." It was his way of saying sorry about Ramirez.

"Okay—you meet me back here after you've set up." Kumo was uncertain. She liked to work with Motler—worried about depending on him too much. She thought about the project they were working on together, a chill ran down her back.

"See ya kid. I hate setting up. If only the fucking bastards would let us leave the stuff up instead o' tearing it down every time," he grumbled as he strode off dragging his equipment and making the sounds of a pup with cans tied to its tail.

Kunio said nothing, turned and headed toward her locker in a nervous, slinking walk. The back of her head was throbbing, her tongue was burnt, and her throat hurt from the chicken-shit, Pink Fly. She was glad for the shark-skin which made her whole body a weapon. She'd fought Pinkies before and didn't relish it. She planned to stop the escalation by hitting the Pinks hard the first chance she got.

She slammed her code-key into the scarred, steel doors. They showed no new signs of a break-in but there was a dried bloody streak under the lock. The door popped open. To her relief it was all there, her holographic material with the chips of data, her permit for selling and her gaudy market mask.

She took a small pot of oil and a rag and smoothed her scuffed, clone-leather outfit. It was a sort of black-brown one-piece and the leather was patterned and molded to the shape of exposed muscle tissue. Across the stomach and other vulnerable areas Kumo had sewn some metal clasps and buckles. Over her head she pulled the heavy native-style market mask. It was a black wolverine head with yellow stripes. It was hinged on four sides. Attached to the hinges were strings that ran down the sleeves of the performer and tied to the middle finger. When the finger was jerked, the strings pulled the hinges and they would spring open. Under the top layer, a second and third mask could be revealed. She straightened it on her shoulders.

The pianist, David, shook his/her head, as s/he watched Kumo put on her disturbing mask.

"You look obscene," s/he called to Kumo as she walked up. Behind, him/her, a group of artists pushed a genuine acoustic piano to the market center.

Kumo pinned him/her with the wolverine's furious, painted eyes.

David's pale face blushed and his/her heavy-lashed lids closed softly over gray eyes. A concert pianist—disowned by family because of his/her sexual gender—that is—both genders. His/her full pouting mouth took in the station with a hunger and horror. S/he coughed.

"Better get something for that cough—" Kumo scolded. "S'koshi has algae syrup."

David made a gagging noise and Kumo laughed.

"It was Swanie, you know . . ." Tears glassed David's eyes and s/he gave a shuddering sigh.

"Hai, what of it?" Kumo interrupted with irritation. The pain in her gut returned, sharp, as if she had gulped glass shards. She knew perfectly well Swanie was David's current.

"What of it! It was Swanie, that's what." S/he looked at her so desperately Kumo wanted to smash David's face. It was stupid to become attached here—in this place.

Station bells announced the opening of artists' market and David began to move off. S/he paused. "Did you finish those holos you promised me?" David gave Kumo a dove-eyed stare and put on his/her beautiful, white fox mask. David was wearing a bandoleer of shining white rat-skin purses. They were empty at the moment, and flapping in the brisk breeze that gusted through the market.

"Yeah, I finished em." Kumo tilted her head.

David blew her a kiss. "Bring them by tonight," s/he coaxed as s/he turned to walk away.

Kumo shrugged and gave David's rounded buttocks a hard stare. It was a little too close this time. She'd have to be more careful.

David turned back to her. "Yes, that's right, Mr. Kumi. Just what are you doing about all of this blood?"

Kumo spat. "Let the bastard howl after me and I'll send him home with his tail up his ass," Kumo hissed. She was tired of dealing with people, with David, Motler—the other artists.

The first thing she always did was have a look. She had her own way of finding out if dreams came true. Market was already in full swing. Chips were beaming out shards of bright, tinny music, cheesy organ chords, and synthesized calliopes, mixed with bells, flute and drums.

A huge cable of shiminawa, decorated with cloth, plastic fruit and origami papers, fluttered in the breeze. Strings of red, gold and blue dangled baubles of plastic koi, and the face of Daikoku. Lucky dice and shogi hung off the richer stalls. Ema boards fluttered off even the poorest stalls. All Kumo had for her stall were a few omamori for general good luck. In omamori, she didn't believe in specifics.

Through the crowd, she spied Tommy's karakura ningyo squeaking away on their recycled gears of wood and plastic. Most of their bodies were crafted from ancient enamel appliances. In groups of three, they jerked and crept. She sidled close to one and rapped on the top of its head.

An ancient piece of music, *Karakuri,* was wheedling out of its audio. Its huge, blue, headlight-eyes lit up.

"Konnichiwa! Hello! Wouldn't you like to take me home as your own private slave? I can do anything. I'm solar-powered. You can turn me off with this key." It dangled a chuck key in front of her. "Let's start home. Just give my price to this handsome red ningyo beside me."

The salesbot karakuri, lumbering and friendly looking, had a way of moving which discouraged vandalism or rip-off.

"Do you take messages?" Kumo asked it.

"Of course." The ningyo was beginning to wheel away.

"You tell Tommy this. Anta ga dame desu yo."

Some customer's children were shrieking and playing kagome and dragging synthsilk koi kites in the filth of the market. They surrounded the karakuri with squeals of delight.

Kumo moved toward the booths full of mingei, either Japanese or American folk art. She stopped and watched a potter wheel his pot in the old way. Even washi was offered here. Kumo stopped in front of a stall with rice paper, just as she did every market day, to stare. Paper, canvas, these things were so rare.

Kanda, the rice-paper artist, laughed at her. "Hey, you, Tanuki-girl, get away from that kozo. In a million years you could never afford this."

"Jitsu wa . . . you ought to be smart and buy that sign from me," Kumo insisted.

Kanda laughed, his black teeth showing through the mouth-hole of his papier mâché mask. "Why do I need holo shoji? I have the real thing right here." He showed her a beautiful rice-paper window. Kumo drooled and sucked the saliva back into her mouth.

"It looks like something to eat."

"You have the mouth of a tigress."

Kumo looked past Kanda for Kai—the kokeishi salesman.

"So where is Kai? He gave up on kokeishi?"

"No, no. Kai," Kanda motioned Kumo a little closer, "he has business in Chuugoku."

Kumo stared a second. "Yeah all right. That's good, eh? Very good. And what about you Kanda, you have business there too?" Just enough sarcasm had crept into her voice.

Kanda laughed. "Perhaps. I have a few cousins there. They have a lot of business. Maybe I see you there too."

Kumo shook her head. "Chuugoku-go o hanashitte imasen."

"That doesn't matter. Just speak Japanese."

Here Kanda laughed and threw something at her, a small, crumpled, blue tsuru. Kumo ducked, caught it in mid-air, and put it in her pocket.

"On second thought, this looks too good to eat," Kumo said and moved away. "Chuugoku de aimashoo!"

"Kono ama!" Kanda cursed her soundly, but with good intent.

People had gotten used to Kumo's trickster habits. She would heckle the GAP until they got mad enough to throw something at her to scare her off. Many of these craft artists, liking custom, just threw something as soon as she announced herself. Occasionally they threw rocks, filth, or cups of urine, but sometimes they threw a piece of ware she could sell later, or even a bite of edible food.

Kumo found what she was looking for today. Am empty stall that should have been selling Japanese wares. Every couple of days it was the same. Everyone had business in China—or somewhere else.

This was the rich end of market, the place where assistants to the Ningen Kokuho worked. Kumo frowned at the long line of real bamboo stalls, overflowing with color, good scents, and richly colored synthetic cloths. Of course all the folk crafts looked much the same as they had for years, both the Amerikan folk arts and the Japanese. Nothing had changed in the crafts. Kumo went to the stalls of the lacquerware artists, her second love, but she passed by quickly as she saw her favorite box, a make-i with a maple leaf and crescent moon, was sold now.

Kumo checked the government-approved art section as a matter of principle. She wanted to see who ripped her off, how and why. The customers were Mickey-san denizens temporarily bored with their eggsuits. Like terrible exotic birds, they dressed in gay costumes of brightly colored mawai robes worn over calf-length, close-fitting cotton pants. They flocked to the high-art stalls, with pieces of work, to consume or destroy.

Kumo searched the walls carefully for something even vaguely reminiscent of Dori. In the sixth cubicle she found it; a kinetic sculpture like a piece of caramel, tan and sweet, with a good clean line.

Satisfied, she bit back a smile and pushed through the crowd again. Her eyes were misty. No murderer had grabbed Dori, only an impersonal swindler.

Kumo stooped to look at a plastic limber jack, with its only wood a thin laminated plank. Amerikan folk art seemed somehow pitiful to the kana of the Japanese. She ran a gloved finger along the booth and then jumped when she heard a yell directed at her.

"Hey!"

Kumo thought, at first, that it was the artist who hollered. But he was looking at her from behind a sort of primitive cowboy bandanna mask. She nodded at that with approval. He jerked a thumb to one side and she looked over to see Mikans dashing toward her with lite mikes and ammi cameras. She jumped to one side and pushed through the crowd, too late. One Mikan grabbed her elbow firmly.

Kumo turned and hissed angrily. "Sawannai-de! Don't touch me."

She twisted her arm in the Mikan's grasp and he let go with a whiny "Owwww."

By then, four other Mikans had surrounded her and were sticking their ammi cams in her face.

"Hey, we just want a moment of your time—just a minute."

"Fuck off, Godkillers." Kumo shoved one backward, hard, but his friends caught him before he fell.

"Sister, you must talk to us," one of the Mikans pleaded with her. Kumo couldn't tell which; they were all identically dressed in tangerine coveralls with ninja masks. "You have to talk to us."

"It's no good," said another. "We know who you are." "Muko itte yo. Get lost, cream-dreams." KunHo stepped forward with yellow-jacket behavior, assertive—no-nonsense. One of the Mikans lowered his voice, spoke conspiratorially, "You are the Messiah's Mary Magdalene."

"*Nan*'?" Kumo hissed in confusion and annoyance, the bland, orange faces pressed at her like foam puppets. Kumo wanted to put them off, and fast.

"A curse on your mihon!" Kumo had had some trouble with Mikans before. Tommy had given her something to stop them, yet they were back, aiming their miserable ammi cams and lite mikes. Still, the Mikans faded like orange smoke. Kumo silently cursed the market and moved on. This, she thought grimly to herself, is a very unlucky day.

She went back to her locker, tiredly picked up her ungainly booth apparatus and dragged it to her usual spot. She gave an explosive hiss at yet another irritation.

A glass craftsman in a pierrot outfit was set up in her space. His droll, ceramic mask flashed in her direction, leveled a stare and turned back to the wares.

Kumo had already had a bit of trouble with the cops this month—but she was getting hungry, so she dropped the booth and a long, thin blade whispered open in her hand.

Before she pounced, Motler brushed past her and swept his meaty forearm across the glass counter. The shattering baubles masked the sound of the bottle breaking in his hand where jagged ends gleamed a warning.

"Dame-yo! No, no, no, we can't 'ave that," Motler bellowed. "This won't do. We can't have craftglass by the holographic imagery. Some poor customer might get confused and kick over yer stand thinking it were just a hologram."

The craftsman swore in fear and indignation. "Hey what do you think . . . ," he started to protest and saw the jagged end in Motler's bloody grip. Motler made a quick lunge and fabric and skin tore soundlessly. The craftsman's coverall was covered in Chinese blood-blossoms—now the only color on the grey morning.

A Friendly Navvy sauntered over but his suit-strobe was off.

"Shokumujinmon?" he asked. "Kisoku ihan da yo?"

"No, there ain't no trouble, officer," Motler replied casually. "This fine gentleman and I were helping this young lady set up her booth and he accidentally knocked over a tray of jam jars."

"Soji o shinasai! Clean it up!" he ordered. The craftsman hesitated, so the Navvy took an aggressive step forward. "Itta tori ni shiro yo!"

"Hail," said the craftsman, tossing Motler an obscene gesture and slinking off to search for some cleaning device.

The Navvy stood staring at Kumo a moment—then moved off. Motler was a favorite with all of them. He shamelessly bullshitted all the cops, entertained the artists with stories and songs, and made more money than all the rest put together. A bullet-ridden television set on ancient *Ratbone* wheels took the place the cop vacated.

"Konnichiwa. Hi there. Need a hand? Puis-j'aider? Do you want some help?"

"Shove off," Motler muttered and kicked the screen with a heavy boot. It cracked and the set wobbled on in the wake of the cop.

A few seconds later some styrofoam floats in geometric shapes came by, whistling. "Hey—over there! Look over here!"

The glass craftsman went back over to the far section of the market—away from the artists' quarter. Kumo watched his absurd costume weaving in and out of the artists and craftsmen. She marked him well because she knew she'd be seeing him again. Probably when she least expected it.

Motler hawked and spat. "Wot's that asshole doing? Any tame cat in a circus knows his own spot."

Kumo shrugged, she was overwhelmed and embittered by the morning and already grimly predicting she'd sell no chips this day. No chips, no food, damn.

Motler sensed her tiredness and helped put up the stand without a word. Hers was a simple affair with a holoflag consisting of a trio of red and white koi swimming in circles above her booth. The sights and the sounds of the market pressed in on her so she let Motler do the job of setting up the chips and sound equipment and roping off the area to alert customers that inside that braided boundary—anything might happen.

"Motler, anta wa mimashita o Dori-san desu ka?" She gave him a straight stare.

He shook his head slowly. "Not a sign of her, I hope she ain't orffed by that maniac." He gave Kumo a brief look of affection. "You know, I reckon that mask actually improves your image. Come on over later— I've got something I want to show you." Motler patted her shoulder.

"Sure." Kumo nodded, but she had no intention of doing so. Something was different about Motler. And she had a feeling he knew all about Dori but wouldn't tell her. Kumo felt at once sad and depressed. "Arigato," she added as he walked away. A gleam caught her eye and she stooped down. A piece of broken glass was on the ground, a paperweight halved. One side was totally crushed, the other somewhat chipped. It had an S-shaped pattern in the crystal hemisphere. She kicked it and it skittered under her booth.

Across the market, she could hear a passel of brats on a field trip, cruising the displays. These kodomotachi had no manners and had virtual free rein out of class. The harried sensei herded them along, but didn't attempt much more. Kumo could hear metal falling and some controlled cursing.

Kumo put up a holo sequence. She smiled with irony as the first image came up, a large carafe of red, plum wine. It suddenly exploded and some near passers-by ducked from the shards of light dangerously spraying in every direction. A solid pane of glass formed then shattered, as if by bullet impact. The holo zoomed on the image, a spun-sugar spider web. A soft spider climbed the web, froze into white crystals and fell. The white spider was in the shadow of the white web. She stood staring at it a moment.

The group of schoolkids in padded olive jackets and white cloth masks came squealing to her roped area and dived under and over it like a mass of squirming pollywogs. Their mouths were stuffed with Hello Kitty bubblegum and Golden Boy stick candy. They fastened their steely eyes on Kumo's spider. She swallowed a mouthful of envious saliva. She knew they were just making the rounds. Her number had drifted into their clammy, white hands. She hissed and grimaced ferally to the guardians who stood outside the rope, clutching it nervously.

"Go ahead now, children—ask." The tallest of the guardians spoke up. She pushed the children slightly forward and they made the merest of bows.

"Tell us about your youth!!" they shouted in unison with harsh, metallic voices.

She sneered at them. "When I was young we lived on a reservation," she said in a low conspiratorial voice.

"Liar, liar!!" the brittle little clams screamed.

"It's true. We had a cow, that's right, a fat cow. And golden horses." The image was all too real for Kumo. She longed for it like the taste of wild strawberries—a taste that was missed and could not be synthesized with any satisfaction.

"Nyahhh haaaah! And Henny Penny?" they jeered.

"Yes, and fat white chickens, with hair on their feet. And they laid blue and pink eggs." The white spider faltered, metamorphosed into a giant white rooster.

"Filthy liar!!" The chorus echoed throughout the station. The children jumped up and down pointing at her. David was walking by and stopped to stare at the rooster and the kids.

"I slit the scrawny necks of chickens and lapped the blood." The rooster's head flew off and a shower of vermilion splashed down in harmless light.

The children all screamed and yelled for the Friendly Navvys but the flak-jacketed officers skirting the edges of the market only gave them cold stares. David shook his/her mask and Kumo grimaced and jerked her head at the Navvys. Sometimes she felt it was difficult to tell which of them were actual humans and which were the aerial watchdogs.

The children all screeched with laughter and ran to badger someone else. The teachers straggled behind.

She yelled after them. "And a black cat, a big black cat with no tail, no tail at all," she mumbled the last part. She was fuming, wished to spin them by the heads, their skinny necks all cracking in unison. The holograms and lasers sliced the dense market air. The odor of sanpuru oysters and sushi fell all around them in thick bars of green scent.

David trotted off.

Kumo heard a sound and spun around. One of the children was still standing there. He had taken his mask off and was staring at her with large black eyes. He had bit into a candy stick and half of it hung from his lip; the other half was in his fat fist.

"Hey kid," she said, a little edgily.

The boy looked at her with, Kumo knew, wonder. Kumo snorted. "Get lost, kid. Get after those other drone clones." She sniffed.

The kid didn't leave, he just stood there, staring, with his mouth open and the half stick of Golden Boy dangling from his sticky mouth.

"Hey, wanna see something son?" Kumo spoke with a hint of honey. The kid gave a tiny nod, as if a little breeze had rattled his head.

"You know why I wear this kinda mask, don't ya?" The kid let the breeze ruffle his head no.

Kumo's mask seemed to stare at him long and meaningfully, until he looked down and dragged his foot in the scurf. Then she edged toward him, squatting lower and lower as she walked so that she was almost on his level. She lifted her hands and began to dance, slowly and menacingly. The boy's hand and mouth let the broken rolls of candy fall. Kumo didn't react, though she noted it. A sharp note from a Japanese flute whistled shrilly and her mask sprang open.

The boy screamed and fell flat on his buttocks.

Kumo moved toward him and tilted her head so that he could see the second layer of masking. A pair of heavily clawed wolverine paws were resting over the face of the inner mask. Kumo sidled forward until she was leaning over the fallen boy. The paws jerked away from the inner mask so that another mask, a human face, was revealed.

The boy yelled again and put his hands over his face. He struggled with himself like this a moment, the wind swaying him like a young sapling. Then he put his hands down. His eyes were averted. He scrambled to his feet and dashed off into the crowd, blindly, slammed into an artist with a bristling insect mask, fell, jumped up again, and tore after the rest of the students. Probably, Kumo thought, wailing and sniffing all the way.

Kumo laughed dryly, and refastened her market mask. She bent down and picked up the sticky candy from the soot-blackened bricks. She wrapped the blue paper crane around it. Bangohan. Maybe ocha.

Flighty, bewildered, customers came to stare at the holos. They were mesmerized by the images, but uncertain. Unlike the craft, this high-art had no noticeable practical value. Kumo had many customers, but few buyers. She didn't hawk, but stared at them all balefully if they made too much noise and disturbed her while creating a new piece.

A couple of intense hours later, JuJube came by carrying a raft of daruma dolls. These were legless round dolls with red and gold coloration and blank white eyes. He threw them down next to her booth and held out his hand.

"I'm Mr. Ducats today, Kumi." He spoke in his sweetest sympathy-asking voice. Kumo had kept the mask open so the inner face showed.

Kumo whistled through her teeth in annoyance. "What the hell you doing that for—you crazy?"

"I can't seem to sell anything lately—my heart ain't in it." His shoulders slumped.

Kumo nodded. "You been one too many times to the Bell Factory?"

JuJube swallowed. "You won't say anything?"

"Course not." She gave him a look of disdain nevertheless.

Here it was create or die—even the Navvys went for that. Poor JuJube wouldn't last long.

"You selling?" He looked at her, hopeful as a tick. Very different from the JuJube at the bento stall.

"Hah!" Kumo couldn't care less about it in some ways. She only saw it as a performance anyway. She could lure them in—vampirize the energy—but rarely the pockets.

"I saw that guy over there staring at the white spider sequence." There was insect lust in Jujube's voice.

Kumo looked over, saw a thin, rich and rotten in a soft half-face mask—and spat. "He can't have it."

"Why not?" JuJube was hungry for this bite of commission.

Kumo tilted her head to show mistrust. "I don't like him."

JuJube pressed close to her and shook her arm. "Don't say that! You owe it to me, Kumo. Gimme 40 per cent."

An angry spark flew from her eyes—but she sighed and reached into her pocket. "All right gimme that daruma doll." She picked out a medium-sized one and drew a red slash across one blank eye. "For luck," she said, and tossed the doll back to JuJube.

JuJube nodded, looked at the credit board. It was up. He ran to Motler. If he could make it to the exchange before the money went down—he would make profit. Kumo looked at the smoke-colored man who wanted to buy her work. She'd sold to him before, several times. In fact, other than the genetics, who seemed to follow her with a kind of cult addiction, the grey man was her most frequent customer. He wore a mask that covered half his face, and an outfit of grey suede. He was driven in a grey aircar by two velvety-black guards. Of any one thing in Ded Tek, this man frightened her the most. She turned and looked full at him. The thin man stood, staring straight back at Kumo for awhile before fading away like mist.

If Kumo made credit she usually ran it herself, safe on account of Uchida's dog-killing device. But she didn't want to let JuJube down. The stench, cold, and clang of the Bell Factory still gelled in her mind. In the end, the day turned out better than it started. Kumo had a broken stick of candy for dinner, and the sale of a piece. She decided to take her good luck to Motler and so after putting up her stand, holos, and heavy market mask, she headed toward his stall.

On the far side of market she noticed she was moving parallel to a woman in a caramel-colored coat who walked swiftly and self-assuredly. A stray dog about its own business, she too was headed toward Motler's stand. Kumo followed from a safe distance.

The woman turned and slipped over to Motler's steaming display of rat's organs dipped in bioplast. She reached over and patted Motler on the back, and they began to talk earnestly and at length. Kumo noted this, wanting to join in the fun, but something held her back. The woman motioned Motler to leave with her and a call died on Kumo's lips as Motler laughed, throwing a tray full of reject clone eyes into the air. They flashed like silver as they tumbled down.

Across market, in a booth especially assigned to the Mikans, the ammi cam rolled, the Mikans talking to nothing—no one. The initial gasps and "Lord have mercies" died away, leaving only a special knowing look in each set of eyes.

Biskaabiiyang,
"Returning to Ourselves"

Terminal Avenue

EDEN ROBINSON

(1996)

> I made a very conscious decision to marry an Indian woman, who
> made a very conscious decision to marry me. Our hope: to give
> birth to and raise Indian children who love themselves. That is the
> most revolutionary act possible.
> —*Sherman Alexie*

AN ACCOMPLISHED AUTHOR of Aboriginal horror, reenvisioned Canadian gothic, and (post)colonial experimentations in works such as *Monkey Beach* (2000) and "Dogs in Winter" (from *Traplines,* 1998), Eden Robinson says, "Speculative fiction appeals to me in the free-for-all tumble of ideas you get to mash together. Sometimes it's incoherent and messy, but it's always fun."

"Terminal Avenue" engages Scott Bukatman's concept of the technosurrealism that underlies the nightmarish dream-worlds and phenomenological inside-the-mind-horror of recent genre-bending sf. It takes place in a near future after the Uprisings, when Native reserves have been Adjusted and Peace Officers prey on Indians caught outside their assigned urban areas. It plays with scientific understandings of black holes and event horizons, at once commenting on the metatextual level of language and typical sf tropes while satirizing the genre, much like William Gibson's "Gernsback Continuum" deconstructed and refurbished pulp sf and fantasy. Here in "Terminal Avenue," the witticism of whose life ends up in the black hole and who observes whom from a safe distance encompasses *biskaabiiyang* and the decolonizing of "returning to ourselves," as the alien worlds of the Peace Officers and the Aboriginals collide.

Beyond the imaginary glint of sf-futuristic worlds, the story explores the literalness of metaphor, a typical sf device, to implode this future tale with the traditional Heiltsuk sense of parallel worlds appearing on the horizon, so that the historically forbidden potlatches of the 1880s, the severe government crackdown on Native practices in the 1920s, and the military-peace-keeping restrictions at Oka of the early 1990s literally "reappear" at Surreycentral in genuine cosmological opposition to the robin's egg blue uniform world: Indigenous worlds and perceptions might as well *be* the moon to anyone observing from the outside.

Robinson offers a snapshot of violent oppression glossed by reflections that reveal the colonized state of mind. Events in the narrative span no more than a few minutes: From the closing line of the second paragraph ("The uniforms of the five advancing Peace Officers are robin's egg blue, but the slanting light catches their visors and sets their faces aflame") to the closing line of paragraph fifty-eight ("The Peace Officer raises his club and brings it down"), we are privy to the memories and musings of Wil, a Native Canadian who suffers a beating because he's transgressed the physical boundaries imposed on Indians, in order to visit a nightclub called Terminal Avenue. There he is used to putting on a show for voyeuristic white patrons, in which he is strip-searched, beaten, and abused as part of their evening's entertainment: "He knows that he is a novelty item, a real living Indian: that is why his prices are so inflated. He knows there will come a time when he is yesterday's condom." The masochistic impulses that drive Wil from Vancouver Urban Reserve #2 through dangerous, off-limits areas to meet his dominatrix lover at the nightclub are fundamental to his Indian identity. Defeat and adaptation, in fact, are central ingredients to the story, as every male Native portrayed—Wil's father, his brother Kevin, and Wil himself—suffers physical abuse at the hands of the automaton Peace Officers. It is as if Wil's turn has finally come around.

The story concludes with Wil's memories of a boat ride to a secret potlatch in Kitamaat, where the familiar and comforting images of

Native self-conscious traditionalism can unfold (albeit clandestinely, so that government aircraft cannot detect the ceremony) one final time before the family moves to Vancouver "to earn a living." "This is the moment he chooses to be in, the place he goes to when the club flattens him to the Surreycentral tiles. He holds himself there, in the boat with his brother, his father, his mother."

Will this beating kill him or simply "adjust" him after the example of so many others? Or is it, in fact, Wil's way of seeking restoration, in the Heiltsuk spirit of *hailikila,* "healing." Wil's choice not to back down from the beating suggests the possibility of overcoming the psychological denial of the brutality and violence facing urban Aboriginals on Terminal Avenue in Vancouver. His further choice to be transported to a parallel world of ceremonial tradition (far outweighing any pretenses of other-government-specified "sovereignty") suggests this intrinsic Heiltsuk/Haisla healing, a way of transcending mere bodily existence to seek a life of self-respect and awareness.

His brother once held a peeled orange slice up against the sun. When the light shone through it, the slice became a brilliant amber: the setting sun is this color, ripe orange.

The uniforms of the five advancing Peace Officers are robin's egg blue, but the slanting light catches their visors and sets their faces aflame.

*

In his memory, the water of the Douglas Channel is a hard blue, baked to a glassy translucence by the August sun. The mountains in the distance form a crown; *Gabiswa,* the mountain in the center, is the same shade of blue as his lover's veins.

She raises her arms to sweep her hair from her face. Her breasts lift. In the cool morning air, her nipples harden to knobby raspberries. Her eyes are widening in indignation: he once saw that shade of blue in a dragonfly's wing, but this is another thing he will keep secret.

*

Say nothing, his mother said, without moving her lips, careful not to attract attention. They waited in their car in silence after that. His father and mother were in the front seat, stiff.

Blood plastered his father's hair to his skull; blood leaked down his father's blank face. In the flashing lights of the patrol car, the blood looked black and moved like honey.

*

A rocket has entered the event horizon of a black hole. To an observer who is watching this from a safe distance, the rocket trapped here, in the black hole's inescapable halo of gravity, will appear to stop.

To an astronaut in the rocket, however, gravity is a rack that stretches his body like taffy, thinner and thinner, until there is nothing left but x-rays.

*

In full body-armor, the five Peace Officers are sexless and anonymous. With their visors down, they look like old-fashioned astronauts. The landscape they move across is the rapid transit line, the Surreycentral Skytrain station, but if they remove their body-armor, it may as well be the moon.

The Peace Officers begin to match strides until they move like a machine. This is an intimidation tactic that works, is working on him even though he knows what it is. He finds himself frozen. He can't move, even as they roll towards him, a train on invisible tracks.

*

Once, when his brother dared him, he jumped off the high diving tower. He wasn't really scared until he stepped away from the platform. In that moment, he realized he couldn't change his mind.

You stupid shit, his brother said when he surfaced.

In his dreams, everything is the same, except there is no water in the swimming pool and he crashes into the concrete like a dropped pumpkin. He thinks of his brother, who is so perfect he wasn't born, but chiseled from stone. There is nothing he can do against that brown Apollo's face, nothing he can say that will justify his inaction. Kevin would know what to do, with doom coming towards him in formation.

But Kevin is dead. He walked through their mother's door one day, wearing the robin's egg blue uniform of the great enemy, and his mother struck him down. She summoned the ghost of their father and put him in the room, sat him beside her, bloody and stunned. Against this Kevin said, I can stop it, Mom. I have the power to change things now.

She turned away, then the family turned away. Kevin looked at him, pleading, before he left her house and never came back, disappeared.

Wil closed his eyes, a dark, secret joy welling in him, to watch his brother fall: Kevin never made the little mistakes in his life, never so much as sprouted a pimple. He made up for it though by doing the unforgivable.

Wil wonders if his brother knows what is happening. If, in fact, he isn't one of the Peace Officers, filled himself with secret joy.

*

His lover will wait for him tonight. Ironically, she will be wearing a complete Peace Officer's uniform, bought at great expense on the black market, and very, very illegal. She will wait at the door of her club, Terminal Avenue, and she will frisk clients that she knows will enjoy it. She will have the playroom ready, with its great wooden beams stuck through with hooks and cages, with its expensive equipment built for the exclusive purpose of causing pain. On a steel cart, her toys will be spread out as neatly as surgical instruments.

When he walks through the door, she likes to have her bouncers, also dressed as Peace Officers, hurl him against the wall. They let him struggle before they handcuff him. Their uniforms are slippery as rubber. He can't get a grip on them. The uniforms are padded with the latest in wonderfabric so no matter how hard he punches them, he can't hurt them. They will drag him into the back and strip-search him in front of clients who pay for the privilege of watching. He stands under a spotlight that shines an impersonal cone of light from the ceiling. The rest of the room is darkened. He can see reflections of glasses, red-eyed cigarettes, the glint of ice clinking against glass, shadows shifting. He can hear zippers coming undone, low moans; he can smell the cum when he's beaten into passivity.

Once, he wanted to cut his hair, but she wouldn't let him, said she'd never speak to him again if he did. She likes it when the bouncers grab him by his hair and drag him to the exploratory table in the center of the room. She says she likes the way it veils his face when he's kneeling.

In the playroom though, she changes. He can't hurt her the way she wants him to; she is tiring of him. He whips her half-heartedly until she tells the bouncer to do it properly.

A man walked in one day, in a robin's egg blue uniform, and Wil froze. When he could breathe again, when he could think, he found her watching him, thoughtful.

She borrowed the man's uniform and lay on the table, her face blank and smooth and round as a basketball under the visor. He put a pain-stick against the left nipple. It darkened and bruised. Her screams were muffled by the helmet. Her bouncers whispered things to her as they pinned her to the table, and he hurt her. When she begged him to stop, he moved the painstick to her right nipple.

He kept going until he was shaking so hard he had to stop.

That's enough for tonight, she said, breathless, wrapping her arms around him, telling the bouncers to leave when he started to cry. My poor virgin. It's not pain so much as it is a cleansing.

Is it, he asked her, one of those whiteguilt things?

She laughed, kissed him. Rocked him and forgave him, on the eve-ning he discovered that it wasn't just easy to do terrible things to an-other person: it could give pleasure. It could give power.

She said she'd kill him if he told anyone what happened in the playroom. She has a reputation and is vaguely ashamed of her secret weakness. He wouldn't tell, not ever. He is addicted to her pain.

To distinguish it from real uniforms, hers has an inverted black tri-angle on the left side, just over her heart: asocialism, she says with a laugh, and he doesn't get it. She won't explain it, her blue eyes black with desire as her pupils widened suddenly like a cat's.

The uniforms advancing on him, however, are clean and pure and real.

*

Wil wanted to be an astronaut. He bought the books, he watched the movies and he dreamed. He did well in Physics, Math, and Sciences, and his mother bragged, He's got my brains.

He was so dedicated, he would test himself, just like the astro-nauts on TV. He locked himself in his closet once with nothing but a bag of potato chips and a bottle of pop. He wanted to see if he could spend time in a small space, alone and deprived. It was July and they had no air conditioning. He fainted in the heat, dreamed that he was floating over the Earth on his way to Mars, weightless.

Kevin found him, dragged him from the closet, and laughed at him.

You stupid shit, he said. Don't you know anything?

When his father slid off the hood leaving a snail's trail of blood, Kevin ran out of the car.

Stop it! Kevin screamed, his face contorted in the headlight's beam. Shadows loomed over him, but he was undaunted. Stop it!

Kevin threw himself on their dad and saved his life.

Wil stayed with their father in the hospital, never left his side. He was there when the Peace Officers came and took their father's statement. When they closed the door in his face and he heard his father screaming. The nurses took him away and he let them. Wil watched his father withdraw into himself after that, never quite healing.

He knew the names of all the constellations, the distances of the stars, the equations that would launch a ship to reach them. He knew how to stay alive in any conditions, except when someone didn't want to stay alive.

No one was surprised when his father shot himself.

At the funeral potlatch, his mother split his father's ceremonial regalia between Wil and Kevin. She gave Kevin his father's frontlet. He placed it immediately on his head and danced. The room became still, the family shocked at his lack of tact. When Kevin stopped dancing, she gave Wil his father's button blanket. The dark wool held his smell. Wil knew then that he would never be an astronaut. He didn't have a backup dream and drifted through school, coasting on a reputation of Brain he'd stopped trying to earn.

Kevin, on the other hand, ran away and joined the Mohawk Warriors. He was at Oka on August 16 when the bombs rained down and the last Canadian reserve was Adjusted.

Wil expected him to come back broken. He was ready with patience, with forgiveness. Kevin came back a Peace Officer.

Why? his aunts, his uncles, cousins, and friends asked.

How could you? his mother asked.

Wil said nothing. When his brother looked up, Wil knew the truth, even if Kevin didn't. There were things that adjusted to rapid change— pigeons, dogs, rats, cockroaches. Then there were things that didn't— panda bears, whales, flamingos, Atlantic cod, salmon, owls.

Kevin would survive the Adjustment. Kevin had found a way to come through it and be better for it. He instinctively felt the changes coming and adapted. I, on the other hand, he thought, am going the way of the dodo bird.

*

There are rumors in the neighborhood. No one from the Vancouver Urban Reserve #2 can get into Terminal Avenue. They don't have the money or the connections. Whispers follow him, anyway, but no one will ask him to his face. He suspects that his mother suspects. He has been careful, but he sees the questions in her eyes when he leaves for work. Someday she'll ask him what he really does and he'll lie to her.

To allay suspicion, he smuggles cigarettes and sweetgrass from the downtown core to Surreycentral. This is useful, makes him friends, adds a kick to his evening train ride. He finds that he needs these kicks. Has a morbid fear of becoming dead like his father, talking and breathing and eating, but frightened into vacancy, a living blankness.

His identity card that gets him to the downtown core says *Occupation: Waiter*. He pins it to his jacket so that no one will mistake him for a terrorist and shoot him.

He is not really alive until he steps past the industrial black doors of his lover's club. Until that moment, he is living inside his head, lost in memories. He knows that he is a novelty item, a real living Indian: that is why his prices are so inflated. He knows there will come a time when he is yesterday's condom.

He walks past the club's facade, the elegant dining rooms filled with the glittering people who watch the screens or dance across the dimly lit ballroom-sized floor. He descends the stairs where his lover waits for him with her games and her toys, where they do things that aren't sanctioned by the Purity laws, where he gets hurt and gives hurt.

He is greeted by his high priestess. He enters her temple of discipline and submits. When the pain becomes too much, he hallucinates. There is no preparing for that moment when reality shifts and he is free.

*

They have formed a circle around him. Another standard intimidation tactic. The Peace Officer facing him is waiting for him to talk. He stares up at it. This will be different from the club. He is about to become an example.

Wilson Wilson? the Officer says. The voice sounds male but is altered by computers so it won't be recognizable.

He smiles. The name is one of his mother's little jokes, a little defiance. He has hated her for it all his life, but now he doesn't mind. He is in a forgiving mood. *Yes, that's me.*

In the silence that stretches, Wil realizes that he always believed this moment would come. That he has been preparing himself for it. The smiling-faced lies from the TV haven't fooled him, or anyone else. After the Uprisings, it was only a matter of time before someone decided to solve the Indian problem once and for all.

The Peace Officer raises his club and brings it down.

*

His father held a potlatch before they left Kitamaat, before they came to Vancouver to earn a living, after the aluminum smelter closed.

They had to hold it in secret, so they hired three large seiners for the family and rode to Monkey Beach. They left in their old beat-up speedboat, early in the morning, when the Douglas Channel was calm and flat, before the winds blew in from the ocean, turning the water choppy. The seine boats fell far behind them, heavy with people. Kevin begged and begged to steer and his father laughingly gave in.

Wil knelt on the bow and held his arms open, wishing he could take off his lifejacket. In four hours they will land on Monkey Beach and will set up for the potlatch where they will dance and sing and say goodbye. His father will cook salmon around fires, roasted the old-fashioned way: split down the centre and splayed open like butterflies, thin sticks of cedar woven through the skin to hold the fish open, the sticks planted in the sand; as the flesh darkens, the juice runs down and hisses on the fire. The smell will permeate the beach. Camouflage nets will be set up all over the beach so they won't be spotted by planes. Family will lounge under them as if they were beach umbrellas. The more daring of the family will dash into the water, which is still glacier-cold and shocking.

This will happen when they land in four hours, but Wil chooses to remember the boat ride with his mother resting in his father's arm when Wil comes back from the bow and sits beside them. She is wearing a blue scarf and black sunglasses and red lipstick. She can't stop smiling even though they are going to leave home soon. She looks like a movie star. His father has his hair slicked back, and it makes him look like an otter. He kisses her, and she kisses him back.

Kevin is so excited that he raises one arm and makes the Mohawk salute they see on TV all the time. He loses control of the boat, and they swerve violently. His father cuffs Kevin and takes the wheel.

The sun rises as they pass Costi Island, and the water sparkles and shifts. The sky hardens into a deep summer blue.

The wind and the noise of the engine prevent them from talking. His father begins to sing. Wil doesn't understand the words, couldn't pronounce them if he tried. He can see that his father is happy. Maybe he's drunk on the excitement of the day, on the way that his wife touches him, tenderly. He gives Wil the wheel.

His father puts on his button blanket, rests it solemnly on his shoulders. He balances on the boat with the ease of someone who's spent all his life on the water. He does a twirl, when he reaches the bow of the speedboat and the button blanket opens, a navy lotus. The abalone buttons sparkle when they catch the light. She's laughing as he poses. He dances, suddenly inspired, exuberant.

Later he will understand what his father is doing, the rules he is breaking, the risks he is taking, and the price he will pay on a deserted road, when the siren goes off and the lights flash and they are pulled over.

At the time, though, Wil is white-knuckled, afraid to move the boat in a wrong way and toss his father overboard. He is also embarrassed, wishing his father were more reserved. Wishing he was being normal instead of dancing, a whirling shadow against the sun, blocking his view of the Channel.

This is the moment he chooses to be in, the place he goes to when the club flattens him to the Surreycentral tiles. He holds himself there, in the boat with his brother, his father, his mother. The sun on the water makes pale northern lights flicker against everyone's faces, and the smell of the water is clean and salty, and the boat's spray is cool against his skin.

from *Almanac of the Dead*

LESLIE MARMON SILKO

(1991)

> The Anglo-European analytic philosophy of rugged individualism,
> empiricism, logical positivism, and arid scientific objectivity—the
> philosophy that informs the secular side of Manifest Destiny—
> when put in contact with holistic, spiritual, telluric Indian culture,
> leads to a subversion of Western knowledge.
> —*Brewer E. Fitz*

IN *ALMANAC OF THE DEAD,* Leslie Marmon Silko (Laguna Pueblo)
rewrites the history of the Americas by predicting an Indigenous revolution that straddles the US and Mexican border. This transnational
revolutionary vision paradoxically combines collective political force
with distinct tribal autonomy, suggesting the kind of "tribal interna-
tionalism" that Shari M. Huhndorf discusses in *Mapping the Americas: The Transnational Politics of Contemporary Native Culture* (2009).
Fundamentally advancing a prophecy of the survival of Native rather
than European societies as a Marxist revolution in the hands of the
Indigenous, the novel finds its antecedent in precontact writings of
the Mayan codex (three surviving Maya screenfold books extant today).
It traces the stories of Lecha and Zeta, Yaqui women and leaders who
"possess large portions of a fourth Maya book, which survived the
five-hundred-year-war for the Americas."[1]

These keepers of the codex are detailing the final days of the 1990s on the cusp of transition to a new century. Published in 1992, the novel thus follows the early-eighties trend in cyberpunk to set sf tales in the near future rather than millennia removed. In Silko's projection, Indigenous peoples all over the Americas are converging: they come from the lake country of Canada, from the alleys of New Orleans and the swamps of Florida, from the islands of the Caribbean, representing a diversity of Native tribes and bands, Louisiana's Black Indians, and the descendants of rebel slaves of African and Native blood who together cross racial and national boundaries. Unnamed and unguarded millions pour over the borders, and no fences or walls will stop them. The growing influx of "illegal immigrants" constitutes "a Native American religious movement to reclaim the Americas from the destroyers," prompting the US government to make Tucson "command headquarters for all US military forces assembled along the Mexican border." Across the Southwest, law enforcement officials are empowered to stop all brown-skinned people to demand ID, foretelling the national contentiousness that Arizona created in 2010 with its controversial immigration policy proposals Senate Bill 1070 and House Bill 2779.

The codex originates as Mayan glyphs, but with each keeper's notes on the continuing history of the Indigenous peoples of America, the writing changes. Mayan was transcribed phonetically by Indians who had learned classical Spanish, then translated into Spanish, and finally, as the notebooks made their way in the twentieth-century to present-day Tucson, were translated into English typed out on a word processor. Soon enough, the implication follows, the Mayan prophecies will occupy cyberspace as well. It's worth noting how Silko links this emphasis on the literacy of Indigenous peoples to the Laguna Peublo:

> The king of Spain had granted the Laguna Pueblo people their land. The Laguna Pueblo people knew their land was protected by a land grant document from the king of Spain. The Anglo-Americans who swarmed into the New Mexico Territory after 1848 carried with them no such documents. The Pueblo people fared better then other tribes simply because of these documents. The land grant documents alerted the Pueblo people to the value of the written word; the old books of international law favored the holders of royal land grants. So, very early, the Pueblo people

realized the power of written words and books to secure legitimate title to tribal land.[2]

The knowledge of the past histories of fighting back and resistances throughout time is a necessary component of predicting the future, the real purpose of the almanac. The excerpt provided here once again invokes the Wovoka Ghost Dance to illustrate how time is on the Indigenous side despite Eurowestern misconceptions that the Ghost Dance failed because its effects were not immediate. Here, Silko chips away at global capitalism, as eco-terrorists share their plans to debilitate the space stations and biosphere penthouses that billionaire tycoons have launched into orbit in an effort to escape the failing Earth that their greed has consumed. Silko puts it succinctly in *Gardens in the Dunes* (1999): "The invaders made the Earth get old and want to die." In *Almanac of the Dead,* the fight for Indigenous land reclamation and tribal sovereignty is a matter of planetary survival.

Medicine Makers—Cures of All Kinds

Lecha could only shake her head in wonder. She had never seen German root doctors or Celtic leech handlers before. But most of the new-age spiritualists were whites from the United States, many who claimed to have been trained by 110-year-old Huichol Indians. Lecha searched the schedule of conference events for familiar names. Scheduled in the main ballroom that morning had been the following lectures:

> Tilly Shay, colonic irrigation therapist, editor of the *Clean Colon Newsletter,* discusses the link between chronic constipation in the Anglo-Saxon male and the propensity for violence
>
> The cosmic Oneness of Red Antler and White Dove (adopted members of the Abenaki Tribe). "Feel the nothingness of being through the emanating light of the sacred crystal."
>
> George Armstrong—Intuitive Training and Meditation Power Sites
>
> Jill Purcee—Tibetan Chanting
>
> Frank Calfer—Universal Experiential Shamanism

Lee Locke—Women's Spirituality

Himalayan Bells—A Rare Concert at 2 p.m., Poolside, Donations Soundscape, Rainbow Moods, Cosmic Connection, and the New Age: Where Next for Healing? 8 p.m., Tennis Courts.

It would have been difficult to overlook Wilson Weasel Tail's portion of the program schedule because it filled half the page. Lecha had to laugh; Weasel Tail really knew how to get people's attention:

Stop time!
Have no fear of aging, illness, or death!
Secrets of ancient Native American healing
Hopi, Lakota, Yaqui, others
Kill or cripple enemies without detection
Summon up armies of warriors' ghosts!

Lecha glanced at a clock: there was half an hour before Weasel Tail spoke. Lecha had felt her heart beat faster when she read the last line in Weasel Tail's program about summoning armies of ghosts. Who had spiritual possession of the Americas? Not the Christians. Lecha remembered their mother had forbidden old Yoeme to slander Christianity in their presence, but of course that had not stopped Yoeme from telling Lecha and Zeta anything she wanted when their mother wasn't around. According to old Yoeme, the Catholic Church had been finished, a dead thing, even before the Spanish ships had arrived in the Americas. Yoeme delighted in describing tortures and executions performed in the name of Jesus during the Inquisition. In a crude catechism book Yoeme had even showed them pictures, wood-block prints of churchmen burning "heretics" and breaking Jews on the wheel. Yoeme said the mask had slipped at that time, and all over Europe, ordinary people had understood in their hearts the "Mother Church" was a cannibal monster. Since the Europeans had no other gods or beliefs left, they had to continue the Church rituals and worship; but they knew the truth.

Yoeme said even idiots can understand a church that tortures and kills is a church that can no longer heal; thus the Europeans had arrived in the New World in precarious spiritual health. Christianity might work on other continents and with other human beings; Yoeme did not dispute those possibilities. But from the beginning in the Americas, the outsiders had sensed their Christianity was somehow inadequate in the face of the immensely powerful and splendid spirit beings who inhabited the vastness of the Americas. The Europeans had not been able to sleep soundly on the American continents, not even with a full military guard. They had suffered from nightmares and frequently claimed to see devils and ghosts. Cortés's men had feared the medicine and the procedures they had brought with them from Europe might lack power on New World soil; almost immediately, the wounded Europeans had begun to dress their wounds in the fat of slain Indians.

Lecha had not appreciated Yoeme's diagnosis of Christianity until she had worked a while as a psychic. Lecha had seen people who claimed to be devout believers with rosary beads in their hands, yet they were terrified. Affluent, educated white people, upstanding Church members, sought out Lecha in secret. They all had come to her with a deep sense that something had been lost. They all had given the loss different names: the stock market crash, lost lottery tickets, worthless junk bonds or lost loved ones; but Lecha knew the loss was their connection with the earth. They all feared illness and physical change; since life led to death, consciousness terrified them, and they had sought to control death by becoming killers themselves.

Once the earth had been blasted open and brutally exploited, it was only logical the earth's offspring, all the earth's beings, would similarly be destroyed. The international convention had been called by natural and indigenous healers to discuss the earth's crisis. As the prophecies had warned, the earth's weather was in chaos; the rain clouds had disappeared while terrible winds and freezing had followed burning, dry summers. Old Yoeme had always said the earth would go on, the earth would outlast anything man did to it, including the atomic bomb. Yoeme used to laugh at the numbers, the thousands of years before the earth would be purified, but eventually even the radiation from a nuclear war would fade out. The earth would have its ups and downs; but humans had been raping and killing their own nestlings at such a rate Yoeme said humans might not survive. The humans would not be a great loss to the earth. The energy or "electricity" of a being's spirit was not extinguished by death; it was set free from the flesh. Dust to dust or as a meal for pack rats, the energy of the spirit was never lost. Out of the dust grew the plants; the plants were consumed and became muscle and bone; and all the time, the energy had only been changing form, nothing had been lost or destroyed.

Lecha had to laugh to herself. The earth must truly be in crisis for both Zeta and Calabazas to be attending this convention. Calabazas must be getting old because he had been listening to his loco lieutenant, Mosca, who had wild stories about a barefooted Hopi with radical schemes, and new reports about the spirit macaws carried by the twin brothers on a sacred journey north accompanied by thousands of the faithful.

The hotel conference rooms and lobby areas were swarming with people of all ages and origins. Lecha could sense their urgency and desperation as they milled around ushers who collected ten dollars at the entrance of the ballroom where Wilson Weasel Tail was scheduled to speak. Lecha saw a hotel conference room full of women chanting over and over, "I am goddess, I am goddess." In the next room freshly cut evergreen trees were tenderly arranged in a circle by white men wearing robes; it looked as if tree worship was making a comeback in northern Europe. In the corridors there were white-haired old hippies selling cheap crystals and little plastic bags of homegrown chamomile. There were white men from California in expensive new buckskins, beads, and feathers who had called themselves "Thunderroll" and "Buffalo Horn." African medicine men seven feet tall stood next to half-pint Incas and Mayas selling dry stalks of weeds wrapped in strips of dirty rag. Lecha watched for a while; she had watched the hands. The hands had gripped the cash feverishly as they waited for their turn; old Yoeme used to brag that she could make white people believe in anything and do anything she told them because the whites were so desperate. Money was changing hands rapidly; fifties and hundreds seemed to drop effortlessly from the white hands into the brown and the black hands. Some bought only the herbs or teas, but others had bought private consultations which cost hundreds of dollars.

Lecha had not been able to get close enough to the Incas or the Mayas to hear what they were saying. Two interpreters appeared to be attempting to translate for the crowd, but they had momentarily been involved in disagreement over the translation of a word. Lecha could not help noticing a short, wide Maya woman who seemed to be studying the crowd; suddenly the Maya woman had turned and looked Lecha right in the eye. Yoeme used to warn them about traveling medicine people, because witches and sorcerers often found it necessary to go to distant towns where their identities were not known. Lecha turned and saw a woman holding a walrus tusk, surrounded by spellbound listeners. Lecha's heart beat faster and she felt a big smile on her face; she would have recognized that Eskimo anywhere!

Rose had talked to Lecha as if the crowd of spectators had not been there. The more Rose seemed to ignore the people, the more quiet and intense the crowd had become as they sought to hear each word between the two short, dark women. Rose had begun talking about the years since Lecha had abandoned the dogsled racer for warmer country and faster men.

Rose had learned to talk to her beloved little sisters and brothers who were ghosts in blue flames running along the river. Of course Rose did not speak to them the way she was talking to Lecha now. The blue flames burned with a loud blowtorch sound that would have made words impossible to understand even if her sweet ones could have talked. But no sounds came from their throats; when they opened their mouths, Rose saw the words written in flames—not even complete words, but Rose could understand everything they had to say.

Lecha had felt the crowd press closer, but at that instant, Rose stood up and caused the spectators to step back quickly and respectfully. Rose pointed at a big suitcase near Lecha's feet. Rose lifted the lid; inside, all Lecha saw were white river pebbles and small gray river stones. Rose nodded at the rocks and then at the well-dressed young white people lining up obediently to buy whatever the Yupik Eskimo medicine woman had to sell. "Some of us are getting together later in my room," Rose said, "after Weasel Tail and the Hopi speak. Room twelve twelve."

The Return of the Buffalo

Wilson Weasel Tail strode up to the podium and whipped out two sheets of paper. Weasel Tail had abandoned his polyester leisure suits for army camouflage fatigues; he wore his hair in long braids carefully wrapped in red satin ribbon. Weasel Tail's voice boomed throughout the main ballroom. Today he wanted to begin his lecture by reading two fragments of famous Native American documents. "First, I read to you from Pontiac's manuscript:

"'You cry the white man has stolen everything, killed all your animals and food. But where were you when the people first discussed the Europeans? Tell the truth. You forgot everything you were *ever* told. You forgot the stories with warnings. You took what was easy to swallow, what you never had to chew. You were like a baby suddenly helpless in the white man's hands because the white man feeds your greed until it swells up your belly and chest to your head. You steal from your neighbors. You can't be trusted!'"

Weasel Tail had paused dramatically and gazed at the audience before he continued: "Treachery has turned back upon itself. Brother has betrayed brother. Step back from envy, from sorcery and poisoning. Reclaim these continents which belong to us."

Weasel Tail paused, took a deep breath, and read the Paiute prophet Wovoka's letter to President Grant:

> You are hated
> You are not wanted here
> Go away,
> Go back where you came from.
> You white people are cursed!

The audience in the main ballroom had become completely still, as in shock from Weasel Tail's presentation. But Weasel Tail seemed not to notice and had immediately launched into his lecture.

"Today I wish to address the question as to whether the spirits of the ancestors in some way failed our people when the prophets called them to the Ghost Dance," Weasel Tail began.

"Moody and other anthropologists alleged the Ghost Dance disappeared because the people became disillusioned when the ghost shirts did not stop bullets and the Europeans did not vanish overnight. But it was the Europeans, not the Native Americans, who had expected results overnight; the anthropologists, who feverishly sought magic objects to postpone their own deaths, had misunderstood the power of the ghost shirts. Bullets of lead belong to the everyday world; ghost shirts belong to the realm of spirits and dreams. The ghost shirts gave the dancers spiritual protection while the white men dreamed of shirts that repelled bullets because they feared death."

Moody and the others had never understood the Ghost Dance was to reunite living people with the spirits of beloved ancestors lost in the five-hundred-year war. The longer Wilson Weasel Tail talked, the more animated and energized he became; Lecha could see he was about to launch into a poem:

> We dance to remember,
> we dance to remember all our beloved ones,
> to remember how each passed
> to the spirit world.
> We dance because the dead love us,
> they continue to speak to us,
> they tell our hearts what must be done to survive.
> We dance and we do not forget all the others
>   before us,
> the little children and the old women who fought
>   and who died
> resisting the invaders and destroyers of Mother
>   Earth!
> Spirits! Ancestors!
> We have been counting the days, watching the
>   signs.
> You are with us every minute,
> you whisper to us in our dreams,
> you whisper in our waking moments.
> You are more powerful than memory!

Weasel Tail paused to take a sip of water. Lecha was impressed with the silence Weasel Tail had created in the main ballroom. "Naturopaths," holistic healers, herbalists, the guys with the orgone boxes and pyramids—all of them had locked up their cashboxes and closed their booths to listen to Weasel Tail talk. "The spirits are outraged! They demand justice! The spirits are furious! To all those humans too weak or too lazy to fight to protect Mother Earth, the spirits say, 'Too bad you did not die fighting the destroyers of the earth because now *we* will kill you for being so weak, for wringing your hands and whimpering while the invaders committed outrages against the forests and the mountains.' The spirits will harangue you, they will taunt you until you are forced to silence the voices with whiskey day after day. The spirits allow you no rest. The spirits say die fighting the invaders or die drunk."

The enraged spirits haunted the dreams of society matrons in the suburbs of Houston and Chicago. The spirits had directed mothers from country club neighborhoods to pack the children in the car and drive off hundred-foot cliffs or into flooding rivers, leaving no note for the husbands. A message to the psychiatrist says only, "It is no use any longer." They see no reason for their children or them to continue. The spirits whisper in the brains of loners, the crazed young white men with automatic rifles who slaughter crowds in shopping malls or school yards as casually as hunters shoot buffalo. All day the miner labors in tunnels underground, hacking out ore with a sharp steel hand-pick; he returns home to his wife and family each night. Then suddenly the miner slaughters his wife and children. The "authorities" call it "mental strain" because he has used his miner's hand-pick to chop deep into the mother lode to reach their hearts and their brains.

Weasel Tail cleared his throat, then went on. "How many dead souls are we talking about? Computer projections place the populations of the Americas at more than seventy million when the Europeans arrived; one hundred years later, only ten million people had survived. Sixty million dead souls howl for justice in the Americas! They howl to retake the land as the black Africans have retaken their land!

"You think there is no hope for indigenous tribal people here to prevail against the violence and greed of the destroyers? But you forget the inestimable power of the earth and all the forces of the *universe*. You forget the colliding meteors. You forget the earth's outrage and the trembling that will not stop. Overnight, the wealth of nations will be reclaimed by the earth. The trembling does not stop and the rain clouds no longer gather; the sun burns the earth until the plants and animals disappear and die.

"The truth is the Ghost Dance did not end with the murder of Big Foot and one hundred and forty-four Ghost Dance worshipers at Wounded Knee. The Ghost Dance has never ended, it has continued, and the people have never stopped dancing; they may call it by other names, but when they dance, their hearts are reunited with the spirits of beloved ancestors and the loved ones recently lost in the struggle. Throughout the Americas, from Chile to Canada, the people have never stopped dancing; as the living dance, they are joined again with all our ancestors before them, who cry out, who demand justice, and who call the people to take back the Americas!"

Weasel Tail threw back his shoulders and puffed out his chest; he was going to read poetry:

> The spirit army is approaching,
> The spirit army is approaching,
> The whole world is moving onward,
> The whole world is moving onward.
> See! Everybody is standing watching.
> See! Everybody is standing watching.
>
> The whole world is coming,
> A nation is coming, a nation is coming,
> The Eagle has brought the message to the tribe.
> The father says so, the father says so.
>
> Over the whole earth they are coming.
> The buffalo are coming, the buffalo are coming,
> The Crow has brought the message to the tribe.
> The father says so, the father says so.
>
> I'yche'! ana'nisa'na'—Uhi'yeye'heye!
> I'yche'! ana'nisa'na'—Uhi'yeye'heye!
> I'yehe'! ha'dawu'hana'—Eye'ae'yuhe'yu!
> I'yehe'! ha'dawu'hana'—Eye'ae'yuhu'yu!
> Ni'athu'-a'u'a'haka'nith'ii—Ahe'yuhe'yu!
>
> [Translation]
> I'yehe'! my children—Uhi'yeye'heye'!
> I'yehe'! my children—Uhi'yeye'heye'!
> I'yehe'! we have rendered them
>   desolate—Eye'ae'yuhe'yu!
> I'yehe'! we have rendered them

desolate—Eye'ae'yuhe'yu!
The whites are crazy—Ahe'yuhe'yu!

Again, when Weasel Tail had finished, the ballroom was hushed; then the audience had given Weasel Tail a standing ovation.

"Have the spirits let us down? Listen to the prophecies! Next to thirty thousand years, five hundred years look like nothing. The buffalo are returning. They roam off federal land in Montana and Wyoming. Fences can't hold them. Irrigation water for the Great Plains is disappearing, and so are the farmers, and their plows. Farmers' children retreat to the cities. Year by year the range of the buffalo grows a mile or two larger."

Weasel Tail had them eating out of his hand; he let his voice trail off dramatically to a stage whisper that resonated throughout the ballroom speaker system. The audience leapt to its feet with a great ovation. Lecha had to hand it to Wilson Weasel Tail; he'd learned a thing or two. Still, Weasel Tail was a lawyer at heart; Lecha noted that he had made the invaders an offer that couldn't be refused. Weasel Tail had said to the US government, "Give back what you have stolen or else as a people you will continue your self-destruction."

Green Vengeance

There were forty-five minutes of recess before the Barefoot Hopi made the keynote speech. Lecha had searched until she located Leta, sitting with her computer expert, Awa Gee. Awa Gee had intercepted a coded fax message that the eco-warriors planned to make a surprise appearance at the healers convention. Zeta looked exhausted and nervous. Neither of them had had much sleep since the shooting.

Ferro had not known his lover was an undercover cop. But then Lecha had not known Seese had kept a kilo of cocaine in her closet either. Secrets and coincidences involving cocaine didn't surprise Lecha anymore; how odd that Zeta seemed so upset. Lecha whispered in Zeta's ear, "What's the matter?" Zeta had looked around, then leaned close and whispered, "I killed Greenlee yesterday." Lecha nodded. So the time had come.

Ferro was the problem now; Ferro had loaded a junker car with six hundred pounds of dynamite to park outside the Prince Road police substation. Zeta had tried to persuade Ferro to hold off retaliation at least until the preparations she and Awa Gee had been making through the computer networks had been completed. They only needed time for Awa Gee to run Greenlee's access numbers, but Ferro had refused to listen. Still Ferro couldn't make a bomb that size overnight. Awa Gee's guess had been it would take a week for a competent bomb maker to load the car properly and wire it correctly to the detonation device.

Just when Zeta was beginning to think the holistic medicine convention was a bust, a great commotion had developed near the steps to the ballroom stage and podium at the far end. Zeta and Lecha had both stood up, but they were too short; Awa Gee leaped up on his chair where he could see over all the heads. "There!" Awa Gee said. He excitedly patted Zeta on the shoulder. "I told you they'd come!"

The two eco-warriors wore ski masks and identical camouflage jumpsuits; they did not appear to be armed and Zeta saw no bodyguards around the podium. The eco-warriors had motioned for the audience to take its seats, and there on the stage with the eco-warriors Zeta saw the Barefoot Hopi impeccably dressed in a three-piece suit and tie and wearing Hopi moccasins instead of boots or shoes. The Hopi stood close to the eco-warriors, who were listening intently to the Hopi. The rumors about the alliance between the Hopi's organization and the Green Vengeance group apparently were true. Zeta was in agreement with the tactic. Green Vengeance eco-warriors would make useful allies at least at the start. Green Vengeance had a great deal of wealth behind their eco-warrior campaigns.

A convention organizer had announced the Hopi was going to introduce a special unscheduled appearance of Green Vengeance, who came with an urgent message. The noise in the main ballroom and in the corridors outside had hushed as the Hopi approached the microphone; a buzz of whispers began as the Hopi had pressed a button on the podium, and a giant video screen lowered to the center of the stage.

"Friends, you have all heard state and federal authorities blame 'structural failure' for the collapse of Glen Canyon Dam. Now you are about to see videotape footage never before made public by our allies on earth!"

The ballroom's overhead lights had dimmed, and a jerky sequence, videotaped from a moving vehicle, filled the giant screen. The soundtrack and any voices on the videotape had been deliberately removed. The brilliant burnt reds and oranges of the sandstone formations and the dark green juniper bushes flashing past appeared to be Utah or northern Arizona. Next came interiors of motel rooms with figures in ski masks and camouflage clothing standing by motel beds stacked with assault rifles and clips of ammunition. The camera had avoided the masked faces and focused instead on the hands carefully arranging black boxes in nests of foam rubber; the foam-rubber bundles were packed carefully inside nylon backpacks. A close-up of a black box before its lid was closed showed a nine-volt battery and wires. On the worn gold motel bedspread, the hands had strung the six backpacks together with bright blue wire. Awa Gee leaned over and whispered in Zeta's ear, "I can't wait to see this!"

Next, the screen had been filled with highway signs and US park service signs; in the background was the huge concrete mass that had trapped the Colorado River and had created Lake Powell.

GLEN CANYON DAM; the sign had filled the entire screen. Next the concrete bulwark of the dam came into focus; tiny figures dangled off ropes down the side of the dam. At first none of the park service employees or bystanders and tourists appear to notice. Then the camera had zoomed in for close-ups of each of the six eco-warriors, each with a backpack loaded with explosives in the motel room. Zeta had been thinking the six resembled spiders on a vast concrete wall when suddenly the giant video screen itself appeared to crack and shatter in slow motion, and the six spiderlike figures had disappeared in a white flash of smoke and dust. The entire top half of the dam structure had folded over, collapsing behind a giant wall of reddish water. Zeta heard gasps from the audience.

"A massive structural failure due to fault asymmetries and earth tremors," the eco-warrior said in mocking tones amid the excited voices and cheers. Zeta looked around; the audience was on its feet. "Your government lies to you because it fears you. They don't want you to know that six eco-warriors gave their lives to free the mighty Colorado!" The audience cheered. The eco-warrior handed the microphone to his partner. Zeta glanced at Awa Gee, who sat motionless, spellbound by what he was seeing and hearing.

The eco-warrior who spoke next was a woman. She spoke calmly about the choice of when and how one was going to die. She continued calmly, relating the states of awareness she had passed through; for a time, she said, she had not wanted to resort to the destruction of property or the loss of human lives, but after their beloved leader had been murdered by FBI agents, her eyes had been opened. This was war. The new enemies, she said, were the space station and biosphere tycoons who were rapidly depleting rare species of plants, birds, and animals so the richest people on earth could bail out of the pollution and revolutions and retreat to orbiting paradise islands of glass and steel. What few species and what little pure water and pure air still remained on earth would be harvested for these space colonies. Lazily orbiting in the glass and steel cocoons of these elaborate "biospheres," the rich need not fear the rabble while they enjoyed their "natural settings" complete with freshwater pools and jungles filled with rare parrots and orchids. The artificial biospheres were nothing more than orbiting penthouses for the rich. Three thousand eight hundred species of flora and fauna are required for each artificial biosphere to attain self-sufficiency. Eco-warriors had infiltrated the artificial biosphere projects at all levels; plans had already been made for the final abandonment of earth. At the end, the last of the clean water and the uncontaminated soil, the last healthy animals and plants, would be removed from earth to the orbiting biospheres to "protect" them from the pollution on earth.

The eco-warrior paused to clear her throat. People in the audience raised their hands frantically to ask questions, but she ignored them. "All orbiting telescopes and space stations will be turned back on the earth to monitor the human masses for as long as they survive. The orbiting biospheres will require fresh air and fresh water supplies from time to time; giant flexible tubes will drop down from the sky to suck water and air from the earth. If the people on earth attempt to destroy or sabotage the giant feeding tubes, lasers from satellites and space stations will destroy the rebels and rioters." The eco-warrior paused, then shouted, "This is war! We are not afraid to die to save the earth!"

"Hard act to follow," Lecha had whispered to Zeta as the warriors left the stage.

Zeta had read the messages Awa Gee had intercepted from the

eco-warriors. The eco-warriors had lost their beloved leader to a car bomb. They were determined to give him glory. They were determined to turn out the lights on the United States one night. They were determined to destroy all interstate high-voltage transmission lines, power-generating plants, and hydroelectric dams across the United States simultaneously. Their scheme did not seem quite so improbable now that Zeta had seen the videotape. The six kamikaze eco-warriors disappearing into the collapsing wall of Glen Canyon Dam was a stunning sight, Zeta agreed. No wonder the US government and Arizona state authorities had blamed the destruction of Glen Canyon Dam on "structural failure." Naturally the authorities had feared copycat bombings of hydroelectric dams.

Awa Gee knew from the intercepted messages the government had begun sweeping arrests of all persons affiliated with environmental action groups; even people with the Audubon Society and the US Forest Service employees had been accused of being "secret eco-warriors." Awa Gee was always reminded of South Korea when he heard about mass arrests by police. The United States had been different when Awa Gee had first arrived from Seoul by way of Sonora. Awa Gee remembered that back then the world economy had still been riding on the big wave; to Americans, Awa Gee had looked Japanese. Back then, all the Americans had been able to talk about were Japanese cars this and Japanese cars that. Love-hate between Japan and the United States, two countries Awa Gee had despised for their racism and imperialism. Zeta had thought Awa Gee could not hope to get much help from the eco-warriors now that the government had begun to round up all of them for "protective custody." But Awa Gee thought about the situation differently; the police had only caught the law-abiding eco-warriors with families and jobs. Awa Gee didn't think people with jobs and families were worth much as subversives anyway.

Awa Gee had high hopes for these Green Vengeance eco-warriors. Green Vengeance was hard-core; one of the eco-warriors who had died blowing up Glen Canyon Dam had been a gay rights activist ill with AIDS. No wonder government authorities had denied all reports of sabotage or loss of human life at Glen Canyon Dam's collapse. Awa Gee had intercepted the gay eco-warrior's last message to his family, colleagues, and friends. Awa Gee had kept the computer readout of the eco-warrior's message although he knew it was risky to keep such evidence.

> Dear lovers, brothers, mothers, and sisters!
> Go out in glory!
> Go out with dignity!
> Go out while you're still feeling good and *looking*
>   good!
> Avenge gay genocide by the U.S. government!
> Die to save the earth.
> Mold long underwear out of plastic explosives and stroll past
> the U.S. Supreme Court building while the justices are hearing
> arguments. Bolt in the exit door and flick the switch! Turn
>   out the
> lights on the High Court of the police state!

Awa Gee believed very soon these last remaining eco-warriors would push forward with their plot to turn off the lights. From messages he had intercepted he had concluded that a good many eco-warriors had gone underground at the time their leader was assassinated. Awa Gee decided he would help the eco-warriors turn out the lights, although they might never even know Awa Gee's contribution. The regional power suppliers had emergency generating plants and used sophisticated computer systems to deal with brownouts, storms, or other electric power failures by automatically rerouting power reserve supplies to black-out areas and by switching on emergency power-generating systems. But Awa Gee had already developed a protovirus to subvert all emergency switching programs in the computers of regional power-relay stations. Awa Gee's virus would activate only during extreme voltage fluctuations such as might occur after the coordinated sabotage of *key* hydroelectric dams and interstate high-voltage lines across the United States. To destroy every last generator and high-voltage line would be doing the people a favor; alternating electrical current caused brain cancer and genetic mutations. Solar batteries were the wave of the future. The plan was a long shot; Awa Gee was counting on the "cost cutting" of the giant power companies to curtail or cancel auxiliary emergency systems. But if the plan worked, if the lights went out all over all at once, then the United States would never be the same again.

from *The Bird Is Gone*

A ~~Monograph~~ *Manifesto*

STEPHEN GRAHAM JONES

(2003)

> The condition of postmodernity has already been a part of Native
> life; the key is to reaffirm and go beyond this postindian condition.
> —*Gerald Vizenor*

SET IN THE FUTURE when the Dakotas are Indian Territory again,
Stephen Graham Jones's (Piegan Blackfeet) *The Bird Is Gone: A ~~Monograph~~*
~~graph~~ Manifesto (2003) ups the ante of science fiction skewed through
Indigenous eyes. The Mayan calendar date of December 23, 2012, "supposedly the end of this world, the beginning of the next," has come
and gone, and the US government has enacted a so-called Conserva-
tion Act restoring land to the Indians in an effort to reestablish bison
herds on the Great Plains. Post-cyberpunk reverberations quickly
accrue in this future where Traditionals now cling to their microwaves
while Progressives live on the grassland with the buffalo.

With new treaties "something changed. In the ground. A deep rumbling . . . and there were headlights, millions of them, streaming toward the Dakotas." The promise of restoration leads to a "Skin Parade,"
as Indians from all over rush back to the restored Territories. Toll-
booths guard entry into their land. Only Indians may freely pass, while

anthropologists attempt to sneak in disguised as day-use-ticketed tourists. Jones centralizes intersecting stories of these dispossessed/repossessed at the Fool's Hip Bowling Alley, the futuristic equivalent of the medieval Ship of Fools allegory.

The novel offers no easy answers about the consequences of tribal sovereignties. Some who embrace Indian Territory in the spirit of political excitement experience profound side effects like the "refurbished vanishing Indian syndrome." Removed from the white world and no longer privileged as the exotic other, now that she lives where everyone is Native, one young woman clings to a fence so that she won't disappear, telling herself "not to look to either side—not to believe the stories—that the Old Ones are out there on their unshod horses, with their lances and their scalps, and their downturned mouths. Watching. Waiting. Not saying anything yet." Others like the young girl featured in the following excerpt have quite a different reaction. Jones says this about the passage:

A lot of *The Bird Is Gone* is having fun with the present, kind of exaggerating it, saying what-if, having some butterfly-effect fun, and then extending all that out into a ridiculous future. But parts of it, like this one, try to go back, explain away the past. Which, the Lone Ranger being an android, a manbot, an automaton, I mean, that's the only thing that makes even partial sense to me. Or, the only thing that makes sense and allows Tonto some dignity, as the real puppet master here, doing good but shielding himself from the glory and all that goes with that: having to wear the white hat, sit so right up in the saddle. So, yeah, I was laughing the whole time I was writing, and, yeah, it's got to be science fiction—the whole novel's alternate reality—and, that's what I grew up reading, what I still read, what I aspire to write when and if I ever get good enough. Science fiction, it can instill a sense of wonder in you like no other mode, no other genre. You can crack one denim panel on one person's back, somebody you thought you knew, and like that the world has to shift all around you, to accommodate this possibility. Doesn't that girl in that scene say just a little "oh," when she sees what's really going on? That was me.

♃

Suddenly Tonto turns his head to the darkness. It's empty, quiet, and then a girl steps out.

"I didn't hear you," he says.

She shrugs. Her shoes are in her hands.

"Can I?" she says, looking down at a saddle propped up as a backrest.

"Free country," Tonto says. But he's smiling. The girl sits down.

"You don't talk the same," she says.

"Sit um down?" Tonto tries, handing her his cup.

She looks off. The horse stamps again, blows.

"Silver?" she asks.

"More like white."

And now the Lone Ranger's gloved hand twitches. Like a wave. The girl waves back, her fingertips drumming the ground too.

"You even wear that at night?" she asks him—the mask—and reaches across the fire to touch it. Or his cheek. But Tonto shakes his head no.

"All these strong, silent types," she says.

Tonto has his cup again.

"I used to listen to you, you know," she says. "On the radio."

Tonto narrows his eyes at her.

"The *radio*," she says, with her whole mouth, then leans over, touching her ear to the ground for *listen,* looking at him with a question mark.

He can see down her bodice, now.

"Rad-ee-o," he says.

"But it was real, too," she says. "Like I always thought there was this third horse running behind you—both of you—with like a boom, a *mic,* tied to its saddle horn . . ."

Tonto looks out to the horses, then jerks beck when the Lone Ranger's leg spasms. The rowel of the spur digs into the packed dirt.

"He alright?" the girl asks.

"Hard day," Tonto says.

"Guess so," she says, then touches her own face for him, Tonto, like he's got something there.

"Thanks," Tonto says, and moves his cup to the other hand, touches his fingertip to his cheek like she is.

It just makes it worse, though.

Now his war paint isn't symmetrical.

He looks at his hand, at her. With a question mark.

Before she can answer, though, the Lone Ranger speaks: "When the chips are down, Tonto, well, sir, now that's when the buffalo's empty."

His voice is mechanical.

"Got ya," Tonto says, fingershooting him across the fire.

The girl is looking at both of them now.

She touches the Lone Ranger's boot with her foot. It rotates without the leg. Tonto closes his eyes, opens them.

"Hard day?" she says.

"Miners," Tonto says. "A stagecoach."

She's still staring at him.

He smiles. "I can hear them coming from miles away, you know."

She nods.

Tonto rubs his eye, smearing the paint. Staring at nothing, the emptied coffee cup hooked on his finger, his hand on his knee, his leg propped.

"You shouldn't drink so much," she says.

"I don't like to sleep out here," Tonto says.

"But you're . . . Indian."

Tonto smiles, nods.

The sky yawns above him.

"When the chips are—" the Lone Ranger starts to say again, but Tonto stomps his foot on the ground.

"*Hi-ho Silver!*" the Lone Ranger says instead, raising one gloved hand above his head.

"That really him?" the girl asks.

Tonto nods, watches her.

"Want some more?" he asks finally, swirling the grounds in the bottom of his cup.

The girl nods, then flinches when he braces himself to stand.

"It's okay," he tells her, but keeps both hands up as he backs into the darkness. A horse whinnies. Supplies touch each other with a tin sound, muffled by leather. This is 1890. Tonto walks back into camp with a bag labeled COFFEE. He tosses it down onto the Lone Ranger's lap. The Lone Ranger stares at him. Tonto stares back.

"It's okay, really," the girl says, "I can come—" but Tonto shushes her.

"*Coffee*," he says. To the Lone Ranger.

But the Lone Ranger just sits there.

Tonto shakes his head.

"This always happens," he says.

The girl doesn't ask what.

A horse stamps just past the firelight and a boom lowers over them. They both see it.

"Shh," Tonto almost says, holding a black finger over his lips.

"So . . . ," the girl says, "a stagecoach . . . ," and Tonto nods, rolls his hand in the Indian signal for more, cover him, and as she recounts the episode he creeps over behind the Lone Ranger, opens a panel in the back of the denim shirt.

The girl catches her breath.

Tonto stares at her, red and green lights blinking off his face.

She closes her eyes, continues: ". . . and he was on the rocks like that. *Dry gulch!* Sam yelled—I think that was his name—but it was too late . . ." Tonto smiles around the knife in his teeth. His hands are deep in the Lone Ranger's back. The black paint is grease.

The girl is crying down the back of her throat and talking around it.

"Okay," Tonto says to her, holding his palm out.

She trails off, leaving someone midair. Tonto closes the panel, coughs to cover the click.

"How," he says, walking back to the fire, looking down at the Lone Ranger, "coffee."

The Lone Ranger's face snaps up. The domino mask. All the fringe.

"Coffee?" he asks, his voice deep and heroic.

"More like it," Tonto says.

He squats down on his haunches.

"I always thought you sat like that," the girl says.

She sits down like him, like a little girl, and before them the Lone Ranger stands, dragging his rotated boot, and goes through the motions of coffee.

"Delicious," the girl says when it's done, holding her cup with both hands.

Tonto nods, blowing steam off his own, never looking away.

The Lone Ranger tips his crisp white hat to him, says ma'am to the girl.

In her cup is a silver bullet. She spits it into her palm.

"Oh," she says.

She looks to Tonto.

"It's real," he says, "that part."

"*Hi ho Si—*" the Lone Ranger starts, but Tonto slaps the ground with his palm, stopping him mid-sentence, his arm on the way up.

The rowel of one of his spurs is left spinning.

Tonto pinches the bridge of his nose hard. The girl closes her hand around the bullet, holds it close to her chest.

"Thank you," she says, then looks up to the Lone Ranger, standing over her. Behind him one of the horses drums its hoof on the ground and the Lone Ranger moves the arm by his side, straightening it out behind him.

Again; again.

The girl smiles, sweeping her eyes across the dark prairie to see who might be watching.

Tonto shakes his head, leans back against his bedroll.

"What is it already?" he says, not quite grinning around his cup, and, her voice small like a question, she says it, and the night pares itself back down again, to a campfire, a domino mask, two white eyes looking out of it in terror.

from *Star Waka*

ROBERT SULLIVAN (NGĀ PUHI)
(1999)

"Contact" has been a problematic word for us, not to mention a
traumatic experience, but perhaps we are at a historical juncture
where tribal experience can be strengthened and challenged by
contact rather than simply diminished by it. Perhaps even, instead
of being on the receiving end of contact, we can become the
contactors instead of the contactees in ways that emphasize
sharing rather than displacing.
— *Craig S. Womack (Creek First Nation)*

ROBERT SULLIVAN (Ngā Puhi, Maori iwi of the Northland region of
New Zealand and of the South Island iwi kai Tahu) sets the epic poem
Star Waka in 2140 AD, a future where the Maori waka, or canoe,
transforms into a starship. His sf foray reflects *Kaupapa Maori,* an effort
to combat the dehumanizing effects of colonization by maintaining
the Maori language, culture, teachings, and philosophy. Sullivan has
emerged as a significant Maori poet whose numerous collections, including *Jazz Waiatu* (1990), *Piki Ake!* (1993), and *Captain Cook in the
Underworld* (2002) explore dimensions of contemporary urban Maori
experience *and* traditional (iwi-based) tribal power bases, including
local racial and social issues. The *Oxford Companion to New Zealand
Literature* remarks on the postmodern feel that Sullivan gives to Maori
histories and stories. As Linda Tuhiwai Smith (Maori) might say, such
work has the effect of exacerbating "the reach of imperialism into our
heads."

Sullivan clearly finds sf an effective means for contemporary renewal of iwi *tino rangatiratanga,* Maori self-determination and sovereignty relocations. A recent collection, *Voice Carried My Family* (2005), contains the notable alternative history entitled "London Waka": on February 6, 1870, the waka Pono sail down the Thames, take the capital, and London falls to the Maori, "who sack the seat without mercy." The Maori quickly gain alliance with a quarter of the people of the planet "by emptying the spoils of the British Museum" and returning them to their rightful owners. In an ironic reversal of actual history, the waka invaders offer aid to this reimagined England, as the last lines of the poem suggest: "We expect they will benefit from limited self-government in the long term./A restoration project is under way to ensure the survival of their language."

Star Waka hints at the puzzlement of building and restoration, individually and collectively, contemplating not only how "to ask for sovereignty and how to get from policy into / action back home," but also the troubling feasibility of colonizing other planets with "our spacecraft *waka.*" How does one break the cycle of the darker undersides of colonization itself and yet have the freedom to relocate, renew one's own stories, erect *marae,* sacred places infusing everyday living, and celebrate *tino rangatiratanga?* How does one as iwi, people of "going back to the bones," remain iwi, that is, return home after traveling? Expanding in the space-time folds of Ranginui's cloak or Great Skyfather's folds, the poem defies the complacency of sf that offers only a wildly imagined future. That is the excitement and depth of Indigenous futurisms—the responsibility of each moment, each fold, each time, imagined or not, because each imagined moment contains within it *already* our presence, not our absence. The visibility of Indigenous space-time creates an event horizon we can all slip into, a responsibility we all share: to "confiscate the rocket ship," go space waka, and sing *waiaita* to the spheres.

♪

2140 AD

Waka reaches for stars—mission control clears us for launch
and we are off to check the guidance system

personally. Some gods are Greek to us Polynesians,
who have lost touch with the Aryan mythology,
but we recognize ours and others—Ranginui and his cloak,
and those of us who have seen *Fantasia* know Diana
and the host of beautiful satyrs and fauns.

We are off to consult with the top boss,
to ask for sovereignty and how to get this
from policy into action back home.
Just then the rocket runs out of fuel—
we didn't have enough cash for a full tank—
so we drift into an orbit we cannot escape from
until a police escort vehicle tows us back

and fines us the equivalent of the fiscal envelope
signed a hundred and fifty years ago.

They confiscate the rocket ship, the only thing
all the iwi agreed to purchase with the last down payment.

it is feasible that we will enter

space
colonize planets call our spacecraft *waka*
perhaps name them after the first fleet
erect marae transport carvers renew stories
with celestial import

establish new forms of verse
free ourselves of the need for politics
and concentrate on beauty

like the release from gravity
orbit an image until it is absorbed
through the layers of skin

spin it
sniff and stroke the object
become poetic

oh to be in that generation
to write in freefall picking up the tools
our culture has given us

and to let them go again
knowing they won't hit anyone
just stay up there

no longer subject to peculiarities
of climate the political economies
of powers and powerless

a space waka
rocketing to another orb
singing waiata to the spheres

Notes

Imagining Indigenous Futurisms

1. Drew Hayden Taylor, *alterNatives* (Vancouver, BC: Talon Books, 2000).

2. The term *Indigenous* throughout this book references the kind of breadth that Simon Ortiz (Acoma Pueblo) gives it: "I have been using the word Indigenous more because while we are Native or Indigenous to the Americas, in terms of the world, there are Indigenous peoples all over the world, the people of Africa, the people in the Mid-East, the people in the Pacific, Indigenous peoples that are in the forefront of changing the world. If Western culture is dissipating and eventually falling apart, Indigeneity is very much going back to the roots, but going back toward a way in which the earth is in relationship to us and we with it in a very reciprocal way. We're not just using the earth to be our technological Garden of Eden. The earth is not necessarily under our control, but the relationship is one of responsibility, so that relationship is [a] creative one." "Simon J. Ortiz, In His Own Words," Evelina Zuni Lucero's interview in *Simon J. Ortiz: A Poetic Legacy of Indigenous Continuance* (Albuquerque: University of New Mexico Press, 2009), 163.

3. Joy Harjo's original coinage of "Skin thinking" or "thinking in skin" quickly accrued multilayered meanings of Native "intellectual sovereignty," inviting, in this case, readers to enjoy not only the pleasurable levels of cognitive dissonances grounded in sf and speculative fiction but also the commitment to embodiment, fusing our bodies with our intellects connected to material realities, a "map to the next world." See Robert Warrior (Osage), "Your Skin Is the Map: The Theoretical Challenge of Joy Harjo's Erotic Poetics," in *Reasoning Together: The Native Critics Collective,* ed. Janice Acoose, Lisa Brooks, Tol Foster, and Leanne Howe (Norman: University of Oklahoma Press, 2008), 340–52. Skin thinking also has the implications of reading stories with the richness and awareness of the specific tribal frameworks relationally within an intertribal setting, or as Tol Foster (Anglo-Creek) puts it, "fires that travel," a cosmopolitan tribal tradition (i.e., not

a universal pan-tribalism but a readiness to perceive interactions and negotiations of Skin thinking). "Of One Blood: An Argument for Relations and Regionality in Native American Literary Studies," in ibid., 276–78. Thinking in Skin additionally concentrates on reading writers of Indigenous nations within the networks of intertribalism, as Lisa Brooks (Abenaki) urges. "Digging at the Roots: Locating an Ethical, Native Criticism," in ibid., 234–64. Thinking in Skin is a relational framework of Native thought and one that is helpful for the increasingly global network of Indigenous intellectual exchanges and storytelling.

4. John Rieder, *Colonialism and the Emergence of Science Fiction* (Middletown, CT: Wesleyan University Press, 2008). While he supplies a necessary caveat in attempting to define genre itself or a contested arena such as sf, describing it as a "web of resemblances . . . an intertextual phenomenon always formed out of resemblances or oppositions among texts," Rieder nevertheless contends that sf becomes complicit in the colonial gaze (1–2, 18). Note that Adam Roberts's *The History of Science Fiction* (Basingstoke, U.K.: Palgrave Macmillan, 2005) divides sf into stories of travel through space, of travel through time, of imaginary technologies, and utopian fiction; he devotes several chapters to much earlier forms of sf that can be set side by side with classical Greek and Roman literature but invariably agrees with Rieder when approaching nineteenth-century sf, which represents "in some cases, a direct mapping of Imperialist or political concerns" (88).

5. Roger Luckhurst, *Science Fiction* (Cambridge: Polity Press, 2005), provides an excellent study of the cultural history of sf but slips up when he demarcates: "The different experience of time associated with modernity [and therefore, sf writing, the emphasis of his book] orients perceptions towards the future rather than the past or the cyclical sense of time ascribed to traditional societies" (3). This would unintentionally omit much of Native sf whose futures very much are thought experiments about recycling space-times or parallel worlds.

6. Nalo Hopkinson writes in her own introduction to *So Long Been Dreaming: Postcolonial Science Fiction and Fantasy*, "Arguably one of the most familiar memes of science fiction is that of going to foreign countries and colonizing the natives, and as I've said elsewhere, for many of us, that's not a thrilling adventure story: it's non-fiction, and we are on the wrong side of the strange-looking ship that appears out of nowhere" (Vancouver, Canada: Arsenal Pulp Press, 2004), 7.

7. Mark Bould, "The Ships Landed Long Ago: AfroFuturisms and Black SF," *Science Fiction Studies* 34, no. 2 (2007): 182. For a discussion of the "merging of African and Native American traditions formed in the New World," see Jonathan Brennan, *When Brer Rabbit Meets Coyote: African–Native American Literature* (Champaign: University of Illinois Press, 2003): xiii. The seminal work on the topic is Jack Forbes's *Africans and Native Americans: The Language of Race and the Evolution of Red-Black Peoples*, 2nd ed. (Champaign: University of Illinois Press, 1993). See also Joanna Brooks, *American Lazarus: Religion and the Rise of African American and Native American Literatures* (New York: Oxford University Press, 2007).

8. De Witt Douglas Kilgore, *Astrofuturism: Science, Race, and Visions of Utopia in Space* (Philadelphia: University of Pennsylvania Press, 2003), 29 and 213. The

parallel experiences of African and Indigenous diasporic peoples are hinted at throughout sf, as in Ben Bova's *Mars* series, which elicited Kilgore's comments. There a Navajo geologist inadvertently brings Navajo ways of sovereignty to a desolated and arid Mars whose aboriginal inhabitants are long gone. Pursuing the implications of these theories, De Witt Douglas Kilgore explains the cultural relevance of sf in dealing with issues of race and ethnicity: "What is at stake for me is the shape of the future: whether or not we can imagine, in any meaningful way, a future that both reflects and influences the complex realities of a complex world. . . . Are peoples of color equals in the space future vision or only clients who may visit the frontier as long as they behave? Can a nonwhite character carry the visionary burden of the space future in a medium that is often considered the exclusive preserve of white males?" (3).

9. Taiaiake Alfred, *Peace, Power, Righteousness: An Indigenous Manifesto,* 2nd ed. (New York: Oxford University Press, 2009), 165.

10. Victoria de Zwaan, "Slipstream," in *The Routledge Companion to Science Fiction,* ed. Mark Bould, Andrew M. Butler, Adam Roberts, and Sherryl Vint (New York: Routledge, 2009), 500–504.

11. Damien Broderick, *Transrealism: Writing in the Slipstream of Science* (Westport, CT: Greenwood Press, 2000), 21.

12. John Gribbin, *In Search of the Multiverse: Parallel Worlds, Hidden Dimensions, and the Quest for the Frontiers of Reality* (New York: Allen Lane, 2009), 63.

13. Gerald Vizenor, *Fugitive Poses: Native American Indian Scenes of Absence and Presence* (Lincoln: University of Nebraska Press, 1998), 15.

14. Ibid., 51.

15. Istvan Csicsery-Ronay Jr., *The Seven Beauties of Science Fiction* (Middletown, CT: Wesleyan University Press, 2008), 218, 220.

16. Lisa Brooks, *The Common Pot: The Recovery of Native Space in the Northeast* (Minneapolis: University of Minnesota Press, 2008), 4–10.

17. Csicsery-Ronay Jr., *Seven Beauties of Science Fiction,* 157.

18. A starting point, though, could be any works by Keith James (Haudonasonee) or any by Gregory Cajete (Tewa from Santa Clara Pueblo Nation), but especially, perhaps, *Native Science: Natural Laws of Interdependence* (Santa Fe: Clear Light, 2000).

19. Wendy Makoons Geniusz, *Our Knowledge Is Not Primitive: Decolonizing Botanical Anishinaabe Teachings* (Syracuse, NY: Syracuse University Press, 2009). This work expands on *gikendaasowin* and notes historically that the "search for botanical knowledge helped to drive the force of European colonization in the Americas and around the world. Many 'explorers' and their sponsors sought the economic opportunities brought by 'discovering' previously unknown plants and botanical knowledge" (16).

20. Andy Duncan, "Alternate Histories," in *The Cambridge Companion to Science Fiction,* ed. Edward James and Farah Mendlesohn (Cambridge: Cambridge University Press, 2003), 217.

21. Cited by Deborah L. Madsen, "On Subjectivity and Survivance," in

Survivance: Narratives of Native Presence, ed. Gerald Vizenor (Lincoln: University of Nebraska Press, 2008), 65–66.

22. Patrick B. Sharp's *Savage Perils: Racial Frontiers and Nuclear Apocalypse in American Culture* (Norman: University of Oklahoma Press, 2007), 172.

23. Linda Tuhiwai Smith, *Decolonizing Methodologies: Research and Indigenous Peoples* (London: Zed Books, 1999), 39.

24. Isiah Lavender, *Race in American Science Fiction* (Bloomington: Indiana University Press, 2010).

25. Amy Ransom, "Oppositional Postcolonialism in Quebecois Science Fiction," *Science Fiction Studies* 33, no. 2 (2006): 291–312.

26. Michelle Reid, in *The Routledge Companion to Science Fiction,* ed. Mark Bould, Andrew M. Butler, Adam Roberts, and Sherryl Vint (New York: Routledge, 2009), 256–66.

27. Rieder, *Colonialism and the Emergence of Science Fiction.*

28. Veronica Hollinger, "Science Fiction and Postmodernism," in *A Companion to Science Fiction* (Oxford: Blackwell, 2005), 232–47.

29. Larry McCaffery, *Some Other Frequency: Interviews with Innovative American Authors* (Philadelphia: University of Pennsylvania Press, 1996), 293.

Gerald Vizenor, "Custer on the Slipstream"

1. James Patrick Kelley and John Kessel, *Feeling Very Strange: The Slipstream Anthology* (San Francisco: Tachyon, 2006), vii.

2. Ronald Sukenick and Curtis White include Vizenor's story "Obo Island," from *Griever: An American Monkey King in China,* in their 1999 anthology *In the Slipstream: An FC2 Reader* (Normal, IL: FC2, 1999).

3. Kelley and Kessel, *Feeling Very Strange,* viii.

Diane Glancy, "Aunt Parnetta's Electric Blisters"

1. Jennifer Andrews, "A Conversation with Diane Glancy," *American Indian Quarterly* 26, no. 4 (Fall 2002): 656–57.

2. Ibid.

Simon Ortiz, "Men on the Moon"

1. "Nana" here refers to the grandfather. The term is used reciprocally for both grandfather and grandson throughout the story.

2. Elizabeth Ammons offers a fascinating analysis of these futurisms in "*Men on the Moon* and the Fight for Environmental Justice," in *Simon J. Ortiz: A Poetic Legacy of Indigenous Continuance,* ed. Susan Berry Brill de Ramírez and

Evelina Zuni Lucero (Albuquerque: University of New Mexico Press, 2009), 287–313.

Nalo Hopkinson, from *Midnight Robber*

1. José R. Oliver, "The Taino Cosmos," in *The Indigenous People of the Caribbean*, ed. Samuel M. Wilson (Gainsville: University of Florida Press, 1997), 142–43.

Gerald Vizenor, *Darkness in St. Louis: Bearheart*

1. Hartwig Isernhagen, *Momaday, Vizenor, Armstrong: Conversations on American Indian Writing* (Norman: University of Oklahoma Press, 1999), 125.

Archie Weller, from *Land of the Golden Clouds*

1. Brian Attebery, "Aboriginality in Science Fiction," *Science Fiction Studies* 32, no. 3 (November 2005): 401.
2. Joan Gordon and China Miéville, "Reveling in Genre: An Interview with China Miéville," *Science Fiction Studies* 30, no. 3 (November 2003): 365.

William Sanders, "When This World Is All on Fire"

1. Emmet Starr, *History of the Cherokee Indians and Their Legends and Folklore* (Oklahoma City: Warden, 1921), 9.
2. Daniel Heath Justice, *Our Fire Survives the Storm: A Cherokee Literary History* (Minneapolis: University of Minnesota Press, 2006), 138.
3. Renard Strickland and Jack Gregory, "Emmet Starr: Heroic Historian," in *American Indian Intellectuals,* ed. Margot Liberty, 104–14 (St. Paul: West Publishing, 1976), 111, cited in Justice, *Our Fire Survives the Storm,* 139.
4. Louis Owens, *Mixedblood Messages: Literature, Film, Family, Place* (Norman: University of Oklahoma Press, 2001), 227.

Leslie Marmon Silko, from *Almanac of the Dead*

1. Leslie Marmon Silko, *Yellow Woman and a Beauty of the Spirit: Essays on Native American Life Today* (New York: Simon and Schuster, 1996), 158.
2. Ibid., 159–60.

Source Credits

Gerald Vizenor, "Custer on the Slipstream." Reprinted by permission of the author.

Diane Glancy, "Aunt Parnetta's Electric Blisters." Reprinted by permission of the author.

Stephen Graham Jones, from *The Fast Red Road*. Reprinted by permission of University of Alabama Press.

Sherman Alexie, excerpt from *Flight*, copyright © 2007 by Sherman Alexie. Reprinted by permission of Grove/Atlantic, Inc.

Celu Amberstone, from *Refugees*. Reprinted by permission of the author.

Gerry William, from *The Black Ship*. Reprinted by permission of the author.

Simon Ortiz, "Men on the Moon," from *Men on the Moon: Collected Short Stories*, by Simon Ortiz. © 1999 Simon J. Ortiz. Reprinted by permission of the University of Arizona Press.

Nalo Hopkinson, from *Midnight Robber*. Copyright © 2000 by Nalo Hopkinson. Reprinted by permission of Grand Central Publishing.

Gerald Vizenor, from *Bearheart*. Reprinted by permission of the author.

Andrea Hairston, from *Mindscape*. Reprinted by permission of Aqueduct Press.

Archie Weller, from *Land of the Golden Clouds*. Reprinted by permission of Allen and Unwin.

Sherman Alexie, "Distances," from *The Lone Ranger and Tonto Fist Fight in Heaven*, copyright © 1993 by Sherman Alexie. Reprinted by permission of Grove/Atlantic, Inc.

William Sanders, "When This World Is All on Fire." Reprinted by permission of the author.

Zainab Amadahy, from *The Moons of Palmares*. Reprinted by permission of the author.

Misha, from *Red Spider, White Web*. Reprinted by permission of the author.

"Terminal Avenue" by Eden Robinson, copyright 1996 by Eden Robinson. Reprinted by permission of the author.

About the Editor

Grace L. Dillon is Associate Professor in the Indigenous Nations Studies Program at Portland State University in Portland, Oregon. Her PhD is in literary studies with emphasis on sixteenth-century (early modern) literature, while her current research focuses on science fiction (sf) studies. The two points are not so distant as one might initially imagine: (post)colonial studies fits naturally with sf paradigms of first contact and marginalized or "alien" cultures. Her scholarly agenda reflects personal origins: of First Nations Anishinaabe descent, her family moved transnationally between Garden River Reserve, Ontario, and Bay Mills Reservation in the Upper Peninsula of Michigan. An abiding interest in issues of indigeneity or "place" is easily seen throughout her publications and presentations. She is the author of *Hive of Dreams: Contemporary Science Fiction from the Pacific Northwest* (Oregon State University Press). Her work appears in diverse journals, including *Foundation: The International Review of Science Fiction; Extrapolation;* the *Journal of the Fantastic in the Arts;* the *Historical Journal of Film, Radio and Television;* and *Renaissance Papers.*

About the Contributors

Sherman Alexie (1966–) grew up on the Spokane Indian Reservation, a bit shy of fifty miles from Spokane, Washington. An avid reader as a child, Alexie embraced education early on, excelling at both academics and sports. His basketball skills inspired his breakout novel, *The Absolute True Diary of a Part-time Indian*. Subsequently he became a prolific writer, attending Gonzaga University and Washington State University, where he found himself inspired by a poetry class. Leaving WSU with a BA in American Studies, he received the 1991 Washington State Arts Commission Poetry Fellowship and the 1992 National Endowment for the Arts Poetry Fellowship. Building on this prestige, he has emerged as a powerhouse poet and fiction writer, publishing numerous books as well as dabbling in cinema with noted Cheyenne-Arapaho filmmaker Chris Eyre; their collaboration *Smoke Signals,* a movie based on one of Alexie's short stories, garnered the Sundance Film Festival Audience Award and Filmmakers Trophy in 1998. He followed this with his own adaptation of *The Business of Fancydancing*. Known for an outstanding stage presence, he is a regular, entertaining, and inspiring speaker and presenter. Among his numerous awards is the 2007 National Book Award in Young People's Literature and the 2010 PEN/Faulkner Award for his collection of short stories *War Dances*. Alexie lives in Seattle with his wife and two sons.

Zainab Amadahy (1956–) is a mother, writer, and activist. Her publications include the novel *Moons of Palmares* (Sister Vision Press, 1998) as well as an essay in the anthology *Strong Women Stories: Native Vision & Community Activism,* edited by Kim Anderson and Bonita Lawrence (Sumach Press, 2004). Most recently Zainab has contributed to *In Breach of the Colonial Contract* (edited by Arlo Kemp) as co-author of "Indigenous Peoples and Black People in Canada: Settlers or Allies?"

Celu Amberstone, of mixed Cherokee and Scots-Irish ancestry, was one of the only young people in her family to take an interest in learning traditional Native crafts and medicine ways. This made several of the older members of her family very happy while annoying others. Legally blind since birth, she has defied her limitations and spent much of her life avoiding cities. Moving to Canada after falling in love with a Métis-Cree man from Manitoba, she has lived in the rain forests of the West Coast, a tepee in the desert, and a small village in Canada's arctic. Along the way she managed to acquire a BA in cultural anthropology and an MA in health education. For the past eight years she has been a frequent contributor to the SF Canada professional writers website. Her latest novel, *Taste of Memory,* published by Kegedonce Press, will be published in 2011. Celu loves telling stories and reading. She lives in Victoria, British Columbia, near her grown children and four grandchildren.

Diane Glancy (1941–) is Professor Emeritus at Macalester College in St. Paul, Minnesota, where she taught Native American Literature and Creative Writing. She was the 2008–2009 Visiting Richard Thomas Professor of Creative Writing at Kenyon College. A new collection of nonfiction, *The Dream of a Broken Field,* is forthcoming in 2011 from the University of Nebraska Press. In 2010, Mammoth Publishers in Lawrence, Kansas, published her latest collection of poems, *Stories of the Driven World.* Her 2009 books are *The Reason for Crows: A Story of Kateri Tekakwitha* (SUNY Press) and *Pushing the Bear: After the Trail of Tears* (University of Oklahoma Press). In 2009, Salt Publishers brought out a commentary on her work, *The Salt Companion to Diane Glancy,* edited by James Mackay. In 2007, University of Arizona Press published a collection of her poems, *Asylum in the Grasslands.* Her 2005 books are *Rooms: New and Selected Poems* (Salt Publishers), *The Dance Partner: Stories of the Ghost Dance* (Michigan State

University Press), and *In-Between Places: Essays* (University of Arizona Press). Glancy's novels include *Stone Heart: A Novel of Sacajawea* (Overlook Press), *The Man Who Heard the Land* (Minnesota Historical Society Press), *Designs of the Night Sky* (University of Nebraska Press), and *Pushing the Bear: The 1838–39 Cherokee Trail of Tears* (Harcourt Brace). In 2009, she received an Expressive Arts Grant from the National Museum of the American Indian to write a creative history of Native American education called *The Catch*. She made her first independent film in 2010, *The Dome of Heaven,* about a mixedblood girl who wants to go to college. The film won the Best Native American Film at the Trail Dance Film Festival in Duncan, Oklahoma. She currently lives in Shawnee Mission, Kansas.

Andrea Hairston was a math/physics major in college until she did special effects for a show and then ran off to the theatre and became an artist. She is artistic director of Chrysalis Theatre and has created original productions with music, dance, and masks for over thirty years. She is also the Louise Wolff Kahn 1931 Professor of Theatre and Afro-American Studies at Smith College. Her plays have been produced at Yale Rep, Rites and Reason, the Kennedy Center, and StageWest, and on public radio and television. She has received many playwriting and directing awards, including a National Endowment for the Arts Grant to Playwrights, a Rockefeller/NEA Grant for New Works, a Ford Foundation Grant to collaborate with Senegalese Master Drummer Massamba Diop, and a Shubert Fellowship for Playwriting. Her first novel, *Mindscape,* was published by Aqueduct Press in March 2006. *Mindscape* won the Carl Brandon Parallax Award and was shortlisted for the Philip K. Dick Award and the James Tiptree, Jr. Award. "Griots of the Galaxy," a short story, appears in *So Long Been Dreaming: Postcolonial Visions of the Future,* an anthology edited by Nalo Hopkinson and Uppinder Mehan. In March 2011, Ms. Hairston received the International Association of the Fantastic in the Arts Distinguished Scholarship Award for distinguished contributions to the scholarship and criticism of the fantastic.

Nalo Hopkinson was born in Jamaica of Taino-Arawak lineage and draws frequently upon Caribbean history, language, and oral and written storytelling techniques to craft her speculative science fiction and fantasy. She received the John W. Campbell Award for Best New Writer and the Ontario Arts Council Foundation Award for Emerging Writers. *Brown Girl in the Ring* was nominated for the Philip K. Dick Award in 1998 and received the Locus Award for Best New Writer. *Midnight Robber* was shortlisted for the James Tiptree, Jr. Award in 2000 and nominated for the Hugo Award for Best Novel in 2001. *Skin Folk* received the World Fantasy Award and the Sunburst Award for Canadian Literature of the Fantastic in 2003. *The Salt Roads* received the Gaylactic Spectrum Award. *The New Moon's Arms* received the Aurora Award (Canada's reader-voted award for science fiction and fantasy) and the Sunburst Award for Canadian Literature of the Fantastic. Hopkinson is thus the first two-time winner of the Sunburst Award. She is the daughter of Guyanese poet and actor Abdur Rahman Slade Hopkinson. Holding Seton Hill University's master of arts degree in Writing Popular Fiction, she also teaches writing in a variety of international programs and has been a writer-in-residence at Clarion East, Clarion West, and Clarion South. Additionally, she is one of the founding members of the Carl Brandon Society, whose mission is "to increase racial and ethnic diversity in the production of and audience for speculative fiction."

Stephen Graham Jones (1972–) is the author of seven novels and two collections, and has at least three more novels currently in press. He also has published some 130 stories, many of which have been included in best-of-the-year anthologies. Jones has been an NEA Fellow, a Stoker Award finalist, and a Shirley Jackson Award finalist, and has won the Independent Publishers Award for Multicultural Fiction. Jones earned his PhD from Florida State University and is now Professor of English at the University of Colorado at Boulder, where he teaches in the MFA program.

Misha Nogha (1955–) was born in St. Paul, Minnesota, of Nordic and Métis ancestry. She attended Eastern Washington University, Portland State University, and Eastern Oregon University, and has earned degrees in English Literature and Secondary Education, with endorsements in Language Arts and French. Misha has studied Cree medicine path and Seidr, an ancient form of Nordic shamanism. Her short story "Chippoke Na Gomi" (1989) was featured in the 2010 *Wesleyan*

Anthology of Science Fiction, putting Misha in the company of "over a 150 years' worth of the best science fiction ever collected in a single volume." Currently at work on *Bell Factory,* the sequel to her acclaimed *Red Spider, White Web,* she lives with her husband and four children in Cove, Oregon.

Simon J. Ortiz (1941–) grew up in the Acoma village of McCartys (Deetseyamah), a part of the Eagle clan (Dyaanih hanoh), of Acoma Pueblo Native American decent. Close family and community ties gave him the opportunity to retain the Acoma language (Aacpumeh dzehni), which also mixes English and "Acomaized" Spanish. The importance of traditional language perhaps has underpinned much of his writing aesthetic, as so many Indigenous and Native authors have lost their original languages through the colonizing process. Even as a youngster he planned on a writing career, despite the cultural attitudes at that time that limited Native peoples to manual and menial labor. Nevertheless, he struggled through these obstacles to become a major voice for Indigenous and Native rights and sovereignty. He succeeded at Ft. Lewis College, the University of New Mexico, and the University of Iowa, where he was made a Fellow in the International Writing Program. His writing awards include the Lifetime Achievement Award from the Native Writers' Circle of the Americas (1993), and he teaches regularly at numerous universities across the United States.

Eden Robinson (1968–) grew up near Kitamaat in British Columbia, Canada, of combined Haisla lineage on her father's side and Heiltsuk on her mother's. Kitamaat remains home to seven hundred members of the Haisla nation, with approximately another eight hundred living off-reserve. Robinson's youth in Haisla territory near Kitamaat Village exposed her to the profound beauty of the forests and mountains of the central coast of British Columbia, an influence easily seen in her numerous short stories and novels. Her first novel, *Monkey Beach,* immediately established her importance in the writing community, winning the Ethel Wilson Fiction Prize and making the short list of finalists for a Giller Prize as well as a nomination for the International IMPAC Dublin Literary Award. Her collection of stories *Traplines* won the Winifred Holtby Prize for the best first work of fiction in the Commonwealth and was a New York Times Editors' Choice and Notable Book of the Year. She holds a BA and started the writing master's program at the University of British Columbia after *PRISM International* (UBC's literary journal) published her first story. Among only a handful of Canada's first female Native writers to gain international attention, Robinson recognizes her importance as a role model for emerging authors.

William Sanders (1942–) served in the US Army Security Agency during the Vietnam War. Besides soldiering, he has at various times worked as a musician, a construction laborer, an encyclopedia salesman, a traveling preacher, and a dishwasher. In 1973 he took up writing, first as a sports journalist, and then, in 1988, turning to fiction. He is the author of twenty-two published books. His stories have been nominated for various awards, including the Hugo and the Nebula, and he twice received the Sidewise Award for Alternate History. A definitive collection of his short fiction, *East of the Sun and West of Fort Smith,* was published in 2008. Now retired, he lives in Tahlequah, Oklahoma.

Leslie Marmon Silko (1948–) is of so-called mixed heritage, combining Laguna Pueblo, Cherokee, Mexican, and white pedigree that prevented her from reveling in the rituals of her Native peoples, even though she grew up near the Laguna Pueblo Reservation in New Mexico. It may be this very denial of rights to heritage that has made her embrace her Laguna Pueblo roots and work fiercely to become one of the preeminent voices of Native literature in the United States. Her books include *Ceremony* (1977), *Almanac of the Dead* (1991), and *Gardens in the Dunes* (2000). Her most recent work is the provocative memoir *The Turquoise Ledge* (2010).

Robert Sullivan (1967–) is a Maori poet with numerous publications and awards to his credit. He is emerging as one of the significant voices in Indigenous arts and letters. A graduate of Auckland University, he has authored such books as *Jazz Waiata* (1990), *Piki Ake* (1993), and *Star Waka* (1999). Sullivan is currently Assistant Professor of Creative Writing and Pacific Literature at the University of Hawaii, Manoa; editor of the online *Trout;* and a registered librarian. He is coeditor with Albert Wendt and Reina Whatiri of *Whetu Moana: Contemporary*

Polynesian Poems in English (2003), the first anthology of contemporary Indigenous Polynesian poetry in English edited by Polynesians.

Gerald Vizenor (1934–), American Book Award winner, is Distinguished Professor of American Studies at the University of New Mexico and Professor Emeritus at the University of California, Berkeley. Anishinaabe and an enrolled member of the Minnesota Chippewas, White Earth Reservation, he has published over twenty books on Native American and Indigenous issues ranging from literary and cultural criticism to fiction and poetry. A member of the Native American Renaissance, he has emerged as a definitive voice representing Native intellectualism. His distinction between Native victimry and Native survivance is a mainstay of Indigenous thinking as the world turns toward global unity in this century.

Archie Weller (1957–) is an Aboriginal author who was born in Subiaco, Western Australia, and grew up in bush country just south of Perth. After a brief foray into institutional higher education at the Australian Institute of Technology (now Curtin University of Technology), Perth, he left academia to write full-time. His first novel, *The Day of the Dog* (1981), confronted urban oppression with sardonic humor. Next up, his short-story collection *Going Home* (1986) brought him national and international acclaim, leading to more poems, plays, and film scripts commissioned by organizations that seek to address the contemporary Aboriginal experience and to mainstream Aboriginal authors in global discussions of cultural studies.

Gerry William (1952–) is a member of the Spallumcheen Indian Band in Enderby, British Columbia, Canada. Gerry has had numerous poems, essays, and short stories published in journals. His first novel was the science fiction novel entitled *The Black Ship* (Theytus Books, 1994). Gerry completed the next two books in that series and has submitted the entire trilogy, entitled *Enid Blue Starbreaks* for consideration to Baen Books. Gerry has written a historical novel, *The Woman in the Trees* (New Star Books, 2004), which describes first contact between the Okanagan Indians and European settlers in the nineteenth century. In the past year Gerry has written the first draft of the sequel to *Woman in the Trees* and hopes to submit it for consideration by the fall of 2011. In addition, Gerry has completed the first half of a new novel set in the same time period as *Enid Blue Starbreaks*. That novel describes the conflict between humans and the Nordells, a species briefly referred to in *Enid Blue Starbreaks*.